CAUSE AND EFFECT

KIND HEARTS AND MARTINETS BOOK 1

PETE ADAMS

Shallow men believe in luck – strong men believe in cause and effect

RALPH WALDO EMERSON

I dedicate this book to my family who have been behind me, pushing me; I was on the platform of Waterloo Station at the time, and of course Charlie, our Border Terrier; is he Martin...? Perhaps...?

ACKNOWLEDGMENTS

I am indebted to the support of Jan East who helped me along, storyline comments, poof reading, and in the first instance, helping me self-publish.

PROLOGUE

CLASHES OF STEEL AND SCREAMS PIERCED THE NORMALLY
tranquil night air of the leafy, salubrious Portsmouth suburb of
East Cosham. The locals had long been concerned about the
dodgy Christians in 33 Acacia Avenue, but, in true British
middle-class reserve, complaints to the authorities had mainly
been tutts and an occasional polite letter or two; suggestion of a
working group, maybe? Reports to police, largely ignored,
"With the Government cutbacks, resources are tight and
getting tighter."

Now, their worst fears are come to pass, ruffians with large
bladed poles, defending number 33, clash with men armed
with scimitars. By the time the police arrived, the skirmish was
over. Four youths seriously injured, taken away by ambulance,
the remaining protagonists melted into the borders and shrub-
beries. Streetlights, out for months, replaced by a strobing blue,
faces of residents looking out windows; most cowered.

As it became clear the area was safe, peace, if not tranquil-
lity restored, so it was disturbed again by harrumphing and

other such expressions of indignation, mention of letters, values of property and self-interest. "Hadn't they warned the authorities?" "Didn't you write a letter?" "No, I thought you did?"

———

'HALLO, CHAS.'

Chas jumped.

'Blimey, Mr Masters, you scared me.'

'Working late?'

'Finishing these bikes, they're going out tomorrow,' Chas explained.

'Not till late, but thanks,' Brian Masters, owner of Bazaar Bikes, said, turning to leave. 'See you tomorrow.'

Jeez, that was close, Chas thought, scared. How did he get in so deep?

———

OSAMA HELD HIS SOBBING WIFE, a peculiar sight, this mammoth wobbly woman being cuddled and comforted by a diminutive matchstick man who, despite being of distant Pakistani origins, presented his British stiff upper lip. His son is missing, but what can he do about it?

———

THE ELFIN-LIKE GIRL could not remember when she had last worn clothes or felt safe. She was afraid now as her mother lifted her to hide behind some boxes. 'Be very still, Meesh, and not a peep,' her mother whispered. Meesh nodded, couldn't remember the last time she had spoken. The light went out, the door remained open. She had no sense of time, heard a shot, her mother scream. Mesh's scream stayed inside of her, where it remained as she saw the man put the knife into her mother, felt her bowels open, and worried about the noise.

PART ONE

CAUSE

ONE

BATTLE OF ACACIA AVENUE
POLICE - where were they?
Bernie Thompson: Portsmouth Evening News, crime reporter.

Four youths were injured in a gang incident last night in the usually peaceful suburb of East Cosham. George Rattle, Chairman of the Local Community Policing Committee, said, "The fight was vicious and people were scared. Why did it take 15 minutes for the police to respond?"
A Police spokesman said, "The response time is under investigation." An anonymous but reliable police source said, "We're sorry residents felt threatened, but what do they expect with Government cutbacks forced on an already stretched Police service? If it is any comfort to the residents, who returned a Tory MP, we are all in this together."
The Chief Constable commented, "The Police do not

comment on Government policy." When pushed if his force was under strength, he said, "The force struggled with all it was charged to do even before the cutbacks." The Head of the Community Policing Committee for Portsmouth, Captain John V. Littleman RN, said, "The Police may be understaffed, but in-line with Government policy to involve more volunteers, good people are helping in admin posts, freeing up officers for frontline work." He has called a special meeting of the committee, made up of senior police officers, Councillors, and volunteers like himself. "Government policy is working," he said, "and being implemented with full vigour in |Portsmouth."

———

'JANE, MY OFFICE,' AND TURNING ON HER HEEL, Detective Superintendent Amanda Bruce squeaked across the polished floor of the community policing room, jerked the door open, and disappeared along the short corridor and into her office at the front of the police station.

Jane continued his reverie, induced, he says, by his cycle ride into work on a glorious late spring morning. At 59, Detective Inspector Jack Austin felt his morning assertion (he meant exertion) due to his competitive nature, racing often unaware opponents, generated a creative frivolity, his juice moment, referring to his brain activity, not the sweat; others referred to that.

Spinning Jack's chair, Detective Sergeant Josephine Wild, nicknamed Jo-Jums, cautioned,

'Pumps looks serious.' The Superintendent's nicknames were Mandy Pumps or Mandy Lifeboats, courtesy of Jack Austin, who nicknamed everyone, saying, "That's yer moniker, son, so lump it." Everyone was son to him. You had to lump that as well. Jo-Jums, also known as Mumsey, which described her comely appearance as well as her instincts, asserted her matriarchal caring role of her frequently distracted, often errant, boss, shook her head and tutted, which usually did the trick.

The Superintendent reappeared, 'Jane, when I say step into my office, I mean now, not when you felt like it,' stayed, hazel eyes flaring green within her angry face; Jack liked that face.

Languidly, and in his most refined voice, 'Miss Bonnet, I seek first to deteriorate your intonation, thus relieving me of the burden of assuming your iron on a morning when my mood is elevated and my eyes are brightened by exercise, and, what's the magic word?'

As funny as his *Pride and Prejudice* misquotes were, Jack Austin being Mr Malacopperism, Jo-Jums noted the impeccably coiffed, sharply dressed, high-achieving, fifty-something, strong Superintendent, appeared edgy this morning and not so sartorially smooth. Jack remained unruffled. He relished his nickname, *Jane*, frequently regaling one and all with bastardised Jane Austen quotes such as, "Your family, they are well?" the expected response, "Yes, quite well." However, this morning, Jack was insensible to the precarious signals.

The Riot Act was interrupted by the whistled theme from *Z-cars*, a vintage BBC police drama only Jack remembered, heralding Hissing Sid, the station desk sergeant. 'Jane, I need you downstairs to sort out bleedin' Dixon of Dock Green.' Sid acquired his moniker because he hissed the C in CID, although he was a lanky, skeletal, middle-aged snake of a man, so covering all bases, Austin would say.

'Siderney...' Austin's posh voice, '...the magic word?'

'Christ's sake, Jane, Pleeeeeeeasssse,' Sid hissed, a drawn-out whiney, sycophantic enunciation, reflected also in Sid's body language that naturally simpered.

'Righteeho, but I may have a previous engagement with Superintendent Pumps.' Austin replied, fluttering his one eye, pleased with his response, didn't look around, he knew others liked it too. He had a sense for these things to the extent he told people he was blessed.

Resigned, Sid slithered out as Mandy bashed Jack on his head with a rolled-up newspaper, and mimicking Sid, 'Pleeeeeeeasssse, Jane, pretty please with brass knobs,' and whacked him again.

Feigning a serious head injury, 'Be right with you, sweet'art.'

Jack's juvenile behaviour irritated, but Mandy liked him, irritated her more. A tall man, six-four and straight backed, his dad had been a Marine, a tad overweight, he erroneously thought, and definitely ugly, though he argued his face had character, Austin was a charismatic cockney barrow boy, and he called her beautiful, a real woman, which she liked. Mandy was tall herself, five-ten, and in reasonable shape for fifty-three, but beautiful? She considered her nose too big, but Jack would say it was one of the things he liked most. Mandy had known Jack nine years since coming to Portsmouth, she, a single parent of two children, Jack an evident strong bond of love with his wife and their two kids. He'd been devastated when Kate died three years ago; even now she knew he grieved.

She paced back to her office.

TWO

JACK SAUNTERED THE CORRIDOR, KNOCKED POLITELY, opened the door, and Martin zeroed in on Mandy's crotch. 'Can we not meet without your dog?' Mandy exclaimed, brushing Martin away with an affectionate scratch of his head.

Austin Martin, a proud and scruffy, ginger-haired Border Terrier, his nose not appreciated, trotted on, any idea Mandy's crotch worth sniffing, a coincidental thought, and settled himself beside his master. Jack sat upon the spare, straight-backed, orange PVC chair that resided on the far wall. Jack felt the comfy seating in front of her big desk put him at a psychological disadvantage; low, reclining backs made him appear awkward and feel small.

Jack wasn't an office man, preferring the social amenities of a communal space, but Mandy's office had one coveted feature, a large south-west facing window, affording a view of a mature, leafy tree. He settled, in order to take pleasure in the solar benefits of this window and the hypnotic dappling leaf shadows on the moss green carpet, like a forest floor he supposed; Jack was a town man, but he'd seen *Robin Hood*. The combination of agitated, sparkling dust motes, a whirligig leaf pattern on the forest floor, had a soporific effect on Jack, or would have, were it not for Mandy asserting herself. He adjusted his seat so his scarred and empty right eye socket faced her, leaned back, enjoying the warmth of the sun on the varicose veins of his outstretched legs, raised his arms behind his head and closed his eye, just for a bit; it didn't look like he would be called upon to say much.

In the spirit of the never-ending exchanges between the two of them, Mandy positioned herself in front of the window, forcing him to look at her into the sun with his good eye, and she criss-crossed the strong sunlight, beating her leg with the rolled-up newspaper. 'Ah, attack out of the sun,' a casually murmured thought as Jack slipped into a daydream, warmed by the radiant heat and the sight of this magnificent woman, in her prime, every inch and curve his Isle of Portsea, Sophia Loren.

Hissing Sid popped his head around the door, saw Superintendent Amanda Bruce musing, bashing her leg with a newspaper, hips swaying in the sunshine, and DI Austin slumped in the most incongruous part of the office, his extra-long bare legs stretched outright, and Martin looking as if he was seated at Wimbledon.

'Bugger off, Sid,' Mandy and Jack said, Martin barked out of synch, and Sid slithered off. Mandy launched into Jack, pacing, every now and then pointing the newspaper, eliciting defensive grumbling from Martin, whose perceived role in life was to defend his master when he was not paying attention – a full-time job. In reality, however, Martin was a recommendation by the police psychiatrist to calm Jack, a noted Berserker, a trait people believed the cause of his severe facial disfigurement, his right eye glassed berserking in a pub fight.

Jack lived with a gruesome, puckered layer of sunken skin in his redundant eye socket, a vertical, silvery, raised scar from his forehead to the top of his cheek. No eye patch, he wore the disfigurement with perverted pride, adding character to a face he considered handsome. If asked, he would say he was a Buddhist, but was C of E, Church of Egypt, and allowed this minor imperfection to his counter-dance. The normal response to this was Twat, and what's a counter-dance? One tended to ignore his face-saving diatribe of *Strictly Come Dancing* on shop counters.

Ordinarily Jack was a calm individual, rarely flustered, always witty (he thought), happy, whistling and singing, jovial to the point of causing everyone else to go berserk. Extraordinarily, he survived all attempts at censure, allowing his natural instinct for humour to smooth over his pathological hatred of the "pompous, self-important, doctrinaire, up their own arses, bureaucrat wankers," quoting *Mary Poppins,* whom he also said was *Truly Scrumptious.* Jack was a team player as long as he was captain, but how did he survive the bureaucracy? A "higher power" he would say. "You'll get your comeuppance one day," people said, and maybe he would eventually have to take early retirement, another of his great jokes at 59, aware he was reckless, which he put down to the loss of his wife. People said he'd gotten worse since Kate Austin died. He cared not, thought if he was a ship, rudderless and at sea, he would get back to harbour. "You're a natural survivor, Jane" and replying by rote, "Not sure I want to survive," the melancholic Jack, ever present, an emotional man not frightened to show his feelings, some say rare in a copper, especially the crying.

'Earth to Austin, are you listening, what're you thinking?' Mandy asserted into Jack's ether.

Groggily, he replied, 'Amanda, sweet'art, I was thinking of your lustrous hair, how it sways with your body. In the sun it glows album. You're fifty-odd, an age where a woman may worry about lines, and you do have a few...' acknowledging his

13

powers of observation, '...but they radiate your womanly beauty.' Mandy stopped pacing. Martin flipped his grizzled muzzle. 'You have magnificent hips and an arse like a scrumptious apple, a womanly figure silhouetted by the sunshine behind you, and I imagine your olive skin, in cream silk underwear, full Alan Wickers, stockings and suspenders, where the button gives the tell-tale hint beneath your skirt,' he was quite breathy.

Smoothing her skirt and feeling dim-witted for walking in front of the window, she shuffled aside.

Responding to the familiar watch-out growl from Martin, Jack stirred to see a stunned Superintendent, mouth agape as if someone had unsuspectingly kicked her backside, 'Did I just say...out loud?'

Martin barked Der.

Mandy countered, 'You did, and I see an old man with floppy, unkempt hair and a gammy eye. A man who has never matured, a senior police officer no less, sprawled in an ill-fitting England rugby shirt that displays his beer belly off to revolting effect.' She paced energetically. 'A shirt incongruously worn with spindly, sticky out arms that makes him look like a drawing by a five-year-old, magnetically pinned on the fridge by a Mother who would pin anything their child did on the fridge and say, how lovely.' She changed her tone, settling into her rebuke, 'Then we come to the lower part of you, Jane. The piece-de-resistance making you truly God's gift to women, the *Morecambe and Wise* khaki shorts, so voluminously baggy around the leg holes I inadvertently glimpsed your revolting bits and pieces. Why shorts when you have legs choked with varicose veins, and why Jesus sandals with your revolting big toe sticking out wrapped with toilet paper and sellotape? What happened to your toe?'

Martin was impressed; he'd not heard such a fantastically

devastating attack on his master since his mistress had died, God bless her soul; Martin was Catholic.

Jack reacted, 'I'm not God's gift to women. I prefer to think I was sent by the devil to tempt womankind, and I dress to tone down my overwhelming magnet, and I like to air my various...' Martin sniffed Jack's toe, and reassured of the loyalty of his hound, Jack continued, '...a fat eejit in an eclectic buggy ran over my toe. I did a pretty good job bandaging this morning, mind you, with all the government cutbacks the NHS will soon be a DIY, Dad's Army.'

Mandy detonated, 'Ah ha, J'accuse mon petit turd,' the newspaper making contact as Jack felt his chest for an imminent heart attack, 'cutbacks, the very topic....' the phone rang, she picked up. 'Amanda Bruce...Fuck me, Sid, what part of he will be down when I've finished with him do you not understand?' She listened. 'I don't care if I didn't say that...' Jack and Martin shared a conspiratorial glance, '...piss off, Sid,' and she put the phone down probably harder than was absolutely necessary to break the connection.

Jack thought he ought to say something; he instinctively knew what to say to a woman. 'Well, that's fecked the mood. I may be wrong, but I think I detected a concoction?'

Martin knew his master's conversations with the human opposite sex rarely had a satisfactory outcome, so he let out a strangled whine to indicate he was generally on his master's side, but in this instance... Mandy rolled her eyes, exasperated, but smiled. Martin was no expert in human behaviour, preferring to sniff another dog's bottom, but his master was right in one thing, "You just never know."

'Sort out Dixon, and, Jane, we need to have a serious conversation,' and she emphasised her point by brandishing the newspaper. 'Sid also said your dad phoned, what's that about?'

He flinched, put that down to Florets, 'Did he say dad or father?'

'Dad, now get out, and I think you mean Tourette's,' she replied, the rolled newspaper no longer threatening. Raising himself and making for the door, Martin took advantage of the mood of bonhomie to pad over to Mandy's crotch. 'Bugger off and take this flea-bitten hound with you,' Mandy's dramatic effect mitigated as she crouched and gave Martin a flea-bitten hug.

Jack sensed a sexual paroxysm; was that the tell-tale sign of a suspender button? Martin was licking Mandy's nose; she cooed. 'He's been licking my toe.'

Mandy leapt, heaving, and chortling, Jack and Martin departed, heading to a rendezvous with Hissing Sid and Ha Ha Dickey old chap, a meeting that would turn out to be more significant than he could imagine.

THREE

Approaching the bottom of the two flights of stairs to the station reception, 'Jack Austin, Olympic champignon,' he'd seen his son do this, easy-peasy, jumped the last three steps whilst swinging off both handrails.

Spread-eagled on his back, Jack had a faraway view of the stairs ascending as if to heaven. Heads hovered, not Gods, but the pale, emaciated, red-lipped, crescent-mooned face of Hissing Sid, and the rounded, florid, face of Dickey; Martin managed a lick when he could get his snout in. The twanging Pompey (Portsmouth) tones of hissing Sid burst his fantasy, 'Y'alreett, Jane, nasty bang, needs a few stitches you dooos,' and imitating the sentiment was the lyrical Welsh inflection of Dickey, but it was Martin's slobbering that brought Jack to his senses, that, and a celestial view up Amanda's skirt as she leaned over the upstairs landing, an Olympian Goddess.

'Oooh err, I prefer cream silk...' Jack said, unable to stop himself, '...sorry, florets...'

'Jane Austin, you're a twat,' Mandy said and tossed her head for a parting shot, 'you're disturbed, and so am I to put up with you and your Tourette's,' and she disappeared, shooing the team back into the CP room.

Jack's developing Superintendent fantasy was spoiled by Dickey's hymns and arias, 'Yer Jane, it's Mickey Splif's boy, Keanu, you knows 'im, a good lad, and Gail will go barmy, and his dad, well, he's a bit fed up. Osama says he'll 'ave the fucking bastard, but I didn't fink Muslims swore, anyway, if you're in the family way you often fancy something weird, my Dyliss fancied coal and not cause she's as Welsh as me neither, something in it, Amfracite? So, Bombay mix and pineapple chunks, stands to reason?'

Sid inveigled in a Dickensian, very 'umble way, 'Bombay Mix or the contents of the till...' Jack thought, it's like Stratford-upon-bleedin'-Avon here, '...a crime, is a crime,' and rising, he struck a pose the Bard and *Mincing-International* would be pleased to see.

'There's never a Z-*car* around when you want one,' Jack thought and said, to whomever might be interested, as he was mainly talking to himself, 'should it not be Mumbai Mix now?'

Martin was relieved his master was back to normal. Lifting his star-swimming head, Jack looked through the glazed screen into the spacious reception lobby, where, in assorted states of merriment, was Mickey Splif with his son Keanu, WPC Alice *Springs* Herring, gorgeous in her uniform, standing next to a spotty drip of a youth in a suit from Sainsbury's, who could only be the duty solicitor, and everyone stood clear of *Little shoe big shoe*, the *Big Issue* salesman. What was immediately obvious, though, was everyone could see up his shorts, which didn't worry Jack unduly, except Alice was laughing uncontrollably; a minor dent to his ego.

'Dickey, old Chap, a hand-up, and, Sid, a plaster for my forehead, please,' Jack said, fingering a gash on top of a bump, oozing blood, which would likely be gushing if Martin had not been licking it.

"Ave to be toilet paper and sellotape, we got no plasters,' Sid replied, disappearing.

Toilet paper and sellotape on my toe and now my head, Jack thought, and promising himself a couple of Paracetamol like it was a pint after work, he went into the reception vestibule to be assailed by a plethora of pleas.

FOUR

'Cod and Chips twice please, Sid.' Jack thought Sid, behind his counter, looked like he was serving in a fish and chip shop.

'Heard you the first time,' Sid's conforming response.

Pondering the universe like a space chicken, and based upon the grating quotient of his blossoming headache, Jack faced the most significant noise source. 'Oi, I want my pand,' a circumspect, *Little shoe Big shoe* said. Not a nickname, but a quote from the street corner salesman for the *Big Issue*, a paper sold by people who need a hand up from life's misfortunes. For the newspaper vendor's style, Jack would forgo his pound and buy a magazine off Little Shoe, who would hold up a baby's shoe saying, "little-shoe," then the magazine, "Big-Issue." Jack ordinarily would avoid these salespeople and then feel guilty; "The price you pay for being a socialist," he would say, "wouldn't see a Tory-boy worrying." Jack never saw any reason why he shouldn't generalise. 'My pand?' a quieter, questioning look on the down and out man.

Jack gave him an old-fashioned look, and at nearly 60, most

of his looks were old fashioned. He tried as often as possible to create new ones, but when pressed for time, he rolled out the old ones. "A bit like his jokes," Mandy would say, but just now, Jack's headache was biting at his good humour, and pointing to Little Shoe, 'Right, you, what's a pand?'

'It's wot you owe me, Guvna,' Little Shoe's snapped reply.

'First of all, my dear old chap, I'm not your Governor, and the inclination I am indebted to you to the tune of one of our Majesty's sovereigns leaves me somewhat perplexed.'

Martin looked at Dickey, who looked at Sid, who looked at Alice, nobody looked at the gentleman of the street or the suit from Sainsbury's, but between them all, you could see them thinking, "Oh no, it's Mr Darcy," and tittered.

In an *Eliza Doolittle* moment, Little Shoe said, 'You 'ad one of me *Big Issues* this morning and scarpered wivout payin', and I wants me spondulics.'

Jack recalled, he'd taken a *Big Issue* that morning having stopped on his bike at traffic lights, meaning to pay of course, when the cyclist he'd been racing passed him looking back and smiling as the lights changed. Naturally, Jack engaged in hot pursuit, regardless the runaway was thirty years younger, had a Claude Butler supersonic ten thousand-gear, mega bike, and wore tart cycling clothes. 'Sod, I forgot,' Jack said, rattling loose change in his pocket as a pretence or prelude to paying, but largely buying time. 'Pay the man, Sid,' Jack said, disappearing to find an interview room, calling Dickey, Keanu, and Mickey Split to follow.

Martin was comfortably seated in the smallest interview room in the police station, oppressive, no window, no ventilation, painted institutional green base and cream upper walls, reminding Jack of school corridors of the 1950s, he reminisced, enjoyed reminiscing. He shoved Martin off his chair, and ignoring the canine sulk, they settled around the old wooden table covered in an imperfect *fablon* covering, a sort of sticky back plastic from the seventies, meant to protect the table and brighten the place up, but only gave suspects something to do, picking at it. The chairs were also old, wooden, and specially designed with varying leg lengths so they wobbled.

There was a timid tapping at the door, 'Yoh,' Jack's *American cop*, nobody was impressed, reinforcing his view American police only look good on telly.

The door opened and the suit from Sainsbury's, a beanpole youth with greasy, jet black, lank hair that draped over his forehead causing a major eruption of spots, popped his pimply head around the door and nervously spluttered, 'As duty solicitor, I should be present.'

Mickey Splif said it for everyone, 'Fuck-off before I get *Rin-Tin-Tin* to give your bollocks a seeing to.'

Martin assumed an air of indignation. Jack made a mental note to tell Martin, *Rin-Tin-Tin* was a famous dog in the fifties; how come he got a sensitive dog, and a guilt-ridden Catholic to boot, Jack thought as the pimply solicitor withdrew, relieved. Putting his head in his hands, causing blood to ooze into the toilet paper, Jack mumbled, 'Constabule Dixon, what's got your goat this morning?'

Mickey Splif looked hesitant, 'Mr. Dixon, you got a goat?'

Keanu and Dickey tittered.

Mickey was a likeable, weaselly rascal, slight and short, the complete opposite of his wife, Gail. He was known as Mickey Splif as his phizog appeared always vacant, but he just had a lugubrious style about him that was the vogue in the seventies, presumably what the long-suffering Mrs Splif saw in him. Well, she must have seen something because they had ten kids, and if the nicking of the Mumbai Mix to go with pineapple chunks for Keanu's Mum was any measure, likely another was on the way.

The Splifs, like many on the council estate where they lived, were interrelated with the criminal underbelly of Portsmouth, but this family had not a criminal bone in their collective body, which was why Jack had excluded Hissing Sid and his charge book. Keanu, looking like a dozy, lanky, skinny alien, but with no aerial on his head, was a good lad.

'Shall we get on?' Jack said, distracted, looking at the blood on the palm of his hand and feeling faint.

Dickey, in his Welsh modulating tones that Jack found hypnotic, related the story of how Mr Ali, affectionately known as Osama by locals and even Mrs Ali, caught Keanu nicking a bag of Bombay Mix. Jack once had to explain to the Chief Constable, "Osama, it's not about political correctness but being able to laugh at yourself; quintessential Englishness, see? A bit like I'm known as *Jane* and you, Chief, as *Sitting Bull*." Jack often thought he should have been a Dimplemat.

Melodic Dickey asserted himself into Jack's outspoken thoughts, explaining Keanu was not denying the offence but begged extenuating circumstances. Mickey put his hand up like he was in class, an effect Jack noticed he had on people, which he ignored, of course, also like he did with most people.

Jack turned to Keanu, 'D'you do this, son?'

'Yes, Mr Austin, me mum wanted Bombay Mix with her pineapple chunks, there was nobody there to pay, so I legged it,' Keanu answered, looking every bit the child just turning fifteen.

'That's fievery, you dipstick!' Jack startled himself, wondering where his aggression came from. Tears appeared in Keanu's eyes, in Dickey's as well, romantic and soft-hearted, the Welsh, Jack thought, staving a tear himself. Thinking a hard-man image suited him, he slapped his hand onto the *fablon*, everyone jumped, and Martin did two circuits of the table at breakneck speed, barking, which brought in Sid.

'What's up?' Martin slowed, looked up.

'Sid, Keanu and me are going to see Osama,' Jack answered.

'We not charging him then?'

'Feck-off, Sid.'

Sid slithered from the room, a defeated look on his skeletal face, and as his bony bum disappeared around the door, he murmured, 'My name's not Sid.'

Jack phoned Jo-Jums, 'I'm off to Osama's, what's going down, apart from Pumps on the towpath. What's that about?'

'Mandy, not a clue, theft of bikes, riveting, why I followed you to Community Policing. Alice Springs had some ideas, shall I talk to her?' Jo knew he would say yes and had already got the ball rolling, knowing Jack encouraged initiative if he couldn't give a toss.

'Yeah,' Jack said, realising he was encouraging initiative, not that he gave a toss.

'D'you need some help at Osama's?' Jo added, knowing also Jack would want to do this himself.

'Nah, but tag Spanner, got potential that girl. In fact, get her on our team; despite the baggage of her family, she's made it clear she's her own gal, diplomanic as well.' Jack sometimes called Alice *Springs* Herring *Spanner*, said her lips made his nuts tighten.

Jo-Jums disapproved, knew resistance was futile, but was intrigued. 'I agree about Alice, but what makes you say this, and do you mean diplomatic, and tag?'

'That's what I said, diddli?' Jack replied, explaining further, 'She just got a butcher's hook up me shorts and didn't laugh, and I know she'll not say anything, good girl that.' He hung up, and turning to the Splifs, 'Keanu, go with Dickey in his car, I'll cycle and meet you at Osama's.' Jack was issuing orders on the move, sort of multitasking.

Jo enjoyed a laugh; Alice was sitting beside her having shared the shorts moment.

'What about me?' Mickey Splif asked, his Eeh-haw face on, to a disappearing Jack, schlepping with Martin through reception, Dickey complaining about the room in his car, a distant and ignored voice.

'Oi, my pand?'

'Sort this bloke, Sid.'

Sid's rejoinder faded into the car park ether as Jack unlocked his bike whilst reading an attached note from Bad. Commander Manners was known as either Good or Bad. The note, threatening dire consequences if he locked his bike up beside his car again, was from Bad. Jack scribbled a repost, stuck it on the Commander's windscreen, and cycled off. Martin, in the front gunner's seat, an orange box that Jack had secured to the pannier frame with a combination of rusty brackets and duct tape, sat proud on Jack's son's old Noddy and Big Ears baby quilt, which, to Jack's continued amusement, had PC Plod facing out. The wind in his face, whistling, Martin's face nudging the breeze, Jo-Jums and Alice Springs leaning out of the first floor window jeering, *"Dinah, Dinah, show us your leg,"* Jack thought, it doesn't get much better than this, gestured two fingers behind his back, unaware his euphoria was about to be shattered. His life changed forever.

FIVE

No immediate competition on the horizon, Jack pedalled at a relaxed rate, the morning still bright. He loved his adopted City of Portsmouth. Even cycling up into the north, arguably less attractive than Southsea, where he lived close to the seafront, he saw much to contribute to his sense of wellbeing. Portsmouth was flat, making cycling easy, which allowed Jack time to indulge his favourite pastime of daydreaming, marginally more favoured than *rememincing*, mainly because he couldn't spell reminisce or say it. He had many arguments of justification for his love of daydreaming; thought processing, a form of meditation, but whatever reason he was using at the time, he did it because he loved it and looked for any opportunity to indulge. Mandy said it was the natural state of a man, a vacant mind, but what did she know; probably why Buddhist monks were men, Jack would say to himself, would be one himself only orange didn't suit him, or was that Gerry Kitchener?

Jack cycled lazily, sometimes wonky, which he called multi-directional; hand gestures, tooted horns, occasional shouts, all ignored, this was a good morning, and he would not allow the intolerant to spoil it for him. He turned off the main drag into a parade of seedy shops where the Asian Emporium took up three units. Osama's shop was alongside an off licence, an irony Jack thought, the other side a betting shop, even more ironic. A tatty hairdresser advertising in its window a special for manicures completed the line-up. Jack pushed his bike to the nearest lamppost, and Martin sprung from his orange box and marked the post as his territory. Jack locked the bike and a sulky Martin to the lamppost; well, it was his territory.

Osama's expansive frontage display offered all kinds of fruit and vegetables that Jack hadn't a clue to the identity. To Jack, the Asian Emporium looked chaotic, sacks of rice here, and in another part of the shop, more sacks of rice, interspersed with sacks of rice and fragrant and the not so fragrant commodities that served the Asian community, strong in this part of town and well-integrated. No ghettos here. Jack liked the Pompey people; they got on with life, rubbed along.

Martin gave Jack an old-fashioned stare, shrank as he sensed Jack's thoughts, and goldfish-like, forgot his concerns, attracted to a poodle tied up outside the off-licence. 'Leave it out.' Jack couldn't stand poodles and made a mental note to get Martin's eyes tested. Dickey arrived, parking the ridiculously small patrol car. Keanu exited nimbly, Mickey Splif languorous, Dickey puffed and blew invisible steam from his inflated red cheeks and pursed lips, 'Get a bike or a trumpet, Dickey,' Jack called out.

'If they gave me a proper car...people will think you're barmy talking to Martin like that, Boyo.'

Jack screwed his good eye up as he looked into the sun, 'Dickey-old-chap, my dog is my soul mate, my muse, did you know Shakespeare had a Border Terrier, did you know Martin sniffed Mandy's crotch this morning?' Jack's face beamed pride; a two-point rejoinder.

In his grumbling Welsh baritone, Dickey looked at Martin, 'You lucky, lucky bastard.'

No mention of the Bard, I work with Philistines, Jack thought as he heard the incongruous Pompey accented voice of Osama, or as Sitting Bull would say, Mr Ali. "Allo, Mr Austin, lovely day, in it.' Jack looked down on the diminutive Osama's joyful smile and sparkly teeth, his thin face animated, wide brown eyes contained by squinting into the bright sun that illuminated the pencil thin moustache balanced on the edge of his lip, held in place by a hooked nose. A slender man in baggy white linen garb, upside down pie-dish cloth hat, and black waistcoat, a natural born Portsmouth lad whose manner conveyed energy and goodwill, though Osama's demeanour changed in an instant when he saw Keanu with Dickey. 'Bloody Nora, why's that boy not in prison, in it?'

Jack loved to hear the second and third generations of Asian people speaking, not only in the local accent but with the Asian idiosyncrasies, it was all he could do to focus on the point. "No change there, then," he could hear Mandy saying in his head; he'd drifted off again.

'A word in your shell-like?' Osama appeared nervous, a normal reaction when the police call unexpectedly, Jack thought, but his eye was twitching; Jo's caustic comments intruded, "Well, he's obviously guilty, nick him now." Jack would explain his non-existent eye twitches when something is not right, and the fact Jo-Jums is never around when he had got it right just meant she should get out more.

'Mr Austin, you alright?' a polite Osama asked, nervous, shuffling his soft-shoed feet. Maybe it's the police car parked outside, Jack thought, Osama kept looking at it. 'Can we talk out here, lovely day, in it?'

Irritated, Jack returned his gaze and thoughts to Osama. 'Yes, yes, let's go in and have a cup of tea over the rice sacks, so oriental; slow boat to India or something like that?' Osama, thinking it should be a boat to Pakistan, went off in one direction, Jack another. 'I meant these rice sacks,' Jack said, rolling his eye to the ceiling that had posters of Asian scenes, women in saris. Jack's mind flitted, should be Burkhas, he thought, falling over another stack of rice sacks.

'Sorry, Mr Austin.'

'Osama, what's up?' Jack gave him the quizzical eye, he only had the one and making it quizzical involved a momentary blurring of his vision, his explanation for the rice trip, an outspoken thought.

'Nuffing, in it.'

'Is it, I don't know, in it,' Jack, getting into the swing. 'You look upset. Mickey Splif's family are the good guys, what d'you say we give Keanu a break, eh?'

'Okay, right oh, in it,' Osama agreed, turning to go deeper into the store, conversation over.

'Old yer camels Osama, what 'appened to the 'aggling?'

'Stone me, Mr Austin, it's you what says stop 'aggling and get on with life, in it. Yeah, he's good kid, bye. I'm needed in the back, in it.'

Jack's eye twitched. 'Osama, I want you to give Keanu a Saturday job. Let him hump things for you, stack shelves, what d'you fink?'

'Yeah, whatever, Mr Austin.'

'He can start Saturday morning, okay?'

'Yeah,' and Osama made it away, stumbling past more rice sacks.

Back outside, Jack's eye was on red alert; he had to act. 'Mickey, get lost; Keanu, you're off the hook, but so help me...' listened, '...I will come down on you like a ton of...' he heard

29

something, '...ton of rice, and you've a Saturday job, and don't let me down.'

'Fanks, Mr Austin, you're a diamond geezer,' Mickey said.

Jack felt good, did a forward defensive cricket shot, and clicked his tongue.

'Good shot, Jane,' Dickey said, by rote.

'A push into the covers, a single, I think.'

Keanu didn't look so pleased; it was a good shot as well.

'Yeah, fanks, Mr Austin, can't work in there, it stinks.'

Jack was pre-occupied, told them to bugger off, and called Dickey to one side. 'Osama seemed troubled. I think he's in the process of being robbed. You go round the back, cover the rear and call for back-up, I'm going inside. I'll confront them when we have the support in place.' He looked inquisitively around, and so did Dickey, mimicking the look. 'Go on,' Jack ordered, annoyed Dickey was copying his looks.

SIX

Jack puffed out his chest, sucked in his stomach, but it hurt after a few minutes, so he deflated; only works on girls anyway, he thought, sensing an adrenaline rush. Stealthily Jack bumped around the rice sacks, edged along an aisle to another stack of rice sacks, stopped to listen; the rice was quiet, but he could hear raised voices from the rear, stressed, the level rising with shouts of "Osama!" "Oh no, please!" Unable to control his red mist, Jack charged the door to the warehouse, screaming, a fleeting thought he was berserking, but he couldn't stop, even if he tried; a symptom the Doc had said. The door collapsed, fell askew, twisted and swayed on one hinge. He heard Osama scream, and in a blur saw Mrs Ali on a pile of rice sacks, her legs in the air. Mrs Ali's paroxysm in tempo with the modulation of sirens, whereas Osama, his trousers warming his ankles whilst his dick cooled, was panicking, completely out of time, Jack thought.

Dickey came in through the back door as the squad car pulled up. The beached whale that was Mrs Ali moaned, and Jack noticed her thin lips, submerged in a pumpkin face, were turning blue. Jack realised what was happening, and pointing to Osama's bits and pieces, 'Put that away and move over.' He scrambled over the rice sacks to give Mrs Osama the kiss of life, his hands sinking into soft flesh as he adjusted her head, a sense of slow motion, reconsidered going in, saw the moustache, smelled stale onions, and in a *Sam Peckinpah* moment, did it.

The back-up officers burst in, weighed up the situation as trained officers, ripped Jack off and dragged him, scraping his exposed knees across the rough concrete floor and pushed his face into a box of overripe mangos, holding him down. All Jack's struggling could merit him was increased grazing to his knees and a feeling of suffocation, except for a passing ironic thought he had recently been to a Hindu wedding and really liked the magno squash.

Dickey stepped in as Jack was being handcuffed. 'About time, Dickey, what you been doing?' Jack exclaimed, spluttering mango snot, coincidentally enjoying a fruity mouthful, making a mental note to take some 'magnos' away with him.

Dickey restraining a laugh, 'Phoning an ambulance for Mrs Ali, though I think it's just shock and possibly pneumonia of the arse, and its mango.'

Osama began to pull up Mrs Ali's huge knickers. Jack watched the mainsail being hoisted and illogically thought of Mandy, when he said he liked the larger knickers he had in mind the French kind, this was something more from Black and Edgington the tentmakers. Jack couldn't stop thinking about Mrs Osama's knickers, thought about the mouth-to-mouth, her moustache, the onion breath, and combined with a nose full of mango, he started to feel sick, and with a devilish grin, 'Right, think I'll mosey back to the ranch.'

Dickey replied, a sideways glance to Mrs Ali, whose colour was returning, 'We should maybe debrief with Osama and his wife before we disappear?'

Wobbling his grinning head, a finger to his lips as though indicating a discreet titter, Jack said, 'Not sure debrief is an appropriate, Dickey,' looked to Osama, 'call it quits, eh? And don't forget Keanu Saturday morning.' Osama looked fit to explode, hopping foot-to-foot in his fetching ankle warmers, which only served to broaden Jack's smile, seemingly not appreciated. There's no pleasing some people, Jack thought, irritated by this, and before Osama could gather himself for a verbal repost, Mr Darcy headed him off at the pass. 'Mr and Mrs Ali, may I ask if this is a reglear event in the Asian Hemporium...' Jack was speaking posh, '...and was this the distraction what allowed Keanu, a self-confessed crap tea leaf, the opportunity to half-inch the bag of Mumbai Mix?' He thought about raising his one eyebrow, and they say he can't multi-task. 'If you get my grift?' Jack prevented a reply with his hand up in the classic police, traffic control manner. He looked in front of him, thought his hand looked good, and said to the confused company, 'I'd have made a good point duty cop, eh, Dickey?'

The patrolmen were clearly itching to get back to the station to begin spreading the word of coitus-interruptus Jane, and Dickey pressed, 'Mr Darcy, you were about to say something?'

'Oh yes,' Jack replied, 'Mr and Mrs Ali, I caution that if you partake of conrural, conjag...' he paused, '...shagging during trading hours, can I recommend you get some more staff so a mince pie can be kept on the place, and it would help if you were up for a bit of nooky with the Missus the form would be to give a little knowing look next time?' Jack demonstrated the knowing look, a tilt of the head, a nod and a fingertip touch of the nose. The patrolmen and Dickey acknowledged this was how you should do it. Jack was pleased; he was good at looks.

Mrs Ali was tearful, but Jack thought, all things considered, this was better than expiring on the sacks of rice and getting her carted off to the mortuary. Jack hated mortuaries; the smell made him feel sick and not a little scared; shed load of ghosts there, stands to reason. Mrs Ali took control, the patrolmen made their excuses and left, while Jack, Dickey, and a cowering Osama faced the short, moustachioed fat woman who commanded attention, exhaling the essence of an onion patch, hands firmly planted on her expansive hips. How do they do it? Jack thought, I could outrun her any day of the week, but stood fixed to the spot. 'So,' she said. So, Jack thought, she's going to get going in a minute. 'So, why d'you break our door down and come in screaming bloody blue murder, in it?'

Jack mused, other pictures in his mind, then, blimey she's expecting an answer. 'Mrs Ali, I thought you were being robbed, heard you screaming and thought I'd better do something, quick. Can I take some magnos please?'

Mrs Ali switched on the waterworks. Jack looked at Dickey, edging out of the line of fire to another stack of rice sacks. 'Oh, you lovely man, in it,' Mrs Ali sobbed, 'you did that for us, did you hear that Osama?' With a look of despairing hope on his face, Osama shuffled to join Dickey. Mrs Ali whispered in Jack's ear, 'Help us, Mr Austin?' Bugger that, Jack thought, 'Oh, Mr Austin, how can we thank you?' A bag of magnos would be nice, he reflected. 'You've hurt yourself.'

Realisation dawned, Jack's adrenaline levels plummeted, pain shot to his legs as he observed two substantially grazed knees and a steady flow of blood washing his shins, and combined with the mango perfume, his nausea reach critical. Jack had often thought he could have been a doctor if he could overcome his fear of blood; add to that essence of mango. 'Let me deal with that, Mr Austin, I don't have any plasters, but I could put some toilet paper and sellotape on until you get back to your police station, in it,' Nightingale Ali said.

Jack thought, does nobody have plasters? Cutbacks, he

supposed, instantly recalling he'd said that to Mandy and she'd gone ballistic. Bet she wants to talk about redundancies, bringing in Big-Society volunteers. How bloody ironic, the Big Society, big only for those who had a job, Jack was thinking, which helped distract him from Mrs Ali's unintelligible whispering and energetic medical ministrations. 'Kin hell, Mrs Ali, Ow!'

Mrs Ali mouthed, 'Stop moaning, you baby,' then, 'Please help us,' she cooed, as maternal instincts took over the kneeling, plump woman, but Jack couldn't help noticing she could see up the leg of his khaki shorts and was not shy at letting him know, or was she saying something else, maybe he should get deaf aids? Is there anybody in Portsmouth not had a gander at me privates today? Which brought him back to Mandy and the cutbacks, early retirement for you, Austin, he thought and felt his face tighten into a barely concealed grin. Jack was one of those rare coppers who had lasted the distance. "Never let the grass grow under your feet, embrace change and move on," was his maxim, not appreciated by his colleagues who viewed him as a dinosaur, an amusing one, granted, but a dinosaur nevertheless.

How wrong they were, only last week Jack said he needed a computer specialist, had in mind WPC Way Lin, had already spoken to her and she'd readily agreed, even done three evening classes, probably four by now. When asked if she was up to it, Jack proudly responded he'd asked her to Google the football results and let him know how Millwall had got on, and in thirty minutes, like a flash, she was there. The smugness lasted some time.

Squatting, Mrs Ali continued to cause knee havoc whilst playing I-spy bits and pieces, all the time mouthing something. Jack was oblivious, thinking if cutbacks were the problem, why had Mandy told him to take on Dave Manners, a raw detective constable? Not a polite request as he was the son of the Commander, but the kid showed promise, though as there were already so many Dave's in the force, Jack called him Nobby.

'There, Mr Austin,' Mrs Ali had finished and struggled to stand.

Jack thought he may need to ditch the shorts and wear long trousers, or he may become the laughing stock of the police station, and in his frontier gibberish that only a few aficionados understood, he thanked Mrs Osama. Mrs Ali didn't understand, smiled, winked, and tilted her head, gave him a bag of mangos and kissed him. Her moustache tickled, onions again as she whispered something bordering on his gibberish, which he respected, even if he didn't understand, assuming it was the Pakistan border, and that seemed like a good time to make his move back to the station, his deckchair, a smoked mackerel and mussel salad beckoned, as did the mangos.

———

OUTSIDE THE SUNSHINE lightened Jack's mood. He unlocked his bike, freed Martin, and planted him in the front gunner's seat. His mobile gave out a strangled summons. Jack struggled with technology, and once mastered did not consider it necessary to be forever changing, and as a consequence of age and poor stewardship, his mobile phone was a sight to behold. He argued it was a study in duct tape and elastic bands and will likely find its way into the Tate Modern that he pretended to hate but actually loved. "Pretentious, tow-rag artists" he would say, jealous he'd not done this. Jack considered himself a frustrated artist to which Mandy would say, "Piss Artist," but then she was a Philistine, a beautiful one, no doubt, but no sense for the arts. 'Why change it if it still worked,' his spoken thoughts to a bored Martin who grumbled a suggestion to answer the phone.

Settling on his saddle, which involved major bottom jiggling, revolting cheek adjustments, and giving Martin a sideways look, he squashed a finger through the sellotape onto the answer button. Jack noticed Mandy's name on the cracked display. 'Babes, before you say anything, all's sorted; Keanu's got a Saturday job, and I'm up for the Queens Gallantry Medal,' he chortled nervously, mainly to reassure Mandy. He knew girls needed a man to reassure them every now and then, liked a joke as well, and they say Jack Austin doesn't know women?

Mandy replied, 'What're you talking about, and I certainly do need reassuring. The Commander, Serious Crime, and Cyrano are here, and the balloon's gone up.' She paused, and the timbre of her voice modulated. 'What have you done, and please, do not let me down.' No attempt in disguising her dread.

'I was going to have my smoked mackerel and mussel salad,' Jack answered, 'some fresh magnos, a ziz in my deckchair. tart without me, I can catch up, maybe over a drink tonight?' Just before she hung up, he could hear some ripe expletives, thinking this was the only woman who could hold a candle to his Kate.

SEVEN

DESPITE MANDY'S CALL, OR PERHAPS BECAUSE OF IT, JACK cycled slowly. Something not right at Osama's? Grinning, *Mary Poppins*, 'Storm brewing over Cherry Tree Lane,' he said to himself, 'Spit spot,' chortling as he pulled up at traffic lights, wiggled on his saddle to save scratching his bum with people looking, and waited for the lights to change, old-fashioned looks from a driver and passenger in an adjacent car, spotty youths with their music up loud. To Jack, all youths were spotty, even if they had perfectly clear skin. Balancing on his pedals, Jack leaned across and rested his forearm on the car roof, and leaning in, 'Turn it up, son, I'm a bit Mutt and Jeff.'

The passenger intimidated, Jack's eye in his face, the driver not so much. 'Some Vera Lynn, Granddad?' The lights changed, and the car drove off. Jack, pushing himself upright, was left chuckling and feeling there was hope for the younger generation, he peddled off.

JUST AFTER 2 PM, Jack locked his bike beside the Commander's car; mussels, mackerel, and his deckchair beckoned. Jack regularly took naps, input from the police psychiatrist, "Eat properly and, if you can, have a siesta. The Italians know what they're doing, Jane." So now, Jack's "deckachairo" moments are heralded by, "Just one Cornetto or wotsamatterwivyou" and he certainly felt better; the trick cyclist may not be an ignorant tart after all?

———

THE STATION CONFERENCE room was on the top floor of the four-storey utilitarian building, central to the facade, and dominated by a full-width window that looked onto the front car park and entrance below. Mandy was chatting sociably with Commander Manners, casually rubbernecking to look out at her tree and wanting to see when Jack arrived, finding it hard to disguise her misgivings.

Jamie Manners was a pleasant man who had the look of a tall *Captain Mainwaring*, round glasses on a round face, more chins than a Chinese phone book, and a terrible comb-over hairstyle that regularly flopped three or four lengthy, matted strands, to be immediately flicked back with a practiced hand of *Bowyers'* sausages. He had a good heart, but the stresses of police seniority caused unexpected mood swings. Jack called them his PMT moments, and Jamie would laugh or rail depending on his good or bad mood, 'Everything alright, Amanda?'

Mandy snapped out of her daydream, 'Fine, Sir, just wondering how long Inspector Austin will be,' but she'd just seen him locking his bike up where he shouldn't.

'Aren't we all,' Manners responded, conjoined with a grunt from drugs and a scowl from the sissy who continued to draw hangmen on his notepad; had to be Jack he was drawing. The head of Sissies, (Jack's name for Serious Crime), DCI Paul Willie, and the head of drugs, DCI Bob Appleby, sat around the table. Naturally, Jack had a nickname for Paul Willie, and that was Paolo, and this irritated DCI Willie. Jack's mature response was "tough-titties." Jack was not vindictive, but Mandy knew he had little time for Paolo, considering him more concerned about his sartorial style and arse protection than policing, frightened to take a chance lest he be ridiculed. "Not what being a team player was about," Jack would say, and he would know? Mandy was dreading the meeting; Paolo was prone to lording it over Jack. She stole a look and could see that in the nearly four years he'd been running Sissies, Paolo's sharp suits were more figure hugging. Jack would say, "Been sitting on your arse too long and become a couch potato copper." Oh my God, she thought, I'm sure he will say this.

Jack thought he knew these people and would say, "Apart from the up their own arses, martinet wankers, everybody is redeemable," apparently another quote from *Mary Poppins*, but Paolo? She had her doubts. She was put in mind of an *Alan Bennett* monologue where he described sitting with his mum and dad and they would sketch a random person's character and life, all from their imagination. Jack thought *Alan Bennett* would have made a good copper, except, and like Jack, he would likely feel sorry for people and let them off; another worrying fault of Jack's, especially for a copper. Amanda felt warm inside, recalling Jack's Alan Bennett on Paolo.

Paolo left school unfulfilled, disappointingly average, a Billy no Mates. So, he assembled an elaborate façade, the suits an integral part. His Mum stopped him going into the military, knowing if he shot someone, it would devastate her son, a minor redeemable feature.

In the police, if you keep your head down, do well in an

average way, crawl up the appropriate trouser legs, you will climb the ladder. Acknowledgement, in a way, but to reassure yourself, you are bossy to the people beneath your rank. Eventually, you rise further and have real power but not a clue how to use it and still no respect.

Life passes you by, colleagues have families, but you have not, so you get an off-the-shelf bride, but you need to grow with these things, not parachute in. Things fall apart, and you cling onto hope, and all you want to do is have a pint with your non-existent mates to complain affectionately about the Missus and kids, but it will never happen.

So, the system developed a police officer in a position of power who feels he needs to wield it and would not begin to know how to empathise. Had he not been steered severely by his mum, Paolo probably would have been a cycle path, by which she knew he meant psychopath, *but in the event, he is a sociopath, a man to be pitied, in need of a hug.'* Mandy would feign being sick.

She looked over to Paolo, weight going on, medium height, brown hair with flecks of grey, non-contentious styling that had probably not changed since he left school, everything medium or average. Bob Appleby, however, was a completely different type, laid back as if he'd never heard of nervous energy. Lean, tall if he didn't slouch, alabaster skin with a permanent five o'clock shadow and a shock of unruly black hair atop a narrow face. He had a bony frame, not unlike Sid downstairs, though Bob's had a hint of the muscular. The first thing you noticed, apart from his big feet, was his immense roman nose. Aqueduct, Jack called it, meaning aquiline, and he called Bob *Cyrano.* Good humoured banter, although Cyrano's wife never liked Jack; you either love Jack or loathe him. "Just like Biggley," Jack would say, meaning Wickham, and not Bingley, in PP (Jack was fed up with saying *Pride and Prejudice*; apparently all the youngsters called it PP now).

———

Sᴀᴛ ᴀʀᴏᴜɴᴅ ᴛʜᴇ ᴛᴀʙʟᴇ, Paolo showed off his numerical prowess counting fingers. 'One, I cannot see why we're waiting, and two, why we are waiting for Bozo Austin?'

Commander Manners looked up. 'Amanda, where is he again?'

With an undisguised expression that said, "I've told you a million times," exacerbated, having to deal with men, 'I'm not fully briefed, Sir, but Inspector Austin has just foiled an armed raid on a local supermarket. I've just noticed him cycle in.'

'What, single-handed?' the Commander asked.

'Well, he has Martin in the front gunner's seat, but yes, he cycles it on his own,' Mandy replied, chuckling.

'No, I meant the raid.'

'Sorry,' a mocking curtsey, 'I understand so. George Dixon called for backup, but the perpetrators escaped, I think?'

'Typical wooden top, he go in gung-ho with Spotty Dog?' A smug Paolo remarked, making a reference to *The Woodentops*, an old children's television programme oft referred to by Jack in his *Watch with Mother* moments; a term also used for dopey constables, wooden tops. Spotty dog was a woodentop Jack would imitate, and everyone would laugh, not because it was a good impression, most people had not even heard of *Watch with Mother* let alone seen *The Woodentops*; it was just the way he did it. He was a clown, and Mandy felt a warm sensation inside of her.

She looked sternly at the Sissy. 'I understand the situation escalated, and he had to go in. So, Sir, I'm a bit light on the details, and as much as I enjoy humiliating Inspector Austin, I am rather impressed, and furthermore, I hear he saved the wife of the proprietor with mouth-to-mouth before the paramedics got there,' and Mandy applied her schoolgirl, *told you so* look and sent it to Paolo with *brass knobs* on.

A loud jeer resounded, and the Commander knee-jerk jumped and looked out of the window. 'Our hero returns, and the bastard's locked his bike up by my car again, how many times do I have to tell him. I even left a note on his bike this morning.'

'You left him a note?' Mandy could not disguise her look of horror.

'Yes, it clearly says my parking bay.'

'Yes, Sir,' Mandy made a mental note to check Jack hadn't left a note back.

The Commander conjured a sneer. Mandy thought, Jack would say, "It's Bad Manners," recalling his maxim, "he can go from good Manners to bad Manners without the wind changing direction." *Mary Poppins*, he said, but with Jack, you never knew. It was Jack who insisted *Mary Poppins* gets PMT, his reasoning being she only reluctantly joined the people on the ceiling for a laugh. Mandy was snapped back to reality by an even bigger jeer. The Commander stared in the direction of the CP room, his lower jaw sagging. Mandy was tempted with "Close your mouth, we are not a codfish," but thought better of it. After all, *Mary Poppins* was only in her head. 'I'll make sure Jane comes straight away, Sir,' and she dashed off. Spit spot, giggling, as she stepped in time down the stairs to the CP room to be confronted by a Roman orgy; couples in suggestive poses, and Jack, hands on his hips.

'Droll, very droll,' he said and played an imaginary cricket shot.

'Good shot.' The Superintendent was there, which brought the room and Martin to attention, a couple of barks, largely doggy Tourette's. She thought about Martin, anything out of the ordinary and he would launch into multi-directional running and simultaneous barking. Last Christmas after a tipple of the Commander's sherry, she gave Jack a hug and a kiss, which excluded Martin, naturally, as he had dog breath. Martin proceeded to bark and hump her leg. Mandy had been embarrassed at the jeering, and Jack's comment to a room full of half-pissed coppers, "Martin's only doing what I would like to do." Mandy blushed just thinking about it, but boy did she recover. "You only want to fuck my leg?" she'd responded, and he'd whispered into her ear, "Nice save, love your perfume, is it Opium?" How did he know these things? He was your average dipstick bloke, but at times, he impressed.

The scene in the CP room righted itself. 'I won't ask what you are doing, but will ask what you are all doing here?' Mandy announced.

Jo-Jums assumed the role of spokesperson, a role as a mother of four she was used to, a strong presence and people listened to her. 'We were called back, can you tell us what's happening, Ma'am?'

Jack was alerted. 'Who called you back? It wasn't me.'

'No, Jane, I think you were otherwise engaged,' Jo-Jums fired back. An immediate chorus of "Ooh err Matron" ensued.

Mandy took back control. 'Right, get on with something, and you, Jane, the conference room now, pretty please with red injuns on top.'

'Be right with you, Ma'am,' Jack smarmed back.

Mandy was halfway up the stairs when she thought, bugger, I've just mixed my things, and that note of respect from Jack, trying also to bring an image to mind; toilet paper and sellotape on both knees, as well as his big toe and forehead, were Jack's shorts that filthy this morning, and what was that orange stuff around his neck, a scent of mango? Not unpleasant, maybe Dolly was using a different polish?

Dolly was the pensioner cleaner. Jack insisted only Dolly clean his CP room and the floor be polished, the only place in the station that received this loving attention. Mandy wondered, even old girls, smelling ever so slightly of urine, fall in with what he wants. Mind, I don't suppose it would be long before he's smelling of his own wee, and she made a note to save that one up. Holding that thought and the giggle that went with it, Mandy re-entered the conference room.

'What larks, Pip.'

Mandy looked at the Commander askance. 'You like Dickens, Sir?' thinking Jack is getting through to the Commander, and this will stop Billy Bunter minus the school cap.

'Don't know, never been to one,' at which Manners rolled up laughing, joined by the sycophant Paolo.

Mandy looked at Cyrano, a despairing visage, 'Nuff said.' Cyrano, a man of few words, and Mandy thought, I'd take that right now.

EIGHT

Clutching his family-sized Tupperware lunch container, and a smaller one for Martin, who was not keen on salad, Jack clumsily opened the conference room door. Martin passed by, intent on Mandy's crotch, while an affronted Lord Snooty Paolo injected into the disturbed atmosphere, 'What's that dog doing here?'

Jack, distracted, looking for somewhere nice to eat his lunch, opined, 'I'd say he was investigating the Venus areas of my beloved Superintendent.'

Oh Christ, Mr Turnip head, Mandy thought, pushing Martin away, giving his scruffy head an affectionate scratch, heaven help us.

Commander Manners stepped in to deflect the inevitable altercation. 'Jack has his dog as a recommendation from the police psychiatrist, so roll with it, please.'

Mandy rolled with her eyes to the ceiling, here we go, except there was a knock at the door, and bone-man, red-lipped, gobshite Hissing Sid, poked his head round the door. 'Sorry, Sir, message for Jane...' He paused, waiting for the nod from the Commander; Jack was still considering his seating options. 'Your dad rang, again, will try to get you this evening; urgent. Michael's home from school, he's got dinner...' Sid referred to his notes, '...Loch Etive trout from Waitroses, timed for....' notes, '....6.30, he's having a break then will get on with his homework, which he's doing with Colleen.'

Mandy thought, what does it say about this man, his teenage son, nearly eighteen, was reporting in, doing his homework and cooking dinner. Jack, but mainly Kate, she suspected, had done a good job.

'Cheers, Sid, now feck-off,' and still deciding on his seat, Jack looked at DCI Willie and, in a florid, overly mannered deckachairo Italian, 'Eh, Paolo, whattsamattawivyou, you isa startin' to lookalika my Mama,' and reverting to his natural cockney, 'put on a bit of weight, my cowson, comes from sitting on yer arris all day. Still got that Thai bride? Get *Ting Tong* to let the seams out.'

Mandy, still processing someone telephoned saying he was Jack's dad, knowing his dad had died six or seven years ago, recalling how upset he'd been, was shocked back to reality when she heard him say more or less what she had predicted, and her eyes hit the ceiling, again. Jack pulled up a seat for Martin, arranged a seat for himself so that he had to squash against Mandy's leg. She gave him, in return, her old-fashioned look before shuffling her chair away, giving Cyrano the same look. 'Move up, big nose, I don't fancy your legs.'

With hardly any discernible movement, Cyrano responded, 'Leave that for Martin?'

Oh my God, the Christmas story has got around the whole force, and after what seemed like half-an-hour, they were all seated, including Martin not so patiently waiting for his lunch.

Jack politely acknowledged DCI Appleby with a nod and a

mutter, 'Cyrano' and an equally muttered "Jane" from Bob Appleby.

'Austin,' the commander said.

'Commander,' Jack said.

'Austin.'

'Commander.'

'For God's sake, please,' Mandy interjected, thinking the chuckling Commander was as bad as Jack.

Unmoved, Jack plonked his and Martin's lunch on the table, retrieved a spoon from his back pocket, which revolted Mandy as Jack was known for the occasional ripe fart, blaming Martin of course. 'Commander, don't mind if we eat our lunch, only we were somewhat preoccupied this morning?'

Paolo was about to object when the Commander replied, 'Not at all, Jane, I think we would be rather churlish to refuse after this morning's heroics.'

Martin had already snaffled his mackerel and, along with Mandy, was eying Jack's salad with disgust. Noting it was Good Manners, Jack mumbled his *Godfather* impression, 'Eh, Paolo, you wanna getta me a glassa water?'

'Fuck-you,' Paolo replied, not a hint of Italian.

'Get him some water, Paolo,' the Commander ordered sharply, and the Sissy shuffled to the water tower while Mandy mimicked Martin and sniffed the air, only she did it with a little more decorum; fish, she expected, mango again, not unpleasant. 'Paolo, tell us why we're here, please?' the commander requested.

Paolo smarmed, and in his fatally flawed way, paused too long, allowing Jack with a mouthful of mackerel and mussels to interject, 'I know why we're here,' studying his pot to see what he might select next.

'You do? Then why didn't you tell me when I phoned just now?' Mandy rounded on him, and Jack chewed, while Martin chased his box around the table top with his tongue and farted, only a bit, but discernible because Martin turned to look at his bum, shocked a police dog could do such a thing, and in a meeting?

Jack, still with a partial mouthful, 'My dearest Governor, I recall our telephone conversation was rather one-sided.' Mandy, diverted by Jack's food-stuffed grin, leaned back in her chair and called it a draw.

'Okay, clever Dick, why are we here?' Paolo spluttered, his face reddening.

'Keep your girdle on, Paolo,' Jack reacted, taking another mouthful and turning to Mandy, 'many a true word, eh?' This time Mandy got full on mackerel, mussels, red onion, and mango, and something else that made her feel sick. Jack noticed, 'Sorry darlin', Martin just let one go, better make a run for it, eh?' and Martin snickered.

Focused on mackerel and mussel edging in his teeth, Mandy still registered Jack's aside about Paolo's increasing weight. Pots and kettles, she thought, but annoyingly, he had that *Jack Nicholson* effect; some men grow old, run to fat, and still look good, but women! She thought affectionately of Jack's compliments, the way she looked, that he had always liked older women; well, you can't have everything. She was aging, saw it in the mirror every morning, but Jack looked good, if you got past the ugly, not that she would tell him. She'd once told him he sang and whistled beautifully, obviously a mad moment, as he sang and whistled all the time and people frequently told him to shut up, and he would say, "Detective Superintendent Amanda Bruce says I have a lovely voice and whistle beautifully," so the last thing she was going to say was Jack carried his weight well, whereas Paolo's weight was definitely going to put Ting Tong and her sewing machine to the test sooner rather than later.

'Well?' Paolo asked.

'Well,' Jack said.

'Jack!' Mandy reacted, accompanied by a stare that could tear the skin of yer.

'Sissies and Cyrano?' Jack, obliging, 'A new drugs firm on the block. Two gangland skirmishes, drugs related? I don't think so.' He ran his tongue around his mouth. 'The sissies have been rattling cages in the badlands to no avail. Hardly surprising, this is too sophisticated for the gangland Herberts.' He paused, combining dramatic effect with the opportunity to pop a couple of mussels into his mouth with his fingers, savoured them, but unluckily for Mandy, he turned to her. 'Got my taste for mussels from my dad. He was from the East End of London and every Sunday morning he would...'

Mandy interrupted him, not relishing the view or the smell. 'Yes, I know, fried mussels and bacon and you sat down with him before the other kids got up, and close your mouth we are not a codfish,' punched the air and said, '*Mary Poppins*, Yes,' before she realised it.

'Well done, Amanda,' the Commander added, blushing, thinking he'd better get this meeting over lest he took some banter home; what would Dorothy think?

'If, Commander, I may be allowed to continue,' Jack said, none too pleased with the smug look on Mandy's face as she mouthed, "535 nil." The Commander nodded to Jack and smiled at Mandy. 'Commander, will you tell Paolo why Martin and I are here, why you've waited through my lunch and not even mentioned I've locked my bike next to your car?'

Mandy stifled a giggle, and an exasperated Commander asked, 'And why have you been invited to this meeting?' It was Bad Manners, the wind must have changed, and Jack wet his finger, put it in the air, and gave Mandy a knowing musselly grin.

'Simples,' Jack said, and Mandy's audible intake of breath was noticeable, as she thought, in response to her success in *Mary Poppins*. Jack was about to launch into *Alexander the Meerkat*; Jack could not get anywhere near that voice.

Paolo blew, 'What's so fucking simples.' Nope, Mandy thought, Paolo can't do *Alexander* either.

'Now, now,' the Commander said in a platonic tone; wind veering, 'Jane, stop winding Paolo, I mean Paul, up, and tell us, please.'

'Simples,' this time it was *Alexander,* 'you want me to solve this for you.' Jack, satisfied with the response, went back to his lunch, and Martin put a paw onto his hand as if to say *Atta boy*. Paolo fumed, Cyrano smiled inscrutably, and the Commander put a hand on Paolo's shoulder. Not the kindly gesture of Martin's paw, it was a firm grip. Mandy inadvertently relaxed, but Jack had not finished. She tensed, starting to feel sick; nerves, or was it the mackerel, mussels, mango, red onion, Martin's fart, or the acidic aroma of salad cream?

The Commander commanded, 'If we can all calm down,' looking at Paolo, aware everyone else was quite calm. 'Paolo, what strategy you propose, please,' Manners stressed the please, a firm intonation that could not be confused, but Paolo would not be Paolo, and Jack would not be Jane, and the Commander would have to be incredibly naive if he thought that would be it.

Paolo could not resist a dig, 'Will you be taking notes, Jane? I see you've plenty of toilet paper, but no pencil.'

'Are you going to be saying anything relevant?' Jack reacted, and with hardly a pause, 'this is what we'll do...'

Paolo banged the table, leapt, and in a whiney schoolboy tone, 'This is my show, tell him, Commander,' a stiff arm and index finger pointing at Jack.

'Sit the fuck down, Paul, Paolo, or whatever your bloody

name is, and let Jane have his say. He has at least done some solid police work today,' the Commander asserted, metaphorically blowing smoke from his two-fingered pistol.

Dumbfounded at the Commander's reaction, Paolo lowered himself into his chair, hissing indignation as, simultaneously, his ego deflated, a stony look through his joined-up eyebrows. Jack looked equally mystified, and Mandy, sensing a looming disaster, shifted her seat back just a little. Even Martin shrank into his chair, a known cowardy custard dog.

'My guys are already on this,' Jack opened up, casually.

'They are, why haven't you briefed me?' Mandy responded indignantly, straightening in her seat.

'I would have this morning, sweet'art, but you were too busy peeking up me round the houses.'

Mandy blushed, it was more than a glance up his shorts, and smiling sweetly in a radioactive, syrupy, Southern Belle voice, she replied, 'Impress us, please.'

So Jack continued, assuming it was now 535 all, 'I've got Jo-Jums and Nobby following up leads; Spanner's a go-between the local rogues. I want to open up the back part of the CP room that's been closed since the bloody cutbacks,' got himself side-tracked, 'I never voted for them you know, but I bet half of you did. Well, not smiling now in your feckin' Big Society Masonic lodges, are you?'

Mandy liked it when he said "feckin'," it was something he picked up from his love of *Father Ted*; Cod Irish he called it, and she smiled.

'Jane, we're aware of your political views, keep to the script, please, and keep the expletives, Irish and English, to a minimum,' the Commander said.

'Is Paolo taking notes, Sir?' The suppressed giggles blew, and the atmosphere was disarmed, with the exception of Paolo, who fumed. 'As I was saying,' Jack was getting into the swing, swaying his arm and pointing with his spoon that had half a mussel held there only by the viscous strength of the tiniest amount of salad cream. 'I'm going to open up the old squad room; the Sissies can go in there, they will be in nobody's way in that part of the house.' Mandy thought, nice Jack, *Lady Catherine de Burgh.* 'I want Frankie drafted in to work with my computer officer, Confucius.'

Mandy put her hand up and immediately thought, what am I doing. 'I yield the floor to the pervert in the corner.'

Not to be diverted, and leaning towards Jack, hands flat on the table, and despite the pong, she asked, 'When did community policing get a computer officer, and Confucius?'

Jack sat back and grasped his hands behind his head and applied a smug smile, 'Superintendent, darlin', if I'm to run an efficient community policing department, clearly I need a computer expert, Der.'

Paolo sniggered but kept his counsel. Mandy thought she should probe but was wary, 'Confucius?'

Holding his hands up as if to stop a barrage of critical comment, 'Way Lin, and before you say it, I know we should call her *Wailing Wall* or the *Wall of China*, but I settled for *Confucius,*' and he nudged Mandy with his elbow, which she returned in good measure along with a frigid stare. Jack laughed nervously; Mandy had some devastating looks. The Commander seemed distracted, looking down his nose trying to remove a part of a mussel from his uniform jacket, indicating Jack should get on with it. Jack did, 'Frankie, a Met computer whiz, will hook up with Confucius; you and your mob Cyrano can camp in with me, as needs be.'

Cyrano, with minuscule amounts of body movement, chuckled, demonstrating just how much he was enjoying himself, aware Paolo wanted the incident room to be set up at his nick in Cosham. 'Okay, Jack,' Cyrano replied, and pitching in with the fun, 'you got this, and working it from Kingston is good, near the docks and bandit territory.'

Jack started to get up. 'No way I was gonna be cycling up to Cosham,' and showing his Tupperware box to everyone, 'probably won't eat anymore; want some?' greeted by unified retching, 'suit yourself. Commander, d'you want to see Nobby?'

'Good idea,' the Commander answered, rising enthusiastically. 'Amanda, will you join me, and you chaps,' pointing around the table, 'sort out the incident room, toute suite.'

'Ah, *Chitty Chitty Bang Bang*, Sir, nicely done,' Mandy said, and Good Manners bathed in his inadvertent glory.

Jack buzzed down the stairs and, entering the corridor, noticed a scurry of activity in the CP room. He ducked into the toilet with Martin, leaving the door ajar. As the Commander and Mandy approached, Martin and Jack looped behind them as the commander opened the CP room door and Jo-Jums jumped, 'Boo!'

Jack bent over in hysterics; toilet paper popped off his knees and blood cascaded down his shins. The Commander bellowed, 'Fucking kids!' and stomped off, accidentally treading on Jack's bad toe causing him to double over again, this time bashing his head on the closing door. 'Serves you fucking right,' but the Commander felt a mellow warmth, relieved, because his son David had been in on the act, and he could tell Dorothy their boy has a nickname and is fitting in.

NINE

MATERNAL INSTINCTS ON RED ALERT, JO-JUMS SPRUNG TO Jack's side, giggling and cooing as she steered him to his chair. 'DS Wild, I'm not one of your brood!' Jack retorted and immediately felt a bit Catholic. Jo was a good woman, loyal colleague and, in his way, he loved her. She'd worked with him in Sissies, and when he was demoted and shifted to Community Policing, she was one of the few who stood by him. In her trademark baggy cardigans, tent dresses, Mumsey stood firm, hands on hips. 'Sorry, Jo,' he said.

Disguising her actions, she kissed him on the forehead, and so all could hear, 'Feck you, Jane Austin, you're a bleedin' wuss.' Tantrum over, normal relations restored, and grinning, Jo made her way to her seat, and everyone breathed.

In the meantime, Mandy returned from the Ladies producing a roll of toilet paper and collected the sellotape. Jack hissed as he examined his knees then his toe, laid back, and put his handkerchief to his bleeding head. Peeling a strip of sellotape, Mandy said, 'You put your head back for a nose bleed, dinlo, and don't look to me to get the bogeys out of your cut; that hanky is filthy.'

He bolted upright, 'You say the nicest things, bacon-bonce.'

'Bacon-bonce?'

Panicked, and not wanting people to think Oldtimers had set in, 'Just made it up.'

Too late, Dolly was in, 'No you didn't, we used to say that all the time in the fifties.'

'The 1850s, Dolly?'

The Dolly and Jack banter would have continued if Mandy had not said, pleasantly, 'Sorry, Dolly, we've things to sort before we go home tonight.'

'That's alright, dearie, I was going to clean next door first, least that's what Jamie said to do. He was in a good mood, d'you tickle his fancy?' Dolly remarked as she went off chortling and spraying, Jack thinking his office might be no safer than Chernobyl.

Mandy thought about the highly polished floor of the CP Room. Jack had apparently been offered a carpet as this voluminous, old and tired room still had the original plastic tiles. He'd refused, and playing the old cockney boy, said he preferred the "Oil clorfe," or to the posh, linoleum. Dolly loved the floor, polished it regularly to a beautiful shine, and Jack would say, "Look at that, real working class, proud of what she does, happy with her lot but wanting the best for her kids," and he meant it; Dolly was his girl, and woe betide anyone who upset her.

Mandy summoned the team to the jumble of tables Jack had dubbed the "chaos table." Jack decided he needed his deckachairo, offered up a token *Cornetto* and, complete with fresh toilet paper and sellotape, but still clasping the blood-soaked handkerchief to his forehead, he sat, feet up.

Wotsermatterwivim, Mandy thought, looking around at the

team: Jo-Jums; Nobby; the beautiful Alice Springs; Half-bee who was DC Eric Timpson; Kettle, a tall slender black man, not a huge intellect, posh, deep voice, real name Russell Hobbs; and Wally, a bear of a man whose real name was Ken Burke. 'Where's Biscuit?' she asked. Biscuit was a Detective Sergeant, recently transferred from vice to work with Jack. Biscuit said he liked his nickname, preferred it to ginger nut, which was the unsubtle epithet given him in vice; he had an abundance of curly, ginger hair. His real name, Brian Smith.

'Biscuit's on something for me, Mands,' Jack answered, though he did wonder where he was.

Mandy continued, 'Jo, where are we, drugs and the gang assaults?'

The question hung in the stilted atmosphere, Jack looked sheepish, and Mandy thought the delay was because Jo-Jums needed to shuffle her thoughts and reply in her usual succinct manner, but instead, Jo replied, 'Begging your pardon, Ma'am, and I appreciate having to look up the leg Jane's shorts can be a mite distracting, and please pardon my French, but what the feck are you talking about?'

Jack took his legs off the table and wrapped up the ends of his shorts, miffed, 'That's not French, it's Irish,' he said, 'and why's everyone looking up me shorts? You could always look away, Jo.'

Never one to be bested by Jack, Jo retorted, 'I was intrigued, you seem to be covered in toilet paper, including a big lump sticking out your arse.'

Mandy had been around Jack and Jo for many years and would not let this spat distract her; this was either a play on *Father Ted* or Jo really had no clue as to what was going on. Jack was sweetness and light, having taken his legs off the table, stepped out the deckchair and settled in his wheelie chair, and she knew, this was not *Father Ted*.

Jack shaped to speak when there was a faint scratching at the door; Jack ignored it. Mandy thought, did he ignore it or did he not hear? He started to speak, scratching again, 'Come in,' he had heard. Nothing, a continued scratching, Martin was alert, ears pricked. 'Come in, for Christ's sake,' a distinct tutting from Dolly next door.

Mandy admonished him with her eyes and went to the door, shaking her head. Hovering in the doorway was a flat screen atop a box of tricks encircled by a pair of spindly arms. The machinery spoke, 'Scue me, bu' I go message you wan' me.'

Jack shouted from his chair, 'Confucius? Come in, sweet-'art, and put your stuff over there.' Jack waved his hands indiscriminately around the room that clearly Confucius could not see as Confucius couldn't see anything over her burden, but it was clear also Jack had not a clue where Confucius would be working; not his problem.

'Let me help you,' Mandy offered.

'Oh, fang you, Ma'am.' Yep, this is Confucius, who put her stuff down in a space along the back wall, and standing beside Jack, she started to talk about getting a ping slip from Hiss Sid and "Not know wot it mean." Jack had conspiratorially asked Sid to use the pink *Post-it* so she would say "Ping," not being the most politically correct man you would ever meet.

'Jane can't see out of his right eye, love.' Mandy said.

'Oh, solly about eye, sir, does hurt?'

'Only when I laugh, but it does help me to sense when something is amiss.'

"Like shagging," a unified chorus from the team.

Confucius shuffled to Jack's left side, and he could see Way Lin's four-foot-nothing, skinny frame, round face with *John Lennon* bottle glasses and distinctive teeth; well, not four-foot, more like five-foot, but if you could not exaggerate in this life, what is there left to live for, Jack thought, exaggerating to himself.

'Solly, sir, I no unerstan why I here?' and Way Lin looked in horror at the toilet paper, sellotape, and the blood saturated, bogey-ridden, handkerchief, 'Is this joke, sir?'

'What, the toilet paper or the job?'

'Ah, bofe, I fin.'

Jack answered using his kind and sensitive voice, usually reserved for kittens and villains, accompanied with his universal wry smile, 'Way Lin, you wanted to do more in computers?' Way Lin was confused, and Mandy wondered if Jack came up with Confucius because she was Chinese or whether she was just confused. 'You've been working with Hissing Sid, right?' Way Lin nodded. 'Well, he's recommended you, so what d'you say?'

'I only done free eve classes and Googled Millwall for you, sir,' Way Lin answered.

Mandy gripped the edge of her seat; it stopped her leaping up in dismay. She'd seen Jack, over many years, do some daft things, but wondered if this time he'd lost it, big time. He'd clearly not briefed his team, hijacked the investigation for what can only be called a cowboy outfit to run, and apart from Paolo, everyone was up for it. She shook her head slowly and jumped with everyone else as Jack all of a sudden leapt up and strutted; it was his look *how masculine I am* walk; she was reminded of John Wayne with a carrot up his arse.

'Don't worry your little cotton socks, Confucius babes, you'll be working alongside Frankie, a real computer expert, and you'll love her too,' and he nudged Confucius with his elbow, and she went flying across the room as Jack's one eye winked; and they say he can't multi-task.

Amid the team's confusion, and the patent fear on the

puffed oval face of Confucius, Dolly shouted from the other room, 'You will, she's lovely.'

'Dolly, why don't you put your cleaning stuff down and join us,' Mandy called back.

'I would if I thought I'd hear something interesting, dearie,' the faint, almost feeble reply muffled by a hiss that signalled the death knell for the Ozone layer.

Mandy put her hand to her forehead, apart from Jack's not particularly subtle reference to Frankie's sexual preferences, and the fact he thought the two girls would get on famously, in more ways than one, it would appear he had also discussed this with Dolly. She felt obliged to reassure Way Lin. 'Jack's right, Way, you will...'

Way Lin interrupted, 'Oh no, I call Lin, no Way.'

Jack resisted the obvious comment, and Mandy appreciated it. 'Okay, Confucius,' and Jack winked with his good eye, 'Jack is right, he and Dolly, by all accounts, Frankie is the best.'

Mandy stood, stretched fully, arms and legs akimbo, and Jack thought, there's never a sunny window when you need one, and talking into a yawn, 'Why don't we all meet up tomorrow morning, get the ball rolling. Before then, perhaps Jack will tell you all what he just told the Commander, why you lot should be leading this feckin' investigation with the world's best feckin' computer expert on the team.' Way Lin mewed as Mandy sat back down, sighing loudly, which set Martin running back and forth.

'When time?' Jack asked, rubbing his hands together, thinking he'd gotten away with it, which caused Martin to stop, his dog aware he rarely got away with anything.

Nobby, keen to impress, 'I can do 6.30, Guv.'

Jack swung his gaze around the room and settled to lecture the new boy. 'Nobby, Nobby, my boy. Are you married?' Jack shook his head as though what he was going to say was obvious.

'Of course not, I'm not sure you would get on with her guide dog...' paused for laughter, flicked his hand in receipt, '...and how many children do you have? How many American Cop TV shows d'you watch?' Nobby was looking worried. Jack gestured his bloodied head to Jo, 'Take Jo-Jums, she and her husband have to get up before the four kids, get themselves ready, then get the kids up and abluted.' Mandy smiled; she'd not heard Jack say that for a while. 'Then she gets them breakfasted while Tanner does the lunches; on a copper's salary, you can't afford school dinners, not with this government anyway...' He paused to look around to see if he could spot a closet Tory in his team. 'Then you have to get them to their different schools, always assuming they're all well, and one doesn't want to go, and you suspect it's because they're being picked on, and what can you do about that?'

Jack took a deep breath, intending to move on, put his hand up to stop Nobby from talking, looked at his hanky and planted it firmly back on his forehead, out of sight out of mind, another Jack maxim. 'As you go through your career, you'll meet coppers who will imitate the yank cop shows on the telly and tell you that you need to work all the hours God sends. All that will get you, old son, is a divorce, unhappy kids that resent you and the police, a shorter career than you imagined, and you'll likely drink yourself into an early grave.' Still with his stopping traffic hand up, 'You'll meet coppers who will tell you to distance yourself from what happens, not to take anything personally. You'll witness black humour at a murder scene, but all that will get you is more of the same.' His arm was hurting, so he swapped it, propped the new one with his other arm, this replacement hand wavering with the bloody hanky. 'Nobby, to be a good copper, you've got to empathise, and when it's shite you feel, you have to grow with that. You need a home and a family and someone you can share the good and the bad times.

You've got to be there, because it'll not happen otherwise, and you can't do that working all hours. You need to understand people, what makes them tick, and, when you've done all that, you Nick the feckin' bastards.'

Everyone chortled, except Dolly, who stood unnoticed at the back of the room. She walked to Jack, who stood to greet her, towering over the diminutive cleaner, and she cried into his ballooning waist; Jack had saved her son from drugs, gangsters, and the gutter. Dolly's son was now an accountant, and if rumours were to be believed, Jack had helped fund him through college. Here ended Nobby's lesson.

Jack collected Dolly's sprays and, hugging the old girl, Martin following, quiet, they left the room that was Jack's room, it sparkled and gleamed; it was loved.

TEN

Jack saw Dolly off as Sergeant Dawson was preparing to take over Sid's fish-and-chip counter in reception. Dawson didn't have a nickname, probably because he worked the night shift, something he professed to like, and if you knew his missus, you might be tempted into the graveyard shift yourself, even the grave. The nearest Jack got was, "Have a care, Dawkins," from PP, but it never caught on.

The telephone rang, 'Jack, your dad,' Dawson called, gesturing with the phone.

'Told you, Jane, a man saying he was your dad,' Sid mumbled from behind his hand, getting ready to leave.

'It's not that I didn't believe you, Sid, but considering my dad shuffled off his mortar-foil many moons ago, I was not in a tearing hurry to have a conversation with a bleedin' loony. Put it through to the back office please, Dawkins.' The phone in the back room remained silent. Jack shouted, 'In your own time, Dawkins,' and decided to ignore the muttered expletives as the phone was ringing, 'Dad, feeling better?'

'Jane, sorry about that, but I knew you received calls from the father, so I thought this would get your attention.'

Jack recognised the voice, 'Biscuit, you dinlo, why not call and say it was Biscuit; where are you?'

'Jane, we need to talk and not in the office. I'm not sure who we can trust.'

'Bit minternational man of mystery, eh? I'll be down the seafront walking Martin about 8.30, getting dark then, so will suit your clanbestine requirements?'

'Okay,' Biscuit said, hanging up.

Jack spoke to the dialling tone, 'Would be useful to have your number.'

Jack returned to reception where Nobby was kicking his heels while Dawson roughhoused with Martin. Jack couldn't resist, 'Have a care, Dawkins.'

'Sir, a word?'

'Nobby, I'm running late and Michael's cooking.'

'Michael's cooking?'

Nobby was not spotty, he had a fresh-faced complexion, which Jack assumed was because his mum was always scrubbing it. It was, though, a nice face, slim, his build more the athletic Dorothy than the *Billy Bunter* of his dad. Nicely turned out, tall, a good-looking lad, smart, polished shoes he noticed even at the end of the day. 'Why so surprised? You need to get out from the apron strings, but not before your mum's taught you to cook. So, what can I do for you?' Jack's patience was ebbing.

'I wanted to apologise. A lot of strings were pulled for me, and I know you resisted, but Dad said you were the one to learn from. He did add I should filter out the shite, but in my view, Sir, and from the little I have seen and heard from others, this is what makes you who you are.'

Jack yawned, it had been a strange day. 'Nobby, six-thirty tomorrow?'

'Yes, sir,' excitement scrawled on his cherub face.

'Come in and set up the crime wall.'

'Thank you, but...' he looked nervous, '...I've never set one up before.'

Jack put his arm around the lad's shoulder, felt his eye getting heavy, his energy had been sapped, and he still had to overthrow the government. 'Go home and sit with your dad, talk to him about what you've heard so far, and listen to what he says. Your dad, before he became a twat, was a good copper, and for the record, I resisted like mad taking you on, but now I'm glad. So, feck off, I'll see you early tomorrow.'

'Will you be in, sir?'

Jack groaned, 'I've got to finish Dolly's cleaning of the Sissy room.'

Jack watched Nobby disappear up the stairs he had fallen down this morning, admiring the sure-footedness of the young, but inwardly, knew he still had it.

'You're a softy, Jack.'

'Yeah, Dawkins, but don't tell anyone.' Jack peeped a discordant whistle, and Martin leapt off the counter, scampered through the entrance door, to be lifted into the front gunner's seat. It was chilly, so he put on his bright red eejits anorak with hi-viz vest. Kate used to say he looked like an eejit in it; he missed her. Daylight fading, he switched on his flashing front and rear lights, screwed up the note from the commander, and cycled off whistling, singing, and talking to himself; just what he needed, a good chat and a sing-song on the way home, and he sensed his anger rise as he thought about the Coalition Government; his mind turned from *The Sound of Music* to sedition.

ELEVEN

Jack locked his bike in the forecourt garden of his semi-detached Southsea house. This had been the family home, and since Kate died, it had become his pain and his comfort, an old house of classic proportions, cream painted render and expansive Georgian sash windows. Jack thought it was like a happy face, comfortably familiar when you got to the big brass door knocker, Kate's insistence. He used to say how he liked her knockers; she laughed! He certainly knew how to amuse women.

Michael opened the door before Jack could get to his keys; Martin rushed in having had a wee and a smell in the bushes. 'Leaving your bike outside, Dad?'

Taking off his coat, 'C&A's later,' Jack's term for the Crown and Anchor pub, and bending and oomphing, his shoes not complying, he squeezed out an unnecessary explanation, 'to plot the overthrow of the government.'

'Hello, Mr Austin,' it was Michael's girlfriend, Colleen, from Irish parents, so Jack's Cod Irish was really appreciated;

don't ask, Jack just knew these things. 'Hallooooo, Martin,' and Martin was at the crouching Colleen's crotch; they got on well, and why not, it was a lovely crotch.

'Colleen, call me Jack, or Jane, please.'

Colleen took in the picture of her boyfriend's dad, a composition of eejit shorts, mango, toilet paper and sellotape, and focusing, was that bogeys in drying blood on his forehead? She was off to medical school with Michael soon, so Jack assumed she was interested in bogeys. 'Okay, ah, Jack,' but she could not stop looking at him. Jack noticed but was also aware he was good looking. 'You are good looking, Jack. I see where Michael gets it from.'

'Did I just...?'

Colleen smiled. Michael was back having tidied his dad's shoes after he'd thrown them, intending for them to learn a lesson and not to be stubborn in the future. 'Michael's cooked a beautiful dinner, err Jack.'

'Cosmic, darling. I'll just change; had the piss taken out of me all day for some reason.'

Colleen ventured a mention of the preponderance of toilet paper and sellotape that preoccupied her vision, 'What happened?'

'You went out like that this morning, didn't you, Dad?' Michael answered.

'Yeah, minus the magno,' Jack replied, proud his son had inherited his own powers of diluted observation, 'time for an Eiffel Tower, son, wash the day off?'

'If you hurry, Dad.'

Jack went upstairs, shaped to go to the front room he shared with Kate, but he had given this to Michael to use as a bed / sitting room to entertain his mates, which these days was more often than not just Colleen. Shortly after Kate had died, he moved to the back bedroom. It wasn't bad, close to the bathrooms, and if there were people staying he could generally make a dash for the toilet in the middle of the night without having to put his dressing gown on, but truthfully, the other room had too many memories. Jack stripped, appreciating his vision of loveliness in the full-length mirror as he pulled himself to his full six-foot-four, contracted his stomach, patted, 'Jacko, you've still got it.' He checked, no toilet paper sticking out his bum, 'Jo-Jums is good', and dashed to the wet room, ducked under the shower, screamed as the hot water hit his head wounds, his knees, and his toe.

Scrubbed up, Jack put on a frayed denim shirt, his favourite, a pair of tired cream chinos and fun socks, penguins and dogs, which he didn't like, but Colleen had got them for him at Christmas. He grabbed his tan, brogue, dealer boots to protect his toe and make him look roughty-toughty, and carried them downstairs. Colleen spotted the socks, smiled, said nothing. And who said Jack Austin knew nothing about women? Michael brought the fish out, the vegetables already steaming in their serving dishes. Michael was a good cook. Kate and Jack had always cooked properly, and it was a rare day they did not sit around the table. Jack looked at his son, the dopey teenager, disappeared, and from his chrysalis, a new man was born; welcome back Michael, a pity Kate was not here to see.

'How was your day, Jane?' Colleen asked, embarrassed using the nickname.

'Not much to report. Mandy Lifeboats had a flea up her arris this morning, brandishing last night's evening news. Present company expected, Colleen, never sure I've understood women.'

Smiling at the malacopperism, Colleen replied, 'There was an article by your mate Bernie about a fight in East Cosham, and he quoted an anonymous police source that basically said tough shite the police were late, I didn't vote for the government. I'm not paraphrasing well, but Mandy may have thought the quote came from you?'

Jack chortled as he savoured the last of the fish. 'That was good, son,' and making a smacking noise with his lips, apparently like his Dad used to do, Jack got up. 'I'm gonna walk Martin,' and Jack slipped on his red eejits anorak, removing the hi-viz vest; he didn't want to look an eejit. Said his goodbyes and headed out the door with Martin going bonkers.

'Martin excited?' A neighbour. Jack liked his neighbours, apart from the local snooty Duchess, who thought she ran the street as a mediaeval feudal manor, and occasionally Colonel Blimp. 'God save me from arseycrats and military types,' Jack said, agreeing with himself; he was an agreeable chap, he thought as Martin pulled for all he was worth. They headed to the seafront, Jack whistling, singing and talking to himself, Martin making hoarse choking sounds, not unlike Jack's singing.

As he crossed the expansive common before the seafront, Jack reflected on the events of the day. He now knew what was bugging Mandy, and Bernie will likely be in C&A's tonight. He'll see Biscuit in a minute, but something bothered him about Osama's. Paolo was antsy, and Jack smiled; he'd robbed the case for the hell of it, but it could be convenient, and didn't law and order begin and end with community policing? The Government may be saying involve ordinary people, but you can't fool Jack Austin, and he checked to see if his nose grew. 'Come the resolution, brothers,' Jack said, punching the air, causing Martin to stop and look. Martin knew Jack had been distraught at the election of a Tory Prime Minister, enabled by a Lib Dem Muppet, and he worried for his master.

Feck, I need a bit of sedition tonight, Jack thought, noticing he was walking briskly when he'd promised himself a saunter, part of his anger management. Oh well, start that tomorrow. Biscuit would be just around the bend of the promenade.

TWELVE

It was cloudy, the full moon obscured, but the diffused light was enough for the flat sea to give off that shifting sheen Jack loved, leaning on the promenade railings, looking out to the Solent, while Martin sniffed every blade of grass, crook and granny. After a while he realised his vacant gazing at the shipping, their lights moving slowly across the water, the twinkling from the Isle of Wight, some lights from the nearby Spitbank fort, had allowed time to pass on. He whistled discordantly for Martin, 'Where the hell is that dog?' Looking for the flashing collar light in the near darkness, Jack began to get angry, so Martin nudged Jack's leg as if to say, "I've been here all the time numpty."

Biscuit was late. Jack hurried off the common, rummaged for his phone, cursing he didn't have Biscuit's number. Stood under a streetlight, the light on his phone didn't work anymore; probably needed a new bulb. The elastic bands and duct tape meant it was a delicate to use, but he was able to call Kingston Police Station, and the night deteriorated.

'Kingston police.'

Jack thought he knew everyone at Kingston. 'Who's this?'

'Who's this?'

'I asked first,' Jack said. She hung. He dialled again, his phone flagging, and he made a mental note to get some more duct tape as well as a bulb.

'Kingston police.'

'This is Detective Inspector Austin, I need to get hold of Biscuit, I mean Detective Sergeant Brian Smith. Can you give me his mobile number please.'

'Are you the funny guy that called just now?'

Jack was irritated. 'I am, and you should not hang up on calls, it might appear odd to you, but it could be important—'
She hung up.

He rang again. 'Kingston police.'

'This is DI Austin, do not hang up.'

The telephonist got her retaliation in first.

'Listen, I don't know who you are, but I'm volunteering for this work. That means I am not getting paid. I am giving up my free time to pitch in and help this country due to the dire straits the Labour Government left us in.'

Jack could feel the hairs on the back of his neck stand up, the feckin' Big Society had reached his Nick. The bile in his stomach bubbled; this was his Labour Party she was talking about, not that he was a member, wasn't even sure they would want him, and in his view, it was the greedy Tory bastard bankers who got the country in this mess. His eye was giving him gyp. 'I'll say again, this is DI Austin, and I need to get hold of Detective Sergeant Smith. It's urgent; I need you to give me his number.'

'I cannot give out numbers, how do I know who you are?'

'Put me through to Dawkins on the front desk.'

'Aha, if you worked here, you would know his name was Dawson,' and she hung up. This used to be easier, he thought as he rung back.

'Kingston police.'

'Listen, darlin', phone Sergeant Smith and tell him to ring DI Austin, take down my number, and if you can't get hold of him ring me back, comprendeh!' He thought, nice touch that, Mexican, sure the telephonist had not detected he'd incorrectly used his Gestapo accent.

'You, sir, are not a pleasant man,' must have picked up on the Gestapo, 'why do you not phone his wife?'

'What?'

'Sergeant Smith's wife has been calling saying he was expected home.'

'And what did you say?'

'I told her he was likely in the pub with his colleagues, like they do on the telly.'

Jack sighed. 'This, lady, is real life, and believe it or not, coppers are not always down the pub,' but she'd hung up again just as he realised he was about to go to the pub. 'The Big Society. Help!' he shouted to the black sky, and Jack thought he saw the couple crossing the zebra crossing nod in agreement, but if they walked that fast in the dark, they could trip.

———

JACK LOCKED his bike to his regular lamppost outside C&A's and made a call to Mandy while Martin cocked his leg. 'Christ's tits, you've wee'd your way around the seafront, surely you can't have any left.'

'Jack, I've just got into the bath, and the last thing I need is you winding me up about weeing around Portsmouth. You were bang out of order today, and I've just heard that rather than being a hero at an armed robbery, you interrupted Osama and his wife shagging on the rice.'

'To be fair, Mandy love, I never said that.'

'Yes, but you never said, "oh, I just interrupted some shagging, and there were no armed bandits." '

'No, you got me there, Amanda.'

She noted with a catch in her breath he had called her Amanda. Jack could hear the gentle lapping of her bath water, and his mind went a bit haywire. 'What is it, Jack? I don't like it when you go quiet on me; it's unnatural.'

'I was imagining you in your bath, and me in with you. I'd appreciate it if you didn't make me have the end with the taps.'

He heard her sigh, it echoed, 'If I wanted you to have the taps, you would have the taps, but as it happens, my taps are on the side, and before you say you'll be right up, I'm picturing you in the bath with your sellotaped toilet tissue toe hanging over the edge because you don't want to get it wet, two bony scrawny knees also with bog roll and sellotape, varicose-veined skinny legs folded double so they would fit in, and a head that must have been bashed around about a dozen times today and, unfortunately, not one of those times was me.'

There was a short silence. 'You imagined me in with you.'

'Jack, I'm trying to unwind.'

'I'll take a rain check, suppose a fuck's out the question?'

An exasperated sigh and agitated water. 'Jack, why did you call?'

The end of the conversation was nigh, he had a sense for these things. 'I'm worried about Biscuit. He was the one calling saying he was my dad.'

'Well, now I'm worried about him.'

'No, he was scared, Mandy. I arranged to meet at the

seafront, only he didn't show. I phoned the nick, and some tart answered who said she was one of Mackeroon's volunteers saving the country, said Biscuit's wife had been calling, expecting him home. Telephone tart suggested he would likely be down the pub like all other coppers. Mandy, what's happening?'

'Big Society volunteers. I'll make some calls, where are you?'

He mumbled a response. 'Err, just going into the pub, but I'm meeting to talk sedition,' he replied, as though this was a reasonable thing.

'I'm going to pretend I didn't hear that, now get off the line and leave your phone on.'

'Wilco, Ma'am, roger you and out,' and he hung up to dodge Mandy's repost, and man and dog went into the pub.

———

C&A's was a quiet, old-style, English local, no music, and a friendly landlord and landlady. The long, narrow bar had its inconveniences but meant you were easily in touch with the other regulars. Sidling along this bar, Jack acknowledged greetings from friendly faces, and as he approached the counter, Bruce the landlord was filling Martin's bowl with cooking bitter, Martin's favourite; it was weak, so he didn't get too pissed. Jack's drink came second. It's a dog's life, he remarked to himself as he always did. Jack called out to his table of co-conspirators, they all had full glasses but had a drink off him anyway, except Bernie, who wanted a cheese sandwich. 'I asked if you wanted a drink, not a four-course bleedin' meal,' Jack responded curtly to the dishevelled reporter.

'Cheese sandwich?' Bruce asked.

'Yeah, old cheese and no pickle, got any stale bread?' Then Jack's standard, 'How much? How Much!' and paid, he always did. He needed more exertion classes, and lifting the drinks over heads and around bodies, 'There you go, you greedy bastards, and there's a cheese sandwich coming for the gutter press.'

'You prolong active life, Jack,' Bernie said, quoting back one of Jack's expressions that drew on a dog food advert for *PAL*. It amused those present except Martin, who looked up from his bowl, thinking *PAL* would be nice, better than the dried crap he was forced to eat. Jack had heard this all before, and many times, especially after Martin had had a drink.

Jack supped a satisfying draft of beer and scanned his co-conspirators. Bernie Lebolt, a medium-height fella, fair hair going grey, no surprise at just over 50, but still thick, the hair but Jack did wonder. Bernie showed the wear and tear from smoking sixty a-day, dishevelled clothes stinking of fag ash and sweat; Jack thought Bernie cultivated his reporter look. He had no woman, no surprise there.

What could you say about the intellectualising Brainiac, a University lecturer? Jack would say, "Shut-up, Brainiac, we've come out for a larf," thinking it odd Brainiac didn't enjoy his jokes, nice bloke, bushy academic beard, struggling to disguise flaky skin below that made you marvel at the stomachs of women.

Pin Head was a short nervous man, dead skinny, dead ugly, like a shrivelled prune, and dead jumpy; they called it St Vitas dance in the old days, sitting still only when it was his round. Brilliant sense of humour, which Jack thought essential with his condition, but you had to concentrate as he bounced all over the place.

Then there was the evangelical Jon-Bob and Mary-Bob, husband and wife with the look of the Von Trapp family; fortunately, C&A's didn't have a puppet theatre, although he'd often noticed them eying up Bruce's curtains, probably to make play clothes. A nice couple, though irritating, finishing each other's sentences, but it was fun distracting them and observing their frustration when they messed up.

The good thing about all Jack's fellow conspirators was they could sit all evening and not say a word to each other, enjoy a few beers, leave and say they'd had a good night. One of the qualities of a good English pub, sublime nothingness, companionable and comfortable silence, and despite the desperate need to overthrow the Government, this was one of those nights where little would be said. Mackeroon could sleep safe; Jack's thoughts were of concern for Biscuit and miffed Bernie wanted a cheese sandwich.

A murmuring, much like *hubba, hubba*, energised the comfortable silence, and Jack took in the vision of loveliness that was Alice Herring, framed in the portal to this fine, but ordinary, hostelry. Alice was scanning, looking for someone, and when her eyes alighted on Jack, she wiggled her fingers as if saying hallo to a two-year-old. Always intimidated by women, which he never acknowledged, Jack lifted his arm and mimicked a finger wiggle in response; reduced to a quivering imbecile by a girl, Jack Austin, what are you man or moose?

He did a moose sound, trying to get his deep voice going as Alice wafted like a wood nymph would if there'd been a carpenter around, making her way in a sensuous slow motion, passing by stunned men and envious women. Alice swivelled her beautifully rounded hips, tightly contained in Levi's, and sat on Jack's lap, stroked his face with her right hand, slipped it around his neck, and pulled his face to hers. She hugged and kissed his disfigured cheek, lingered around his neck, and breathed in like she was enjoying his scent in an oxygen tent; and Jack, being only human, was affected by this and not just in the cheek, neck, and ear department, wondering if Alice was asthmatic.

She surfaced, a stunned silence in the bar. 'Jack, is that your telephone?' but that was on the table, was she stupid? She kissed him again; so what if she was learning impaired. 'My oncle Alf wants to meet you at the Mother Ship,' huskily said. A *Star Trek* aficionado could be convinced this was a temptress alien luring him back to her spacecraft for scientific experiments, except Jack knew Alice Herring's uncle was Alfie Herring, a villain shading the likeable rogue side of dangerous, and the Mother Ship was Alfie's local pub in bandit territory. 'Spit-spot,' and she made to lift off his lap.

'I'll need about ten minutes before I can respectably walk out of here.'

Alice smiled sweetly; make that fifteen minutes. 'Mandy's in for a treat, but I have to admit, I'm wet.'

'You are?'

'Yeah, Martin's been licking my hand.'

Jack slumped. 'Alice, babes, I'd love to meet your oncle, but I'm not up to cycling all that way, and my bike's outside.'

She looked into his swimming eyeball, and he readied himself in case she sat on him again. 'Is it?'

Aware of the silence, the thumping pulse in his ears, Jack gathered his anorak and used it to cover his embarrassment, croaked, 'Police work,' and bent double, shuffled to the exit as bright red as his eejit coat. As he stepped outside, so the jeering started, quietly at first, and reaching a crescendo of, "*Get em down, you Zulu warrior, get em down...*" 'They always sing that when I leave. I think it's juvenile,' Jack said.

The cool air worked wonders for Jack's bits and pieces, but what really did the trick was his bike had been stolen. "Bastard," he said, several times.

An amused Alice suggested this was not likely to get his

bike back. 'Jump in my car; we can report it tomorrow morning.'

Like a Buddhist mantra, Jack repeated "Bastard" as he climbed awkwardly into Alice's old mini, bending his stiff, wounded knees. Martin pushed past to get on the front seat; he liked to pretend he was driving. 'To the back, hound,' and Martin weighed up the prospects before bounding into the back seat, and the mini gave a throaty roar as Alice screeched off. Jack thought he would liked to have had a conversation with Alice, sort of post-coastal, but was too scared, looked back to Martin, legs akimbo, claws out and thoroughly enjoying himself. Feckin' dogs!

In what seemed like a lifetime, but probably only a nanosecond, they pulled up outside The Mother Ship, completely the other end of the City. An attractive Hansel and Gretel, figurative pub from the outside, Victorian, glazed ceramic tiles, frosted windows, acid etched, but that was where the fairy-tale charm ended; this was a bandit pub, in bandit territory, and he was a cop Hansel and didn't think going in with Gretel would help. Jack thought he must be mad; this was not the sort of place you go in if you were a copper, except Alice, who was Alfie Herring's niece.

The Herrings were one of the big Pompey *Families*, related to the Splifs along the way somewhere. They were everywhere, and Jack began to rethink his concept of community policing, getting out meeting the people, but then he had in mind nice, civilised people, not Herberts. A bit like being a doctor. He always thought it would be okay treating nubile young women; after that, it went downhill, even if you could stand the sight of blood, and Jack couldn't, even struggled with the odd magno. I wonder if my bike's in here, he thought.

Alice had parked and wafted across the road, feline, a sensual walk, pushing a barrage of intoxicating perfume. She patted Jack's backside, 'Come on,' and breezed into the pub. Fearless Martin, the wonder police dog, was in like a rat up a drainpipe; the door slammed in Jack's face. Thinking he may have lost the impact he wanted, he gingerly pushed open the door, his bum feeling odd, as did his kissed other cheeks.

THIRTEEN

MACHINE GUN FIRE GREETED JACK ACROSS THE CROWDED and hostile bar; Uncle Alfie was laughing and playing with Martin; Alice giggled at his side. A cheer mutated to a jeer when people spotted Jack; he wasn't sure how to read this. Oh yeah, fuzz alert, but he brazened it and moved into the crowd wishing he had Harry Potter's invisibility cloak.

A thug with one brain cell blocked his way. 'Well, if it ain't dead eye Dick.'

Jack thought, he had to be Slytherin. 'Jack, but you can call me Jane,' Jack said, feeling more than a bit Hufflepuff.

One cell started making pig noises. 'We don't like pigs in here.'

To which Jack replied, rather wittily, he thought, and with no hint of the fear he felt in his watery bowels, 'Darcy, I would not be as fastidious as you for a kingdom,' his best Biggam.

One Cell, obviously inspired by PP, moved onto creative thinking, 'You're doing my fucking 'ed in copper,' obviously Wickham; you see, are you not diverted?

Alfie diverted his way through the testosteroned melee and directed himself to the skinhead. 'Now, now, One Cell,' blimey that was his name, 'Jack's my guest, got that.' Alfie was quite clear in what he meant, and turning from One Cell, 'Fanks for coming, Jack, sorry about the bleedin' Nazis. Come, sit, what d'yer want to drink?'

Still beside One Cell, Jack replied in his best Hufflepuff voice, 'Campari and soda, please, Oncle Alfie.' Had Mandy been there she would have rolled her eyes, again.

'Fuck off,' Alfie shouted and, turning to the bar, 'pint of best, my table.' He was talking to Len Bone, the fat greasy landlord in a dirty vest that seemed to stop just beneath a fine set of man boobs, supported by a thick black belt that held up huge shiny arsed trousers.

As they sat, Alfie looked at Jack quizzically, 'You really want a Campari, Jack?'

'No, that was for One Cell's benefit,' and Alfie's machine gun, fitful laughter, was enthusiastically enjoined by the other customers, although clearly none of them had any idea what the joke was. Alfie was about the same age as Jack and had to be a good villain to survive this long, with the patent respect. Always smartly dressed in a suit, Italian, slim tie, straight out of the sixties. He was short, and that made Jack think of small-man syndrome, but Alfie had the personality, presence, and presumably the backup, to overcome any deficiencies in the height department. He was a man to be respected, whether good or bad, but Jack liked him.

Jack took a long suck of his pint. He needed this following the kiss with Alice, strange feeling that, her driving, One Cell, he had an odd sense of elation, he might get out of this pub alive. Mickey Splif sidled and sat. Alfie's eyes swivelled in their sockets like a ventriloquist's dummy, and Jack had to stop himself laughing, which morphed into concern Alfie was having a stroke, when Alfie's lips screwed and he started speaking out of the side of his mouth, 'Good fing you did for Mickey's boy. You're a diamond, and that's sayin' somfing for a filf. Got the lad a job with Osama as well.'

Something was brewing within Alfie, Jack thought, and it wasn't a fart. But it was a fart, and he let it go by lifting one of his substantial cheeks off the chair, and the parping noise and aroma received respectable acknowledgement as the toxic miasma pervaded the bar like a nuclear cloud. Jack was put in mind of Mrs Ali's breath as he laughed and gagged with the rest, then shut up with the rest. The gangster's face gurneyed to release confidential information, 'I wantsyer to see Mickey's missus, 'ave a cup of splosh, she wants ter fank yer, personal loike.'

Looking at Mickey, aware all eyes in the pub were on him, and every one of them watering due to the chemical reaction of bad eggs and onion, Jack replied, 'Really? There's no need.'

But clearly there was, 'No, yer missing me drift.'

'I'yam, I finks I'yam?' Jack couldn't help mimicking out the side of his mouth.

'I'm sayin' go see Gail, make like you're having a good chinwag, you might need to take some antidote for the tea wiv yer,' and he laughed, which was a cue for everyone to start breathing again and laugh with him. 'When you've spent a respectable time, take a gander at a terrace of houses down by the community centre,' and at that, he touched his nose, apparently knowingly. This was clearly the signal for something dodgy but was also the signal, beware shagging in progress. Obviously universal, Jack thought, but he was intrigued, for Alfie to speak to him in a very pointed way meant this was something important, and he was about to question further when there was a blood-curdling squeal.

Jack knew Martin had been hurt and, looking up, saw his

dog fly across the room, hit the distant wall and slump to the floor. Alice attacked One Cell, and Jack, in a berserking mist, saw another skinhead go after her. He was out of his bench seat, on top of one table then another, drinks spilled, glasses smashed as he launched himself at the now two skinheads attacking Alice. His fists and feet flailed, and the two lads had no repost, taken more by surprise than by Jack's pensioner brute force, on the floor having the lights kicked out of them, not moving.

Instinctively, Jack moved to One Cell, pulling Alice away as he went in battering and kicking. He scurfed the brawny yob against the bar, held him, and time stood still, then out of the blue, Jack nutted him. One Cell's nose split and teeth broke, reminding him of his mum's best rag and bone china when, as kids, they played football in the living room. He heard in his mind his dad call "Cups," even One Cell was shocked, but not as shocked as he was when Jack tipped him over the bar as Len Bone looked around for the cups.

Jack clambered over the bar and hoisted One Cell by the scruff, shoved his shaven head into the washing up sink, holding him under the dirty water, bloody bubbles surfacing. Alfie was calling to Jack, 'S'alreet, you've done im, ease up he's not werf it, old bill's on its way.'

Jack released a limp thug, who slithered to the floor. Alice zipped around the bar, grabbed One Cell, laid him out and started to pump, then amazingly gave him the kiss of life, those lips that had kissed him now on this bottom feeding lowlife. One Cell was recovering as the police burst in, weighed up what was happening, grabbed Jack, and frog-marched him through the pub door, Jack protesting he was a police officer and the arresting officers' laughing, as they thrust him into the meat wagon. Martin was limp and lifeless, blood dribbling from his mouth.

After a short drive, the van halted, 'Out you come, sunshine,' and strong arms steered Jack forcefully from the van to the desk in the custody room; public enemy number one. He'd been taken to Cosham nick, and when the custodian sergeant appeared, Jack thought, I know him, but what's his name?

"Allo, 'Allo if it isn't Jane Austin, shag spoiler and pub brawler extraordinaire. Welcome, Jack, my old cocker, been read your rights?'

Summoning deep reserves of energy, 'Rights, you plank, I'm on an enquiry,' Jack pleaded.

'In the Mother Ship? A quiet drink and a chat with those 'ardened crim-types?'

Jack remembered this bloke now, Nitty Norris, corpulent rugby ball-shaped body with a complementary football head with wisps of hair that seemed to move in a wavy motion, and along with his mystic ping pong ball eyes, the effect had a tendency to mesmerise Jack. 'Listen, Nitty, I'm entitled to one call, right, well, call Superintendent Bruce. I've got her number on my phone.' He took his phone out, and it completely disintegrated. 'Feckin' duct tape.'

'No worries, Jane, I'll call Kingston and get her number.' Oh no, Jack thought, and sure enough, ten minutes later, Nitty came back. 'What's going on in your nick, all I got was this snotty bird who kept hanging up and saying she and Mackeroon were saving the world.'

'Nitty, lock me up, I'm tired and shagged out, but do me a flavour, get hold of Alfie Herring and ask how my dog is, please.'

Nitty's face changed, he might not like Jack, but everyone loved Martin, there was immediate concern. 'I'll do that, I'll get one of the boys to drive you home, or do you need casualty?'

Shaking his head, 'No fanks, Nitty, just me hands are scraped to buggary and my toe's about to fall off.'

'What's that, gout?'

'Yeah, Nitty, goat.'

FOURTEEN

Portsmouth Evening News
Mother Ship Pub Brawl
Crime reporter: Bernie Thompson.

*A police spokesman said officers were at the scene
within a few minutes of receiving the call from landlord,
Len Bone, but could not comment on the cause of the
fight, which was the subject of an ongoing investigation.
The three injured persons, taken to QA Hospital, were
known members of the National Front and will be questioned by Police.*

*There is no local Community Policing committee in this
area, but the Chairman of citywide community policing,
Captain John V. Littleman RN, said, "There is a two-tier
society developing where the working-class areas get a
rapid response police service, but the middle classes,
those who actually pay their council taxes and are law-*

*abiding citizens, have to put up with a reduced police
cover and are at risk daily from the riff-raff."*
*Captain Littleman is tipped to be the next Conservative
candidate for Portsmouth North.*

———

Sparrow's fart. Jack wobbled beside his bed; he
ached and deep breaths hurt. In the bathroom mirror, he
thought, if seen in a prudential light, the damage to his black
and blue face seemed superficial; physically a wreck, ego intact.
He suppressed tears, thinking of Martin. Alice had telephoned
in the night; she and Alfie had taken Martin to the animal
hospital over the hill in Wickham. He was concerned, he did
not trust Wickham, the slimy snake out of PP, but Alice reassured him it was an animal hospital. Alfie had found out where
the vet lived, who got out of bed to deal with Martin. Jack
wondered if he should inquire as to what threat or benevolence
Alfie had to bestow, but Alice volunteered her uncle had given
the vet five grand in cash and no other option.

Jack was touched by Alfie's generosity, ignored how
someone can have five grand in their pocket and what else was
needed to induce the vet to get up? Leave that for another day,
or never, probably a horse head in his bed. Alice had gone on to
say Alfie felt responsible for what had happened and would
take care of any costs for Martin, who had several broken ribs
and was being kept in for monitoring in case he showed signs of
internal injuries. The prognosis was he would be sore, but okay
in three or four weeks. Jack asked about visiting hours, and
she'd laughed, "Anytime you want, even if you have to get the
vet out of bed."

Jack showered. 'Bugger shaving, I'll have to look trendy,' he
said to the wreck in the mirror. Binned his ruined clothes,

thought about the cycle ride into work and remembered his bike had been nicked. 'Bastard, bastard, bastard.' Did he stamp his foot? Lucky it was the good one, the other was likely tantrum sensitive. It was Friday, he would drive into work, and in the afternoon get down to Bazaar Bikes and get himself another second-hand bike, an orange box from the greengrocers, and get Martin's front gunner seat sorted over the weekend; shame about the Noddy blanket.

Downstairs by 6.30, he looked like a battered cartoon character. He'd taped up his toe and put on his builder's, steel toe cap boots he'd bought for when he went on demonstrations and people were apt to tread on his size-twelve feet that stuck out at a quarter-to-three. En route to the kitchen, he decided not to make his muesli and have a canteen fry-up. Jack always bought the ingredients for his muesli and made it up just how he liked it; Kate had pushed him to look after himself. Funnily enough, although he said often man was not born to eat bird seed, after a while, he got to like his muesli and frequently told his colleagues where he bought the ingredients and how he made it himself, describing the recipe and process. Although they gave the appearance of being bored rigid, Jack knew it was just a front, and probably they were doing the same at home.

Having said that, and to himself, every now and then Jack would have a full-English fry-up in the police canteen, especially if he was a little down, his comfort food; and as he approached the kitchen, his mouth was already watering. He needed comfort and quickly but saw Michael had made his muesli and had left a note, "You said I could have the car today, wake me up before you go go."

'Sod it,' and Jack called a cab, decided to let Michael know about Martin tonight, and he was in the station just after seven, having forgotten to wake Michael before he went, went and eat, eat his muesli.

THE SCENT of hardened arteries pervaded the halls and corridors of this ugly police station, built for utility, not aesthetics, but Jack, perversely, loved it, and he put this down to a long working relationship with the building, flickering lights, scuffed walls and dangerous stairs. Bit like his community policing room Dolly made shine, a real woman's touch, and he thought of Mandy touching him, then Kate, Martin's licks, and this made him crave comfort even more. The melancholic Jack Austin surfaced, but as his psychiatrist had said, if you want comfort food, you obviously need comforting. The good thing about head doctors was they gave you really good excuses, and Jack used and embellished them all.

Dawson was uncomfortable as he watched Jack enter the police station. Jack was aware he would have learned of last night's fracas from the desk sergeants' grapevine. Dawson struggled, what to say, so Jack let him off the hook, 'Morning Dawkins, suppose you heard about last night?'

Gripping the edge of the counter, a nervous tick in one of Dawson's fingers Jack thought would come in handy picking his nose, the sergeant replied, 'Sorry to hear about Martin, how is he?'

'No, I meant someone nicked my bike.' More fingers joined in, so Jack let him off again, confident he'd saved Dawkin's nose. 'Martin's in a bit of a two and eight, but unless he has internal injuries, he'll be okay, thanks for asking.'

'He's a lovely dog.'

'See the Commander's in, what's happening?'

Dawson relaxed enough to release the counter. 'D'you mean apart from you taking the Mother Ship and half the Nazi party down last night, not much. The Commander's in with

Nobby,' a warm smile, and Jack felt kindness to the man who had to go home and preferred to stay at work.

'I'm going to the canteen.'

'Okay, Jack.'

———

'JANE,' Jean shouted, slipping out from behind the servery, wiping her hands on her apron and calling to the ladies of the canteen. Jack watched the sensitive animated face approach. Jean was head canteen bird, and next to Jo-Jums, was Mumsey personified, bleach-blond, frizzy hair, blue eyeliner, a wrinkled but warm face that reminded Jack of the prunes he put into his muesli, and frankly, this is what he needed this morning, Jean, not the prunes. She was not the rounded Mumsey, but the sparrow stick version, a bit like Dolly, he thought as he heard Jean's Pompey chimes approach.

'Said he'd be in for his comfort food,' and the ladies in the canteen, all shapes and sizes, surrounded Jack, circled their matriarchal arms around him and hugged, asking after Martin and squashing him in all the wrong places. It hurt, was comforted, started to cry and couldn't stop. Jack sensed the ladies retreat. Mandy stared from the doorway; he stared back, looked at his feet, his arms involuntarily wind-milling. He put his head to one side in a, *I cry, so what can I tell you?* She opened her arms; message received and understood.

'Come here, you big lummox.' He ever so slowly walked to her open arms, comforted he was her lummox, and Mandy embraced, hugged, and cried with him. 'I'm so sorry, I phoned the vet, Martin will be okay.'

'You phoned the vet?' muffled, he had his head on her shoulder and was thinking about seeing if he could snuggle into her breasts.

'Yes, I was concerned.'

Postponing his mammary mission, 'How d'you get the number?'

'Alice phoned.'

'Didn't ring to see how I was.'

'How are you?'

'Well... I hurt,' so she hugged him, he winced, but nobody appreciated good wincing.

After a period of sobs, ouches and mumbles, a resounding clap of hands made Jack jump, and it irritated as he had his head resting on Mandy's bosoms.

'Jack, full-English?' Jean took control. Mandy put a finger up to indicate, for her too, and they went to a far corner table, sat and stared out of the window, across the room, the floor, ceiling, anywhere but into each other's eyes, or his one. They ate their breakfast in companionable silence; Jack finished off Mandy's spare sausage and hash brown. She said nothing, which was a bleedin' miracle in itself, he thought. Mandy shooed people away, eventually whispering they should go upstairs.

'Ooh err matron.'

'You're better,' she responded, standing.

He placed his hand gently on the top of hers, and she sat, engaged his eye. 'You think I'm a loose cannon.'

'Think!' Things were certainly returning to normal.

'I need your help, Amanda,' she knew it was serious, he had used her full name, 'you think I blagged the investigation that I know nothing about what's going on. Not true.'

Leaving the table was no longer an option; she also liked the feel of his hand, and the look as his eye held hers. 'What is it, Jack?'

He took a deep breath, 'I asked Biscuit to join our team, and now I'm worried, he's on the missing list.'

'You suggesting Community Policing can be a danger to your health?' her gentle laugh stifled; he was serious.

'Depends, what you knew?'

'Jack, how do you know all this?' Her turn to be serious.

He thought she looked beautiful, wanted to kiss her. 'Can't say, but I want you to run with my calls this morning. Paolo's going to want to lead, and I'm going to let him.'

'You are?'

He looked at her as if to say, *Yeah, Yeah*. Mandy made to interrupt, but he put his hand on hers again. She felt a jolt of electricity. Jack noticed it as well and warmth bathed through him; for a moment, he didn't feel so alone. 'Paolo will lead off with strategies, blah, blah, I'm going to ask for Alice and Nobby, and two squad cars on alert, just in case.'

Putting her other hand on top of his and gently gripping, 'Jack, I will back you because something is going on. I also know it generally revolves around you, and I don't want you hurt. So yes. By the way, did you know the Commander is in this morning? Is that also something to do with you?'

He nodded.

FIFTEEN

In what looked like a new shiny suit, Paolo had installed himself in front of the crime wall and arranged the chairs to face him, nervy. The Commander had stayed, and he braced for a confrontation as Jack, and when this did not happen, he was palpably disconcerted.

'Eh, whattsamattawivyou, why you no makatha starta?' Mandy said with a chuckle.

Jack loved Mandy's sense of humour; the Commander was also tickled. Paolo enjoined the exuberance, and his team followed. Confucius was wary. Frankie patted her hand and whispered something; Frankie had moved in, was moving in.

Paolo kicked off, smarmily, 'I see someone's got the crime wall going, nice attempt. We'll sort that, show you how it's done.'

Mandy interrupted, 'Commander, d'you want to stay behind, find out where you went wrong?' Paolo choked, and it dawned on Mandy, Jack had set this up the previous evening, bringing the Commander together with his son. She stole a glance, Jack was smiling, she liked his smile. Shite teeth, she thought, knocked about he always said, but a lovely smile if you screwed your eyes up. Paolo stammered excuses, Mandy listened and imagined, in the same position Jack would have gone to PP, quoted some extended bastardised text about meeting Wickham in Mereton, he called Worthington, or something equally stupid, and by the time he'd finished, he would have defused the situation; the difference between the two men. Mandy was proud of Jack, although her gut instinct informed her, trouble was brewing on Cherry Tree Lane, but where from? She looked around with her, wary head on.

Paolo restarted, 'There's a new drugs outfit in town, which is why I have invited Cyrano to assist...' Cyrano flinched, but let it go. Paolo unaware. '...How is the stuff getting in and where's it going, Cyrano anything to add?' Cyrano shrugged, Paolo gathered himself. 'My team will work strategies, any questions?'

Jack resisted, left it to Mandy. 'That's it, is it?'

A ripple of laughter, and Paolo realised what seemed like a punchy and succinct briefing to him when he rehearsed it in front of the bathroom mirror this morning, despite being hurried up by Ting Tong, was in reality, lacking. 'Well, early days, I expect we will start to build a picture as the investigation gains momentum.'

Mandy pressed, 'What about Community Policing?'

Paolo responded sheepishly, 'Ma'am, I expect Jane to organise his team into basic ground research. Intel from the street, any ideas here, Jane, apart from smashing up pubs, Nazis and coitus interruptus, your contribution, I am sure, will be valued.' Paolo sneered, it came naturally to him; a ripple of laughter confined to the sissies, supporting their man.

You patronising gobshite is what Jack wanted to say, but instead, in a polite and civilised manner, worrying Mandy and everyone else. 'Ma'am, I would like Alice Springs and Nobby with me this morning. Springs is briefed,' he looked at Alice, 'can you bring Nobby up to speed?' Alice nodded. 'Jo-Jums, I'd like two squad cars at the ready, then if you could head up a team to look out for Biscuit, please. He didn't show last night. He was worried about something, what were his enquiries? Biscuit is missing, and I fear for his safety...' he paused, allowing Paolo to steam, '....I'm not convinced this is about drugs, although drugs are certainly involved, maybe funding something. My gut instinct? It's about power. On the streets? Who knows? The key question will be who and what are they intending to do with this power? So listen up for shifts, anyone uncomfortable, has anyone new surfaced?' Jack allowed a little time for this to settle while Mandy confirmed he could have all that he wanted. 'Cyrano, you okay teaming up with Jo?'

'Sure.'

'If I might make a suggestion,' Jack followed on, 'sound out known drug barons, suppliers and street infrastructure because you can be sure they're looking for these guys just as much as we are. Sit in on the interrogation of the East Cosham gang members, please, although this doesn't gel, there's something else there, religion, radical Christians? What the hell?'

'Okay, Jane,' Cyrano moved, settled, probably exhausted.

Jack moved on, 'Frankie and Confucius, money movements. Port Authority, check on ferry traffic, anything odd? I've a feeling this is small. If we can crack this, we might just find out what's really brewing, but my bet is this will be only the start.' He called out to the ether, 'Frankie, can you get me a new idiot proof phone, please. Mine, for some inexplicable reason, gave up the ghost last night.' Frankie gave Jack a knowing glance, an American rolled salute, and this surprised Mandy; it was familiar?

Paolo grudgingly admired the way Jack had taken control, but needing to get the knife in, swung his arms around to enlist everyone in his question, 'Jane, enlighten us, what do you think is going on?'

Jack rubbed his stubbly chin, thought he must look like one of those male models. He noticed Mandy giggling and realised he'd spoken his thoughts but ploughed on, 'Happening? Don't know, but let's be clear,' he panned his one eye, 'not a word outside this team, something is not right in our State of Denmark. I believe Biscuit found something and has been nobbled before he could tell me last night. So the investigation stays here. Are we right on that?' A healthy chorus of agreement flattered Jack, but he already knew he was good at rallying the troops. 'Any questions?'

'Just one, Jane,' the Commander, 'is the wall okay?'

'Yep, exactly how we want it, thanks, Jamie, and you, of course, Nobby. Oh and, Commander, I don't want any volunteers in the chain of communication, please.'

The Commander looked shamefaced. 'Noted, heard about last night. God save us from do-gooders.'

'It's not the do-gooders, Jamie, it's the government cutting costs and at the same time passing responsibility to the people, and making us feel grateful for the opportunity; don't play cards with Mackeroon or Blogg. Okay, let's get to it. Jo-Jums my back up; Alice, brief Nobby; and stab vests.' The Commander blanched, 'I'll look after him,' and patted the Commander on his shoulder.

'I know you will, Jack, I know.'

Jack mouthed a thank you to Mandy, touched her shoulder, and got a warm smile in return as he telephoned the vet.

'Martin is pretty knocked about, but thankfully he may not have anything seriously wrong internally. We operated last night to manipulate his ribs and dislocated jaw, stitched the knife wound on his back leg. I will keep him for about a week, let me have your mobile number, and I will call if anything changes,' the vet said.

Jack gave the vet Mandy's number. 'When can I see him?'

'I believe the gentleman who arranged for Martin's care arranged flexible visiting. I will give you the out of hours number.' Jack noted this down, thanked the vet. 'Mr Austin, I would like to say you should not take a pet on a police operation.'

Miffed, Jack replied, 'Martin is a police officer, and if you would tell him I've bought some PAL, please, it'll brighten him up.'

The vet was unfazed, 'I do not think tin food is good for Martin. We recommend the Science diet; it is a dry pellet food that will give Martin all the nutrients he needs.'

'Yeah, Doc, don't mention that,' and Jack hung up, did a wheelie on his imaginary motorbike, screeched the tyres, and went out to meet Keanu's mum. He stopped in reception, kept his engine idling as partial reality dawned, his bike had been nicked, how could he have forgotten that? Revved and carried on into the rear car park, trusting in fate, looked around and there was a beat bike used by cycling patrol coppers, that'll do. The beat bike was fantastic, working gears, oiled, so no squeaking. Jack pedalled and felt okay.

Portsea was flat, and cycling was easy, but as you left the island, so the land rose sharply, but what was the odd incline to Olympic cyclist, Bradley Biggins? Up the hill, not bad, Jack thought as he pushed the bike. Nobody watching is the most important bit, did you ever see *Biggins* pushing his bike up a hill? Of course not. Some flat bits that were the approach to Keanu's house, one among many in this council house estate. A spurt of speed and a sharp braking manoeuvre outside the Splif residence, just to show anyone watching he was not to be messed with. He dismounted, realised he had no lock and this was bandit territory; they probably had his old bike. He walked the bike to the front door, rang the bell, it didn't work, tried the knocker, it fell off in his hands, and he was about to bash the door with his fist when Gail appeared. 'Hallo, Gail,' she took the knocker from him, 'stone me, you're gigantic.'

Gail filled the doorway and, with an equally wide smile, invited him and his bike in. 'I 'ope it's not twins, that'll be difficult.'

Shunting his bike into the hall. 'Shut-up, Gail, you wouldn't notice them amongst the ten you already have. Give up the Catholic Church and join me, Church of Egypt.'

Jack laughed but responded to a pronounced, Ahem!

Gail directed Jack's gaze with a nod. 'D'you know Father O'Brien?'

'Christ's Tits, Jesus, sorry, bollocks, feck, did I just say that?'

'You did, Jack, feck is okay, not sure about the Church of Egypt, or even the breasts of our Lord, but it could mean he will embrace and succour you and your camel,' the Father smiled warmly; they knew each other.

'Always the smart arse, Mike, but I'm glad you're here,' his serious head on.

'Martin?'

'He's right poorly.'

The Father nodded, 'I'll say a prayer and light a candle, he's in Wickham, isn't he?'

'How'd you know?'

'Alfie Herring. Ah Jeeez, Jack, everyone knows Martin's a Catholic. Alfie has asked for him to be mentioned in a mass.'

Keanu lumbered in, teenage Neanderthal. 'Huh, Mr Austin.'

'Keanu,' Jack acknowledged the lad, 'not at school?'

'Half term,' grunted, Jack understood, was partial to frontier gibberish himself.

Gail berated her son's manners, 'Cup of tea, Mr Austin?' Father Mike gave Jack the knowing glance; now that's how to do it.

'No, ta, darlin', Alfie said you fancied a chin-wag.'

She cracked her cup on its saucer like it was a lead weight and smacked her lips. 'I wanta fank yer personal like, getting my Keanu off, Saturday job as well, diamond.'

'No fanks needed, hold that job down, Keanu, and do what I asked.'

'Will, promise,' excellent gibberish.

Gail sat opposite Jack, legs wide awake, tucking into pineapple chunks and Mumbai mix, and spectator Jack felt nauseated. Keanu noticed, 'Alfie...show yer houses...community centre; d'you...go?'

Jack grabbed at gibberish salvation, 'Better 'ad, sorry to pebbledash, good to meet you again, Father.'

'God go with you.'

But Jack was already backing his bike out and bumping into everything, including God as he went with him. 'Keanu, where am I going?'

SIXTEEN

'WHAT D'YOU EXPECT TO FIND?' KEANU ASKED AS THEY walked.

'Not sure, but make yourself scarce, got that?' Keanu mumbled a response that Jack assumed was agreement. He could see the community centre in the near distance, a mini, parked on the steep sloping driveway to the car park, gave a quick flash of the headlights. Alice and Nobby in place with a fair view of the frontage of the short terrace of four council houses, set into the steeply sloping landscape. Back garden not covered, but the ground fell steeply away to the rear, difficult for surveillance, also tricky for a quick dash from a nosey copper.

'Righto, Keanu, bugger off,' and Jack rubbed the boy's hair to Keanu's clear irritation; it made Jack smile. A skinhead Jack recognised from the Mother Ship, sat on the door-step, rolling a joint, spotted Jack and went to red alert. 'Oi,' Jack challenged, threw the bike against the privet hedge and loped down the steep garden path and steps, reaching the door as it was closing. 'Hold up son, a word,' and Jack jammed his foot to the threshold and screamed as the door slammed, the lad stopped, temporarily taken aback. He could only have been sixteen, tall, skinny, a bony arse sticking out of low-slung, filthy jeans, a stained elastic top to protruding underpants that clung to non-existent hips, a swastika tattooed arse crack. Jack doubted even Hitler would want this filthy tow-rag with black pegs for teeth.

The boy released the door, and as Jack folded to examine his toe, he dodged the thrown punch; the boy ran. Jack sensed the saturation of adrenaline pervade his body as the arse crack disappeared, heading for the kitchen back door. He limped in pursuit only to meet the boy returning who dipped his shoulder and rammed into Jack's rib cage. As Jack blew and stumbled, his peripheral vision picked up a naked woman with a tiny baby clutched to her breast, deadly still on the kitchen floor. Jack righted himself, Nobby was framed in the street doorway, and it was difficult to tell who was more startled, but Nobby's, "Oi you," caused bony to leg it up the stairs.

'I've got him. Nobby, check the front room, in the kitchen a woman and a baby, call an ambulance.' Jack took the stairs two at a time, turned on the landing, and looked to the front bedroom to see the skinhead climbing out the window. Breathing heavily, Jack lumbered into the room, his eye was immediately drawn to the bed and Biscuit's bloodied body, the quilt cover black, dried blood, the distinctive ferrous odour. Jack recoiled, but his berserking mist and momentum carried him to the window, clawing at a filthy tee shirt as the skinhead jumped. The drop was not high if you leapt outwards, the front garden rose at a steep slope, and the boy landed and sprawled on the grass. Jack clambered onto the window cill, wriggled his body through the window and launched, expecting to land by the side of the skinhead as he started to rise, but he belly flopped on top, a face full of tattoos and a not too pleasant smell. 'Oomph!' and bony Nazi looked like he might sit this out for a bit.

'Get orf him.' A bloody-nosed, fat bastard, waving a knife, came from the front door. Nobby must have got one on him, Jack thought as he swayed to avoid a swipe of the blade, and leaning back on bony, landed an upward kick into the fat rib cage, twisted, and with his other leg kicked the knife from fat boy's hand; one for the toe caps, a passing thought that maybe he should take the boots back to the shop as his toe throbbed.

Fat boy pushed Alice as he made a wobbly exit from the garden, and she rollypollyed down the grass bank. 'C'mon, Alice, no time for frolicking, cuff bony arse and check on Nobby, I've got the fat bastard.' Jack wasn't worried; he could catch this overweight lump of lard, likely a few joints to the wind, and he gave a confident ambling chase, reconsidering his tactics only when the bastard bent down behind the privet hedge and popped up with the beat bike. 'Oi, me bike,' and Jack gave chase knowing it would be a forlorn hope.

From nowhere, Alice's mini careened across the road into the bike, spinning fat bastard onto Alice's bonnet, and we're not talking Easter, and Jack thought, how come I think these things when I should be focused? But allowed himself a titter while he watched the somersaulting thug-blob bounce off Alice's car, which was fortunate for him because the mini ploughed on over the bike, stopping eventually halfway into the hedge. Momentarily, all was quiet before a metallic scraping as the driver's door pushed against the privet, and Keanu squeezed out, face to face with Alice Springs, busy cuffing bony, who was complaining some fat old sod had just broken his back.

'Nick him, Alice, and see if you can find that fat old sod?' Jack ordered.

The squad cars had swung sideways to close the road. The obese skinhead was stirring, lifting his face, and Jack could see the job Nobby had begun had been substantially enhanced by the road and pavement. Jack contemplated some additional creative boot work for luck, being superstitious, but for a split second couldn't remember which foot had the bad toe; the moment passed and probably his luck with it. 'Cuff him, then come with me,' he called out as the second squad of uniforms arrived, 'paramedics in the house as soon as they get here,' they were arriving as he spoke, 'kitchen, mother and baby, top, front bedroom, gunshot.'

Jack looked at Alice, looking at Keanu, an expression that said, *what have you done to my car?* Keanu, gibberish free, answered the look, 'Sorry, miss, I didn't know what else to do. Aren't you Alfie Herring's whatsername?'

Alice, a tight grimace as she forced her knee down on bony's back, 'Niece. You're one of Mickey Splif's kids, right?' Alice and Keanu were having their little chat as Nobby stepped from the house, he had a slash across his shirt sleeve, and blood was dripping from his lower arm.

'Keanu, take my handkerchief and wipe your prints off the steering wheel and anything else you touched,' and just as Jack was about to add get off home, an enormous woman determinedly waddled in and dragged Keanu from the car, clipped his ear, dragged him two more yards, stopped, hugged, clipped his ear again, then dragged him once more. Gail took Jack's handkerchief from Keanu and threw it on the floor, 'Where d'you get that filfy rag?'

'Gail, go easy on the lad, and that's Alice's hanky.' Jack turned to Nobby, bleeding onto the front step, and before he could cry, 'Nobby, paramedic. That's it now, well done, son.'

Nobby looked relieved. 'House is clear except for the top room at the back, it's locked, and I think Biscuit's dead on the bed upstairs.'

Alice dragged bony to the car and looped the cuffs to the

steering wheel. 'Don't go anywhere, gorgeous,' and shouted after Jack, 'Jane, wait for me.'

'You talking to me, Ms. Springs, only I thought we had a lovely thing going in C&A's last night, and within a few minutes, you're kissing an 'orrible skinhead on the floor of a pub, and now you're whispering sweet nothings to a tattooed Nazi.'

She looked at him with a familiar, don't-be-an-idiot look she reserved for men. 'I was undercover. Still, best not to tell Mandy, eh?'

'What's Mandy got to do with it?'

'Sir, you can be such a tosser, and my handkerchief?'

The paramedics had already entered, one team in the kitchen, another set to go up the stairs. 'Front room, Barry, back room's not clear yet.'

'Gotcha, Jane,' Barry the paramedic replied.

Climbing the stairs, Alice pushed in front of Jack. 'Alice, it's bad luck to cross on the stairs.'

She stopped for an instant, then carried on, calling back, 'Protecting the elderly, and I think it's if you're going in opposite directions. I grew up in a house like this. There are two rooms at the back, a big bedroom and a box room.' Standing on the landing, outside the two rear bedroom doors, Jack could sense Biscuit in the other room, and he racked his brain, what else could he have done? He was not a guilt merchant, but he had to think these things through in order to move on. Alice poked her head into the bathroom and heaved; syringes, shooting gear and a lot more. 'Yep, I lived in a house just like this,' she said.

Jack thought he liked this girl, but focused on the rear bedrooms, put his ear to door one, turned the handle, locked. Alice put her ear to door two, turned the handle, locked. Jack made finger gestures, and Alice signalled back she didn't understand. He made all kinds of fiddly idiot gestures, including sticking his fingers up his nose; she folded, smothering her snigger, and as she came back up, Jack kicked the first door in, the second followed. 'Brilliant boots,' he said, a token toe feck, then, 'Oh Christ, Oh dear...' Jack was known for his exaggerations, but sometimes he was the master of the understatement. He looked instantly devastated, 'Paramedics, Alice.'

She'd seen and was ahead of him. The paramedics were coming out from seeing Biscuit. Barry confirmed he was dead as they peered into the larger of the back bedrooms. On the floor were three women and two children, naked, the air fetid with the stench of shit, piss, and vomit, a comatose skinhead on the floor. Jack tip-toed into the room, and from behind the door, another skinhead launched himself. Jack straight armed and the man was down; the toe cap made sure he stayed. 'Didn't see a thing, Sir,' Alice said.

'No, but you have to be impressed.'

'Looked like he was totally stoned, still won't say anything,' and turning in the doorway, she instructed a uniform officer to get both skinheads cuffed as she checked the women and children. Barry was calling in, requesting more ambulances.

'Alice, have you got your phone?'

'Yes,' she was subdued, her eyes beginning to puff.

'It takes photos, right?'

'Yes.' He flicked his head towards the room, 'Get a couple of snaps then let the paramedics get to work.' He stepped out as Alice commented "Snaps?" and Jack went into the box room, aptly named as it was floor to ceiling with boxes. Jack opened one, full of flier leaflets, a headline in black on a white surround, red highlights as if blood was dripping off the ends of the letters;

DEFENDERS of ENGLAND

KEEP ENGLAND FOR THE WHITE ENGLISH
Let the streets run with blood

THERE WAS MORE, and not Shakespeare. Inflammatory stuff. Jack pocketed the leaflet; he would read it later, but knew what it would say, and turning to leave, he looked at Alice, 'What?

'Listen.'

'Sorry, darlin', I'm a bit Mutt and Jeff.' Then he heard it, faint, a whimper. Jack moved a few boxes and revealed a pair of startled, petrified, emerald eyes in a cherub face. A tiny emaciated, naked girl. Jack thought, six, maybe eight years old. She could not have hidden herself, could never have lifted one of these boxes. Someone had deliberately concealed this girl; to save, or punish? A question for later, the girl's shock and fear was palpable, had she even blinked?

Jack tried to offer as many comforting words as he could, 'It's alright, you're safe now, I'm a policeman. I'm here to help you, sweet'art.' She understood. Feck, he had automatically thought they'd stumbled upon people transporting foreigners, Caucasian, European, maybe Romanian, but no, this girl understood him. Shifting more boxes, calling more comfort to the girl, he cleared a space, and on his knees, he approached at her eye level. She had pissed and shit in the corner, was covered in it, how long had she been here? He tried to show no revulsion.

'Please, mister, don't hurt me.' Faint but clear, and definitely English. Jack hummed a tune and intermittently gave more reassuring words. He opened his arms; he saw the strength drain from her emaciated frame as she fell into his embrace. Jack's mind buzzed, I'm going to cry, what's happening to me? Was this his midlife crisis? He cuddled the girl, denying his thoughts, a rancid smell, heart in front of his other senses. Little pats and tiny kisses, he continued to hum his tune, gazed back at Alice, dry racking breaths at first, but inevitably his tears came in floods. Slowly he stood, sobbing, crushing the girl in his arms. 'Are you moy dad?' whispering in his ear, shallow, moist breath. 'Dad, I wants to go.'

Alice whispered, 'Pompey accent.'

Jack nodded, hugged the girl covered in her own waste, opened his jacket and wrapped it around her, tight. She responded to the comfort and snuggled her head into the crook of his neck. He was unsure whether to press his head to her, to offer additional reassurance; he'd not shaved that morning and was cautious of her delicate skin. He chose to go for comfort, and Alice nodded, understood his dilemma and approved his decision. There was a commotion behind, 'Close your eyes, darlin'. I'm taking you somewhere safe.'

She screwed her eyes, nose, and her mouth at the same time, like they were joined, clutched tight, and Jack's breathy sobs convulsed his body as he backed out of the room, his left hand over the back of the child's head so she could not turn and see what lay around her. Jack saw past Alice; paramedics triaging, calling, working, asking, and praying? Shocked but professional, 'Thank God for those guys, paid a pittance, taken advantage of by the government and even abused by some people, but who do we call in our hour of need, not Big Society volunteers, that's for feckin' sure.'

Alice touched his arm, 'No time for politics, Jack,' and he walked the landing, carefully watched his feet down the stairs, whispered, 'Nearly outside, sweet'art. I'm taking you to an ambulance and hospital.'

Faint again, 'I wants to be wiv you.'

'You will, darlin', you will.' Christ I must stop crying, he said to himself, as he thought, what to do? He started to hum a tune, a beautifully lyrical piece of music, and it was calming the girl. A uniform held the latch of the street door, and placing his lips to the ear of the girl, 'We're going outside now, there's a lot of police, ambulances and noise, but you're with me, and you're safe, okay?' She managed a nod of her head as she packed down against his chest. He responded, wrapping his jacket tighter, and she sighed; incongruously, she had sweet breath. He exchanged a glance with the constable, the door opened, and they were hit by a cacophony of shouts, blue lights flashing bright in what was now a gathering gloom. He looked to the leaden clouds; rain, any minute. Keep calm, if only for this girl's sake; God love her. The press and TV observed and recorded him talking to himself and crying as he traversed the path and up the steps.

A robust lady ambulance officer, Australian accent, green fatigues, approached and tried to take the girl who let out a piercing scream: 'Noooooooooo!' Jack's girding of loins and stifling of sobs was lost, get a grip, but he failed. He sobbed into the flashing cameras. The Aussie shielded them as best she could, softness in her face for Jack, wasted on the girl, snuggled into Jack's chest.

'Let her stay with me,' Jack said, then talking to the girl, 'Shall we get into the ambulance and let the nice lady take a look at you?'

Mew, 'No.'

Jack looked to the sky; he had to think practically, the girl is the most important thing, and climbed into the ambulance and sat. Gail's smothering presence dominated his emotions and the cramped ambulance; how on earth did she slip through the cordon, but this wondrous woman will likely amaze right up to her last breath.

'It's okay, little one, let me see your face, oh you are such a pretty girl aren't you.' Maybe it was Gail's Pompey accent working the miracle, or maybe the earth mother, but there were signs. 'What lovely hair you have.' Jack thought it was mousey, but supposed mousey could be lovely. The ambulance woman draped a bright red blanket on what remained of the distance between the distended, pregnant belly of Gail and her knees. 'My name's Gail, sweet'art,' she said, close in on the child's face, smelling her and planting little kisses on the cheeks. Tiny tears appeared, and Gail picked them up with the end of her finger and put them to her own mouth. This continued for some time before the spindly arms left Jack and reached out, Gail gathered the girl to her lap and wrapped the blanket around her.

Jack blubbed. Gail put her hand on his, how do mothers do this, they're like octopuses. 'We're going to the hospital together, love, I will not leave you, but we've got to let Jack go so he can catch the bad men, okay?' A mew, a nod.

Gail flicked her head, Jack kissed the girl on her forehead and whispered, 'You're a beautiful girl, and I love you,' backed out of the ambulance, stumbled down the steps, grabbed the side rails just containing his cussing, and then he melted. His supposed tomfoolery caused Gail to laugh, and after a moment, so did the girl; nothing like a clown, why do women always laugh at me, Jack thought, but it was worth it to see a sparkle in the girl's green eyes.

The ambulance doors closed and it drove away.

SEVENTEEN

'Well Jane, another wagon of shite?'

Jack knew the voice, didn't want to turn and present his emotionally ravaged face to the assembled press. He spoke to the disappearing ambulance, 'Paolo, thank God you're here.'

'Jack.'

This time he turned, 'Amanda?'

She took in his look, 'Jack, take Paolo and me around the scene, then casualty, get checked out. Is it true about Biscuit?'

Jack nodded, 'Amanda, get someone to check the rest of the houses in this block.'

She put her hand up like she was stopping the traffic. Jack was inexplicably offended, the hand came down onto his and gripped; it was all he needed, all he needed ever, loneliness and grief was shredding his heart. Jack felt tired and emotional, tried to convey this to Mandy, but she was focused, not unreasonably, and he knew this, but unreasonably he resented it; was he expecting special treatment?

'When you're ready, Jane.'

There were times when the nicknames haunted him, times

when he wanted to be Jack, and with Amanda, also unreasonable. He trudged to the house with Mandy and Paolo in tow, and that is what it felt like, dragging a dead weight, taking them around the house, describing the sequence of events. The paramedics had the situation under control, crime scene tape sealed the front bedroom; his mind drifted.

Mandy noticed, 'Jane, focus, please.'

He didn't, he couldn't, he was feeling light-headed and nauseous, aware as he grew older he became sensitive of what had been happening to his body over the years, it seemed so logical, difficult to bear, and sometimes he wished he could shut these feelings off, knew this would be impossible, and in his more rational moments, he wouldn't want this, but for now, he wanted oblivion.

On the upstairs landing it was not difficult to see into the scene and Biscuit's prone form; the smell, of course, you never get that on the telly. Mandy took a little time after looking at Biscuit and had heard him express his thoughts. Jack looked at her, she was probably thinking her own thoughts that she did not share, but he could guess; so final, senseless, a family man, the poor wife and the children, who will go to see them with the news? Should it be her, Jack, or someone from vice, although technically he had transferred to Jack's team, so?

'I'll go to see his wife, Amanda.' Her gaze penetrated, grateful he had read her mind, felt bad making him do this tour of the scene, was moved also, he had called her Amanda. She noticed he was not looking well, but this has to be done, and he would know that. 'We have photographs of the scenes here and in the other bedroom,' he said, 'obviously I had to disturb the room for the little girl, and the paramedics...' Mandy nodded.

Alice stepped from the second bedroom, 'One of the women is dead, stabbed looks like, the others, including the kids, look out of it; drugs. Off the record, Barry thought the stains and smells were older, that the occupants of the room may only have been here a short period; suggests a turnover of kids and women, Ma'am.'

Mandy nodded, her mouth was dry, her lips felt like they were cracking; she licked them. 'Thank you, Alice. What do you think, Jack?'

He noticed she had switched to Jack and he felt immediately better, had seen her dealing with the dry mouth, knew what that was like, looked at her lips and wanted to kiss them, to moisten them for her; his senses heightened.

'First of all, this is my case, and who is Barry?' Paolo asserted, agitated.

Jack snapped his head up, immediately calmed, and spoke in a deceptively quiet tone, 'Paolo, this is not about turf or territory. We have a dead copper, and some serious stuff here,' nodding to the bedrooms. 'Barry's a paramedic, we know, he often has an opinion, it's not formal or expert, but it gives us a heads-up at a scene. So, Paolo, initial thoughts?'

Mandy had to hand it to Jack. Whilst being nice and respectful, he had backed Paolo into a corner, but saw, his heart wasn't in it.

'Ma'am, scenes of crime are here, we should maybe let them get on?' Alice interjected.

'Thank you, Alice. Jo-Jums and Kettle are on their way. Paolo, if you are okay, I suggest Jo takes the rear bedrooms, your guys focus on Biscuit. Alice, can you coordinate what needs to be done until Jo gets here please,' and turning to Jack, looking deep into his eye to see how he was, but still talking to Alice, 'Jane said to check the rest of the houses on the block, so organise a few uniforms please.'

'We're already onto that, Ma'am.'

Mandy hemmed, deep in thought, 'Good, where now, Jack?'

Paolo answered for him, 'Back to the station, and let's turn over what we have,'

Mandy was still looking at Jack; he'd not answered.

'Ma'am, I'll see you back there.'

Mandy dismissed Jack's sarcasm and answered her phone, 'Yes, sir, we're just leaving. I wanted Jack to get a once over at casualty, it was hectic here, and I'm worried he took a bit of a pasting last night.' Jack was still in a daze, she did care; why was he so sensitive about her? She was still talking, and he was guessing what was being said on the other half of the conversation. 'Yes, Sir, sorry, Biscuit is dead, gunshot looks like.' She listened for a little longer, 'Just one moment,' she held the phone to her chest, 'how're you feeling, Jack. Jamie wants you back at the nick, he's sitting with Captain Pugwash (this was the nickname Jack had appointed Captain Littleman RN) and a couple of his Committee cronies...' she went back to the phone, 'sorry, Sir, Captain Littleman, yes indeed, heaven fucking forbid, Sir.' She pulled a harrumph face at Jack.

Jack was not responding, looking like he could slide down the wall. 'Tricky call, casualty or Pugwash, Pugwash casualty, chips or no chips?' he said.

'Alright, Jack, you seem okay to me, yes, Sir, he can come back.' Mandy listened intently. Jack thought she's trying to hear what the Commander is saying to Pugwash, satisfied, she pressed end and looked to Jack. 'Get yourself to the nick, I want a case conference straight after lunch, so clear Pugwash ASAP, and let's get some serious work done.' Her phone went again, she was impatient. 'Hello, who, just a second,' she looked at Jack, her face unreadable, 'a Father Mike O'Brien, for you?' She put her hand over the phone, 'Why does he have my phone number? Who is he?'

He looked at her as if she was learning impaired, 'Der! My phone is broken, you know.'

She was temporarily struck dumb by the crazy logic, 'Jack, you cannot do that.'

'Mands, Shush, I'm on the phone! Yes, Mike, what can I tell yer?' he listened, and listened some more, 'hold your Angels, Mike,' and Jack flicked his fingers, 'Mandy, pencil and paper?'

Mandy was not a happy bunny, and this was conveyed in the vehemence of her response, 'I thought all police officers had a pad and pencil?'

He flicked his head in frustration, 'Yes, that's why I'm asking for yours.'

'Paolo, your pad and pencil please,' Mandy said, and before Paolo could be embarrassed, a uniform offered his.

'Mike,' he started to write, 'okay, got it. Mike, will you look in on the girl up at the hospital, tell her I asked after her,' a smile developed into a laugh. 'Brass knobs, Mike, see you at mass,' he handed the phone back. Mandy had to close the call for him. 'Thanks, Mands,' well, she'd called him Jane.

'Mass, Jack?'

'Bless you, Ma'am,' and he sketched a blessing in the air, 'if I go to this meeting with Pugwash, that'll be two days running no deckchair? Just sayin'...'

Paolo looked bewildered, Mandy shook her head. 'Feck-off, and, Jack, shame we couldn't get to Biscuit sooner, but well done here; good call.'

He pivoted on the ball of his foot, not easy in bovver boots despite his ballet training. The stairs and landing were getting congested as he tippy toed. He looked a last time into Biscuit's room, sighed, and glanced towards Mandy. There was no need for words, except she managed some, of course, 'Ballet, Jack?'

'Why do you put up with that idiot?'

'Because, Paolo, he's a good copper...' she paused, watched Jack leave, tugged her bottom lip, '...I think?'

———

Climbing the steep garden slope, Jack met Jo-Jums fuming her way in, 'You knew something, didn't you, because it would have been nice to involve me, and this business with Biscuit?' She looked down at the ground as she kicked her toe against the footpath kerb, subdued. 'Bad business, wife and two kids,' she rallied, 'you knew, Jack?'

He responded politely because it was Jo, gesturing with his head for her to follow him away from the press. 'Sorry, but I wasn't sure what I was going to find, and had there been nothing, it would not have looked good for the team. Anyway, the drug angle is still important.'

Jo was mollified, 'Okay, but I want to be fully briefed, here on in, you forget I know you, and trouble follows you like a, like a... feck, what is it, who cares, but I want you to keep me informed.'

He felt let off. 'The kids and women could be local, not imports, what d'you think that's about? Check local missing persons? I've got to go, I borrowed a bike and want to get it back before it's noticed.'

Jo spun back to him, 'Jack, you plank, Hissing Sid was all over the place looking for that bike, berating the poor constable who didn't lock it up, his defence it was inside a police station not getting him very far.'

He smiled as he pictured the scene, 'I'll sort it.'

'Lord, give me strength,' Jo sighed.

'I'm sure he will, Jo, come to mass with me, bring Tanner and the kids.'

Nothing more to say, they went their separate ways, Jo-Jums thinking he'd gone holy Joe, called back, 'Bad smell.'

'What?'

'Follows you like a bad smell, you stink.'

He looked down at his shirt, smeared with the girl's mess, as he leaned forward up the slope of the garden path, thinking he should retrieve the bike wreckage and scam a lift back to the nick. The crowd was showing no sign of dispersing, the news wagon's still here, irritating, and Jack stood transfixed by the mangled bike when Bernie appeared.

'What's the score, Jack?'

'How d'you get through?' A shrug of shoulders from a uniform. 'There's a press conference late afternoon, so don't bother me, I've got to get this bike back to the nick, and then I've a meeting with Captain Pugwash,' Jack replied, distracted.

'Captain Pugwash?' Bernie's mind ticked over. 'Put your bike in my car, looks like it might fit, now, I can drive you back. I like the sound of Pugwash, and anything else, anonymously attributed of course?'

Jack smiled, saw a solution to his problem for a price he was prepared to pay, 'Bernie, you're a tart.'

———

JACK BRAZENLY CARRIED the bike wreck into the undercover parking bays where he left it. Passed through reception where Hissing Sid was hiding behind his pencil.

'Jack,' Sid said shaking his head, 'nasty... you know, Biscuit. We have prisoners, are they the perpetrators?'

Jack was noticeably subdued, 'Well, they sure as hell knew about it, so make 'em comfortable, Sid, get my drift?'

'I've no idea what you're suggesting?'

Jack leaned on the counter, exhaled loudly, 'Fiddling kids as well, so clear the bottom of the pond for their dinner,' lethargically he shaped to move off, 'and Sid, some bugger's left a bike by the back entrance, get it shifted, I nearly fell over it.'

Sid became animated. 'You're kidding, we've been looking

for a bike all morning...' Jack shrugged, Sid calmed. 'Commander said to go straight up, but maybe you should change your shirt?'

Jack was reminded of the girl. He stopped on the stairs and sat, not wanting to go any further.

Sid simpered, 'You okay?'

He lifted his head from his knees, flicked his floppy hair with his hand and forced a smile, exhaling his words, 'Tough scene. I'd like to have a time where I could feel happy, I miss that feeling; happy,' and his feet on automatic, plodded the stairs. He went directly into the CP room and phoned the veterinary hospital. Martin was making slow but steady progress, probably staying in another four or five nights for observation. Jack's mind responded, I bet he will, courtesy of Uncle Alfie, amazing how snotty bastards become accustomed to the filthy lucre, and reacting to a tap on his shoulder, Jack jumped; shit, I'm edgy.

'Sorry, Jack, how's Martin?' It was the Commander.

'Slow but steady progress. Sorry I didn't come to your office, but I needed to know how Martin was doing, and, well,' he sighed, 'been a difficult morning.'

'No problems, must cost a fortune. I presume you have pet insurance?'

'Sort of, you could say that,' and Jack felt better about Alfie's money. You see, you just need a good explanation, as the psychiatrists would say.

'I'm beginning to hear about this morning, Biscuit, Jeez, hate it when something like this happens. Nobby's okay, thank God. How're you?'

Jack humphed, 'Last night, Biscuit, what we've found, women and especially the kids, suppose I'm fecked. Nobby was good, and Biscuit aside, I suppose we've had a result.'

'Yeah, but you up to meeting Pugwash, you look like shit, and what's that all over your shirt?'

Jack humphed again, but his mood lightened, he liked it when his nicknames were quoted back to him. Pugwash was a classic, based on Jack's memory of an old children's cardboard cut out animation series in the sixties. Pugwash was an inept pirate captain, the names of the characters double entendre, Seaman Stains, Master Bates, and Jack managed a smile as he pictured the chairman of the Community Policing Committee, thinking, I bet he's called Pugwash in the Navy. Captain John V. Littleman RN was a serving Navy officer and, in Jack's view, so full of his own importance he fell between two stools, the inept and a total martinet gobshite. Jack looked at the Commander, okay, he'd not spoken that thought. 'I'll be okay, let's get this over with, I need to focus on the really important things like finding my bike,' but the Commander wasn't listening.

EIGHTEEN

PUGWASH SPRUNG TO ATTENTION AS IF JACK WAS AN Admiral boarding the office, no discordant whistle, just a proffered hand. Not a good sign Jack thought, a bit like the kiss of death when a football club owner announces the manager has his full support. Jack returned the limp, clammy handshake. 'Captain Little...man,' dragging the name. Jack resisted wiping his hand under his armpit, thinking, how can a bloke rise to Captain in the Navy with a handshake like that? Pugwash was a tall, wiry man, about fifty, thinning hair he had cropped, probably ginger at sometime, but despite his height, he did not impress and seemed to know this, leaning forward to greet; must think it compensates. He had a weak chin and a slippery persona, and Jack thought he was like an erect Uriah Heap but without the humbleness, indeed the contrary, he was a self-engrossed martinet.

'Please, call me John,' a cheesy grin, which Jack retuned with brass knobs, thinking, I could throw up all over you mate.

'Then you must call me Jane, John,' Jack said and noticed the Commander roll his eyes, probably wondering why he'd not told him to stay away for a couple of hours. Jack could tell him, a mixture of fear of this naval tosspot, and a lack of empathy due to the rarefied air in the dizzy heights of the police upper chevrons. When do you stop being a copper and become a knob-head? No councillors here, Jack noted, relieved.

Pugwash indicated to sit down, mentioning he probably meant echelons, which Jack ignored as churlish and not at all manly, listening in on his personal thoughts, and not understanding how the Commander could let this man take over his office. Big Society, he supposed, where, in Jack's view, jumped up middle-class turds assumed they ruled the roost regardless of ability to do so, and only because they thought it their birthright. Come the resolution, Jack thought, maybe in C&A's tonight. He thought of Alice, then Martin, the little girl, Biscuit, and his only marginally elevated mood, spiralled.

Jack took the seat by the wall, more or less where he sat when he was with Mandy yesterday morning, only a floor higher, and he looked out of the window. He could see the top of Mandy's tree swaying in a stiff breeze, verdant, that strange sunlight you get when a storm is brewing, and it was. This seat also allowed him to direct his gammy eye to the Captain and his two ladies in waiting, aware they found this discomforting. At a previous meeting they had insisted he wear an eye patch; bollocks, he'd thought.

The ugly sisters were two obese women of a supercilious fat nature, totally obsessed with Pugwash, their officer hero, and from where Jack sat, if he turned his good eye, he could see their arses rolling over the chair sides; they were not comfortable. Playfully, Jack moved some, to see if he could get them to roll over. Now that would lighten his mood.

'Come and join us at the table, Jack,' Pugwash smarmed.

Supercilious tart, Jack thought. 'Thank you, John, but I've got shit on me shirt.'

The ugly sisters sniffed the air; no change in visage.

The telephone rang and Pugwash shaped to pick it up, but the Commander beat him, and with crossed eyebrows and a face that looked like someone had stolen his doughnuts, 'Are you sure one of the patrol cars has not run it over accidentally? Okay, Sid, if I get a chance, I'll raise it with Jack.'

'Problem, Sir?'

The Commander looked to the ceiling for his doughnuts. 'Shall we get on?'

Pugwash was raring to go, 'You can be under no illusion as to why I have summoned you, Inspector Austin.'

'Call me, Jane, and I'm completely at a loss, John, perhaps you'd be kind enough to enlighten me, and as fast as you can, there's a good boy, I'm very busy.'

More eye rolling, and under his breath the Commander tried to get Jack's attention, 'Please, Jack, and your shirt is whiffing.'

Pugwash unfolded a copy of the *Evening News* and made like he was ironing it with the flat of his hand. He pointed to an article, which Jack had not read but surmised the content, 'I'm still unsure of your drift, Captitano?' Jack was thinking of his deckachairo.

'Jack!'

Jack wanted to say to the Commander if the wind changed direction, his eyes would stay like Pugwash's face, which was showing barely contained rage, jaw sinews taut, teeth gritted.

'I will read it to you, Inspector.' And Pugwash read the article after which he sat back, tapped his fingers on the smoothed newspaper, and applied a look meant to convey all should now be completely clear. 'What have you to say, Inspector?'

Jack engaged the captain's eyes. Pugwash dodged them and looked down as if to scan the paper again. 'Well, amateur dramatics are not my thing, but I would say you read that tolerably well.'

'Jack, pleeeeease,' the Commander hissed.

Pugwash's cheeks bloomed as he climbed onto an even higher horse, 'What irritates me most about you, Inspector, is you never learn your lessons. Your arrogance and insolent behaviour a clear indication you have no respect for this committee, and me, as Chairman. You do realise the power I have? It was my recommendation you were demoted from Chief Inspector to Inspector three years ago. The idea of you sitting on this committee, when you grace us with your presence that is, was to enlighten you as to how to conduct yourself in future.' Pugwash stepped off his horse, looking like it was a job well done.

The Commander squirmed as Jack constructed an inquisitive face, checked with his hand, and approved, 'Captain, am I correct in assuming you believe it was me who gave the quote to the paper?'

Pugwash leaned forward, hands flat on the desk in front of him, bum off the chair leaning towards Jack, simultaneously raising his voice to a higher register, seething, 'I know you did, everyone is familiar with your political views.'

Jack felt comfortable he had Pugwash sufficiently riled, twisted his lips, as if to give the impression he was taking the man seriously; he was a good lip twister, practiced in the mirror. 'Captain, I am a police officer of long standing with a good record, which has been, I admit, varnished since you became Chairman of the Police Committee. I will not insult your intelligence by brandying insults other than to say, if I were to persecute a case with the only proof being a Captain in the Royal Navy, *knows so*, frankly, I would be laughed out of court. I'm not sure what it's like in the Navy, although I have inkling, but in Civvy Street, we need proof. I take it you have a signed statement from the journalist to back this up?'

The ugly sisters looked confused, wondering why he would want to persecute a case, but there was hope on the face of the Commander, accustomed to the malacopperisms. Pugwash fixed his grimace. 'No, but I think everyone around this table knows this is you.' He rattled the paper as if this proved his point, and the ugly sisters nodded affirmation; their faces wobbled.

The Commander found some courage, 'Jack makes a fair point, the article does say "anonymous source," so unless you have proof?'

Pugwash shouted his response, 'I will not let this go, Sir. I will be recommending the Inspector is further demoted and I will make this happen.' Pugwash reddened more as the anger flushed through his rusty face.

Jack stood, Pugwash flinched, and the Commander jumped up, thinking Jack was going to punch the Captain, but Jack was calm and collected. He relaxed, ever so slightly; with Jack you have to take respite when you can. Jack spoke, 'Captain, you make a fair point.' There appeared a slight easing of the Pugwash sinews; clearly he did not know Jack. 'I do not respect you, but let me tell you a story. I was asked to attend a school prize-giving recently and the main speaker, who should have been me, of course, was an Admiral in your Navy. The point of his talk to the children was he is often asked what it takes to command his battle feet, or something like that, I wasn't really listening as I had the hump, but the point was, why do men follow him? Was it clearness of strategy? Calmness under pressure? There were a couple of others, but frankly, I was only just getting interested when he answered. "All of these, but you cannot get any of them until you have earned the respect of your spordinates." The point is Captain Little...man, I do not respect you or your position on this committee because you have not earned it, and as for learning my lessons, the only lesson I have learned from you is that it takes a very little man indeed to feel he has to raise himself up by putting other people down. You abuse your power and your position, and as long as you continue to do this, you will never have my respect as a Chairman, but more importantly, as a man. Now, if you will excuse me, I'm in the middle of a serious investigation.'

Jack spun and strode to the door, but before he could get to the handle, the Captain called after him, 'Inspector, may we know the nature of this investigation, the urgency of which compels you to feel it necessary to leave this meeting before I have dismissed you?'

Jack turned, looked at the Commander, and raised his working eyebrow to indicate, *Commander may I?* To which the Commander shrugged his shoulders; what the hell. Jack sauntered back to the table, leaned on it with both hands flat, his arms locked straight, and lowered his head through his shoulders to look Pugwash straight in the eye, a foot from his face, and this meant the ugly sisters had a close up of the gammy eye. They could see every pucker and wrinkle, the white vertical scar that picked up the light, iridescent, the noticeable twitch like the non-existent dead eye was trying to get out and bite them on their snooty noses. Jack swung his good eye to the ladies whilst he allowed his dramatic pause to have the desired effect; they jumped backwards in their seats risking metal fatigue. 'Okay, but if this is leaked to the press, I will know where it came from...' paused for more dramatic effect, and let his eye linger, 'do I have your word on this?' an elevated voice, forceful and direct.

'You do, Inspector, we know how this works, but do you?' Pugwash smarmed, showing he was not intimidated.

'And you ladies?'

'Yes, Inspector,' well-schooled sycophant elephants.

'Last night, somebody stole my bike.' The stunned silence was violated as Jack expelled a raucous guffaw into their collective faces, backed towards the door like he was leaving the presence of the Queen, and for his piece of resistance, and in a highly effected, aristocratic, and effeminate voice, 'I take no leave of you, Sir. I offer no compliments to your family. I am most seriously displeased,' a lovely bit of Lady Catherine De Burgh, PP, probably his best, and Mandy and Jo had missed it. Back to the table in two big strides, 'Goodbye, John.' Jack stuck his hand out, and the Captain, without thinking, shaped to shake, but Jack dodged the hand, laughed at the idiot in front of him, stood to attention, saluted his *Benny Hill* salute, and left, closing the door gently behind him. He had learned a long time ago, a gently shut door said more than the slammed version.

Jack bounced down the stairs and plunged through the door of the Community Policing room; one step inside, he saw the whole team assembled. They had probably been talking things through, but Jack suspected it was the meeting upstairs first on the agenda if the abrupt silence was anything to go by. Jack's first move was to go to Nobby, 'How you doing, sunshine? I was proud of you today.' Nobby reddened, but his chest grew a couple of inches. 'Alice Springs, thanks for your back up, and for last night.' To the team, he waved his arms, 'I apologise for not informing you all. In mitigation, I was playing a hunch, and as Jo-Jums will tell you, those seldom pan out.' Looked to Jo, and swinging his gaze to encompass the team, landing finally on Nobby and Alice, was there something between those two, God help Nobby if there is, 'You see, I get a twitching in my eye, this will not go away, it starts to hurt and then I know...' pause for effect, '...someone is shagging in the back and I can catch 'em at it, so Nobby and Alice Springs, be warned.'

The office erupted into a roar of laughter, which Jack hoped would be audible in the Commander's office, and he was further rewarded to see Paolo enjoying the jest. Nobby blushed and Alice looked at him with affection in her eyes, bless that girl; watch out, Nobby lad, she has her eye on you. Jack remained on his feet and, as the laughter subsided, 'We have serious work to do, but I think a moment's silence to remember Biscuit and his family, God love 'em.'

There was total silence, heads bowed in reflection and respect; this could have been anyone of them.

Pugwash rammed the door open, and it slammed against the wall, he'd come to assert his power. 'Austin, I'm going to have you,' and he straight-arm pointed his finger at Jack as if to explain to everyone who he was talking to, 'you'll be a constable before the week is out,' and he stood rigid in the ensuing silence, not respect, but of dread.

Mandy made to move to Jack, Jo-Jums close behind, the mist had clouded in Jack; the familiar signs recognised, but too late as he spun and lunged, grabbed the lapels of the Captain's jacket and pushed him all of ten feet to the wall. Pugwash back peddling, trying to keep his balance, was slammed against the wall. Jack was spitting bullets and seething hot breath through clenched teeth, drilling invective into the Captain's face, 'You filthy, dirty, cowardly, bollocky, knob-head, wanker of a scumbag, we lost an officer today, murdered, shot on duty, wife and two young kids, a dad, colleague, friend, so stick that in your ship's funnel, and if you ever come into my room mouthing off like you're on a fucking poop deck again, so help me God, I will throw you out of that window. Now Fuck-off.' He released the jacket and pointed to the door, his eye never leaving Pugwash's eyes, sensed his energy dissipating as he turned to the cowering ugly sisters, vigour sapped, and quietly, he said, 'You two, go and orchestrate your Fat-Wah.'

The laughter erupted as Pugwash and the two wobbly women exited.

As the hilarity subsided, Mandy put her arm around Jack's waist, well as far as it would go. 'How're the anger management classes going?' she asked, eliciting another notch of laughter. 'Call me old-fashioned but you may have made an enemy there, and if you want me to tell you where that enmity was made, I think it was, "bollocky, knob-head wanker." ' More raucous laughter that Jack hoped was heard by the terrible trio as they headed off.

The Commander was standing at the door, unruffled. 'Jack, I will do everything in my power to save you. The man is definitely a "bollocky knob-head wanker." Now, can I ask you to get on with the serious stuff and I'll watch your back.'

Nobby's chest grew a little more as the Commander was applauded, remembering Jack had said his dad had been a good copper before he became a twat.

NINETEEN

JACK, SUBDUED IN VOICE AND MANNER, ADDRESSED THE team now seated, 'I can be a tad difficult at times, but I thank you for your support.' Stifled laughter, short lived, Jack had his serious head on. 'We have a hill to climb, and I may have to ask you to jump off a cliff for me, along with other metaphors,' a ripple, 'what we do now, we do for Biscuit, for the women and children. I will not ask you to do anything I would not do myself, it will be dangerous, but know this,' and he looked around, emotion scrawled on his already ravaged face, 'I'm going after the bastards.'

He expects to be able to do what he asks others to do, Mandy thought. Despite his age and being the clumsiest idiot she had ever known, and she feared for him. Jack carried on, 'Paolo, I want to bury the hatchet, and not in your head,' muted laughter, 'this is no time for grudges. We owe it to Biscuit, we owe it to the little girl I carried out this morning, the woman stabbed to death, to get our act together. Paolo, comments please?'

Paolo stood, thinking Jack was alright, took in the faces turning to him now. 'My team will focus on Biscuit, what was he working on? Question vice, they will be expecting us, they will cooperate, but, well, you know, eyes and ears, and I'm happy to defer the ground to you, Jane, but keep us in the loop, please.'

He sat and Mandy rose. 'I propose we skip the group hug,' a stifled reaction, 'team briefings first and last thing unless something comes up. Paolo, Cyrano, and Jane, you report to me, I will keep the Commander and Chief up to speed. If you think you're out of the loop, tell me, do not stew.' She looked to Jack, 'Lay out your thoughts, Jack.'

Jack walked to the crime wall, 'Nobby, you're responsible for this wall, liaise with Sissies on updates.' Nobby nodded to Paulo. 'Cyrano, a small team of bandits, and if I read it correctly, they don't want to get big?' The head of drugs swayed his head. 'Whoever this is does not want to irritate the established criminal cognersentry,' a titter, 'we have several trails to follow,' and Jack signed for Nobby to write on the wall:

'One, Vice, Biscuit picked up something and it got him killed; prostitution, women and children? I'm not convinced this is sex trade, maybe child porn? Talk with crimes against minors. Is this revenue? If so, funding what?

'Two, East Cosham,' Jack shook his head, 'not convinced. Something not right about the

Christian house nearby? The guys this morning, Right Wing organisations?

'Three, Frankie and Confucius, a lot to do, and if you need more kit, Frankie?' Mandy

noticed another familiar exchange. 'Websites, European, local women and children, keep an open mind, missing persons slipped under Social Services radar? Computers records can be manipulated, and Social Services are stretched, even more so these days. Tread carefully, they drop the ball occasionally, but social workers care, it's not fame and fortune, but there may be a rogue? About five years ago there was a stink around the head of Social Services, he sits on the poncey police committee, so I could be prejudiced... it faded to nothing. Find out what it was. If it was something, how did it go away?' Mandy noticed he handed Frankie the piece of paper from the phone conversation this morning, 'Some suggestions.'

'Four, Political, who printed the fliers, who's the organisation behind the rhetoric, are

they targeting something specific? Who are the guys we've arrested, their affiliations? Do they have an end goal, apart from the obvious?' Jack removed another piece of paper from the breast pocket of his rank shirt, and again handed it to Frankie. 'Follow this up, Franks, sweet'art.'

Mandy had to ask, 'Another piece of paper?'

'Don't interrupt my juices, Babes.'

Mandy muttered, 'Farted, have you?' Jack nodded his touché.

'Five, Street, Jo-Jums, any murmurings, discontent? Liaise with Cyrano.'

'Six, Drugs, Cyrano and you, Jo, streets, dealers, users, big wigs, is there word on someone funding civil unrest, minority groups, activists? Just a thought, we have Nazis, is there something left wing?'

Jack checked his fingers, forgot what number he was on, so mumbled, 'S'vnnnnate? 'Lateral thinking, no idea too small, get out of jail free cards, especially if you have any ideas on what this thing is all about.' He pointed to the centre of the chaos table, picked up a sheet of paper and took the marker pen from Nobby's hand, scribbled "any ideas," chucked it into the centre of the table. 'Ideas, write them out and put them here, anyone can pick and sift, anything has merit, Nobby put it on the wall. Aye-than-yow.' It was his bus conductor's sign-off, the team stunned, meeting over as Jack began sifting his multitude of post-it notes, scraps of paper with lists, his personal form of the chaos table. Ordinarily Jack was neat, but his notes and lists were allowed to pile and scatter. Jack had previously explained about chaos theory, but nobody understood. Frankie stood alert, thinking another slip of paper was coming, but it didn't. Jack waved a note. 'Anyone, apart from Alice Springs, I need a lift to Bazaar Bikes?'

'Fat chance me driving you, but I'm still offended. Consider yourself off the kissing list,' Alice said, a wry grin. Mandy stopped in her tracks and looked at Alice. Jack thought, daggers or confusion? Nope it was daggers. Nobby looked jealous.

'Take it up with my cardiganologist, the driving and the kissing, Spanner,' and to Mandy, glibly, 'Still waters, sweet'art.' The hubbub told Jack two things, one, they were working, good, and two, nobody gave a toss about giving him a lift to get a new bike; not so good. 'Right, I'll get a bluebottle cab.'

JACK, waiting for his patrol car taxi, warily planted his elbows on Sid's counter and rested his chin in his hands. Sid mimicked him and mumbled through his fingers, recognising the advantage of his position and the vulnerability of Jack's. 'While you're waiting, perhaps you'd like to watch some CCTV footage? You'll like this, an old bloke rides off on a bike, and later, that same man is seen carrying a lump of scrap metal.' Sid spread his fingers so Jack could glimpse his victory grin, eyebrows arched.

Jack pricked his balloon. 'Sid, I haven't got time to watch telly,' the bluebottle cab arrived, and Jack headed out.

'It can wait, Jane.'

'Don't wait on my account, Sid,' last word, very important. A disinterested observer would call that a draw, but Jack got the impression Sid thought he'd won; amateurs!

TWENTY

THE SQUAD CAR DROPPED JACK OUTSIDE BAZAAR BIKES.
'Thanks, I'll walk to the kerb.' Smiles and hand gestures were
exchanged, the officers drove off, and Jack went into the well-
known second-hand bike shop he'd been patronising for years.
They even did his punctures, Jack tried himself but would
create more holes, and Kate would remark upon the still
deflated tyre, Jack's deflated ego, and refer him to the spoons
and forks in the house that would be bent; he never saw the
need for tyre levers. He was the same at DIY, "destroy it yourself" Kate used to say. He hated work around the house, especially decorating. Some nights he would come home looking
forward to a well-earned sit down in his favourite armchair, an
evening of not communicating, and a wall that was perfectly
okay the night before, had sample paint splotches; horror.

'Landlord, a crocodile bike and make it snappy,' Jack was in
Bazaar Bikes.

Ron Wheelslie, as Jack called Brian Masters the owner of
Bazaar Bikes, jumped up from a bike he was working on,
'Bugger me Jane, you made me jump.' Like everyone Jack nick-

named, Brian Masters was known by all as Ron, his shop as Hogwarts, and frequently get jibes like, "How's Hermione"; pronounced "herm-eee-own", as Jack pronounced it.

Ron was a good-humoured man, about Jack's age, had been there, done that, and his face showed it. A former boiler maker in the dockyard, he was stooped, which Jack put down to either bending over bikes all day or going into the navy ship's boilers to clean them out. Five-foot-nothing, skinny as a rake, he paled like a shadow against Jack, but unlike the elongated Pugwash, this man, despite his diminutive appearance, had presence, and Jack liked him.

'What happened to your bike?'

'Half inched, Ron, probably a student getting home from the pub. So, pray guide me through the wonders of this 'ere emporium of second-hand cycling pleasures, my man. Wouldn't mind some gears that work, tried some this morning and they were brilliant, although the bike was not particularly sturdy. What about these, Ron?'

Ron swung his gaze to a group of three bikes leaning against a wall. 'Just prepped and ready to go, what colour d'you want?'

'Red, Ron, preferably with Scooby Doos on the handle bars, two-tone horn, I am a copper, how much?'

'To you, a hundred nicker.'

'How much? How Much!' traditional response, even for punctures. 'I'll take it now, I'm back to work. I'll drop by next week sometime to get the pannier supports, and if you can find an orange box for Martin in the meantime?'

Ron was reeling from the impact of Jack's visit, 'Back to work, bit late for you?'

'Big show on, watch the news tonight, Pumps is doing the press conference, but I'll be in C&A's later, you up for a bit of sedition?'

Ron shook his head, 'Nah, heard you did alright last night, not so much sedition as seduction, is what I heard.'

'Undercover, Ron.'

'Red anorak, wasn't it?'

Jack smiled, picked up the bike, and helped himself to a padlock. 'Add this on, Ron, I'll settle up next week.'

'If you don't, I'll be straight onto the police.'

'Let me know what they say,' and Jack disappeared out of the door running over the foot of Chas, Ron's only employed help in the shop, least that's what Ron said, but to Jack it looked like the lad ran the show and Ron was the salad dressing.

'Hi, Mr Austin, what you got there?' Chas said, rubbing his foot.

Brimming with the pride of new ownership, 'New wheels, Chas, and I'm eager to make like the wind, little gear changers on the 'andlebars, start knitting the Scooby Doos, I'll be back in next week.'

Chas looked worried, a nice-looking kid, polite and respectful, goes a long way, Jack always thought, slight build, about five-ten, reasonably well-dressed when you think he worked in a bike shop. He never got any of Jack's jokes, and obviously had not a clue what a Scooby Doo was, but you can't hold that against anybody can you? 'But sir, that bike's sold. You can't take it.'

'I can, and I have, okay, Ron?'

Chortling, Ron answered, 'Chas don't worry, we got another couple just like it in the back. See you next week, Jane.'

'Not if I see you first, to the kitchen and put the kettle on,' and Jack shaped like Buzz Lightyear, laughed at his adaptation of the catch phrase, and teetered off on his new, old bike.

'Oi, Monsieur Hulot,' Ron called out.

'Call me Buzz, and tell your mum thanks for the rabbit.'

Ron and Chas watched him bump down the kerb and onto

the road, cars swerving to miss him. 'I'm not sure you should have done that, Mr Masters, and what's this about a rabbit?'

Jack peddled rapidly, never noted for baby steps, Jack was full on, or as Mandy would say, "fall off." He weaved in and out of the traffic and went through the lights where it was clear, a humble Portsmouth cyclist, and took the insults and angry gestures in good heart; people liked a laugh. He whizzed along, but inexplicably was overtaken by a girl; black spandex leggings, lime green Lycra top, goggles, eight hundred flashing lights, a million gears and a beautiful arse. Jack chased her down wondering, pervert or tour-de-France, Jacques Austin? The decision was made for him when she got caught at lights. Jack slowed, and pedalled for all he was worth on amber and flashed past her at green with a sense that as he got older, he was more interested in beating her as opposed to looking at her backside. "A sad old man," Mandy would say, and so would Jack, but not thinking what Mandy was thinking.

As Jack zoomed into the police station car park, he noticed the loop on the bollard by the Commander's car had been nobbled. 'The foot's a game, Watson,' Jack said, invigorated, cycling into the secure compound as if this was his intention all along, and not to park by the Commander's car; pride? He thought of PP, who was proud and who prejudiced? He supposed if he read the book, he might understand, but Jack was a purist, it was the *BBC TV* version for him; *Jennifer Ehle*, a sexy woman, and when her eyes are brightened by exercise, she outshone arsy D'Arcy. Jack was only marginally jealous because Kate thought Colin Firth, especially when he dived into the lake, was "sex on legs." Jack used to say, "Come and watch me down the swimming baths, I'll dive in with me shirt on." "That would be more like whale watching," she would retort; a kidder his Kate, and he missed her.

Ego intact, a little residual melancholia; was that getting

better? Jack locked his bike in the cycle store, and through reception, 'Sid, get your CCTV onto my new bike in case that tea leaf comes back.' Sid looked open mouthed, had no response; amateur, you see. 'Close your mouth, we are not a codfish,' and Jack doubled up in pantomime mock laughter, dived through the doors and up the stairs at a jaunty jog before Sid could respond. 'Who's the daddy?' he said to nobody, which made him think of the little girl; guilt, a touch of Catholicism creeping in there, better watch out, backs to the wall chaps.

Along the corridor, whistling, he bashed through the door to the CP room and was faced by Dolly, hands full of sprays, dusters and mops. 'Shush, Mandy's on.'

Jack wobbled his head and chortled, he was in a good mood. 'I think not, Dolly, menopause is my guess, and I'm not sure you get PMT then, hope not.' Dolly stifled a giggle.

'Shut-up, Jane, we're about to watch the press conference,' Paolo snapped.

'Oooooooh, scratch your eyes out,' and Jack minced around the room to his desk, flicked a cursory look at his notes, shuffled them, and pushed to the front for a prime seat in front of the telly; his seat there waiting for him. The natural order of things, he always said, 'Thought you were doing this, Paolo?'

'The Commander's doing it with Mandy, shush.'

Jack raised his eyebrow, BBC not internal CCTV, relieved he didn't do it, but they hadn't let Jack do one since he called the ITV reporter an insensitive wanker and walked out. On screen they watched Mandy, then the Commander enter, followed by a youth, not spotty, but as Jack had said before, all youths are spotty, it's the only thing older blokes have on them. Stone me, Jack thought, Mandy was gorgeous. Everyone turned. 'Did I just say that out loud?' rolled eyes and a few hand gestures not for the faint-hearted. 'Anyone mind if I see what's on the other side, might be *Countdown.*' Jack's standard joke received the usual groan, but he still said it; he was a tickler for tradition. The spotty youth was talking, and Jack asked who he was.

'Press Liaison Officer,' Jo answered.

Recognition dawned, 'The little tow-rag whose been trying to get hold of me?'

Jo struck, 'Yes, now shut-up, or we'll tell him where you are.'

Jack harrumphed, 'Deal,' and settled to watch the telly.

———

MANDY SPENT a little time introducing the events of the morning, 'Acting on information drawn from an ongoing enquiry, police officers went to an address in Paulsgrove,' she pointed to a picture behind her. 'Recognising a suspect from an assault on a police officer the previous evening, officers pursued the suspect into the house, eventually apprehending him. Another suspect produced a knife and slashed a policeman, threatened a second, who eventually disarmed him, a short chase ensued and that suspect was also apprehended.' She paused, lowered her eyes and introduced a subdued note, 'At the scene, we recovered the body of Detective Sergeant Smith. We also rescued a number of women and children, one of the women was dead. A mother and her baby remain in a serious condition, the remaining women and children are in hospital and are as comfortable as can be expected. A terrace of four houses is undergoing detailed forensic examination.' Energetic shouts, clicks and whirrs ensued, and pressure to answer questions, which Mandy expertly deflected, 'I ask the public to come forward if they have any information about the comings and goings from these properties.'

The Press Liaison Officer jumped in, 'The Commander and Detective Superintendent Bruce will take questions.' Mandy sighed at the enthusiasm of youth, but nodded.

'Superintendent, is it true the police officer was shot?'

'I can't answer that now.'

'Can you tell us if anyone else was shot?'

'We cannot answer that now.'

'Did you recover a gun?'

'I cannot answer that now.'

'Is it true the second suspect was run over by a car driven by a child?'

She halted the quick fire replies to think. 'I'm not sure where you are getting your information, but if someone has evidence, we ask they contact us.'

'Is it true the suspect was about to cycle off on a police bike?'

She leaned back in her chair. 'The bike has disappeared, and we ask the public for information on this also.'

Sid in reception mumbled to himself, 'I know where it bloody is.'

'Superintendent, was the officer leading the operation Inspector Austin?'

'Yes.'

The reporter followed up, 'The news programmes have pictures of Inspector Austin carrying out a little girl from the scene and he's crying, can you comment on that?'

A warm smile radiated how she felt, 'Inspector Austin regularly says to his team they should empathise with the victims of crime. Police work can be emotional at times, and this is a human response. He does not encourage black humour, he asks his officers to feel the emotion, connect with the victim, deal with it, and then, I quote, "Get the bastards." It is not unknown for the Inspector to cry at a scene, we are used to it, and we are proud of him.'

'Commander,' it was the BBC. 'Is Inspector Austin to attend a disciplinary hearing for threatening the chairman of the Police Committee, Captain Littleman, whom the local paper is reporting is known to the police as Captain Pugwash?' There was giggling and scribbling notes to research Pugwash.

Mandy raised her hand for silence, 'A policeman is dead. He had a wife and two small children. A woman died, we found women and children in very poor health and have reason to suspect they have been subject to systematic abuse. What I am saying is, let's keep our eye on the ball, please.' She rose and left, the Commander and the press officer jumped up at the unexpected departure and followed, the combined press corp shouting questions.

Jack leapt from his chair, 'She's our gal. Not sure about Spotty, the little tyke,' confusion as to who Spotty was. 'Okay, men, back to it, anything to report?' Mostly with everyone it was active stuff, not ready to open up, so Jack pushed Frankie and Confucius.

'We have a programme running on the ferry traffic, we'll have something soon.'

'Can we expand that search to types of traffic?'

Frankie spoke, 'Anything in mind?'

'Not sure, but if the drugs are coming in as small amounts, we're looking at something that would ordinarily be anony-mous, can't say much more until it focuses in my own mind.'

'Connie and I are working on tonight. I know what you think, but I don't have much of a private life going anyway,' Frankie said matter-of-factly.

Jack thought, Connie, eh? No private life? 'Well, dead copper, fiddled kids, trumps all, and it's about time you got a private life, Frankie.'

'Working on it, Jane,' she winked. Confucius reddened and Jack was shaken by a raised voice.

'Pugwash, Jack?'

'Amanda darlin', you were terrific, we all thought so, didn't we guys?' A resounding "Yes, Ma'am," in support of Jack. 'It's generally known, you don't have to look at me.'

She grinned, 'Well, everyone across the nation now knows Portsmouth CID calls the head of the police committee Captain Pugwash,' and she put her hand to her mouth to suppress the laugh. It had been a difficult day; she had to visit Biscuit's widow and this was taking its toll, sensed a laugh could turn hysterical. 'I'm guessing, but there may be a little flack coming your way, Jack.'

'Thanks for the heads-up, Mands, any chance we could lump them altogether, save time?' That did it for her, she collapsed, giggling like a schoolgirl. Of course, it was infectious, and strangely, it was Confucius who started first amongst the team, and Frankie put her arm around her and joined in. Jack looked to Mandy, raised his one eyebrow knowingly. The whole team in giggling fits, and Dolly came in dancing with her skirts pulled up showing her long drawers, and it was game over. They needed this, Jack thought.

As things calmed, 'Jack, can I take you up on your offer to come with me to meet Biscuit's widow please?'

He waved his hand, 'Hang-on, Mands,' picked up the phone, dialled, 'Michael, your family, they are well?' Silence, his son knew about PP having been made to watch it many times with his dad, who'd argued that he had watched *Mary Poppins* even more times. 'Set another plate for Mandy, please, we'll be there...' stopped to look at Mandy, she was flustered, looked at her watch and mouthed seven-thirty, '...seven-thirty-ish, be nice to eat together; a lot happened today.' He hung-up.

'He called me a girl's blouse for crying on telly, now all his mates know his dad's a wuss.'

Mandy looked on warmly, 'I think they likely knew that already. Can we go now, please, and thank you for dinner.' She pecked him on the cheek. "Oooh err matron," from the assembled officers, and Dolly. Mandy put her hand up and got the attention she wanted, 'I'm going to boil his arse tomorrow, but today he walks on water, briefing at nine, see you all then.' She turned and flicked her head, and Jack followed, a little puppy obeying. He realised this halfway down the corridor, but will he be allowed to sleep on her bed?

TWENTY-ONE

IN MANDY'S CAR, SHE BUCKLED UP, LAID HER HEAD BACK and sighed, 'I hate going to meet a colleague's loved one. Did you know Biscuit?' Jack remained silent; where women were concerned, he instinctively knew what to do. 'Why? I accept there are the bad guys and us; why kill, why hurt, why abuse? I saw you on telly with that girl, you're a good man and you touch me inside.'

'Touch you inside, Mands? I'm pretty sure I would have remembered that,' again he always knew what to say and when.

'Alzheimer's, Jack,' moment over, and in silence, she drove to Biscuit's home. Mandy was thinking through what she would say, whereas Jack normally said what came from his heart, and besides, he couldn't take his eyes off Mandy's legs. Her skirt had ridden up and he was mesmerised by a sheen; stockings, and for a dirty old man, it didn't get much better than this.

They pulled up outside Biscuit's house. 'We're here, you can stop looking at my legs.' He went to protest, but her smile disarmed him.

The gloom of dusk was reinforced by an overcast sky, the fine weather over. Mandy had gone in and the door was held by the family liaison officer, WPC Forbes.

In the small living room of the terraced house, the widow and her sister sat and hugged; both ravaged with grief. Biscuit's wife was a pleasant-looking woman, would be beautiful in normal circumstances, Jack thought, medium height, as she stood to shake hands, slim, dark mid-length hair, straight, fine and shiny, if she'd been advertising shampoo, she could shake her hair in a carefree manner, but there was nothing carefree this evening. She sobbed into Jack's shoulder, 'Biscuit, you called him, he trusted you, always wanted to work with you again.'

Mandy noted, "Wanted to work with you again," odd?

'Shall we sit Mrs Biscuit?' She laughed and hugged him again. Mandy thought, he just knows what to do. To anyone else, that would have been a huge faux pas, or else he's forgotten her name; I bet he's forgotten her name.

'He found something out and was worried,' the widow said.

'Had he done undercover work before?' Mandy asked.

'Err, can I call you Mandy?' the widow looked quizzically at Jack.

'Please do,' Mandy replied.

'Yes,' and she looked at Jack again, 'he was onto something, and it scared him.'

Jack was tearful. 'We arranged to meet last night, but he didn't show.'

'Did he say anything else?' Mandy felt as though she was intruding.

The widow responded but continued looking at Jack, 'He was protective of his family, and if he thought something would endanger him, he wouldn't say. I wanted him to return to being an ordinary copper, but you know what he was like, Jack.'

Mandy was looking at Jack, looking at the widow, 'I'm going to get who did this and find out why, small comfort, I know. How're the kids?'

'Jack,' she was going to break, her sister tightened the grip across her shoulders, 'the kids, it's not sunk in. They're with my mum, I'll deal with that tomorrow, Cindy will be with me,' gesturing to her sister, and both women hugged and sobbed and Jack joined them. Mandy looked on resigned; Jack was definitely a girl's blouse, but truthfully she already knew this.

WPC Forbes returned with tea and separated Jack from the grieving women. Jack beckoned her to follow them to the door. 'Are you with them all night?'

'Yes, Sir.'

'Make sure everything is locked tight, someone will pick up his home computer, but as a precaution, phone in every two hours and make sure no volunteer twat gives you shite, and let Dawkins know that if you miss a call to get a squad car around, okay?'

'Will do, Sir, you were wonderful tonight, and you of course, Ma'am.'

'Thanks, Babes, get back to your tea, you must drink gallons of the stuff.' She closed the door and he stayed until he heard the bolts strike home.

'Did you mean that?' Mandy asked.

'Yeah, they must drink tea all the time.'

Mandy bashed his arm playfully. 'No, are they in danger?'

'Don't think so, just cautious.'

Jack held the car door for her, she made to protest and let it go. Seated, she buckled up, Jack did the same, slowly, thinking if only Kate had buckled up; Kate never wore a seatbelt, used to say, "If a man had tits, he would've designed a better seatbelt".

'Jack, what are you thinking?'

'You pulled your skirt down, suppose I'll have to talk to you now.' She chuckled and he thought she had the most wonderful smile, her face was aging, naturally, but she must be the most beautiful woman he knew, and in Jack's mind, she was just blooming.

She tugged her skirt, a little, 'Penny for them, Jack?'

'Fuck-off, it'll cost you more than that.'

———

DRIVING up to the rear of Jack's house, they saw someone having a go at his garage door. 'Jack, did you see that?'

They dismissed it and went in. Mandy hugged Michael as he worked at the hob. 'Are you sure you're Jack's kid, you're so good looking.'

'I saw him first Mandy, hands off.' Colleen said, and Mandy hugged her, and Jack tried to press in; the women pushed him away.

'Open the wine, Dad, I've done a chicken stir fry, one mild and one hot Thai, and there's tortilla if you want to roll them.'

'Mmmm, Yumbo Jumbo,' Jack said as he dashed upstairs to change his shirt.

Dinner was messy, on Jack's part, but a tasty affair. Lots of it, and Jack was well satisfied; Mandy ate modestly. Colleen looked at Mandy and how she looked at Jack, and Jack looked at Colleen to see how she looked at Michael. Jack insisted he would clear and Michael insisted back, Colleen interjected, 'Jack, when were you going to tell us about Martin?'

Jack's face morphed, guilt. 'Well...'

Michael put him out of his misery, 'We know, Mandy telephoned, so did Jo-Jums.'

'He'll be okay, son.'

'I know, Dad, we went to see him.'

'You did?'

Mandy relieved Jack's remorse, 'It's okay, you may not have noticed, but what with a major bust, a Brahma of a ruck with Pugwash, a new bike, two briefings, several crying and sobbing incidents, and meeting Biscuit's widow, you've had no time. So, unless you want to turn Roman candle on me?'

'You forgot, Martin was appointed Police Dog.'

'He was?'

'Who did that then, Jack?' Mandy asked.

'I did, and I told the vet to tell him, so if it doesn't happen and with a ceremony, he will be a disappointed hound.'

Colleen and Michael were stunned because this was news, Mandy more so, because she knew Jack would expect her to arrange a ceremony. They sat around the table for another half-hour of convivial conversation, mainly talking about Michael and Colleen going off to college in September together.

Colleen's dad picked her up and looked at Jack in a funny way. 'What the hell was that about?' Jack whispered to Mandy.

'Your son is having sex with his daughter. I remember you with Alana, it was all Kate and I could do to stop you manal-ising the guy.'

Jack shrugged defensively, 'She was only twenty-three.'

'Fathers and daughters, Jack, and if it is any consolation, I feel the same way about my boy, but there is nothing you or I can do about it but be there as a safety net, as you so often say.'

'Fancy a pint at C&A's?' he'd moved on.

'No thanks, I'm off to Bedfordshire,' and she stood and stretched.

'I'll be up in a minute.' Jack said, ever hopeful.

'In your dreams.'

'I don't intend sleeping, for five minutes anyway.'

'Will you ever grow up?'

'No, he won't.' Michael was back from seeing Colleen off.

'Did you give her a big kiss in front of her dad, son?'

'No, Dad, it's bad enough as it is.'

'Michael, you're more mature than your dad. Thank you for a lovely dinner, and Colleen's a treasure, look after her.' Mandy kissed him and followed Jack to the back door.

Jack opened the door and saw a silhouette on his garage roof, 'Oi, you, bugger-orf.'

'Jack, phone it in, this is making me feel uncomfortable,' Mandy said.

'Me too, d'you want to sleep with me tonight, I'll protect you.'

TWENTY-TWO

AFTER WAVING AN EXASPERATED MANDY OFF, JACK phoned the local police; they would keep an eye out.

'Good one on Pugwash, Jane, he's a wanker,' the desk sergeant said.

'That report was anonymous, Johnno, good night.' Next call was to Gail, a nicer call, and he relaxed into his armchair. 'How's our little girl?'

'Well enough,' Gail answered, 'though God knows what she's been through. They've sedated her for the night. I'll go back in the morning.'

'You're a wonderful woman, I'll get to the hospital in the morning as well.'

She was yawning, it made him yawn. 'Goodnight.'

He put the phone down, thought about phoning Bernie, but it rang. 'Maisie,' he listened, and a small tear came to the corner of his good eye. 'Thanks, luv, I'm fine, honest, yes, I will bring her to see you, all the best to Fatso.' Jack hung up and returned the call to Bernie, 'Good one on Pugwash, nothing else, so feck off.'

'Dad!'

'It's only Bernie.'

'Oh, fair do's. I'm off to bed.' They hugged; it was something Jack insisted upon.

———

SPARROW'S FART, six am, Jack woke as usual, no alarm, looked through the curtains to see what the weather was doing, and halfway down the landing forgot; had he looked? Kitchen, 'Mocha pot on, muesli-doosley,' he said to himself and rubbed his hands together 'bloody 'andsome.' His dad always said that. Sunday tomorrow, a fry up of smoked mackerel, bacon, chorizo and mussels, like his dad would do. Jack would normally stay home weekends, but his conscience was plucked, thought of Mrs Biscuit sitting down with her kids; God love em. No call, so they must have got safely through the night. He leaned against the counter, looked out the window, not raining, but it had rained and the sky threatened more. His wet weather gear had been nicked with his bike; he still had his helmet and, stirred from his lethargy, he found it and put it by the door so he would fall over it rather than forget to take it with him, an old trick he used to do a lot, but Kate kept falling over the thing. He'd loved her, but she could be clumsy at times.

'Bathroom; tom tit, rant and rave, Eiffel tower, done and dusted, Hampstead Heaths, bruises bluer around the boatrace, knees on the mend, toe still hurts, knuckles heeling, ego peaking, and body stimulated just by the thought of Mandy in his house last night, a quick look in the mirror, bish-bosh, lubbly-jubbly.' The larks and conversation with himself made him feel better, then he felt miserable, and this is how it was, and even sadder; he was used to it. 'You're fucked-up, Jack,' but he decided to ignore the bloke talking from the mirror; what did he know, and did you see the state of him?

He called a cab, thinking he would cycle home on his new bike, and experienced a childish excitement, left a note for Michael: "Let's have a meal out tonight and give your sister a call; Saturday night's alright, alright." Kate and he always used to use song words in notes, like wake me up before you go go, just a thing, and he always got the words wrong; the melancholy returned, along with the thing. The cab tooted, and he fell over his helmet. Jack really wanted to sit in the back and think nothing, but felt he ought to be sociable, a bit like feeling he ought to buy the *Big Issue*. "People pleaser," the psychiatrist had said. Jack just thought this is what people actually should do, so he got in the front and all the way the cabbie talked about Captain Pugwash, how his dad had told him about it on the phone last night, used to watch it as a kid.

It wasn't Sid or Dawkins on reception. Jack recognised the officer, but struggled on a name. 'Morning, Jane.'

'Morning,' Jack replied, waving his Tupperware box, a look of concern on thingy's face, as if Jack was going to tell him about how he made his Muesli; was that fear? 'Anyone else in?' Why did I say that?

'Nobby's in and the computer girls, don't know their names.'

'Confucius and Frankie.'

'Which one's which?'

Jack turned back, started to say, then realised, left it at that and headed for the stairs.

'Barney Rubble, you call me, but it's actually Bartholomew Kibble; I prefer your version,' Barney called out.

Feck, how could I forget, Jack thought; old-timers, he presumed, maybe he'd been to bed with Amanda and forgotten. He chastised himself and resolved to put her out of his mind, thought he would take a leak but wished he hadn't. If it was only Nobby and the dynamic duo in, then bugger me, Nobby, what has your mum been feeding you?

'I'd give the bog a week or two if I were you, Sir, Dad and I had a couple of beers and a curry last night,' Nobby hollered as Jack, gasping for air, made it through to the CP room.

'No bleedin' kidding, Tonto, you might have posted a warning on the door...'

His fight for oxygen was disrupted. 'Kin hell, Jack, don't suppose you thought about going at home before coming in?' Jack turned to Mandy, offended and innocent, neither expression would ordinarily have washed had not a beetroot Nobby confessed to the crime, but like many boys, he never knew when to stop. Jack made a mental note to pass on his wisdom about how to handle women. If Nobby was getting close to Alice, he would need all the help he could get. So, dipstick Nobby described to Mandy the curry and a few pints. Women never seemed to find this fascinating; Jack supposed men had a higher intellect, forgot what he was thinking, because Mandy looked striking in tight fitting, pale blue jeans and a baggy Arran sweater, and thought his gaze may have lingered too long.

'Close your mouth, we are not a codfish.'

Yep, he had. 'Touché, babes, park yer jacksie,' and he swung a wheelie chair out for her and pulled it next to him.

Mandy swung it away, demonstrably. 'You smooth talking bastard, you had me at touché. So, what's occurring?'

Jack shrugged with his mouth, thought he looked French. Confucius looked like she was going to say something, but couldn't. Frankie rested a hand on her forearm, 'We can tell you what we have now if you would like?'

'Shoot, babes,' Jack replied, and Frankie sighed.

'The ferry traffic search is finished, we need just one thing from you, Jack.'

'What?' Jack was distracted looking at Mandy's jeans.

'What are we looking for?'

Looking up to Frankie, 'God knows, what else?'

'We've trawled known people in white pride-type outfits, last known positions and so on, a couple of our guys downstairs have come up, we'll pass onto Paolo at briefing.'

'Leaflets?'

'A small neighbourhood printer, Wallace and Kettle are calling in.'

'Nobby, please,' Jack gestured with his head to the crime wall.

Frankie continued, aware Jack would remain monosyllabic all the time he looked at Mandy's jeans. 'Looked at Cyrano's druggy names, mainly small time and likely a dead end.'

'Got to follow the string, Franks. Now, the good stuff please?' Jack smiled and looked up from the jeans to Mandy's face, whispered something she couldn't understand but did pick up, "....his computer department," but was never sure when he used his frontier gibberish.

'We followed up your note and have hit several previously unknown cells in the city. The radar is twitching for the spooks, should I make contact...?'

'Anything concrete, if not, no,' Jack replied, back looking at the jeans.

'Sir?'

'Frankie, don't ask, and call me Jane, Jack, or whatever, unless there's a senior officer present.'

'Ahem.'

'Oh, Mands, you're one of the boys,' and he smiled.

Mandy grinned, lips tight. Jack looked, thought for a moment, but all her faces looked good to him. She murmured, 'Don't know whether to be flattered or pissed-off.'

'Flattered, sister,' Jack said, rising from his seat. 'I'm off to the hospital, meeting Gail and hope to get a word with our little girl.'

Mandy told him to park his imaginary motorbike. 'You need social with you when you question her.'

Dismissing Mandy with a hand gesture, he restarted his engine. 'I'm just talking...cor why you no risten,' and he gave her his *Benny Hill* salute, donned his cycling helmet, bent over to tuck his trousers in his socks making loads of oomph's; Frankie signalled all of the lights had gone out. He put on his red anorak with the hi-viz jacket and made his way out, turning as he heard Mandy.

'You don't have much going for you, but when I see you like that, I get really hot.' Frankie and Connie giggled.

'I'm here to fulfil your *Glance Armstrong* fantasies,' he shouted, as he revved up.

'Feck-off, dope.'

And Jack zoomed away, screeching his imaginary tyres. In the corridor, the radiation had still not cleared; a vindaloo, and Nobby went up in his estimation. See, girls wouldn't under-stand that. Down the stairs, through reception, he braked, put his foot out and leaned to one side. 'I knew you were Barney, it was the Bartholomew bit I struggled with.' Face saved, Jack zoomed to the bike shed and collapsed laughing. There was a laminated sign on the door, Jack's face on it.

> *Have you seen this man, bike suspect,*
> *WANTED by the Royal Navy;*
> *contact Captain Pugwash.*

Brilliant, he thought, got his bike out, admired it, sung, *'Flash, aah aah, saviour of the thing...'* Tour-de-France speed trials, as he cycled onto the road unaware of the white transit van that began tracking him. Jack sped through the North End shopping thoroughfare, flicked a look to the sky, he could stop off later and get some wet weather gear, pay Ron. As he approached the Safeway store, he saw Little Shoe Big Shoe, started to wave, when he was hit from behind. Jack spun through the air, crash landing beside Little Shoe, thought, should he buy a *Big Issue*, farted, then fainted.

'An ambulance is on the way. Can you tell me if it's hurting anywhere? You've taken a knock,' a paramedic said as he fitted a collar.

'No kidding, Tonto.'

'I know you from the scene yesterday, Inspector Austin, isn't it?'

Jack lay back, wondering what he looked like in the collar, a Vicar? 'Where's my bike?'

Little Shoe leaned over, 'The bloke in the van nicked it and drove off.'

'What?'

'I got the number, which is more than I can say about my pand.'

Jack ignored Little Shoe's indignation and looked to the paramedic. 'Call this in, Amanda Bruce, tell her to get a search out for the van.'

The medic looked fed-up, like he was being used, which he was of course. Jack used everyone, but he did it with a lot of charm, he thought. 'I'll call it in...' sighed, '...the ambulance is here.'

'What's your name?'

'Well, it isn't Dr Kildare, which is what you called me yesterday, it's John.'

He tapped the medic's wrist, and in his best patronising voice, 'John, express processing at the hospital, there's a good boy,' tried to get up, farted, and fainted again.

TWENTY-THREE

JACK RECOVERED HIS WITS IN A NARROW CASUALTY BED, sounds of hubbub and rustling curtains, beeps, wires coming out of his chest and an irritating clip on his finger. Father O'Brien leaned over and they exchanged whispers, after which the Holy Ghost evaporated. A doctor entered as Jack was talking to himself, developing what Father Mike had related, into his own theory. 'Hold up, Doc, I'm in the middle of a conversation.' The doc asked him who the Prime Minister was. 'Feckin Mackeroon and the slippery bleedin' Blogg, I'm plotting their down fall this evening, so patch me up, Snotty, and get me out of here.' Jack thought the doctor seemed more concerned about his outburst than his wounds. He could hear Mandy outside the curtains, a nurse explaining she had no authority here.

The doctor stepped out, 'You are?'

'Detective Superintendent Bruce,' Mandy replied, struggling to be polite.

'You were on the telly yesterday, Pugwash, what a hoot,' the Doc said, chortling, and became preoccupied with who he was going to cure next. Mandy became civil, never a good sign, and clearly the doc picked up on this. 'Mr Austin has a concussion, there's no serious physical injury. We'll keep him in overnight...' the doc drifted.

'Can I see him, please?' Mandy asked.

'Try not to disturb him, we're waiting for a bed in the assessment unit.'

'Thanks, Doc,' and Jack imagined her sticking her tongue out to the nurse; will she never grow up? He closed his eye in mock sleep and applied his unwell face, sensed her presence, breathed in her perfume as she leaned into him, could feel her warm moist breath on his face as she kissed him on the lips. Jack pulled her down and gave her a deep kiss. She screamed, and the nurse and doctor came running. Jack lay there, cats and cream, Mandy spluttering, 'This man's okay, I want him in my office in an hour.'

'Amanda,' the Cheshire Cat.

'What?'

'Magic word?'

The doc defused the ticking bomb, 'Superintendent, calm yourself.'

Jack patted the bed. 'Amanda.' The doctor left.

'Jack, you gave me a shock...' Her concerned face, and he liked it, made the moaning worthwhile.

She didn't succumb to his smile, odd, he thought, so he resorted to police work. 'They knocked me down and nicked my bike.'

'What are you saying?'

Lovely face, and Jack had to fight the urge to kiss her again. 'Get Frankie to run their ferry info, look for vehicles carrying bikes, small amounts of drugs smuggled within the frames of bikes, families taking bikes on holiday. Little and often can add up.' He was excited and wondered if she understood. 'I got this bike at Bazaar Bikes, would trust Ron with my life, but his assistant, Chas, was keen I didn't take this particular bike, see?' He saw she didn't, so he reinforced the logic, 'He didn't know what a Scooby Doo was, see?' Nope, 'My garage last night? Looking for the bike, see?'

Mandy rubbed her face in thought, and Jack stopped so he could watch, multi-tasking not being a strong point. 'Jeyziz fluid, Jack,' Cod Irish, it warmed him, 'shut-up while I think. I'm off, I'll come and see you later.'

He put his hand on her arm. 'Will you buggery, I'm coming with you, so make some calls,' he stepped off the bed, 'can you help me put me round the houses on?' slipped the gown off, 'oh, my pants as well.'

'Jack, you're revolting,' swished the curtains and left.

Jack was reluctantly discharged, packing some atom bomb Paracetamol, and Mandy drove them back to the station, the briefing shifted to midday.

'I wanted to speak to that little girl,' Jack murmured; she looked at him as she drove, he was subdued.

'I checked on her while you were arguing with the triage nurse. Gail's with her and specialist officers are going to talk to the women and children, you will stay put in the station.' Jack decided he could ignore this, life was about sifting; he had a blinding headache for which the supersonic, atom bombs had yet to deal with. Mandy, sensing he was ignoring her, asserted, 'What if they were after you?'

'Then why take my bike?'

Mandy butted into his elucidating, 'Yes, I've spoken to Michael, he's going to phone Alana. He's worried, so do us all a favour, stay out of trouble and shut-up. I need to think.'

He turned fully so she could see his miffed face; she laughed and told him to feck-off. No appreciation for a sick man that girl, made a mental note to work on his *I'm-not-well* look.

———

IN THE CP ROOM, Connie and Frankie were working the oracle; Nobby, Jo-Jums, Paolo and Cyrano, heads down. Jack pulled up a wheelie chair and by rote spun one over for Mandy. By rote she wheeled it to where she wanted to sit, not squashed next to him.

'Paolo, the interrogations?' Jack asked.

Paolo gave a slightly Italianate, Gallic shrug, which Jack secretly admired, 'Nothing, lawyered up, expensive suit, interesting, eh? We'll charge them and hope for a good follow-up on the murders.'

'When are you interviewing again?'

'Soon.'

'Mind if I sit in? Mandy's not letting me out to play,' Jack chastised himself for reacting like a spoilt child, but thought, she started it, and accidentally said, "Ner."

'Jo-Jums?' Mandy resumed control.

'Wallace and Kettle are at the printers, good Intel from KFC.'

'Whoa, KFC?'

'Komputers Frankie and Confucius, Jack,' Jo-Jums said, matter-of-fact, Mumsey.

'You're making up nicknames?'

Jo, inured to Jack and all his states, continued, 'We're seeing if the printer can ID anyone.'

'Cyrano?'

'Following up the bikes, KFC are looking for regular number plates travelling to and from the continent and a tie-in with the CCTV. We've discussed an approach to Hogwarts but...'

Mandy interrupted, 'Hogwarts?'

'Bazaar Bikes, Jack calls the owner Ron Wheelslie,' she explained.

'Carry on...' Mandy contemplated clumping Jack.

'We've a tail on the assistant, Chas Joliffe, and surveillance on the shop. We think the scam is nicking bikes off the street, sending them over to the continent where they get filled with the stuff, to return with the families to be distributed, and all disguised as refurbished used bikes. Clever, and maybe not as small as you suggested, Jane.'

'So, wait and see?' Jack enquired, holding his head.

Cyrano moved an inch or two, excited. 'Yeah.'

Jack carried on talking to Cyrano, waving his hands to indicate to everyone this was a thought bulletin, 'I still think it isn't just a drugs bust, just as I don't think this is just trafficking, prostitution or porn. My gut feeling is this is funding something. So let's wrap-up what we have and get the extended enquiries underway, which leaves vice, Paolo, any word?'

Paolo swung his chair to look at Jack, 'As expected, they want to make their own Biscuit enquiries, said you'd speak to them.'

Jack remained unfocused, tapped a tune with his fingers, guessed correctly, it was *Doctor Who* and smiled at his brilliance. 'Paolo, let's keep our powder dry; Jo-Jums, find out what you can, if we go in knob-handed, their antennae will start twitching.'

'Okay, do you mean mob? You okay with that Jo?' Mandy summarised.

'Prefer knob,' Jo replied. 'What about the women and children, if they were off the radar, then why? People disappear every day, but it's normally noticed, and local women and children, is that possible, and if it is, how? We need to take a deeper look at social services?'

Jack knew he was right to keep looking at Jo. 'Softly, softly, vice and social services.'

Mandy pressed, 'Jo, contact our team at the hospital, get some personal histories.'

There was a ping from KFC; their equipment had grown to four screens. Sensing the room was focused on them, Frankie and Confucius spun in their chairs, 'Why don't you tell the guys what we have, Connie?' Frankie suggested.

Connie looked nervous, Frankie encouraging. 'We set up program to run multiple trips, repeat car registrations, look for comparison where we have CCTV. We have match on two plates, large family cars, both have bike rack and three bike, we track, and they return to England, one tomorrow and other in four day.'

Jack was animated, 'What d'you think, Cyrano?'

'Put a team on the ferry, and when the passengers are off the car deck, we check the bikes. If we get a hit, I suggest a tracker on the vehicle and follow them when they disembark,' Cyrano responded.

'Registrations for owners?' Jack asked.

'Doing that, but we'll likely find they are dodgy plates and stolen identities,' Frankie answered.

'Cyrano, you okay with manning, monitoring Hogwarts and this ferry business?'

'I'm okay.'

Jack was energised. 'Good, we may just be getting somewhere. Nobby, bring the wall up to speed then get on with whatever it was we agreed you would do, and forget what I said about a home life. That was then, this is now.'

Mandy quietly added, 'Except you, Jane, you're grounded, and if you can take tomorrow off, do that.'

'You and me kid, and *Top Deck shandy*,' Jack ejaculated.

'Jane, deckchair, or home,' Mandy was firm.

Jack shrugged, lollopy, 'I want to see that girl and Martin.'

Mandy capitulated like she knew she would, 'I've stuff to catch up on, then I will take you to the hospital, and the vet, you cannot be trusted on your own.'

'I'm interviewing the skinheads, you're welcome to join me, Jane,' Paolo suggested.

'I will.'

Jack's rising esteem was deflated by Frankie, 'Jane, your new phone.' Frankie held it up to whistles, an iPhone. 'It's synched and ready to go. I'll give you a quick demo.'

Jack felt sick, hated learning new technology, the phone was synched and he was sunk.

TWENTY-FOUR

FRANKIE'S FINGERS FLICKING THE PHONE ICONS MADE Jack feel even greener about the gills. 'Slow down, Franks.' She did, hardly discernible, indicating phone numbers and e-mail addresses he never knew he had, transferred from his computer to the phone. Jack looked, 'Where's my computer?'

'We nicked it, you never use it.'

Miffed, Jack asserted himself into unknown territory, 'I was thinking of doing an e-mail.'

'You can do that on your phone now; Connie and I are here if you need help.' If, he thought, his desk looked bare without the computer, but upon reflection, the last thing he wanted was people thinking he was a nerd, and walking along with the phone out in front of him, his finger moving icons, Jack bumped into the door. 'Watch out for that, Jane.'

'Nice timing, Franks, did you put the settings in I asked for?'

'All there,' she called back, giggling at Jack's discomfiture.

Jack put the phone in his pocket, felt the smooth slim object slide in, better than the feel of duct tape and elastic bands. He had a conspiratorial word with Barney as he passed through reception to the room where Paolo was interviewing the fat skinhead, knocked, and walked in.

'Inspector Austin has entered the room at 11.53 am,' an assistant Sissy said.

'Is it that time already?' Jack said, pulling himself a spare chair, sitting at the end of the table and looking at the skinhead, whose face was a mess. A ponging camouflage vest emphasised, rather than disguised, rolls of blubber, fat legs encapsulated in cargo-pants. Jack knew these trousers, Michael had told him, pockets all over the place, for cargo he imagined; black boots with no laces. The lump of lard lounged silently, smugly, and Jack could understand why Paolo had the hump.

Jack turned his attention to the suave solicitor, slim, works out probably, well groomed, sharp suit. Jack looked under the table, highly polished shoes, shiny buckles like he was King feckin' Charles, back up he inspected the shirt and tie, the finely cut hair, dark, poncy gel; women like running their fingers through that stuff? He knew instinctively women would prefer his hair; experience, he supposed. A nondescript face, ordinary looking, Jack almost felt sorry for him.

'I presume you have finished looking at us, Inspector?' the irked solicitor said.

Jack played with his new phone, 'And your name, Sir?'

'Thackeray, Lionel, solicitor,' the solicitor replied, maximum smarm.

'They call you Len?'

'No, Mr Thackeray.'

'Well, Len, why won't your client tell us who he is and what he was doing at that house yesterday when he knifed a policeman?'

'Mr Thackeray, and my client is denying he attacked one of your men.'

'Len, maybe we've gotten off on the wrong hand, we have fingerprints, witnesses confirming he knifed a policeman, and had he not been so incompetent, he would have knifed me as well. At the very least you can advise him to tell us who he is?'

'Fuck-off, copper,' the skinhead exclaimed.

Jack responded when the rolls of fat had settled, 'Oh, Buddha speaks, and what Carmen are we expecting today, pray?' Paolo was bemused and wondered what Jack was doing, but he had at least got a response.

The skinhead, a bloated and beaten up face, the picture of dimwittedness, turned to his solicitor, 'Who's this Buddha when he's at home?'

'You, since you will not tell us your name,' Jack interjected, smug now, still playing with his new phone.

'It's not fucking Buddha, its Greg Varney.'

Jack looked up. 'Any relation to Reg, you know, *On the Buses*? I 'ate you, Butler.' Jack was doing an impression of Blakey off the sitcom *On the Buses*. There were stunned looks, and Jack thought the impression was good, but it appeared nobody had seen the series.

'What's he talking abowt?' Buddha asked.

Before the solicitor could jump in with a caution, Jack went on, 'Reg, we'll be charging you with assault on a police officer, kidnap and holding against their will women and children, rape of the women and the children, and we have you tagged for the murder of one of the women and possibly a police officer.' Jack looked at Paolo, squashed a grin and scratched his scalp. 'I'm a little rusty on the wording, I'm a pig sty thinker, well, starry thinker as I had a bang on me loaf of bread this morning, but does that sum things up, DCI Willie?'

Before Paolo could ask about "pig sty," Jack's phone rang. 'Oh fuck, this is new, how do you answer it?' The solicitor leaned forward, looked at Jack's caller ID, *Remand Centre*, then in a smart arse manner showed Jack how to slide his finger to answer the call, handed it back with a cheesy grin that reminded Jack of the Prime Minister and his oily sidekick, 'Cheers, Len. Hello, yes, this is Inspector Austin.'

'You do not have to shout,' the solicitor commented.

'Righto, Len.'

'Thackeray.'

'Whatever,' Jack said, then into the phone, 'we have four individuals being charged, sex offences against minors, so we'll need them isolated.' He looked up, Paolo nodded. Jack spoke again into the phone, 'Johnny, if word got out, these lads will be brown bread by morning.' The solicitor put his hand up as if he was in class, one nil, Jack thought, and let him wait while he listened, keeping his hand up in his now well-practiced *Halt the traffic* signal, 'Hang-on a mo, Johnny. Yes, Len?' slightly irritated.

'Thackeray,' shirty; two nil, 'I could not help noticing the caller ID, and I must insist my client has a safe remand cell.'

Jack made some noises in his mouth that he thought were quite good, committed to memory, and forgot them; was it raining this morning? 'Len, can I ask you one thing?'

'Thackeray, and yes!'

Jack applied his *Oooh-err* look, usually reserved for sexual innuendo, but often worked in situations like this; and they say Austin can't multi-task. 'No need to raise your voice, is there?' Jack looked around the table and everyone, including Buddha, nodded. 'Right, who did you vote?'

'What's that got to do with anything?' Len asked, shaking his head in a patronising young conservative way.

'Humour me, Len. Hang on Johnny, be right with you,' Jack laughed into the phone, 'shut-up, you tosspot.'

Frustrated, but thinking he will run this country hick

copper around for a bit, 'I voted Conservative, Inspector,' the solicitor answered.

'Well, Len, I thought so, therefore you will be the first to feel comforted that we are all in this together, the Big Society and all that. You see, the cutbacks have hit the Remand Centre,' Jack pointed to his phone. 'Johnny...' Jack drifted off, leaned back in his chair and looked at the ceiling, a broad smile growing, 'I've known him for...' he scratched his head, checked his fingers for detritus, '...blimey, twenty-five years, hang-on.' Jack got back on the phone, 'Johnny how long...? Shut-up, it's longer than that, we played rugby together more than twenty-odd years ago.'

Len interrupted, typical of a rude Tory boy, 'Inspector, please.'

'Hang-on, Johnny; sorry, Len, it's probably twenty-five years. Johnny was a prop, they get a lot of bangs on the head in the front of the scrum, anyway, a wing of accommodation has been closed, redundancies, reduced capacity.' Jack tried to count on his fingers, but was in danger of dropping his new phone. 'Bloody shame, a double whammy, as the kids say.' Jack looked to Buddha to see if he was impressed he was so up to date with the expressions of youngsters and concluded he must have fat in his brain. 'No staff for special watch prisoners either, see, and the high-risk wing is full, a treble whammy really, because as the eight hundred dip recession hits the normal man and woman in the street, so they feel the need to go out robbing, and we feel the need to nick 'em.' Jack grinned, accentuating his intelligent look with a head wobble, as if he had made an obvious point, then continued. 'I'm sure I don't need to explain this to you, but for the benefit of Buddha here.'

'My name's Greg, not fucking Buddha.'

Jack responded, 'Yes, yes, all terribly interesting, Reg, but as your solicitor will have already surmised, we don't have the accommodation to keep you isolated, so you will have to camp down with the, shall we say, normal criminal types, who, shall we also say, are not overly enamoured with child molesters. The point of ameli...or...dation, I was deluding to...' Buddha was looking glassy eyed, and Jack thought he would introduce a dramatic pause, it would also cover up his not knowing amelioration, take note Paolo, he continued, '...was, that Len, being a Tory boy, would understand we are all in this together, and no more so than you and your mates, sunshine. Excuse me,' and Jack returned to his call, 'Johnny, no, doing the ABC with Buddha. You'll see him tonight, he doesn't seem to understand we can't stop his association with other prisoners.' Jack paused, listening to Johnny, looking at Buddha, the implications sinking in, Der! 'Johnny, no can do.' Jack put his hand over the phone and said to Paolo, 'He's worried, asked if we could hold them at the nick, but I'm not sure that will be okay. Hang on, Johnny.'

Jack got up, opened the interview room door and shouted, 'Barney.'

'What?' a muffled voice in the distance.

'Holding cells tonight, any chance for the perverts and cop killers?'

Barney must have walked into the corridor, he was a lot clearer, 'Not a chance, we expect to be busy, have to charge 'em and ship 'em.'

'Okey-dokey, Barney,' and Jack stepped back in, sat, and stretched his legs. Buddha, Paolo, and even Len moved their feet so he could fit his long legs under the table; three nil. Back to his phone, 'Johnny, you heard, brilliant these phones, iPhone, your missus got one, oh, lah-dee-bleedin' dah, okay, we'll charge the feckin' eejits and get 'em down to you. Do your best, see you.' Jack passed the phone to the solicitor. 'How d'you switch it off?' The solicitor showed Jack how to tap the large red *off* button. 'Cheers, Len. Paolo get these guys charged, and if they're around tomorrow, we can hang the murder on them, pronto Tonto, need you out coppering, not sat on your arse all day.'

Mr Blobby grunted, 'Oi, I 'ave rights, you 'ave to keep me here.'

Jack looked pleased for the opportunity to set the world to rights. 'Indeed, you do have rights, Mr Buddha, and I suggest you or your solicitor write to Mr Mackeroon directly,' it was his Mr Darcy voice, 'see if he wouldn't mind releasing some money so we can staff and run the Remand Centre for you. The only way we can keep you here is if you start talking, got it, you fat paedophile bastard.' Oops, Mr Darcy slipped, Jack calmed in a Hawaiian way, 'Book-em, Danno,' and grinned as he was passing through the door.

Buddha called after him, 'I'll talk, but you keep me here.'

Jack looked back from the door. 'Depends on what you say.' Jack looked at Paolo and nodded to Buddha, 'Okay, Fatty, I'm off to the hospital to talk to the kids you fiddled with, so make it good, and if you don't...' he looked at Paolo '...charge 'em and ship 'em, and if they're around, we'll talk to them tomorrow, after church.' He sketched a blessing and left, feeling holier than thou.

'Was that okay, Jane?'

'Bloody marvellous, Barney,' Jack replied, leaning on the counter, a tired look in his eye. Barney mimicked the lean. 'I try very hard to see the best in everyone, but that fat bastard...'

'Can't save 'em all,' Barney counselled.

'No indeed,' and Jack trudged the hallway, plodded the stairs; he should feel elated but didn't, settled for his old companion, melancholy, felt down in the dumps as he sat in the deckchair, an apathetic Italianate flourish only. He dozed, slept, a dribble of spittle oozing from the corner of his mouth as his head drooped to the side.

He felt the gentleness on his face as he slumbered, sensuous, perfume intoxicating. 'Darling, time to get up,' and Mandy tossed his jacket on his lap, embarrassed at what she witnessed. 'Love the dribble, I cannot tell you what a turn on it is.'

He yawned and stretched, wiped his mouth with the back of his hand, then on his trousers, didn't see the revolted look on Mandy's face. 'Amanda, I dribble for you.'

She restrained an uncouth retort, 'You wanted to go to the hospital and the vet?'

He looked up at her face; he liked it, even upside down, had a perverse thought and felt a charge of energy in his loins and leg departments. 'I do, Ma'am, and I want to sail away with you, to toxic lands and sample their delights and your wondrous body.'

'Let's get going then or we'll miss the feckin' boat,' and she clipped him around the head, and waving his new phone, he followed her to the door where Jo-Jums waited.

'Paolo called up, singing like a canary, he seemed impressed, Jane.'

Jack nodded, 'Frankie, thanks for rigging the phone, seems to have worked,' and headed for the staircase for a Nelson Eddie, 'I'm a calling you, oo, oo, oo, oooooo.' Mandy, at the bottom of the stairs, nodded her irritation as he leaned over the banister, 'You're supposed to sing, I will answer too-oo-oo-ooo.'

She was unimpressed with his lumberjack impression, but she was impressed with his interrogation, and as he tramped down the stairs, 'Heard from Paolo, nice one, Jack.'

'Lumberjack, Mands,' he grinned and tilted his best Canadian head.

Mandy felt lumbered.

JACK FOLLOWED Mandy to her car watching the gyrations of her bottom; how come women's bottoms gyrate and blokes don't? He thought, cranking his neck, looking behind to see if his bum gyrated. Mandy at the car looking back, wondered if he'd hurt his back this morning, 'You okay?'

'Headache, I'll score some atom bombs at the hospital,' and he was asleep before they were onto the road. She chanced a look at him in repose. He was not a looker; she had often said he was a Jack Nicholson type, in that he got away with looking old and overweight with a boyish charm, but looking at him, she thought his face a cross between Geoffrey Rush, the actor, and a slapped arse. She giggled to herself, not classically attractive to a woman, but somehow it was. Get a grip, Mands, she counselled herself, and subconsciously looked at his crotch.

TWENTY-FIVE

THE HOSPITAL CAR PARK WAS CRAMMED. MANDY NUDGED Jack awake, 'I'll drop you and meet you in there.'

'Thanks, babes,' he said, rubbing his recently inspected face.

'What, no diatribe about the scandalous parking charges, and how this penalises the families of the poor?'

He said nothing and it worried her.

Outside the hospital main entrance, Jack exaggerated his fight through the fog of sick smokers. 'What's with you dipstick?' a smoker's retort, a man looking like he was out of a concentration camp, peeking out from behind his wheelie dripstand.

Jack rummaged for his warrant card, gave up. 'You're what's up, pollutin' the feckin' entrance to a hospital so people are forced to walk through your cancerous smog and have to look at your emaciated, cadaverous bodies.' There is nobody more zealous than a reformed smoker; Jack had given up when Alana was born.

'I only asked,' the drip-stand replied.

173

Jack put his finger in the air. 'Ah, *Charlie Drake,* or was that *Bernard Bresslaw?*' But the bloke hadn't heard of either comedian from the distant past, so Jack explained, '"I only asked" another was "Hello my darlings," no, that was *Charlie Drake,* the other one was *Bernard Bresslaw.*'

The Philistine smokers sidled away, and Jack pretended to rub his hands with the alcohol gel; too early for a drink, and he slouched along the hospital corridors eventually finding the lifts.

'I know you?' a lift passenger said.

'I'm sorry, I've a headache,' Jack replied and he had silence; the man did not seem offended. Ding, "Doors opening," 'Well of course they feckin' are,' Jack said in his head, but also out loud, mouthed an apology. Accepted; diplomanic corps, Jack? He eventually found where the girl and Gail should be, approached the nurse and showed his Blockbuster card, said it was *Doctor Who* psychic paper and asked for some Paracetamol and to see the girl.

'You brought her out of the house?' the nurse said. 'Saw you crying on the telly.'

'Yeah,' Jack sighed. She gave him the Paracetamol and strutted to a water cooler. Jack took the pills and slugged the water, the nurse pensive, appraising his physical wellbeing, too nervous to say anything.

The girl was in bed, in a single room, the sheets tight under her chin, her eyes blinked instant recognition as Jack entered. She eased her skinny arms from the binding sheet and held them out. Hesitantly, he went to her and kissed her cheek, leaning past Gail, which, considering her size, was a feat worthy of an Olympic medal. He tingled as a tiny palm stroked his face, 'Are you my dad?'

That tugged, and Gail looked worried about how Jack

would reply. He looked to Gail, 'I hope Keanu went into work this morning.'

'He did, Jack,' and gestured her head to the girl.

'No, sweet'art, I'm not your dad but I wish I was. I'm just someone who loves you very much and wants you to get better.'

He had his reward as she put her arms out again and wet lips slobbered into his ear. 'Meesh,' she said.

'Meesh?'

'My name is Michelle, but call me Meesh.'

Jack wanted to press for a second name, but felt a rising heat in his left leg, thought it might be some reaction to his accident this morning. It got hotter. Is it the left leg if you're having a stroke? But it felt wet. 'Kin 'ell, Gail, you've pissed on me.'

'It's me waters, they just broke.'

'Yeah, and all over me leg, look at these round the houses, clean on this morning.'

Gail grabbed her distended belly, 'The baby's coming.'

Wiggling his leg and trousers, trying to hold the wet material from his skin, 'No bleedin' kiddin',' and he could see Meesh was worried. 'It's okay, sweet'art, Gail's having the baby,' and he noticed a mixture of fear and excitement on her face.

Gail moaned, 'Get someone, Jack.'

'It's okay, they'll dry in a minute,' looked at Gail, 'okay, but should be like shelling peas for you?'

'Yeah, shelling peas, go, before I give you a right hander.'

Waving his leg, Jack loped to the door, looked back and saw Meesh hop out, helping Gail, who had stripped and climbed onto the vacated bed. Jack called to the nurse, 'We need help please, Gail's having the baby, and if you have a hair drier?' The nurse sprung into action, probably looking for the drier, Jack thought.

Back in the room, Gail was open for business, not what Jack had in mind for today, but Meesh seemed galvanised, fussing like a trained midwife. He stood beside the bed and, impressing himself with his sensitivity, he said softly to Gail, 'A doctor's coming.' She grabbed his arm as a contraction came, squeezed, and Jack screamed; so much for feckin' sensitivity, he thought.

Meesh stared. 'Stop being a softy, Jack.'

'Jeyziz, where's that doctor?' More sensitivity; he considered himself a modern man.

'Jack, this is not right,' but Jack was all out of sensitivity.

Meesh was dabbing Gail's forehead, holding her hand. Jack thought she'd better get her hand out of there before another contraction. It came, 'Feck, Gail, look at my arm,' another contraction, another disappointing look from Meesh, who'd had the foresight to remove her vulnerable hand, managed a tut.

In amazement, Jack asked, 'You don't have a grandmother called Dolly, do you?'

'I have no family,' matter-of-fact.

He felt a Roman Candle moment coming, but it was another contraction, and Jack yelled as the doctor entered. The nurse was about to clear the room, but Gail asserted, 'The girl stays, and Jack is my birthing partner.'

'What? I'm not her birthing partner,' he pleaded. 'I can't stand the sight of blood, and my legs are soaking wet and beginning to pen-and-ink,' then falling back on cold logic, 'I've got to take my library books back.'

'Please,' it was Meesh shaking her head like Jack's mum used to do and Dolly still does.

'Oh feck, oh Gail, Jeyziz my arm!' he shouted.

Mandy, strolling down the ward corridor, heard Jack scream and reacted in panic, heard him scream again and thought, should I call for back up? Too late, she burst through the door, Jack screamed; not a contraction, Mandy had made him jump.

Jack resumed his writhing agony in case he got some sympathy, 'What the?' no sympathy then.

'Please,' the doctor said, 'the baby's in an awkward position.'

'Pants, Gail,' a brilliant and quite sensitive idea, Jack thought.

'Pants, you eejit?' Mandy exclaimed,

Meesh explained, 'He means panting breaths.'

Everyone, including the doctor, looked at Meesh, who somehow had taken charge, practicing for when she was a woman Jack thought, still in considerable pain, and miffed nobody seemed to care about him, and more miffed everyone thought panting was Meesh's idea when it was his.

'Here he comes, steady, don't push yet, okay, now, one more, and here...she is.' The doc said.

Jack looked down to the business end, farted, then fainted.

When he came around, Mandy and the doctor were struggling to get him into an armchair. 'If he wasn't so fat, this would be a lot easier,' Mandy said, puffing and wheezing.

Meesh squared up to Mandy, 'Don't talk to moi dad like that.' Pompey accent.

Jack's eye became clearer, avoided looking at Gail lest he faint again.

'Leave him there, he'll be alright,' Mandy said, giving up and returning to Gail, Meesh, and the baby.

Jack looked up from the floor, his leg was wet, cold, and horrible, he was sure his arm was broken, did nobody care about that? Jack noticed the doctor, a young lad with no spots, looked exalted at the birth, and he looked at Mandy too much. 'My first delivery, exciting,' looked at Gail, 'are you going to name the baby after me?' realised his gaff having delivered a girl.

Gail answered, 'No, doctor, I'm naming her after him,' pointing at Jack.

'Jane,' Meesh said, jumping up and down. Dolly had left the child's body, and Jack felt relieved. The *Exorcist* film scared him; just he didn't tell anyone. The doctor looked confused about the *Exorcist* reference, still beaming, and much to Jack's constellation, was looking too closely at Mandy, who was unreasonably beaming back; this was not on, so Jack vomited. The doctor and nurse reacted, Mandy told them he was concussed this morning.

'Then what's he doing out of hospital?' the doctor yelled, and Mandy thought about saying he was, technically, in hospital, but accepted maybe she would have to settle for Jack who stank of sick and had a smelly wet leg; such was her lot.

Jack recalled getting into a wheelchair, Gail telling Meesh to stay with her, as Mandy pushed him to another ward and undressed him; a fantasy come true, but not how he'd imagined it, and if he only knew, Mandy was thinking the same thing.

TWENTY-SIX

'Your partner said you were Church of Egypt, I've amended that to Catholic now.'

'Partner, Catholic?'

'Father O'Brien has been sitting with you, but left to do Sunday morning mass.'

'Sunday?'

The nurse had things to do, 'You've been asleep nearly twenty hours,' and she left.

Jack slipped out a long groan, you're allowed to groan in hospital, but his heart wasn't in it; he felt woozy. 'How's he doing, nurse?' Mandy was there.

'The doctor says he's okay, he's slept a long time, so I think his body must have needed it.' Both women looked at him: one, matter-of-fact; the other, a little love. Jack missed both; you do if you're woozy.

'He's been through a lot lately, God love him. When can he come out?' Mandy asked.

'Doc says now if he's up to it, so let's see, let him sleep.'

Mandy nodded, 'I'll be back in a couple of hours, here's my

card, let me know if anything happens, I'd better get some clothes for him.'

'His son and girlfriend came by earlier and left clean clothes; we've binned the others.' Jack heard and groaned; he hated shopping for clothes.

Mandy saw him stir, 'I'll sit with him for a little, okay?'

No comment, the nurse still had things to do. Mandy held his hand, drifted, then fell asleep with her head on the bed.

'See, she loves your Jack,' Meesh stood beside Gail who had the baby Jane in her arms.

Mandy rubbed the sleep from her eyes. 'Meesh, isn't it?'

'Are you my Jack's girlfriend?' Meesh asked.

'Well, ah,' Mandy was stumped.

'Do you love him, because he loves me?'

Mandy looked long and hard at Jack asleep. 'Yes.'

'Then I love you too.' A tear formed in Jack's good eye. 'He's not really my dad.'

'I know, darling.'

'But he's the next best thing, isn't he, Gail?'

'He is that, sweet'art,' Gail replied, dewy eyed.

Mandy repeated, 'He is that, sweet'art.'

Meesh mouthed, 'He is that, sweet'art.'

Jack heard this exchange and decided not to wake up, but it didn't stop the tear from rolling down; wuss.

———

THE WARD CLOCK SAID FOUR-THIRTY, he rubbed his eye, thought he saw Sitting Bull's squaw sitting beside the bed. 'How are you, Jack? You should sleep, "A great restorer sleep," my husband says, when he falls asleep in the armchair, so I suppose it is, but it does mean we do not get much chance at conversation.' Jack's hallucination offered a doughy smell of baking; is this what you smell before you're about to die, or was that toast? 'Are you okay, darling?' the squaw calling me darling? This cannot be happening. 'I brought some of my freshly baked scones, they insisted at the station this is what you would want.'

Jack laughed; he hadn't laughed so much since his mum caught her tit in the mangle, the Chief Constable's squaw's baking notorious, and she responded he shouldn't have laughed at his mum.

'Mrs Chief,' the squaw smiled at the kindness done to her with this tiniest of epithets, 'you've made a young-looking, middle-aged man very happy. D'you mind if I eat them later, I'm still a bit tom and dick.'

'Pleased to see you laughing.' A wet smacking kiss from Meesh, but it was Father O'Brien doing the talking, not the kissing; the Lord be praised.

'See, he's better, can you come out now, please, Jack, pleeeeease?' Meesh pleaded, 'Uncle Mickey has made a kite and we can fly it on the hill, please, please,' pulling at Jack's hand. Four faces now, the squaw, Meesh, Gail and Father O'Brien, and this became five as Mandy arrived with some flowers, and to Jack's amazement, she pushed through the crowd, gathered Meesh in her arm, plonked her on the bed, and planted a loving kiss on Jack's lips. 'There, that will shut you up,' she gave him the flowers.

He whispered in her ear, Meesh's as well as she was not to be left out, 'Flowers, Mands? I'm not ginger beer, you know.' Meesh tutted; Dolly, it has to be. Mandy play-slapped Jack's face and Meesh smoothed it, to make it better, giving Mandy an old-fashioned look. Definitely Dolly.

'The doctor says you can come out whenever you feel like it,' Mandy said.

'Why didn't he speak to me?'

Mandy smiled, it was obvious, 'He thought you couldn't handle medical facts.'

'Not that spotty kid, cheeky sod.'

Mrs Chief tutted and Meesh saw a kindred spirit in the squaw woman, looked up, tilted her head and smiled. 'He's not my dad, you know, but he loves me very much.'

'I'm sure he does, and who would not love you, darling,' the squaw replied, stroking Meesh's mousey hair that Jack had come to like.

Mandy was talking and Jack was not listening, 'He doesn't have spots, and he's a very nice young man, you could learn a lot from him.'

'Amanda, I want to go,' Jack said in his sickly voice, and Meesh pushed past Mandy, went to the bedside cupboard, and began throwing out Jack's clothes.

'I'll speak to the nurse, come with me Meesh?' The girl chucked the clothes on the bed and Jack's jumbo pants fell on the floor; the Squaw picked them up. Jack sighed as Meesh dashed to Mandy, grabbed her hand, miraculously slowed, and casually they trotted off together. Jack felt amused, whether this was Mandy and Meesh, or the squaw holding his pants, he was not sure, bit of both probably.

Father O'Brien, his sanctimonious head on, 'I've mass in an hour,' sketched a blessing, lingering over the baby Jane. A cue for squaw woman who European-kissed Jack and also left.

Gail took the vacated seat, simultaneously suckering the baby's mouth onto a flying saucer nipple; it was all too much. 'Gail, what's happening with Meesh, where are Social Services?'

'Don't fret, I often foster kids, so she's with me, better than being carted off to a home. She's stuck fast on you and Mandy though.'

'What can I do? She's a lovely kid, but?'

'Jack, find her mother and that will solve everything.'

'Yes, that's what I'll do,' Jack said, 'double whammy, as Michael says; where is Michael?'

'Don't be a plank, who d'you think brought your stuff. Alana's been as well. She's a lovely girl, and so is that man of hers, so cut him a bit of slack.'

'Slack? She's only twenty-five.'

'Talking about Alana again?' Mandy returned.

Matron Meesh climbed on the bed, snuggled into Jack, who subconsciously put an arm around her. 'Alana?'

'Jack's older daughter,' Mandy answered because Jack was close to crying, 'you're going to love her, and my kids, John, he's 20 and Elizabeth's twenty-two.'

'When can I meet them?'

'Soon, darling, very soon,' and Mandy kissed her.

Jack felt he was losing control of his life; no change there then.

————

MANDY HELPED JACK GET DRESSED, turned to put his pants on. 'Jack, stop being a wuss there's nothing I haven't seen before,' Mandy said, giggling. Stone me Old-timer's, Jack thought, struggling with a leg in the wrong pants hole. 'Come here,' and Mandy spun him and Jack tried to gather his bits and pieces, too late. 'Well, halloo, Jack,' she hooted, and he heard Gail and Meesh giggling from behind the curtain; Jack sighed his hospital sigh.

A giggling nurse, popped her head around the curtain, 'Need a hand?'

'No, it's not that big,' Mandy replied. More guffaws the other side of the curtain. Mandy kissed him and whispered, 'For Christmas,' and patted his bum.

'What do I get for Boxing Day?'

'Ha, last word, nice save.' Mandy pulled the curtain back to spontaneous applause. Jack thought it was a bit presumptuous of Mandy to be taking a bow; who was the patient?

She put the rest of his things in a bag, suggesting his hospital pyjamas could be used as a tent by the boy scouts, and Meesh tutted and wriggled; Jack let her tiny hand into his, it felt warm, moist, and sent a shiver up his spine. 'Now this girl knows how to treat a patient,' he said, looking at Mandy who made like Meesh and wriggled her hand into Jack's other hand.

Ego restored, they walked along, the Meesh arm tugged, 'Martin's okay now, and Father Mike said you will let me walk him.'

Jack thought it felt strange to have one hand swing and the other stationery. Gail was close behind, the baby whimpering having lost the space craft of sustenance; home, Jack thought, where is everyone else going?

―――――

Jack was directed to the back seat of Mandy's car, and Gail passed the baby Jane who immediately spewed breast milk onto his shoulder; he made a yeeeuk noise.

'Tut,' Dolly possessed Meesh.

Mandy dropped Gail and the baby Jane home, and onto Jack's; Mandy would drop Meesh off later to sleep at Gail's. They pulled up behind Jack's garage, Meesh not daring to let Jack's hand go as they clambered out. He'd missed this feeling, a child's trust and his consequent comfort. Through the garage into the back garden, Meesh's eyes widened, Colleen appeared and Meesh ran to her open arms, was sucked into a house smelling of roast dinner, it reminded Jack of Sunday lunches when he was a kid; *Two way family favourites* on the radio and he sang, "*With a song in my heart...*" That was it, he didn't know the rest of the words, so he made them up and hummed the other bits. Meesh was at his side holding his hand, humming with him, repeating the wrong words, out of sync. Jack lifted Meesh and she tucked her head under his chin, stroked his stubble, laughed, and rubbed her cheek against it. Mandy wrapped her arms around the both of them and kissed Jack. 'Me, me,' she kissed Meesh.

Jack felt a stirring, was this love, for Mandy? Meesh? 'Show Meesh around, Michael,' Jack asked, and Colleen, Hi Ho'ing and insisting Michael be Dopey, trooped them off. Jack looked into Mandy's hazel eyes, 'I love you,' and they embraced.

'Jack, is that your phone?'

'Can't hear anything.' Mandy tittered; this was getting easier, she thought, and then, I am in deep, but it felt wonderful, didn't it?

They spent a lovely late afternoon and early evening. Michael's roast lamb was delicious, Meesh insisted on having the mint sauce and pickled beetroot Jack always had, and giggled when everyone else made sick noises. Jack's East End of London family always had pickled beetroot on their Sunday roasts. He told Meesh when he was her age he would visit his Nan and Granddad in Stepney, and under one of the railway arches was a beetroot boiler. The road was always stained red, and he used to think it was blood. She absorbed the story with her eyes.

'Lovely,' Meesh said, screwing her mouth at the intense vinegary tastes of the beetroot and mint. She ate it all, blissfully happy, 'My mum's dead, will you be my new mum, Mandy?'

'Oh my God,' Colleen rushed to hug the child.

Meesh slipped from Colleen and went to sit on Mandy's lap. Mandy whispered gently, 'How do you know your mum is dead?'

Meesh looked less frail, not tormented; malnourished, neglected, but an underlying strength of character. She turned from Mandy to the table and declared with force, 'Moy mum put me behind the boxes, and I saw the 'orrible man kill her with a knife.'

Mandy pulled Meesh's head to her breast and held her. 'It's alright, darling, everything will be okay, we'll make sure of that,' and Mandy mouthed to Jack, 'she may recognise the killer.'

'Christ's tits.'

'Tut,' from Meesh, lifting her head momentarily.

'Did I say that out loud?'

'Yes,' Meesh said.

Meesh seemed unmoved, but Jack thought this kid will need counselling, may also be in danger if word gets around she's seen the killer. Michael leapt into action, 'Let's watch *Mary Poppins.*'

Jack gave his impression of the terrible Dick Van Dyke cockney accent, 'Mary Popp-ins,' and started jumping and bashing his legs together, singing *Step in Time,* which Michael thought quite remarkable since he and Alana both knew their dad hated that bit, well, that and the penguins, but then nobody liked the penguins.

Mandy thought there was "Trouble brewing on Cherry Tree Lane" and she whispered to Jack before he flew a kite and fed the birds, 'We need to follow this up, but how?'

He whispered back, 'You know that girl, wotsername-thingybob, child psyche, Kate used to work with her, remember?'

'Jackie Philips, she's probably forty-five, not a girl but a woman, and how can you forget her name when it's virtually the same as yours?'

'Because I've not given her a nickname.'

'You did, Lips, which she told you never to use, and then

Phil, which amused you more than it did Jackie.'

Jack was charged, 'Oh yeah, I'll call her.'

'You have her number?' Mandy looked quizzical, whilst trying to calm and quieten him.

'Kate's old phone book,' and Jack disappeared.

Mandy felt a pang at the mention of Kate's name, they'd been friends, rubbed along, and it was clear Jack worshiped the ground she walked on, but it had been nearly three years and Mandy had decided to release her feelings; maybe she should rein in?

Back with a small black book, Jack stopped to watch Mary arriving on her umbrella, sung *Jane and Michael Banks*, got shushed by Meesh. 'I'll go into the kitchen,' Jack oblivious, and Mandy thought, am I being unreasonable, trying to stop myself from getting hurt?

Colleen was looking at her from the settee, stroked Meesh and Michael as she got up and went to sit opposite Mandy, 'I do believe Jack loves you.'

'Will he ever get over Kate though?' They exchanged a look.

'She's a part of him, can you handle that?'

'Hmmm,' Mandy

'Hmmm,' Colleen; time drifted.

'Oi, shout out to Dad, its *Step in Time*,' and Michael got up with Meesh and started to do the dance, with Meesh giggling as if nothing had happened, the most natural thing in the world, but when will reality set in?

'Like father, like son, you sure you're okay with Michael, Colleen?' Mandy asked.

'I love him, Mandy, he can be as irritating as his dad, but for God's sake I love him, though my dad could kick his feckin' head in.' Mandy laughed. Colleen shrugged her shoulders, applied an inane grin. 'What is life for if not to make sport at our betters? But, Lizzie, you did not seem to enjoy that, are you not diverted?'

Mandy rejoined, 'Yes, I am exceedingly diverted.'

'Brilliant PP girls, okay, Phil's in tomorrow morning at nine-thirty,' and Jack rubbed his hands together, Mandy and Colleen shared a moment, the investigation had killed the afternoon for her, but clearly not for Jack. 'Blimey, have I missed *Step in Time?*' and Jack feigned a disappointed grumpy face; Meesh jumped up and hugged and tugged him to come and join Michael and her on the settee, and as all parents do, he said, 'As soon as this is finished, we need to get you to Gail's for beddy-byes.'

The emerald eyes looked back up at him. 'Oh, I want to stay here.'

'And who will help Gail with the baby Jane?' Mandy to the rescue.

'I forgot.'

Along with a lot of other stuff, Jack thought, but just for now, 'Let's go fly a kite, skittish things, kites.'

'Shush, Jack,' Meesh said, a finger to his mouth.

Mandy felt a jumble of emotions watching the eejits on the settee rumbling around, Jack tickling Meesh under her arms and innocently saying, "What?"

———

JACK CARRIED the sleeping Meesh to Mandy's car. 'Get in the back, you'll need to hold her.' Jack got into the back and put a seat belt over himself and slid Meesh to the side and fitted the centre belt. Mandy watched; again that pang. She drove off in what was for him a comfortable silence, but for Mandy a torture of emotions, looking occasionally in her mirror as he stroked Meesh's hair; she felt wretched.

Gail was waiting for them at the door, Mickey Splif behind, holding the baby. Jack woke Meesh gently, 'We're here, darlin', let's go and see the baby Jane,' and Meesh tumbled with sleepy legs, and Jack holding her shoulders steered her into Gail's waiting arms.

'Take her back, Mickey,' tipping her head to Meesh, 'hold baby Jane on the chair a moment, sweetie.'

Still sleepy, 'Hmmm, bye-bye,' and Meesh wiggled her fingers.

Mandy briefed Gail. 'Poor luv, she can sleep with me tonight,' and shouted to Mickey, 'you're on the settee, babes.'

'Alright,' Mickey replied, disgruntled, but accepting.

They returned to the car, Jack belted up, but Mandy turned in her seat to look at him, 'Don't say a thing, we need to talk.'

He felt the dread all men feel when a woman says, "We need to talk," scrabbling around for thoughts. 'If I don't say a thing, it will be a bit one-sided, won't it?'

She chose to ignore this, 'I love you.'

He dared to interrupt, 'I know.'

'I know you know because I told you this afternoon.' She was irritated; Jack could tell.

'No, I knew before then,' a presumptive victory?

'When?'

'In the hospital, you thought I was asleep,' he relaxed, thinking the talk was over.

'You're an irritating twat, Jack Austin, but I still love you.' Jack went to say something, she stopped him, 'I want you, but I'm not sure you're over Kate, and this is okay. You need to take the time it takes, I will wait. That's what I wanted you to know.' There was a pause and Jack was not sure if he was supposed to say something, and what danger he might be in if he did, he looked for a signal, it didn't come, but Mandy filled the void.

'We should go out on a few dates, maybe the pictures, and not one of those stupid Rom Coms you like. I also want you to know I will continue to beat you up in the office, I don't want people thinking I've gone soft and feeling sorry for me because I love you.'

'You, beat me up?' Jack couldn't resist.

'Yes, Jack, I am continually beating you, in fact, I think this past week alone it was 532 to 2 in my favour.' Mandy was using Jack's persistent quips like, one nil, and sometimes ludicrously large numbers, plucked out of the air, and it was amazing how many people reacted, "It can't be that," and Jack would add another one onto the score and smile benignly.

'I think I must have missed 531 of those, I had it at two-one to me,' he was enjoying this now; there were warning signs, but when you're having fun?

'Jack, I'm trying to be serious.'

'Serious? 532, in your dreams, babes,' he never could get those signs.

'I've said what I wanted,' and Mandy started the car.

'Suppose a fuck's out of the question?'

'Yes, though you were close, you sad bastard.'

'Belt up.'

'I beg your pardon.'

'Put your seatbelt on,' and Mandy laughed, defused again, and as she fastened her seat belt she leaned forward, and saw Gail and Meesh at the top window, peeking around the curtains. Meesh wiggled her fingers and Mandy wiggled hers back; they drove off.

The drive back was quiet. Jack put his hand onto Mandy's thigh, close to the knee, but the thigh nevertheless; a chancy move, but Mandy let it stay there. A few minutes later, she put her hand on top and wrapped his fingers.

TWENTY-SEVEN

J ACK SQUINTED AT THE CLOCK, ANOTHER DEEP SLEEP, NO thoughts of Mandy, Martin, Meesh or Kate. 'Feck,' it was ten to eight, made a dash for the bathroom and ran straight into Colleen. 'Christ's Tits.'

'Not quite, but a fine pair of man boobs,' Colleen was unfazed.

Jack put fingers on his nipples. 'Colleen, what're you doing here?'

Her face, poorly disguising her amusement, 'Michael told my dad he loved me, that we had been sleeping together for a while, and he would like me to stay over. I said I loved him.'

'God! Do I need to take Michael to casualty?'

'No,' Colleen's face showed how happy she was.

Michael was at the top of the stairs, 'I'm okay, he was fine, not like you and Alana, and Dad.'

'What?'

'Your birthday suit?'

'Shite, sorry, Colleen, was on my way for a pony and trap,' and Jack dived into the bathroom.

'Too much information, Dad,' Michael called as he passed by, walking down the stairs.

There was a tap on the door. 'Yes?' Jack answered.

'Jane, if Michael is as lovely as you at sixty, I will be well pleased.'

Jack delayed his poo while he puffed himself up, smiled to the mirror as he heard Michael say to Colleen, 'What d'you say that for, he will continually remind you of this, like Mandy saying he sung and whistled beautifully.'

'But he does sing and whistle beautifully,' Colleen replied.

Jack shouted from the bathroom, 'I heard that, she has a good ear, Michael.'

'Thank you very much, Colleen, you have condemned us and many others,' and he heard Michael saying he'd better warn Mandy.

'Tom Tit, rant and rave, and an Eiffel tower, Hampstead's, Yabba dabber doo,' Jack felt good. Michael shouted up the stairs he would do his muesli, 'I'm in the canteen this morning, son,' Jack called back, 'I feel good, dah dah...'

'Too late, Dad, I don't want you having too many fry-ups.'

He's turned into Kate, Jack thought, a small pang; was that better? Looking in his wardrobe and thinking he'd better go shopping, he chose conservatively, with a small C, no way he would dress as a Tory Boy, heaven forbid; pink or mustard trousers! He looked out the window, cats and dogs, thought of that sunny day, Mandy's silhouette in front of the office window. Is she right? Am I missing Kate, still? His tummy made an involuntary turn as he counselled the face staring back at him from the mirror, 'Do you really want to go on like this? Wasn't it better, just a little?'

———

'You CAN HAVE THE CAR, Michael, I'm getting a cab, I'm down eight hundred bikes.'

'Eight hundred bikes?' Colleen immediately realised her error, hand to her mouth and thought you have to pay attention in this house.

'He exaggerates, darling. Told you a million times, Dad, not to exaggerate.' Colleen removed her hand and allowed herself the previously stifled laugh.

'Crikey, Colleen, that has to be the oldest joke around, you must really love the little tow-rag.'

'I do love him,' and as if to prove it, Colleen got up and kissed Michael, wandered over to Jack, who was putting his jacket on, wondering where his raincoat was, and kissed him on both cheeks, 'and I love you too, Jane,' giggling and pointing to his raincoat hanging in the hall, where it should be.

'Give me strength, you've gone all European.'

Colleen put her finger on his mouth, 'Shut the feck-up.'

'Jeyziz, son, heaven help you.' The cab tooted. 'Okay, tooting back,' which only he knew referred to Totting Bec in London, but that didn't matter, not to Jack in his event garden world, and he rushed out into the rain.

Michael called from the kitchen, 'Avant-garde, Dad?'

The cab dropped Jack roadside. 'I'll walk the rest of the way, it's not like its pissing down or anything,' but the subtlety of Jack's sarcasm was lost on the cabbie. Jack paid and ran to the reception doors, 'Feckety Feck.'

'Cats and Dogs, Jane,' Hissing Sid remarked.

'Cod and chips twice.'

'Heard you the first time.'

'Your family, they are well?'

'Tolerably so.'

Jack shook his coat. 'Thanks, Jane.'

'You're welcome, you needed a wash,' and Jack ran up the

stairs, two at a time as nobody was looking. He tripped at the top step and fell into Jackie Philips.

'Steady on, Jack, you could walk up the stairs like a normal human being.'

Mandy was on it like a flash, 'We're not talking normal,' and the ladies shared a chuckle.

'Phil, you little darlin', how yer diddlin', settled down or still trawling the town for a blind man?' Jack always said this to Jackie, who was an attractive, tall, and elegant black woman, dark brown eyes, hair that had been straightened and worn in a French bun that Jack called a croissant; slim, slimmer than Amanda but not bony, wearing jeans, sweatshirt and trainers; she had style, and Jack liked her.

'Trawling, looking for someone as ugly as you, but so far they're all too bright.' Jackie could match Jack, blow for blow, but knew he had to be standing still to get a shot across his bows, and he was already down the corridor, beckoned for them to follow, pretending he didn't hear. 'Jack!' Jackie stopped him in his tracks, turned a questioning look. Sauntering to him, since he was rigid on the spot, she raised herself to her easily six foot and looked Jack in his good eye, 'This is a difficult one with Meesh and the other children.' She enlightened the startled rabbit, 'Mandy telephoned this morning to brief me, knowing you would have left half of it out, which you did. You need to watch your relationship with Meesh, until we know more.'

'Oh shut-up, Phil, she's just a kid and I'm being nice, right, Mands?' he looked at Mandy beseechingly, 'I'm not being an eejit, am I?' Mandy was silent.

'She may see it differently,' Phil answered.

'Who, Mandy?' Jack replied, and both women sighed.

'Right-you-are, sweet'art, baby steps it is,' and he pushed open the CP room door and held it for Jackie and Mandy, flicking his head so they got a move on, irritating Jackie.

The room was buzzing, 'Kettle, put yourself on mate and make a cuppa Splosh for Phil here. Okay, babes?' Jack looking at Jackie. ''Ave to be monkey tea, no girl grey, I'm afraid.' Jo-Jums was on the phone and she put her hand up to acknowledge Jackie. Jack continued, 'Right, listen up, those who do not know who this is...'

Jo provided him with an admonishing look, 'I'm on the phone?'

But Jack was difficult to stop, 'Well, get off, I want to introduce Phil.'

'Cyrano, I've got to go, I'll speak to you later,' and Jo hung up.

'That was Cyrano? What did he have to say?'

Jo looked to the ceiling, the other women were already there. 'Don't know, bleedin' dipstick, you told me to hang up.'

Jo folded her arms and issued the unspoken dare, and with his best benign face, and leaning slightly back to show how reasonable he could be, 'Yeah, but Cyrano, you could have made an exception.' Every woman in the room knew where Jo-Jums was coming from and shared her frustration, whereas the blokes thought, Yeah, can see that. He ignored it all and pointed to Jackie. 'Anyway, this 'ere is Phil, child Psych, gonna work with us and the kids...'

Jackie interrupted, 'I know most of you and for those that do not, I'm actually Jackie Phillips. Jack, the well-known twat of Portsmouth, calls me Phil, derived from some warped machinations of his brain, but I've been called Sambo and Darkie-girl before and I believe this is a warm and affectionate epithet, but if I find out any different, I'm sorry, Mandy, but I will rip his balls off.'

'Be my guest,' Mandy reacted, smiling at Jack's shocked face.

Jackie continued, 'I am a Child Psychologist and have

worked with the police on a number of cases. I've been briefed on this, and it's a can-of-worms, so, Kettle, I will take that tea if it is still on offer.'

'Yeah,' Jack said, 'get Phil the tea, Kettle, and me a reinforced jock strap.'

Mandy thought, last word again, chuckling, but Jack was waving his hands talking to Jackie now, 'This is Frankie and Confucius my computer team, and Nobby, Good and Bad's lad; where's Alice, Nobby?' The question thrown out, not looking for a reply as Alice came out of the kitchen.

Jackie whispered into Mandy's ear, 'You love this fucking idiot?' Mandy shrugged into her shy and easily startled kitten look.

Jack was leaning over Frankie and Connie. 'Jack, briefing in a minute, and Jackie wants to get up to see Meesh and the other kids,' Mandy called.

Waving his hand behind his back, 'Half a Mo, babes, Connie's printing some pics of our suspects, Meesh may be able identify one as the man who murdered her mum.' The whole room turned to Jack, 'Close your mouths, we are not codfish.' He never could resist *Mary Poppins*, never sure if she was good-looking or whether he just liked the umbrella.

Mandy jumped in, 'Briefing at nine-thirty, where's Paolo?'

'On his way in, Ma'am.'

'Hear that, Connie, way in?'

Another one wasted, Jack thought, but Mandy thought, he's hyper, what's causing this?

'Jane, my office, if you pretty please, with brass feckin' knobs on.'

'Be there directly, Mands.' Mandy gave Jackie a flick of her head and they went to her office. Jack caught them up, 'Phil, you drive this okay, but here are the photos of the blokes in the house.'

CAUSE AND EFFECT

'Shall we get into Mandy's office, and I will take this at my own, or should I say, the kids' pace.'

Jack put his hands up in surrender, 'No sweat, Jacks, let me get this briefing done and I'll come with you.'

'No, you won't,' Mandy reacting sternly, supported by Jackie.

'But I have a bond with the girl.'

Jackie took over, 'This is a traumatised girl who is likely clinging to any life-raft that passes.'

Jack looked hurt, 'But?'

Mandy calmed him, 'Let Jackie see Meesh first, okay?'

Defeated and deflated, in an instant he perked up, 'Okay girls,' stuffed the photos in Jackie's bag; both "girls" looked to the ceiling. Jack shrugged, 'What?'

Jo put her head around the door, 'We're ready.'

'Sit in, Phil, Kettle will have your splosh and you may get a feel for how to handle things.'

'No thanks, I prefer to meet the children and make my judgement without knowing the details of your investigation.' She was firm.

'Fair do's,' he slowed and put his serious head on, 'look, I'm sorry if I'm overbearing, but Meesh made an impact, know what I mean?'

Jackie responded, her sensitive psych head on, 'That may say more about where you are. So, let's just see.'

'What're you laughing at, Jack?' Mandy looked to stop Jackie from being offended.

Still laughing, Jack explained, 'This morning, I made a dash for the bog in me birthday suit and bumped into Colleen, just thought about it.'

'Oh my God, the poor girl,' both women said.

'No, she was fine. Well, get this, Michael only told Colleen's dad he loved her, they were sleeping together, and

197

wanted her to stay the night, and the guy accepted; no casualty, or anything.'

Jackie shook her head, 'Sounds like a well-adjusted man, something you might not understand?'

Mandy smirked, 'He wouldn't, I was around when his girl Alana wanted to move in with her boyfriend. Jack, what happened?'

'What do you mean what happened?'

'You were bollock naked on the landing with Colleen,' Mandy was irritated.

'Oh that, well, she said if Michael was as fit as me at sixty she would be very happy, that stands to reason, but the important thing was she thought I sang and whistled beautifully. I told her Amanda thought so too,' Jack beamed and wobbled his head to convey the point was irrefutably made. Something passed between Jackie and Mandy that was girl's stuff, Jack thought it was generally a look of approval; can Jack Austin read women?

Expelling air from her fulsome lips, made Jack think Jackie was going to whistle, and he tried to think of a tune she might know, 'Mandy, I will go up to see Meesh now, so good luck, and I mean that.'

Jack brushed aside his disappointment about the whistling, 'Thanks a lot, Phil, what tunes do you like?' and as he was already brushing, he brushed aside the querying look from Jackie and moved on, the tunes can wait, and we could always start with Doctor Who. 'Jackie, we must get together really soon, I'm plotting some sedition and the odd demo at C&A's this week, could do with the old shrink angle, know what I mean, nudge, nudge?' and he wiggled his hand under his arm pit and took the opportunity to smell it. It was okay, just, and they say he can't multi-task.

Jackie sighed her reply, 'Jack, I do not want to whistle

"Doctor Who," I am not going to sniff your armpit, Mackeroon is a Twat, Blogg a Twat's assistant, I will not be at the pub with your weirdo, mates, and will not be demonstrating with you either. I will resort to the ballot box.'

Jackie seemed clear, which Jack thought odd, 'Alright, I hope you're not lumping Mandy in with my weirdo mates.'

'No, but I am worried for her.'

'You are, what's up, Doc?' he looked at Mandy, concern on his face.

Mandy told him to feck-off to the briefing, 'I shall be there directly,' she said.

'Little bit of PP there, Mandy babes, not the feck-off bit, but that's what I would have told arsy Darcy, and especially that bloody Wickham. I told Kate right from the start I didn't trust that slimy bastard the moment I saw him in Worthington,' and Jack disappeared as quickly as he appeared. Both women sighed as the pressure was relieved; a common feeling when Jack left a room.

'Certifiable but lovely at the same time, so what can I tell you, d'you think it's easy?' Jackie said imitating Jack's New York Jewish accent, shrugging her shoulders, and they both laughed, 'If you can't beat them..?' and Mandy waved Jackie off and went to join the morning briefing.

TWENTY-EIGHT

PAOLO DEFERRED TO JACK, BUT JACK BEING JANE, 'PAOLO, well done on the interrogation, I hear we have a result.'

'No. Thank you, Jane, your intervention was an eye opener; just the one,' and Paolo grinned. Was that a joke, Mandy thought? Paolo went on to set out what they had achieved. Greg Varney and his cohorts had spilled their guts, but no identity of the main men, Paolo suggesting this may be all they ever knew. The kids and women thought to be no-hopers, picked off the scrap heap and forced to turn tricks, money for the pot, to keep the fascist recruits happy. Paolo agreed this was likely not the driving force, something else was going on, but what?

'Ideas?' Mandy asked.

Nobby put his hand up. 'What if these men were being wound up so they might cause a disturbance, like they did up north?'

Jack spoke, 'Nobby, good point, but what about opposition?'

Nobby reddened, 'I don't understand?'

'People need to rise up against something, but what? Think

about it. We have pretty harmonious race relations in this City. They need tinder for the political spark to light.'

'Bit dramatic?' Paolo commented.

'I know, so let's park that, you have a programme of follow-ups on the skinheads?'

'Park?' Mandy, stifling a giggle.

'Modern lingo, babes, you need to keep up,' and Jack stroked her face.

Ordinarily this would rile her, but this was a loving gesture and she found herself liking it, until she saw the stunned look on the faces of the team. Coughing, 'Right, Paolo, get on with it,' Mandy said, re-establishing her Superintendent credentials.

Paolo set out the follow up plans, names, and addresses they intended to raid.

'Let the docs wean the women and kids off the drugs first,' Mandy suggested. 'If Meesh saw something, there's a good chance one of the women did, just need to convince them they're safe.' Rising from her seat, 'Good work, I've a press conference this evening, so keep me informed.'

The phone went, Jo picked up, 'Okay, Sid, I'll tell him,' she turned to Jack, 'Jane, Father O'Brien asked for you to contact him, soon as.'

Nonchalantly, Jack replied, 'Did he say what it was about?'

Not quite so nonchalantly, Jo replied, 'Oh Yeah, Sid was able to tell me fully in the two seconds I was on the phone.'

Jack was upright now, 'Alright, keep your girdle on, and I'm sorry for interrupting your call this morning.'

Mandy thought, nice save Jack, and Jo responded, 'Thank you, I've spoken with Cyrano, he's on the Pride of Bilbao ferry, the suspect family car is boarded. They've confirmed your theory and they've planted a tracker, a follow up squad will meet the car when it docks. Fake plates, captured identity, so I think the second car will be too.'

'What about the family travelling?' Jack asked, rubbing his chin thinking it made him look intelligent.

'We'll not know until we question them, but I suspect we're talking about a cheap, or free holiday, they leave the bikes somewhere and pick them up later; clever. Cyrano's in touch with the French authorities, talking no arrests, but to watch the next lot and to follow them in France, see if we can get a capture there. We monitor the guys in England.'

'Makes sense,' Jack said.

Nobby looked up as Jack was rising from his seat and stretching, 'Doesn't make sense as a brilliant drugs business, such small amounts, are they not greedy, or is there another motive?'

Jack with an exaggerated yawning voice, 'Good observation; KFC, what do you have?' Jack was now walking like Douglas Bader, distracting Mandy, thinking, surely you do not stretch this much.

Connie answered, 'We look at women and girls rescued in house and they have no record, if we can get some names it will help, Sir.'

Frankie followed up, 'We're looking into social services records for people, especially kids that have dropped off the radar, a long shot, but we're getting cooperation from Social.'

'Sounds the right road, thank you,' Jack fiddled around in his pocket and produced a battered piece of paper, 'have a go at this, just a thought,' and Jack handed Frankie the paper.

Mandy frowned, and Jo-Jums mimicked her.

'Jack, would that be websites, you?' Mandy asked.

'My love, when I'm in hospital it's not all lying around and moaning, although I admit I fantasised about that a lot,' giggles from the younger fraternity, but not from Jo-Jums and Mandy, who had their feminista heads on. 'There were social workers in the assessment wards, I talked to them, okay?' he knew when not to push, but shrugged his shoulders; he was good at shrugging.

Mandy released her breath. 'I believe you, thousands wouldn't; good shrug though.'

'Well, I'm part of the thousands,' Jo remarked.

'Jo-Jums, what news from yonder window breaks in vice?' Jack swerved.

'Not much from the east, in fact we might need you to break Juliet's feckin' window in.'

'I'll do that, Jo,' Mandy said.

Jack jumped in, 'Babes, invite vice here, tell them you want their take on the enquiry, but let the spotlight be here?'

'Something in mind, Jack?'

'Let's just say my eye is twitching.'

Jo looked to the ceiling, but it was full.

'What about the cuppa I just made?' Kettle asked.

Jack pacing anxiously, 'Nothing like a cup of Rosy, lad, have it yerself.'

Mandy clipped Jack on the back of the head, and left.

Jack phoned and agreed to meet Father O'Brien at St John's Cathedral and arranged for a bluebottle cab.'

TWENTY-NINE

Bluebottle cabs dropped Jack outside the Roman Catholic Cathedral. An uneventful trip, the two uniforms prattled on about a hectic weekend at the pubs and clubs, the binge drinking culture, and local demos about cuts in services. They obviously didn't know Jack and his ability to switch off, 'Local demos; must see if I can join in?' he said to himself, standing on the pavement looking up and appreciating the austere red brick Cathedral; he liked the understatement of this building. Similarly, the interior was not as ornate as you might expect for Catholic. He moved towards the rear entrance. Jack had met Father O'Brien here a number of times, this was also Kate's place of worship, where she had prayed with Martin.

He walked slowly through the rear precincts, mainly laid to car parking, and he mused as he sauntered, a sad necessity today, a garden taken up for utility, no longer a space for reflective thought, he reflected, not seeing the irony. Through the rear porch, large gathering room, a constricted corridor, and emerged into the contrasting voluminous side aisles of the Cathedral.

He met nobody as he walked. Pictured Kate in a pew, head covered with a black scarf and bowed, sighed and looked to the soaring roof. When he met Father Mike here in the past, he would usually walk around the inside of the nave and absorb the feeling, aware churches of this style were built lofty and spacious in order to bring the pleasantry to their knees, in awe of God. Jack brushed this aside, but wondered if this effected people still; never seemed to bother Martin.

'Jack.'

Father O'Brien had this knack of being able to creep up on him wherever he might be. Mandy would say get deaf aids, but Mike floated like an angel, though which side did he bat for? The Father was a tall man, about the same age as Jack, a worn, heavily lined face at peace with itself, framed with large black, *Michael Caine* glasses, atop of a snub nose that was well on the way to being a beetroot; too much communion wine. Tall, he had a fading, wiry build, did not carry as much weight as Jack but they shared a pot belly. Jack and the Father went back a long ways, a strong bond, and this man knew Jack, he was intelligent, perceptive, and if you looked into his grey eyes you could see all that.

'So what can I tell yer...?' Jack shrugged, always a little nervous with Mike as if he had authority over him, and he held his hands and arms out in a supplicant manner, '...d'you think it's easy?'

'Walk with me.'

'Take a turn about the room? It can be so refreshing?'

'So our figures may be displayed to their best advantage. I bought *Pride and Prejudice* to keep up, and now we watch it all the time in the Rectory; the initial charm is wearing off,' and with a withering look, Mike stopped the banter. 'Jack, this thing with Pugwash is out of control. We all love a dig at pompous arses, but he's well connected, and, what I'm saying is, you should let me help you.'

'I need help?'

Mike gave Jack his patronising, angelic gobshite look, 'Yes, we cannot afford you on the beat or worse early retirement,' and they both laughed gently at what was a regularly shared joke.

'I don't want to retire.'

'I know.'

'Okay Mike, you didn't call me down here and walk me around like a feckin' eejit just to tell me Pugwash wants to hole me below the water line, I'll take your help, gratefully received, so what's up?'

Jack backed up, Mike was in his face, 'So help me, if you swear in God's house, Pugwash will have to line up behind me, and God for that matter.'

Jack never liked to upset Mike, 'Sorry, think I have Floret's.' Jack meant it, not the Tourette's, the sorry bit. Oldtimer's, yes, but Floret's, no, he would have remembered that.

'Sit down.'

Jack was about to say about feckin' time, but stopped himself, so it wasn't Floret's. The Father sat one place in from the centre aisle and Jack took the end seat, shuffled the pew cushion and stretched his long legs diagonally into the aisle. 'Always promised myself an extra pair of knees if I took up praying,' Jack commented, avoiding looking at Jesus on the cross.

'You could do a lot worse. I had hoped you would follow Kate and Martin into the faith, but enough, first off that was a good thing you did for Keanu, but I'm not sure what you have asked him to do is fair on the lad?' The gobshite angel was back with an admonishing look.

'Mike, I had a feeling at Osama's that's all. It's probably

nothing, but it was there nevertheless,' then something clicked. 'Whoa back Neddy, you knew I was coming to see Gail, didn't you?'

'Jack, it's not just the police I talk to.'

'Well, I know that of course,' he was about to go on about speaking to Jesus, but Father Mike passed him a scrap of paper. He opened it, recognised the handwriting and read, bolted upright, back rigid against the pew, folding his legs back inside and turning, 'Bless me father, for I must dash.'

Mike sketched a blessing, put his hand onto Jack's shoulder. 'Promise me Keanu will be out of the way.'

Jack flopped down, rubbed his jaw, one of his regular thinking habits, 'Blimey, Mike, no chance you could have got this to me sooner?'

Mike sat also. 'Don't change a thing. There's a team close by if you need it.' Jack looked into the eyes of a dear friend and colleague. 'You will do the right thing, and do me a favour, take that girl of yours on a date.'

'How?'

'I have eyes and ears. Kate was the one, but please, move on.'

'It's hard,' Jack was sitting hunched, lanks of hair falling over his forehead, and he felt he needed to pour out what he'd been holding in.

Mike spoke for him, 'I know, you have a strong support mechanism around you, so use it, and I want to see you in church, fake it to make it, or just bring Martin.'

'Mike, we need you at C&A's if only to kerb my swearing,' they both stood.

Mike faced Jack, 'I'll be there. This government is taking a diabolical liberty and crucifying my people, God forgive me.'

'Well said, Mike, come the resolution brothers, and fathers.'

THIRTY

Jack walked from the Cathedral energetically, not his usual saunter. There was a tinkling sound in his pocket, like broken glass; his new phone. With finger and thumb, he picked it out and panicked at the technology, pressed the almost cunningly concealed button; the screen came to life with a picture of Martin. How did that happen, but the picture disappeared, pressed again and Martin reappeared, his head pointing to the slide to unlock, he remembered the pass code, 1,2,3,4, reassured Oldtimers was still a way off. It was a text message; *Back to nick now, Mandy.* A tad fed up she didn't say please, Jack flagged down a passing cab and was soon dropped at the front of the police station.

'You could've walked that mate,' Jack looked at the cabbie and thought no bloody tip for you gobshite, paid the fare and tipped him; he needed more exertion classes.

In reception he checked as to the welfare of Sid's family, 'Mandy's looking for you.'

'Well I hope she's brought condoms, used all mine up at the

weekend.' This made Sid laugh, and that made Jack laugh too, but Sid was still laughing. 'Not that funny Sid.'

'No, it wasn't.'

Jack turned, the weak smile of a condemned man, 'Amanda darlin', knew you were there,' a nervous chuckle.

Hands on hips and feet firmly planted, she allowed herself a half smile, 'I hesitate to say, would you like to come upstairs, and, Sid, you can stop laughing now.'

Jack followed Mandy to the door of the staircase and sped up to squash beside her as she passed through, receiving a strong stare, but a Brahma for Sid; mirth stopped dead in its tracks. Jack deferred to Mandy on the stairs; a polite, dirty old man.

'I know what you're doing you pervert.'

'I have to look where I'm going, Ma'am.'

'Yes, but not yet,' He thought for a bit, then got it.

'Caught up, Jack, 651 to 3 in my favour?' He let it go, was enjoying the view. 'Where have you been, Jack?'

'Praying, Mands,' she should have known better.

In the CP room Mandy rolled the chair Jack had got for her, away from him, ignored his sulking face, she was all business, 'Vice are in at two, KFC have been researching, can you brief us Connie?'

Connie was growing in confidence, 'Seem Biscuit follow up sink estate families, broke and on last leg. Somehow women, some with kid, were lost from social system, worse for them, not even on computer record as though never existed. They were then pick-up by someone who get them hook on drug and pass to guys we have under arrest. We check with Paolo and it tie in, we know this also as uniform police sometime pick-up people and there no record they exist.'

Jack smiled warmly at his Chinese protégé, 'Connie darling, brilliant, now where did you get this info from?'

'You,' Connie answered.

'What?'

Mandy indicated she would take it from here. 'The paper you passed to KFC this morning led the girls, through a maze admittedly, but eventually to Biscuit's computer notes; password protected. But remarkably, that other scrap of paper had a note saying, bread, milk, butter and bacon.'

'Yeah, d'you get what I wanted Frankie?' Frankie demurred; Mandy was in charge.

'A cryptic clue to Biscuit's password and to his notes, all very enlightening, but there is something that confuses me.'

Jack looked at Frankie who did a so what can I tell yer shrug, or was it Gallic. 'What's that, love?' and he smiled; strangely it didn't mollify Mandy.

'Where did you get the paper?'

'I see, and clearly I got it off a bloke in the pub will not do?' he made to be busy elsewhere, but Mandy was not finished.

'Jack, I want you in the interview with vice.'

'My siesta?'

'Out, along with a great many other things, *love*,' she stroked his face, followed with a playful slap and sashayed past, very close. His nostrils got a good dose of her opium perfume, slightly thin at the end of the morning, a blend of the perfume and a real woman; Amandium.

Kettle picked up a call, 'No, Cyrano, she's not here.'

Jack clicked his fingers and waved like mad to indicate he would take this, 'Cyrano, Jane,' he listened and hemmed, 'I'll send Kettle and Nobby, stay safe big nose...Cyrano, there is nothing about my backside that resembles a horse,' and he hung up.

'You sure about that, Jack, you should see it from my side,' Mandy was back.

He addressed her, relaxed, knowing how much she liked a

joke, 'Cyrano needs some secondary tailing as the ferry comes in. He thinks a caravan has something inside it, the dogs picked up a scent, might be nothing, could be something?' He turned away, 'Nobby, Kettle, get down to the ferry port, make sure your fuel tanks are filled and your mum's know you might be out late.' They both reacted enthusiastically. Jack continued, 'Frankie take some notes on this for me please.' Frankie responded with her trademark rolled salute. Jack read it as respectful, knowing he had this effect on women.

Mandy ignored Jack, he had that effect on women as well, 'Take care, don't intercept unless you must, and if you do, call for back up first. We will alert the forces along the route, stay safe.'

'Thanks, Ma'am,' and off they went, two eager young men.

'KFC, coordinate their back up and projected routes, I've a nervy feel about this,' Mandy said.

'Eye hurting, is it, Mandy?' Jack gulped, 'Joke...' he said, feebly.

'I want you now,' and Mandy beckoned him with her index finger.

'Oooh err matron,' childish, Jack thought, but he was nervous, and he followed the vapour trail to her office.

'Stop sniffing and sit down, and not on the chair over there, this one please,' Mandy pointed to the psychologically challenged seats. He collected the PVC one by the wall, and to show his general air of cooperation, he brought it to the front of her desk. 'I suppose that will have to do.'

'651 all?'

She thought better of an official challenge, 'If I asked where that note came from, will I get a truthful answer?'

'No.'

'Okay, but it gives us food for thought for the vice boys.'

There was a knock at the door and Jean from the canteen

poked her head in, 'Cooeee light refreshments,' she called mimicking the *PG Tips* Monkey advert.

'Nice, Jean, don't give up the day job, got the monkey look off pat though,' Jack said.

Jean smiled, gave him a peck on the cheek, ruffled his hair and looked at Mandy, 'Look after him, luv, he's a treasure.' Mandy let a sigh out through her nose, had to, her lips were too tightly pressed together. Jean plonked a large plate of sandwiches in the centre of the desk, handed out two smaller plates like she was dealing cards, left with a casual glance over her shoulder and a cheeky smile at Jack. For his part he raised his hand and wiggled his fingers as if waving goodbye to Meesh. Mandy didn't think it was worth rolling her eyes.

'Well, this is not what I was expecting.'

'I thought we should have lunch together; it's a start,' Mandy answered, removing the cling film, 'let's talk vice.'

'There's no answer to that, luv,' and he grabbed a couple of the dainty triangular sandwiches and a handful of crisps, started eating, thankful Mandy was talking, and wondering how many he could tuck away before he had to reply. Mandy seemed unaware of the sandwich competition; girls, eh.

'Biscuit didn't name anyone in vice, intending to set up a separate case file with us, I presume. I doubt vice have got into his work computer, this was a good encryption.' She helped herself to sandwiches, sensing she needed to, and leaned back, her chair rocked on a spring and she looked at the ceiling, then, bringing her seat abruptly upright, thought she had better grab a couple more.

Pushing a half chewed tuna and mayo into his cheek, like a squirrel, 'I wonder how Phil's getting on with Meesh?'

'There I can tell you something. Jackie thinks Meesh is traumatised, no surprise, closing her mind to a lot of things, but she is also of the view the relationship she has formed with

Gail, you, and me, is sound and we should let things take its path, so we can see her.' Jack expertly retrieved the sandwich from his cheek and chewed. 'Jackie has checked with social on Gail's fostering capabilities, sound also, and they're starting the process for fostering on a longer term.'

'I'm worried about that.'

Mandy knocked his hand away from the sandwich she wanted, 'You concerned if someone knows she could identify the killer she may be in danger?' waving the sandwich, flaunting her success; she was good.

'Precisely, what do you think?'

'I think it's a difficult call, if we secure her it might alert the killer, if we play along casually he may think nothing of it, though I'm worried about the women and the other kids. We have officers at the hospital, but they need to be released soon and we need to keep them safe. Jackie suggested a low secure unit specialising in drug abuse and recovery.'

There was a comfortable silence as they ate, 'Amanda, this is nice having something to eat, just you and me.'

She put her hand up. 'Please, don't say *Top Deck* shandy.'

'Didn't need to, luv, we're soul mates.'

'You think?'

She passed him a bottle of water having opened it for him, wondered why she did that. He took it as normal. They looked at each other with equal intensity, the phone went and broke the spell. 'Amanda Bruce,' she listened, and in a higher pitched, noticeably excited voice, 'Meesh, Jack and I were just talking about you, how are you, you like Jackie?' she listened, 'Yes I know Jack calls her Phil, she tell you that?' listening and mouthing to Jack, 'it's Meesh.'

'No kiddin'.'

'She did? She thought it was funny and so did you? Jack is a dipstick, you know.' Listening for a bit longer, Jack straining to hear, 'I'm not sure that would be a good idea, Jack and I are very busy, yes, put her on.' Mandy looked at Jack, no need to say anything. 'Jacks, hi,' another pause, 'Hmmm, hang on a.' She put her hand over the phone, 'Meesh wants to come in and see us and Jacks thinks this'll be okay. She will be here all the time.'

'Do it, luv, I want to see her.'

Excited, Mandy replied, 'So do I,' put the phone back to her ear and he looked at her mouth as she spoke, watched her lips, fantasising. 'Okay, see you later.'

Mandy had finished eating. Jack was mopping up the remaining sandwiches, but his eye never left hers, 'Jack, be careful.'

He didn't make a joke, 'You too, lover, she's a little angel and I want to see her settled.'

Mandy sipped water from her bottle, 'I like to see a man with an appetite, but there are limits.'

Pretending not to hear, he made a token gesture of leaving a half-eaten sandwich alongside the lemons, thinking, nice touch that Jean. There was a gentle knock at the door and Jean miraculously appeared, 'Sorry, the Commander has asked for sandwiches and this is the only posh plate we have,' she approached the desk noticing all the sandwiches were gone, Jack having eaten the last bit while Mandy was distracted. 'Something wrong with the lemons, Jack?'

Mandy burst out laughing. Jack loved her animated face, 'Jean darling, you're a breath of fresh air, so you are,' his best cod Irish for two lovely women.

'Jack, you do make me laugh,' and he smiled, one of his warmest, and she looked deep into his eye. Jean picked up the big plate, the two little ones, and as she was leaving looked sideways at Mandy, 'Play your cards right, Jack.'

'Jean, he has a hand like a foot, leave the rest to me,' the two women laughed at his expense, exchanged a knowing look, and Jean left. Mandy carried on chortling to herself, Jack just looked, and she held his gaze. It was like that for a little while until Connie poked her round bespectacled head around the door, 'Ferry in, Ma'am.' Mandy waved an acknowledgement and playfully looked at Jack. Bugger me, he thought, butterflies in my tummy, enjoying the feeling. She broke the spell, 'Vice will be here soon, how we shall handle it?'

'Bring them in here. Play it sympathetically, broach the subject of what Biscuit was working on, but do not stress it. We'll need his files, blah-blah. Nothing is going to happen this afternoon, this is sounding out, and they will know this; just you and me.'

'And *Top Deck* shandy, shite, did I just say that?'

'You did, my luv, and tolerably well.'

The phone rang and Hissing Sid announced Vice.

THIRTY-ONE

JACK KNEW AND GREETED THE VICE OFFICERS, 'PEEWEE.'
Peewee was DCI Pete Girdlestone, a tall man, good looking,
mid-forties, dark, you might be tempted to call him suave but
there was a brutal edge. In the past Jack had called him many
names, including brick corsets, but settled on Peewee, as did
everyone else, of course.

Mandy shook Peewee's hand, 'It's okay Jane, Peewee and I
know each other,' shook the other officer's hand, 'Chillyarse,'
she said. DI Dave Winterbottom was not one who could lump
the nickname, given by Jack, but unfortunately for him he had
to; there was barely concealed animosity. Jack's defence, "If it is
said in a Mexican accent, it has a cache, and Chillyarse should
chill out," did not help.

Chilly stepped across Jack to Mandy, shook her hand and
gave her a kiss on the cheek. Mandy was shocked, and Jack held
himself in check, recognising a ploy to wind him up.

'Mandy, good to see you. We should get together and
maybe investigate a social agenda?'

Mandy's fires were stoked, 'Superintendent, to you Chillyarse, and I'm very happy to investigate a social agenda, and when I have that agenda I will roll it up and shove it up your chilly fucking arse. Now, have a seat,' a genteel smile that Jack recognised as definite trouble, as she directed Peewee and Chilly to the psychological chairs.

'Sad news, Biscuit,' Jack said, distracting Peewee, who was staring daggers at Chillyarse, which could not possibly compete with Mandy's refined, shark infested, look. Chillyarse had slicked back thinning hair on a turnip face, a seedy large frame and a persona that made your skin crawl, wearing a tired suit, brought out for this meeting Jack imagined; vice generally dressed casual. Jack knew Chilly was married, but had never met his wife, had kids apparently; no accounting for tastes, and again he marvelled at the stomachs of women.

'Chillyarse,' Jack said in a Mexican accent that only Jo-Jums did better, 'wife and kids, underlay?' Mandy chuckled and eased back in her chair, she liked his Italian accent.

'Divorced, why I thought Mandy might like my company out-on-the-town,' Chilly replied.

'Out on your ear, Chillyarse,' a passable Mexican accent from Mandy.

With placatory hand gestures, Peewee defused the escalating steam generation, aware there was no Martin to calm Jack. 'Sorry about Martin. You we all hate, but Martin's a lovely dog, how's he doing?'

'Thanks, Peewee, he's recovering. There'll be a ceremony soon to appoint him official Police Dog. Mandy, Peewee can come, can't he?'

'Absolutely, I'll send you an invitation etched on a bone,' and Mandy gave Jack the dangerous syrupy look.

'I look forward to that, now what do you want from us? We did think we might take the investigation, but Paolo said it was yours.' Peewee was relaxing, 'Paolo's guys picked up Biscuit's office computer, Chilly went to get his home one and you'd already collected it.'

'First rule of comedy Spike,' Jack said. One of Jack's more obscure phrases that Mandy thought meant *naturellament*. She also thought he's handling this well and would let him run with it. 'Not much on it, porn of course, bet you got a lot on yours, Chilly.'

Mandy thought too soon, and jolted a reply, 'We wanted to chat through the usual, what he was working on, did he come up with anything might cause someone to want to kill him?'

Chilly artificially calmed, 'We deal with serious stuff.'

'Anything significant?' Mandy chipped, 'had to be pretty substantial. We were wondering if he discussed it, after all, it's what I would do, you Jane?'

'Absolutely,' Jack replied, knowing Mandy would be looking to see if his nose grew, 'did he talk to you Chilly?'

Chilly leaned, riled, 'Bit of a loner, you knew him, Jane?'

Finally Chilly had gotten around to using Jack's nickname, something not quite right here Mandy thought, he's nervous, and Jack knew Biscuit?

'Was he Chilly? I had a number of chats about his work, some interesting correlations. Why I suggested he come to CP,' Jack smarmed.

'Corra what?' Chilly demonstrated his general ignorance, and compensating, used aggression instead of acknowledging a failing.

Jack pushed, 'Some interesting links with what we have going, is what I meant, Chilly, we have a special team set up.' Jack allowed his head to convey a relaxed, confident attitude, 'Frankie, you know, and she's teamed up with Confucius, whom I'm sure you've all heard of, down from the Met to plug some juice into the computers, and getting brilliant feedback, which, I might add, is why we wanted you to come in, Chilly.'

Mandy knew Jack's nose would grow any minute and the game would be up.

'What d'you mean, "you wanted me in"?' Chilly rasped.

'You've heard of Confucius, and her work at the Met?'

'Well, yeah, so what?'

Got him, Jack thought. Peewee was interested, sat upright, flicked a glance to Mandy. She responded with a tip of the nose; now she knew how to do it, Jack thought, and not coitus interruptus, Jack thought, not even had any coit to interrupt, leastways, not that he could remember. 'She's uncovered some interesting stuff from Biscuit's office computer, and is on the home one as we speak, encrypted, as you know, Chilly, a damn good encryption as well, as you would expect. Still, she has it sorted, then she would, wouldn't she?'

'Why?' Chilly was aggressive, leaning forward in his psychologically challenged chair, fists balled on his knees, coiled, ready to spring.

'Did you never think Biscuit a bit were?' and Jack waggled his hand, indicating a sharp cookie, laughed at the biscuit, cookie, reference, which was misinterpreted by Chilly.

'Biscuit, were?' and Chilly relaxed a fist to waggle his hand, 'looked a dope, to me.'

'Chilly... how unperceptive,' and Jack put his best Mexican patronising head to one side as if to say, never pegged you for a stupid hombre.

'What d'you mean?'

'Ever felt the need to look over your shoulder, Chilly?'

Crikey, Mandy thought, where is Jack going?

Chilly, looking at Peewee, shifting forward on his seat, 'I'm leaving. Came for a civilised chat and feel like I'm being inter-rogated.'

Before Pewee could answer, Jack was in Chilly's face, 'That's because you are.'

That did shake Mandy, but she nodded sagely to Peewee.

Chilly shrank from Jack's intrusion into his personal space and singular stare, 'You never asked me to come?'

Jack followed on, hardly time for a breath, 'But we expected you.'

Shit Mandy thought, he's winging again, but Chilly reacted. 'Listen you one eyed, old aged pensioner, dick-shit, if you have something, say it, if not, I'm off,' and struggled in his chairs; they were difficult to get out of, low, and the backs sloped.

Peewee pressed Chilly's shoulder, 'Sit down,' and looked to Jack. 'Jack when you say look over your shoulder, d'you mean what I think you mean, and is this tied to the Met?'

Jack looked at Peewee in a knowing way, 'Biscuit and I have had an investigation going for some time, and he was a little more than you thought.'

'You've said enough; eyes and ears?' Pewee said.

'Eyes and ears,' Mandy said to Peewee, not wishing to be left out, but Chilly was reacting.

'Eyes and fucking ears; bollocks?' and Chilly challenged the chair.

'Chilly, calm yourself.'

Chilly looked back to Peewee as he slid his backside forward so it would be easier to get off the chair next attempt, 'Calm myself? I came to help, and find myself a prime suspect.'

'Do you Chilly?' Mandy asked.

'Do you?' Jack enjoined.

'I've had enough of this, I'm off.'

'Sit, Chilly, and that's an order.'

'Well, fuck your orders,' and this time Chilly did push himself off the chair and stomped to the door, yanked, left, and slammed it behind him.

Jack looked at Mandy, then Peewee. There was a piercing

and continuous scream. Jack leapt from his chair calling out, 'Meeeeeeesh,' barged through the door to see Jackie with Meesh, rigid on the stair landing, screaming and pointing at Chilly, who, in return, was shouting at the little girl, telling her to "shut the fuck-up".

Chilly grabbed Meesh. Jack reacted, scrabbled around the front of Chilly's jacket, gripped the lapel and pulled with all his might, and Chilly, an equally hefty man, spun unsteadily on his heels and began to topple towards Jack, the lapel tore. Chilly regained his balance and Jack lunged, Meesh still screaming, Mandy shouting, but Jack's mist was up. The CP room had emptied and was backed up along the corridor, Frankie pulling Jackie, who was tugging Meesh; a tiny mite, but the girl stood her ground, and shouted for Jack.

In his berserking state he heard her call, stopped, and looked. Chilly took the opportunity, a solid punch into Jack's solar plexus, he folded, toppled backwards to the stairs, falling. Mandy screamed. Jack stretched to grasp Chilly's jacket, and as he fell, he pulled. Chilly spun, down the staircase first. Jack fell on top of him, rolled, his head cracked on the concrete half landing. Remarkably, Jack was immediately up on a knee, and in his berserking state, began raining blows on Chilly.

Hissing Sid, with previously unknown strength, pulled Jack off, 'Enough, Jane, enough.'

A moment of utter silence, no movement. Meesh slipped from Jackie's sweating grip and made a run for Jack. Chilly raised himself, snatched Meesh, pushed Sid and Jack aside, and ran down the stairs, the girl screaming and struggling under his arm. Mandy took off like a lioness pursuing her prey, flew past a dazed Jack, and Sid followed. Chilly went through the main reception doors as Mandy was just entering the vestibule. She saw Meesh's head strike one of the doors as it closed, heard her howl. Jack was up, still dazed, but followed Sid and Peewee out to the car park, halted, stunned, an erotic moment, he admitted to himself, but he had just taken a bang on his head, so was excused. Mandy had Chilly in a half-nelson, her legs up and around one side, a knee in his back, Meesh beside her, clobbering. Chilly was raging, Mandy was breaking his arm, then his back, but she did not stop, neither did Meesh. Jack's eyes wide open, the crack on the back of his head forgotten; Mandy's skirt had risen to her hips, she wore stockings; it was a vision.

Sid cuffed Chilly as a number of uniforms arrived. Meesh was cuddling and hugging Mandy, and curiously, neither were crying. Mandy would say later had it been Jack he would have been blubbing and Meesh soothing him. Mandy hugged the tiny girl, hand to the side of her head she felt warm, sticky blood, signalled to Sid with her bloody hand and mouthed, 'Ambulance'.

'I presume you have him fingered for Biscuit's murder?' Peewee said to Jack, observing the spectacle.

'And a bit more, Peewee,' Jack said, looking at the writhing Chilly; Mandy had unfortunately secured her skirt. 'Tip of the iceberg, something is happening, and I'm going to find out what.'

'Whatever you want from us, you will have. Didn't like the bloke, but you never think something like this, do you?'

'No, you don't,' and Jack called out to Sid, 'get the police Doctor to the bastard over.'

'Will do, what about you?'

'Me?'

'You've a cut on the back of your head, bleeding down your back.'

Jack looked to the heavens, 'Blimey another shirt ruined, and look at these round the houses,' Jack smoothed his trousers, 'Christ, I hate shopping.'

The paramedics put a dressing on Meesh's head wound.

Jack sidled up and put his arm around Mandy and Meesh and whispered into Mandy's ear, 'Stockings?'

For his ear only, she replied, 'For you gobshite.' He felt her hot breath and enjoyed an involuntary shiver. Meesh hugged them both; Jack was crying; naturellament.

'Let's get you to hospital, little lady,' the paramedic said.

'Can they come with me?' Meesh pleaded.

'Well he certainly is, that will need a few stitches.'

'You clumsy oaf,' Mandy said to Jack, and Meesh giggled and snuggled into Mandy, easing her into the ambulance; she was not letting this girl go.

Jack followed, 'I know the rules mate, but we need to be together.'

'Your granddaughter?'

Jack smiled, Meesh and Mandy giggled.

———

'CALM BEFORE THE STORM, LUV,' Jack said, prophetic, who knew, but Meesh had certainly calmed in the back of the ambulance, allowing the paramedic to do the observations.

'What, if this is calm, keep me clear of stormy seas, Jack,' Mandy thought she had whispered.

'I mean, this is just the start,' Jack did whisper, shook his head and some blood flicked onto Mandy's hand.

'Jack, your head.'

The ambulance technician passed a gauze pad. 'Hold that on it until I can get to you.'

'You got no loo roll and sellotape?' Jack asked, which got a warm smile from Mandy, otherwise the wisecrack fell on stony ground.

'Tell me later,' Mandy responded, and Jack resolved to do just that, but how much should he say, and just how much can he involve this woman he loved. The prospect of the next few weeks looked grim, and he had only begun to scratch the surface. So many dimensions; red herrings? Jack thought not, and father Mike's sense this was a devious conspiracy being played out in Portsmouth, and with him as the catalyst, was becoming more of a reality. He wanted this woman, yet ironically, for her own safety, he wanted distance from her. And what of the military, what is that all about? Pugwash, a bit of fun, but Jack sensed a malevolent streak in the martinet chairman of the community police committee. A barrier he needed to break down and he had some ideas, but for now, casualty.

Tomorrow was another day, and he will seek his enemy in earnest.

PART TWO

...AND EFFECT

Know Thine Enemy

THIRTY-TWO

CASUALTY WAS BUSY FOR A MONDAY AFTERNOON. THIS'LL get worse, the NHS safe with the Tories, bollocks, Jack thought to himself, 'Tut Tut,' Meesh, mimicking Dolly.

'You're spot on, mate,' a pressured ambulance technician rejoined.

'Did I?' Mandy nodded.

Mandy walked like Long John Silver, sans parrot, dragging a dead leg that had the elfin girl's gangly arms and tiny hands grasping a thigh, her head squashed into Mandy's waist, blood oozing from her temporary dressing and spotting the waistband of her skirt. Mandy's phone rang.

'No mobiles.'

Mandy acknowledged the Jobsworth, and down on her haunches, whispered sweetly to Meesh, 'Sweetheart, go with Jack, I'll just take this call.'

Meesh was ominously showing little emotion as Jack peeled her from Mandy's leg, the fringe benefits of which he had to set aside as his own headache could not be ignored, aware he should be moaning if he was to milk any symphony at all, 'Your legs, okay?'

'Just grazed, you may have to buy me more stockings though.' The accompanying radiant smile warmed him, as did the erotic memory. Meesh tugged Jack back to reality with a tut. This little girl has to be related to Dolly he thought as they were greeted at the nurse station by the senior triage nurse.

'Fallen off your bike again?' he announced, and Meesh put her hand to her mouth and giggled, still no sign of distress.

'Had an argument with a staircase,' Jack replied, and the nurse made a note. 'What's that you've written?'

'We might need to check your coordination, at your age it can sometimes happen your mind is in front or behind your body.'

'Sounds about right,' Mandy had returned, and Meesh promptly detached herself from Jack's tree trunk and suckered onto Mandy's more elegant and shapely thigh; lucky cow, Jack selfishly thought.

'We may have to keep you in since you had a bad reaction to your previous concussion.'

'Not on your Nelly, mate.'

'Tut,' Meesh.

'Jack, I have to get back to the press conference...' she paused, and in a hushed tone, '...message from Connie, things are a bit hectic on *Operation Jane's bike*, what d'you want to do?'

Mandy crouched, 'I have to go Meesh, Jackie will be here soon, okay?'

'Yes.'

Mandy craned her neck to look up at Jack but spoke to Meesh, 'Good girl,' Mandy nodded; Jack was fixated on her legs. 'Earth to Jack, what do you want to do?'

He shook his head, stirring the stars before his eye, 'Jo-Jums can run the op until I get back in a minute.'

'I don't think so, Sir, we will want to keep you in.'

'Please no,' Meesh chastising before Jack had time to cuss.

He held her chin, gently turned her face towards him and looked into her eyes, 'There is someone I want you to meet, her name is Dolly.'

She looked immediately excited, 'Oh good, I haven't got any dollies,' and with a noticeable intake of breath, Jack and Mandy exchanged a glance, it dawned on them this kid had lost her mum, and had nothing, no family that they knew of, not even an old teddy.

'Get going Amanda, we'll watch you on the telly; eh Meesh?' The little girl offered no response, and Jack turned to the triage nurse, 'you'd better get stitching, we have bad guys to catch, and telly to watch.'

'On your head be it,' the nurse was also a comedian.

'And hers as well,' and Jack pulled a funny face, Meesh giggled and robotically followed a nurse into a treatment bay. Jackie Phillips went straight past the agitated triage nurse with just a glance that would freeze Beelzebub in the middle of Hades; a woman on a mission, as she swept and swirled through the exam bay curtains and joined Meesh, brushing Jack aside; he was used to this.

They cleaned Meesh's wound, cutting just a little of her hair away from the side of her forehead and used butterfly tapes to bond the gash. She would have a very neat scar and Jack was pleased, sensing this girl would need as much going for her as possible, growing up. She would have more than enough emotional baggage, when she remembers that is.

'Now you, Inspector,' and so the nurse examined Jack's wound, hummed and aaahed and made faces at Meesh, inviting the inquisitive child to look; it was all getting to be a big game, and at Jack's expense.

'Okay, let's get this done, shall we,' Jack said.

'Ooooh, who's a grumpy old man?' the nurse replied.

'Jack,' Meesh exclaimed through wrinkled lips, a hint of concern.

'Shall we give him a needle, Meesh?'

'Yeah,' cautiously enthusiastic.

'Ah, I'm not good with needles can we just glue it?'

'Don't be a baby, you'll just feel a little prick.'

'That's what I told his girlfriend,' Jackie rejoined. The nurse chuckled, Meesh's wrinkled lips returned.

Jack accidentally saw the needle and when he came round he was in a wheelchair with an all enveloping, swami bandage around his head. Meesh smiled hesitantly. Jack put on what he thought was his reassuringly relaxed face, as it looked like she'd had a fright when he fainted.

'All done, Mr Austin, we do recommend you stay overnight, so we can keep an eye on you, especially after last time.'

'No chance, luv, I have to get back to the station.'

'What about me?'

He carefully smoothed the top of Meesh's head, 'You, me, and Phil, are going to watch Mandy on telly,' and Meesh jumped off the exam couch and grabbed Jack's hand.

———

THE PRESS ROOM WAS FULL, this was becoming a big story, and not just Pugwash, which Mandy had been briefed to avoid. A cacophony of clicks and whirrs greeted her as she appeared, flanked by Commander Manners and Spotty.

Mandy started, 'I will brief you on the latest developments and allow a few questions.' Spotty looked annoyed, he wanted to say this, but snapped his head back to the front; Mandy was speaking again. 'A man has been arrested regarding the murder of Detective Sergeant Brian Smith and a woman, as yet unidentified. We have charged a number of individuals with aiding and abetting a murder suspect, holding people against their will, assault and rape, assaults on minors, as well as assaults on police officers. They are being held on remand, no bail requested or granted.'

Spotty jumped in, 'We will take a few questions,' Mandy ignored his victory smile.

'Superintendent, is the man you have arrested a serving policeman?'

'We're not ready to release that information.'

'Can you confirm if that man is being questioned regarding conspiracy charges?'

A stern, poker face, 'I have told you our line of questioning,' and she thought back to what Jack had been muttering in the ambulance.

Spotty called on Bernie, 'Can you tell us if Inspector Austin was involved in the arrests?'

'Yes. He was unfortunately injured and is at the hospital now.'

'How serious, Superintendent?'

'A bash on the head, so we're not overly worried,' general laughter; Mandy made to stand but there was a call from the floor and Spotty nodded to the BBC.

'Commander, can you confirm Inspector Austin is to face a disciplinary tribunal, and do you have a date for that?'

The Commander shrugged his shoulders to Mandy, 'I can confirm the Chairman of the Community Policing Committee has made some serious allegations, insisting Inspector Austin be made to account for his actions at a tribunal.'

'Can you tell us when, and what you think about this?'

He looked at Mandy again, before returning to face the press, 'A date will be set in the next few days, and I am always saddened when questions are raised about the conduct of a fellow police officer,' he stood, and Spotty called the end.

Jack, watching the TV with Meesh and Jackie, ignored the salient content of the briefing, because he'd noticed Mandy had changed her stockings. She must keep spares in her drawers, and he laughed to himself, drawers, blimey, I must remember that, Mandy will love it.

THIRTY-THREE

Jackie left with Meesh, and Jack was driven back to Kingston Police station by two unhappy uniforms who felt Jack had hijacked their patrol car from the hospital entrance. He had, of course, but nicely, he thought.

Barney manned the station desk, 'Barney, your family they are well?' Jack made his entrance.

'Tolerably well, thank you, Jane.'

'Have you got some atom bomb Paracetamol, I've got a blinder.'

'I'm not surprised, great bandage,' Barney laughed.

'I think the nurse was having a tin-barf, Barney.'

'She won then.'

'Atom bombs?'

'I'll bring them up, but it's not exactly serene up there.'

Jack plodded the staircase, and as he approached the top he saw Mandy's legs, eyed the length of her body through the last few steps, 'Blimey, darlin', d'you live on this landing?'

She opened her arms, 'Come here, you old soldier, come to Mama,' and he went to her and they hugged in that very comfortable silence he noticed had developed lunchtime; what did that mean? She moulded her body to his and it felt good; something not missed by Mandy.

He whispered in her ear, 'You were good on the telly, Ma'am.'

'Mmmm,' she replied, and they made for the CP door, this time Mandy squashed beside Jack as they went through, and shared the joke, 'You up for this, Jack?'

'We'll see.' He didn't know what to expect, but only a token reaction to his bandage? He was peeved.

'You can take that off now,' Mandy said.

'What?'

'The bandage,' Mandy smiled. 'Jackie called, said it was something the nurse, Meesh, and she cooked up while you were out cold. Meesh said you were a wuss,' she whispered in his ear, 'but you're my wuss.'

Jo-Jums was finishing up on the phone, making notes, Wallace and Alice Springs beside her on other phones. 'Jo, kids sorted?' Jack was always concerned about her family life, 'Any chance of a quick up date?'

'Tanner picked them up, thanks. Cyrano's boys followed the principle subject car, straight to Bazaar Bikes, as expected, we have it on Video. He's allowing things to unfold. I've agreed it's his call, his Op.' Jack nodded, pleased at Jo's ability to take control. 'Nobby and Kettle are following the estate car with the towed caravan, which Cyrano suspects may contain explosives. Bomb disposal are alerted and maintaining a discreet distance. We have CCTV from the docks if you want to look.'

Jack shook his head, it hurt, 'No, what else?'

'The car and caravan travelled to Newbury and went into the services. They parked, unhitched the caravan then drove off, Nobby and Kettle are following. They're on the A34, heading to Oxford but traffic is heavy; tail end of the rush hour. Bomb disposal are monitoring the caravan.'

'Nicely handled Jo,' and Jack handed her a bit of paper, 'can you write the reg number, make, and colour, of the subject car please, be your best friend, and what car is Nobby in?' he yawned as he walked to his desk. He made a call and asked Frankie if she had the road CCTV up on screen, she did, two screens, one on the vehicles, one set on the road where the vehicles were expected to travel, as the car got there so she programmed the other screen in front again, and so on. Jack was impressed. The traffic was heavy and slow, 'ETA to Oxford, Connie?'

'We thing fort five min.'

'Any plan, Jo?' Jack asked.

'Cyrano wants it followed, then it will be what it is at the end,' a little short, she was busy.

'Be time for Nobby's tea soon.' Everyone stopped, some *Mary Poppins* mouths, stifled giggles. 'What? Just sayin'.'

Fifteen, twenty minutes, went by and Mandy watched Jack pacing and thought this was not right, she'd noticed Barney bring some Paracetamol, 'You okay, is your head hurting?'

He looked, weighed up the opportunity for symphony, maybe throw in some whinging, but decided maybe later, 'Yeah, a little.'

She looked at his ugly face, deeply carved lines conveyed every emotion he felt, she sidled up and put her arm around his waist, well as far as it would stretch, and squeezed him. 'Mama,' squeezed again, 'Mama,' looked at him, tilting her head, she smiled and mouthed, 'my cuddly teddy bear.'

'Leave it out, Guv, you'll make us all sick,' Jo-Jums had been watching. 'Whoa Neddy,' Jo-Jums had picked up many of Jack's expressions over time, a source of great pride to him, confident it will see her right for the future; he took these things seriously, seeing his staff right.

'What's happening?' Mandy left Jack's waist.

Jo responded, not taking her eyes from the screens, 'Looks like a lorry has gone across the carriageway, this'll hold things up.'

Jack had regained his fed-up face, losing Mandy from his waist, 'Good, we can relax. I need a sit down.'

Mandy said nothing, relying on the eyes in the back of her head to watch over him. Jack made a song and dance, settling into his deckchair, simultaneously singing something only comprehensible to people who understood Italian frontier gibberish.

'Connie, can you get all four screens covering sections of the road please?' Jack asked.

No answer, Mandy interpreted, and Connie began tapping the keys. In just a few days Connie had become very confident on the keyboard. In a matter of moments two other sections of the road came up on screen, Mandy bent down to look closer at the new images. 'What do you think is happening?'

Jo-Jums looked closer, 'Local Bill closing the other carriageway, probably to get emergency vehicles to the scene.'

'They've closed the carriageway, Jack,' Mandy called. He hemmed. She mouthed to Jo, 'D'you think he's okay?'

'Has he ever been?' Jo mouthed back.

'I can hear you two.'

'You can hear bugger all, Deaf Austin.'

'I heard that.'

'He's okay.'

'Mandy look,' a patrol car manoeuvred past the police blockade on the opposite carriageway. The officers hopped over the central reservation and walked along the queue of cars, talking to the motorists. Jack's phone went, he stretched from the deckchair toppled the receiver and picked it up off the floor, only then getting out of his deckchair. Mandy sighed, knowing it was a personal competition to see if he could get the phone without getting up, he had even had a stick with a hook one day, and she wondered how many hours he'd spent dreaming that up.

'Del Boy, whasuuup,' Jack's street talk, which was more like his frontier gibberish, but louder. 'Hang on, Del,' and Jack turned, 'Frankie, sweet'art, blank out a screen and tap this in, please.' He quoted a hot spot address that Frankie typed in slowly because, in-between numerals and letters, Jack was conversing with this Del-Boy. 'Del says hit return, Franks,' and he carried on chatting. 'Mandy? Yeah, thought I might take her to the pictures, know any good films?' He listened, 'You reckon, *Death of the Vampires*, I'll ask, hold on,' and Jack looked up; Mandy was beginning to steam.

'Ma'am, look,' Mandy turned back to Frankie, one of the new screens was showing the faces of drivers. Frankie upped the sound and they heard an officer explaining that a lorry had blocked the road and they may be some time, apologising to the driver. Jack shouted into his phone, 'Del-Boy, give Mandy a wave.' They swung back from Jack to see the officer talking to the drivers turn to face his colleague and wave, speaking into a mobile phone, but also the body camera, 'Mandy Lifeboats, how's you doing, babes,' more excruciating street stuff.

Everyone turned back to Jack and he wiggled his fingers. Del-Boy, to camera and phone said, 'Gotta go, Jack; try that film, Mands, it's well good.'

Jack hung up, the two officers stopped at the suspect vehicle and the camera picked up the occupants. Frankie looked to Jack, 'I presume this feed is going through visual recognition computers somewhere we do not know about?'

'I imagine so,' and Jack handed Frankie a piece of paper.

Mandy and Jo-Jums watched it travel from Jack's outstretched hand to Frankie, who had to come and get it; she was seated and he was standing. Mandy wondered at his cheek, but Frankie was oblivious and commenced tapping. A screen cleared, replaced by an image of processing data, the pictures of the occupants of the suspect car to one side. There were two small square frames at the top of the screen; it had names and personal details beside the portraits. After about ten minutes it was done. Mandy sent a thought transference message, she required Jack's presence. Groaning, he raised himself from where he was now sitting, on the desk counter, onto a wheelie chair and tried to scoot it over but nobody got out of the way, so he couldn't see. He eventually stood, 'What we got?'

'Four suspected Islamic activists, no form, but on the *to-watch* list,' Frankie answered.

Jo's phone went, 'Nobby, I don't know hang on,' she turned to face Jack with a strange look, definitely feminine, but Jack was not sure if it was trouble or something nice. In a fleeting moment he did think, nearly sixty and he'd still not worked that out. Finally, she spoke, 'Nobby says he was told his mum has his tea on the table and should get home now or he will be on the naughty step.' It was a stifled giggle on Jo's face, relief on Jack's, but for everyone else it was a roar of laughter, even Mandy, who was fuming with Jack, but had to laugh.

Jack's phone went and he wheeled back and picked up, 'Well done, Mush, keep me informed... you too with brass knobs, you spotty old fart,' Jack hung up.

Mandy had him in her sights, 'Chief Constable?'

More laughter at Mandy's aside, the mirth lingering, infectious, and moved onto hysterical giggling, and only subsided when Frankie called out, 'The lorry's being moved.'

Jack got out of his wheelie chair, stretching and talking more frontier gibberish, which fortunately Mandy was able to interpret, 'He needs someone to stay to monitor the caravan until the spooks take over; you okay for that Wally?'

'Okay, Jane, err, Mandy.'

'This was a good day men,' Jack followed up, encouraging his troops.

'Men!' Mandy looking insulted along with Jo and Alice; Frankie and Connie were oblivious.

'To me, you're all my men,' and Jack blew Mandy a kiss.

Ruffled, she playfully clipped his head, he exaggerated an ouch, 'Oh Jack, I'm so sorry, I wasn't thinking.'

'Thinking? I got this feckin' great bandage and you forgot?'

'Jack, sorry, does it hurt?'

He feigned a minor collapse, a stoic recovery, and sat back in his chair, 'So the vampire film doesn't appeal?' More guffaws as people prepared to leave, 'Frankie, Connie, go and have a drink, dinner or whatever, a brilliant job. It all starts again tomorrow, for now, it's R and R everyone, Mandy and I are taking a Polar Bear up north, you coming, Mands?'

She put her arm part way around his waist, pulled and kissed him full on the mouth.

"Oooh err matron" resounded.

THIRTY-FOUR

Jack skidded his tyres and righted his imaginary motorbike in one smooth movement, thanks to some good leaning into the corner, and followed Mandy into her office where she collected her coat and threw it onto her desk. 'Park your bike and come here, let's get this bandage off your bacon bonce,' she pulled him to her and began to peel the tape that held the bandage. He responded with his arms tight around her, they kissed and lingered, their mouths opened and Mandy felt her passion rise; him too.

'About time you two got together.' Mandy pulled back, straightened herself and reddened. The Commander followed up, 'Sorry, you did leave the door open. I wanted a catch-up.'

Jack saw Mandy flustered, felt he should take this on, 'Sit down sir, we'll bring you up to speed.'

'Sir, eh?'

'A seat, Commander,' and Jack pointed him to a psychologically challenged comfy chair, pulling the orange PVC chair for himself; serves him right, and looking down on the awkwardly seated Commander, and satisfied with the psychological regime, he briefed. 'You know about Chilly, except Paolo is having difficulty breaking him, he may be relying on intimidating Meesh; the little girl.'

'Scared the bajeezers out of her, did he? What about the drugs?'

'Cyrano's tracked the target vehicle to the bike shop, and he's letting things roll out to see what happens. The French authorities want to see if they can nail the contacts in France or wherever else, so it makes sense to keep it running. Either way, I think it's right we hand that over. The other vehicle was a lucky strike. We had our target nabbed, and as they had an eight hour ferry crossing, Cyrano thought it would be good to let the dogs have a sniff around and they found the estate car and caravan. We allocated Nobby and Kettle,' Jack harrumphed, Nobby was the Commander's son.

'It's okay, his mum called him Nobby the other day,' the men shared a laugh, Mandy not quite so much.

'The caravan was left in the services at Newbury, and is being checked by bomb squad, but really it's the spooks, you know?'

'Yes, I've had the call, the Home Office is mightily impressed the way this has been handled, well done.'

'Mandy's show, but Jo-Jums had a strong hand in there.'

'So, what happens now?'

'Tomorrow is another day. Mandy and I feel we're at the tip of an iceberg, the drugs, the women, the children and the skinheads are not it. Something is brewing, Chilly may know what it is, and even if he does, I would be very surprised if we learn anything from him. There is an organisation, or even one person driving something; civic subterfuge or something else that has not occurred to us yet, funded by drugs and prostitution? Maybe racial disharmony, and we have only hit upon the Nazi side so far, and then why? There has to be something for it to fight against, and for what it's worth, that is Nobby's theory, and I want to run with it; see where it leads us.'

The Commander swelled with pride for his son.

Mandy looked at Jack, 'Why here?'

'The only suggestion I have is Portsmouth has good race relations, no ghettos or lines of tension, unlike Bradford, for instance, which has been targeted, but obviously not had the desired response. I can only think this is the British psyche, "Of course there will be race riots there, there are natural lines of tension", but here, if you can stir something up, it will be noticed, who knows? Where they go after that is anyone's guess, and we will not know until we nail the bastard behind it. I want to codename him Norafarty,' Jack chortled, more to himself. Mandy and the Commander smiled benignly at the juvenile eccentricity, Mandy reassuring the Commander he meant Moriarty. 'Can you ask uniform to let me have details on these little demos going on against the cutbacks?'

'I'll have a look see,' the Commander replied. 'Jack, Mandy, I'm impressed,' and he stood, difficult in the comfy seats, but managed it on the second attempt.

Jack rose to meet the blushing Commander, 'So that's where we are, my head hurts, my heart beats with a passion for this woman, but we have to deliver a Polar Bear to the north.'

'Jack, I will never understand you, but I will fight tooth and nail for you against Pugwash.'

Jack put on his dimwit face, not difficult Mandy thought, 'Going to be a tribunal then?'

'Jack, please, Pugwash is a demonic character, he cannot see any side of any argument other than his own, and everything has to run how he wants it to run; he worries me.'

'A Martinet would you say?'

'I might if I knew what that meant, but I do know his sort will destroy what we have, and I cannot stand by and watch it happen. I will not let you go without a fight.' The Commander left, flushed and determined to get home and find his son; Jack could have told him he would be on the naughty step, but didn't.

Mandy circled her desk to approach Jack, they embraced and immediately returned to the passion that had been interrupted. Jack's breath was in the back of his throat, the butterflies working overtime. He was so in love, never thought this would happen again, but here it was, felt like he was sixteen, decided not to mention this to Mandy, she might think he'd grown up. However, he did feel he could step-in-time, not the best bit of *Mary Poppins* but better than the penguins, nobody liked the penguins, shame though, cause he liked *a jolly 'oliday with Mary.* Mandy took a breath and stepped back a little, 'What, did I...?'

Jack had that look on his face, the one that had grown on her. She nodded he had spoken his thoughts into the kiss and her mouth. She put her hands on both of his cheeks and pecked small kisses on his dead eye, good eye, his nose and then his mouth. Jack was lost, this was full on real woman, and he felt his heart might burst from his body. Slowly, Mandy released him, let him float back down, and in a tender, husky whisper, 'And that is how I have felt for a very long time. Take me to the pictures, not *Death of the Vampires*, something we can talk about. I want to talk to you, I want to know you, and then it will happen. I love you, Jack Austin.' They both calmed enough to walk out of Mandy's office, down the stairs through the reception where they picked up the Polar Bear left by Michael.

'Bravo, you two,' they waved acknowledgement to Barney.

Outside the air was cool, but heralded summer, dusk, that lovely light Jack liked when walking along the seafront with Martin, and now, he looked forward to walking with Martin and Mandy, maybe even Meesh. He chanced his arm, not thinking straight, 'I feel like I'm sixteen again Amanda, I have a fluttering stomach, I'm excited, like I'm walking on air, I love...'

Mandy, surprised at his interruption, turned sharply to look at him when he pushed her hard to the ground. She screamed, heard the shot ring out and scrabbled to a crouch behind the Commander's car. A shot zinged across the bonnet and then another. Jack called out, 'Stay down,' she managed a "No kidding, Tonto".

Barney was behind her, 'Armed support are on their way. Jack what are you doing?' Barney saw Jack crouching, backside in the air, a perfect target, a deformed Hyena, scuttling to the far side of the car park; no sun and consequential deep shadow, but it was the darkest part of the frontage. Jack skirted the perimeter and could see the car, two men, a driver, and a passenger with his feet outside the open door, confidently seeking targets, and why would he not be confident, our police are not armed, so what could possibly happen to them; cowardly bastards. Jack felt his bile rise, tried to control his berserking mist, counted to ten, imagined stroking Martin and the image turned to Mandy, and the anger rose again.

He made a mental note of the car number but knew he would forget it, Oldtimer's? Paranoia, also a sign. This is where Jack thought he wished he knew a bit more about guns, but he hated them, had as little to do with them as possible, even in his past. He thought about the TV shows where the cops always knew how many bullets would be left, but Jack didn't have a clue, couldn't even recall how many shots had been fired. Didn't know what sort of gun it was, except it was silver and was glinting in the glow from the streetlight at the front of the car. Jack was a cerebral man, not a macho action man. Actually, if he was honest, he wanted to go to bed. He felt tired and a little bit sick, his head hurt and the stars were back, floating in front of his panicky eye; was that heart disease?

All the time he was thinking these jumbled thoughts, he was crawling on his belly towards the car. Sparing a moment to look back, he saw Barney stick his head above the parapet of a planter, another shot, drawing fire. Jack continued to crawl, concealed within the anti-vandal shrubs that were scratching him to buggary, Cairo Pantha, or something, so much for his Church of Egypt; who'd be a vandal? The car was only a few metres away. He pulled his keys out, tried not to let them chink, thought about jingle bells at Christmas; focus for Christ's sake. He had a small Swiss army knife. The orange streetlight was behind the car and Jack was in the shadow; he didn't like orange, a colour that didn't suit him; shut-up and focus.

Barney made a run, ducked behind another brick planter, drew more fire, and under this cover and the intense noise, Jack stabbed one tyre, rolled over and hit the other one. The immediate deflation was felt by the occupants, the reaction astonishing. The gunman in the passenger seat made to get out, whilst the driver thought this his cue to make a getaway. No grip from the back tyres caused the car to slew and it clipped Jacks left hand; he screamed.

'Jack!' Mandy's panic call.

The passenger was caught, one leg in the car, one leg outside, his arm twisted in the seat belt causing him excruciating pain, good, Jack thought, and the gunman fired indiscriminately until his ammunition ran out, by which time he had been dragged a few metres and was now on the floor screaming. Jack heaved himself upright, kicked the gun away then kicked the passenger in the face for luck; Jack was superstitious. The driver revved but Barney was there, pulled the door open and had the man half out as he tried to grab a gun; should have worn a seatbelt Jack thought, and thinking that was lucky, he kicked the passenger's head again; you can never have enough luck. Barney seized the gun and had it pointed at the driver's head. The gunman on the floor was stirring so Jack gave him a pearler and waited for new luck to kick in, so to speak. He felt no remorse, the conversation in his head, 'I'm doing this, and there's no mist, so this is what I've missed, and that rhymed, maybe I should have been a poet?'

Barney looked to Jack, 'Poet?'

Jack pointed at the gun in Barney's hand, 'You know how to use that?'

There was a click, 'Safety off, I'm the best shot in my gun club,' and the driver put his hands up.

'Sort of wish I'd not campaigned against gun clubs now, but I will get over it, and probably sooner than I should.' The driver looked confused. 'PP', Jack said, but the driver remained nonplussed, and was less plussed when Jack walked around the car and smashed him in the face. 'Anybody see that? Good, because here's another one, shoot at my feckin' woman.'

'Okay Jane, think I might just see the next one,' but Jack hit him again. 'Nope,' but Mandy had Jack now.

The Commander of the armed support unit called out, 'Nope, didn't see anything.'

'Two sets of cuffs, Cisco,' Jack called.

Mandy turned, 'Cisco?'

'Cisco Kid,' Jack said as if this was all the explanation needed.

'He always calls me that,' Cisco said, 'a cowboy series from the fifties he says, but now everyone calls me Cisco, and I've never seen it.'

'Welcome to the club,' Barney said, handing the gun over, 'bag that, it's evidence. There's another one around here somewhere.'

The man on the floor groaned, his arm was facing completely the wrong direction. Jack looked, farted, and fainted.

'Jack, you wuss,' and Mandy ran to him and squatted beside him, her hand supporting his bandaged head, his left hand appeared broken, and she recalled his scream.

He was coming around as the paramedics and an ambulance arrived. 'Amanda my hand hurts.'

'I know, the ambulance is here.' She stroked his face, he had a look she recognised, 'What?'

'I can nearly see up your skirt.'

She allowed herself a quick sight to the heavens, more out of habit, moved and leaned over a little more to whisper in his ear, 'How's that, can you see better now?' The paramedic was with the gunman on the floor. 'Leave that bastard and get over to this policeman now,' Mandy bawled, concerned for Jack.

'I need to look at this other man, he must have hit the windscreen.'

Jack felt Mandy tense, 'Leave it love, they're like London buses, there'll be another one along in a minute,' and sure enough another was there and it was Barry. 'Bazzer,' and his colleagues shouted, "Oi, oi Bazzer", he'd been appointed a nickname. Bazzer grinned as he took Jack's hand and put something around it that was cool, in a temperature way, but Jack thought it looked quite good as well, but could no longer ignore the excruciating pain beyond the throbbing of his hand; he was scratched all over, and his clothes were torn to shreds. 'Feckin' Cairo Panther,' he said, and Bazzer and Mandy laughed, 'What?'

'It's Pyracantha, bozo.' Mandy answered, loving her dipstick.

The Commander arrived as Jack was getting into the ambulance. 'Mandy, I know you will want to go with Jack, but I need you here to get the ball rolling.'

She was annoyed, 'Jamie.'

Jack put his good hand on hers, 'Mandy you're needed,

come here,' and under the pretence of a kiss, he whispered, 'Ring Father Mike, I need him, please.'

'Jack, it's just your hand falling off, you're not dying.'

Bazzer was looking to close the ambulance door, Jack mouthed, 'Please.'

'Only because you're my wuss,' the doors closed, she took out her mobile and searched for the number he had asked her to store and rang Father Mike O'Brien.

THIRTY-FIVE

'FALLEN OFF YOUR BIKE AGAIN,' THE SAME CASUALTY triage nurse.

'You got no home to go to? Jack replied.

'Can't go home, cutbacks, reduced staff, so no cover, and we have to take up the slack with no overtime payment. They take the piss, and we've no time to demonstrate, cute strategy, eh?'

'Do me a flavour, have a kip before you work on my hand, then meet me and my mates at C&A's for a bit of sedition.'

'I will not be doing your hand, but will certainly meet you at C&A's, but wouldn't it be more convenient to meet here?' They laughed amicably, mechanically. A doctor looked at the hand and scribbled something. Jack was tipped into a wheelchair and was headed off to X-ray, police officers in reception and by the treatment areas, as he was wheeled along; plaudits, pats on the back as he went by. He could hear nurses asking what it was all about, and no doubt it would be ramped up by the uniforms, so when he returned, he would be better known than Thingy Bob, whatshisname?

'Mandy's starting to think you're going Roman Candle, Jack, you'll have to come along for a few Sundays.'

'In your dreams, Mike.'

'How are you?'

'Starting to think the Pugwash tribunal might be a blessing in disguise.'

Mike smiled looking down at him, 'You'll get over it, how did you get those scratches?'

'Some Egyptian plant.'

Out of X-ray, they resumed their conversation as Jack was wheeled to a treatment bay, 'You know Father it's only his hand and a few scratches, he's not about to die.'

Mike looked at the nurse, 'Nurse?'

'Fazacherly.'

'Nurse Exactly?' Jack said.

Father Mike addressed the nurse, 'Nurse Exactly, this man has a calling, just does not realise it, yet.'

The two old pals looked at each other, 'I've a calling alright, a couple of pints in C&A's.'

'Nurse Exactly have the X-rays been sent through?' it was the Doctor, too busy to get involved with banter, but picked up on the nickname.

'I'll check the system, Doctor?'

The Doctor was rubbing his young chin, 'You have some dislocations...' hemmed, '...we can manipulate, some cracking we can do nothing about, and hefty bruising, Inspector, no lasting damage. It will hurt for a while. Nurse Exactly will put on a moulded removable plastic cast to keep everything in place. When that's sorted, we can dress all the cuts and scratches, have you got several hours?' the Doc relaxed momentarily, laughed, 'What happened Inspector?'

Mike answered for him, 'Egyptians,' and the doctor drifted off to cure people, seemingly satisfied with the response.

'Given him the last rites yet?'

'Depends on how angry you are with him Mandy.'

Mandy looked on and smiled benignly, Jack pleased he was wounded; it was like a get out of jail free card. 'All set at the nick, babes?'

Excitedly she responded, 'It is Jack, and you wouldn't believe it, we have spooks camped in the CP room and the only people pleased to see them is Connie and Frankie, and I quote, "They're downloading some cosmic programmes", and this has got them so excited they forgot where they were and Frankie kissed Connie, so I think that's out of the bag now.'

'I know,' Jack said.

'I know you know about Frankie and Connie.'

'No, I know about the spooks.'

'How?'

She looked at Mike, he shrugged, 'Was that Gallic or New York Jew?'

'Gallic.' Mike nodded; good, that cleared that up.

'Mandy sweet'art, look around you.'

She poked her head out of the curtains; 'Oh, Feckin' spooks, inveigle their way in everywhere. I thought they were Doctors,' and she chuckled.

'You can tell Doctors darlin', they're only marginally less stressed than the nurses, that right Exactly?'

Before Exactly could answer Mandy was in, Jack thought she's a bit hyper, but then again, she'd just been shot at, 'Exactly, eh? Please, don't explain, I'm processing enough as it is, not least my man is a tosspot.' Jack looked at Mandy warming at the expressive look on her face, but mainly because she said he was her man; she already knew he was a tosspot.

Amazingly the Doctors did not want to keep Jack in, seemed pleased to be rid of him. He emerged from casualty with a moulded pink, plastic, oversized glove on his left hand, so many little stitches, plasters and tapes, he walked like he'd soiled his underpants. At the exit Jack stopped to talk to one of the spooks who reported they had face recognition on the gunmen, 'Part of a white pride cell; lowlife. The gunman has a smashed arm, they'll have a job to save it, but they're trying. The other bloke will not be as good looking as before. Swears blind he did not hit the windscreen but everyone says he did, so he did. Well done Jane, and Mandy, isn't it? Today, this evening, good job.'

'Thanks, Jimbo, think we have someone rattled?'

They moved off, Mandy started to reply, 'How did you know...?'

Jimbo called after them, 'Del-Boy said you was a banker, think that's what he said.' Jack thought we must all be tired because nobody laughed.

As they left, Exactly handed Mandy Jack's meds, said he thought Jack was a lucky man.

'I know, I could have been shot.'

'No, Jack, you have so many friends, and thanks a lot for "Exactly." How will I explain that to my boyfriend?'

'You won't need to,' Mandy answered.

THIRTY-SIX

JACK WADDLED TO MANDY'S CAR; SHE HELD THE DOOR FOR him. There was a section of cardboard box left on the dashboard, large letters in thick black felt pen, *POLICE if you clamp this I will rip your balls off.*

'Seems to have done the trick, love,' and she smiled as he ooohed and aaahed, winced and complained, into the passenger seat.

'My little wuss,' she whispered in his ear and closed the door gently. All settled, she started the car and took his right hand and put it on her leg, slightly higher than had previously been permitted.

'Lucky I didn't hurt my right hand.'

'Very lucky indeed, Jack.'

They drove to his house in another of those companionable silences Jack thought would come in handy in C&A's. Wondering if he dare move his hand took his mind off the pain. She pulled up behind Jack's garage, 'Not dropping me at the front, Mands?'

She looked at him as she took her keys from the ignition,

'I've been shot at and God knows what else is out there wanting to take a pop, and before you say anything, nothing will happen tonight, and will not, until we have our serious talk, and I've at least been to the pictures with you. Got it?' She looked at his face, curious to see how he took the news.

'Understood, a relief.'

'I beg your pardon?'

'Amanda darlin', I can't move, I'm going to need you to undress me.'

'Okay, but if you give me any lip, I will do it roughly.'

'Oooh err matron,' he squeezed out, trying to ease himself out of the seat.

'Oh, for God's sake, give me your hand and not the pink one.' He groaned, accepting Mandy had limited caring genes, which went along with her patience.

'Michael's right, you're a girl's blouse,' Colleen said, confirming what everyone, except Jack, accepted as fact.

Michael helped his dad, 'We can take him, Mandy.'

Jack looked at his son, then Colleen, a face that feigned innocence, and yet knowing. He stole a glance at Mandy and left it for her to answer; he had head wobbling to do.

'I will be staying tonight,' she smiled, 'not that anything is going to happen, is it, Jack?'

'I have my iron jock strap.'

'Hungry?' Michael asked, embarrassed.

'"Orse between two bread vans, son.'

'You've had a lot of anaesthetic, Jack, don't eat too much or you'll be sick.'

'Mandy, I'm captain Sensible,' and as if to prove it he did the Benny Hill salute with his good hand, which involved saluting with the palm inward, crooked against the forehead, tongue sticking slightly out of the corner of the mouth, and saying with a lisping slur, 'Yeth, thir.'

Michael cooked tagliatelle to go with the sauce he'd made, one of his Dad's favourites, chilli tomato with mixed seafood, extra jalapenos on the side. Colleen put her arms around Michael from behind, cuddled, and kissed his neck, 'She's staying over.'

'Oooh err matron,' Michael pulled her to him, 'he will ruin it somehow.'

'I've no doubt he will,' Mandy was there, 'but, I'm made of sturdy stuff, and put the Jalapenos away. If I'm sleeping with a farting machine, I might need a head start.' Colleen blushed, she could not believe this woman she had grown to consider quite remarkable. Mandy read the thought process, 'Colleen, darling, you need to understand this about men; can't live with 'em, can't kill 'em.'

'I heard that,' Jack shouted from the living room.

'Shut your face, gobshite.'

'But your gobshite, right?'

'You are that honeybun,' she responded in a sickly-sweet manner, bending her knees, winking at Colleen, as she took the bowl of tagliatelle through to the table.

'Oh, great tangled telly,' groan, a predicable joke. 'Misery is optional,' Jack followed up, disappointed the joke unexpectedly dive-bombed. They were all tired, had little energy to keep up with Jack's banal banter, but even so they humoured him, and Mandy observed this was the way with most people; she'd not worked out how he achieved that, yet. Jack thought the dinner felt comfortable except, if he was honest, he was feeling a little nervous about going to bed with Mandy. It had been a long time, and he was not firing on all cylinders. He'd always imagined the first time would be a steamy, passionate event, the thought of performing not an issue, and he would be brilliant; naturellament.

'What're you thinking, Jack?'

'He's thinking about going to bed, Colleen. I know this man.'

'Wrong, babes, I was wondering where the extra jalapenos were,' Colleen put her fist to her mouth to unsuccessfully stifle a giggle. 'Well, okay, I was thinking about going to bed.'

Mandy stood and took him by his good hand, 'I had better get you undressed then, are you okay going to the toilet or would you like me to hold it for you.'

'That's it, I'm officially scared now.'

Colleen and Mandy shared a look, 'Treat-em mean, keep-em keen,' said together.

Mandy was gentle following the torturous trip up the stairs with stick man, 'Where are your pyjamas, Jack?'

'I don't wear pyjamas.'

'You animal, well, I wear nightdresses.'

'Mmmm, I've imagined you in a silk nightie.'

'You'd better buy me some then, or its flannelette for you boy.' She pulled back the quilt and helped him to lower himself onto the bed, tenderly kissing some of his many scratches. She stood back and slowly undressed, 'Not disappointed, Jack?'

'Amanda darling, you are everything I imagined, and more.'

'Right answer,' whispered into his ear as she slid into the bed beside him and snuggled up. He winced, 'I hope it's not going to be like this all night? Oh no, perhaps not.'

Jack flushed, 'You brazen hussy you.'

'Yes, but your brazen hussy, I think?'

'You are right now.'

———

Sparrow's fart and Jack woke first. Mandy was still asleep, it had not been a dream, and they had even made love, uncomfortable for him, and probably not the best experience for

Mandy, but they had concocted he felt. She stirred, found Jack looking into her sleepy eyes. She eased closer and he cursed the Egyptians. Her hands stroked his tummy and he was aroused, lowered his head to kiss her and moved his pink hand out of the way, brought his good hand over, slid down to meet her face and felt her bum and she mewed, 'Right answer,' he said.

'Jack, I want you to court me, I don't want to skip the getting to know you bit.'

He had that look most men have when scratching around for a safe reply, 'I will, just don't tell my mates,' there you go, sorted.

'You are a child, but if it gets me my way, okay.'

Their bodies slid together and Jack sensed the pain ease to be replaced with a tangible rapture. They made slow and gentle love, the only sort he felt able to do, and it was a little better. When they eventually decided to get up, Jack waited while she showered and changed. The other bathroom was being used by Colleen and he thought best not to pollute the atmosphere just yet, he was after all a considerate man.

Mandy padded back into the bedroom, a towel wrapped around her body, another on her head, like a turban. How do women do that? Jack had tried, when nobody was looking of course, and it never stayed on his head or his body for that matter, not that he cared, but on a woman, it looked gorgeous, and on Mandy, sexy indeed. She sat on the edge of the bed, her head to the side, rubbing her hair with the turban; he imagined this is what they did in the Punjab. Jack got out of bed, and naked, waddled to her, bent down, resisting a wince, and kissed her. She put her hand on his bottom, rubbed it gently and he impressed himself. She noticed, 'Have we time?' They did, and Jack felt they were slowly getting to know each other, and it was good.

Mandy thought there is time, and he must be in pain.

THIRTY-SEVEN

THEY STOPPED AT A COSTA COFFEE AND HAD BREAKFAST; Jack his fix of espresso, Americano for Mandy, almond croissants. Jack showed her how it looked like the bun on Jackie's hair, she laughed, he suggested best not to tell Jackie, she agreed, and his fear morphed to a smile. They arrived at the station closer to lunchtime. Mandy tipped her toes and whispered in his ear, 'I'm very happy, Jack.'

With the delicacy of a hippo, Jack nibbled her ear, 'I should hope so, d'you see how much it was in *Costa*?' she kissed him once more, and allowing a discreet distance, they walked in together.

"Ooh err matron" from Sid, they looked at each other and moved along after having greeted Sid politely; his family were well. Up the stairs, Jack a few steps behind, he was sore, which was his excuse, but she liked him looking at her backside. Along the corridor they entered the CP room to a resounding "Oooh err matron" and playing on a loop on a computer screen was Mandy and Jack canoodling in the car park just now. Christ, she thought, looked over at Jack who was waving his pink hand in general acknowledgement.

The twat'll be taking a bow soon, she thought. Then he bowed.

Mandy put her hand up to get some attention. 'I want you to know that once I got past the skid marks, I managed to get into Jack's pants last night for a passable shag, that is all,' there was a cheer, and mimicking Jack, she waved her hand and bowed herself. 'Now, shall we get back to work?'

Jo got straight in, 'Commander said to call him, and, Jack, will you call Father Mike, confession? You might just have something to tell him today,' hearty laughter that warranted a spin in the chairs to look at him. They lived in hope that one day he may be thoroughly embarrassed.

Mandy turned to Jack, 'Do I have any reason to be jealous of Father Mike? I thought those blokes were celibate,' she punched the air as the crowd roared "Goal" and she pretended to dribble a ball, doing some keepy-uppys along the way to the door. Jack tutted, mentioned juvenile behaviour, picked up the phone, sat down with no wincing, after all what was the point, you got no symphony here, he should work somewhere where they appreciated good wincing. Mandy turned at the door and said to anyone who was listening, 'Is there a briefing scheduled?'

'Five, Ma'am.'

'Thank you Nobby, one sensible person, hope your mum didn't keep you on the naughty step too long.' Another big laugh and Jack noted, to his credit, Nobby Manners, the Commander's son, enjoying it too; he will fit in nicely.

Mike O'Brien was on the line. 'Mike, you called?'

———

LATER IN THE afternoon Mandy stood by the door of the CP room and looked in, for something to do. The afternoon had passed in earnest quiet work, it often did after a few days of excitement. Tapping from KFC, Nobby and Alice Springs compiling their reports together, Kettle and Wally doing something on Nobby's wall, she noticed Moriarty was up there, but changed to Bore-a-tarty. Behind the wonky screens a gentle busy murmur from the Sissies. Jo-Jums was writing, probably mapping next moves; a strategy maybe. She needs to be promoted she thought, she's a DI all day long. If Jack gets canned after the Pugwash debacle then she would be a natural to take his place; she felt terrible inside, ached for his pain, even if he did bring most of it on himself, looked at him asleep in his deckchair and not a person fazed by it, nobody resenting he could be pitching in and helping. This was his team, and she felt a sudden anger bordering on rage towards Pugwash. If he brings Jack down, she will get him, even if it's just 12 points on his licence.

Sensitive to Jack sleeping, she turned to a metallic clank, clank, noise to see Dolly with Meesh following, dragging Dolly's aerosol cans like she just got married. As the little girl came through the door Mandy noticed amongst the various cloths, a raggedy teddy bear. Thanks, Dolly. Mandy wiggled her fingers, put one to her mouth, 'Shush, Jack's asleep,' and flicked her head towards the deckchair, the incongruity of it struck her, how on earth did one man affect virtually a whole police force?

Meesh picked up on the signal and tippy toed to Mandy, not realising it was inconsequential, the noise of the trailing cans. Clunking the bag down she grabbed Mandy's leg for a hug; he still slept. Mandy was amazed at how warm inside the hug and the image of Jack made her feel. Dolly registered a look of approval, but Jackie, who had followed them up the stairs, looked from the corridor and warned with her eyes; *not too close*. Mandy knew this, of course she did, but she was only human and her feelings were all over the place right now, witness what she did with Jack last night, and this morning, despite her better judgement telling her to wait, but it was lovely, and it was lovely with Meesh as well; so sod Jackie.

'Meesh and I are going to polish Jack,' and Meesh giggled at Dolly's whispered aside, 'so if you two need to talk,' flicking her head to Jackie. They did, and Mandy lead Jackie into her office giving her the PVC chair which she dragged to the front of her desk.

Forever the analyst, Jackie raised her lush eyebrows, 'Jack always takes that chair. He says I have these two comfy chairs in front of my desk to give me a psychological advantage, they are lower than my own, and the backs slope.'

'And do you?' Jackie asked.

'Maybe, without being aware?'

'As a woman in this job you have to take it where you can. Do you mind if I say something?'

'No, but I know what you're going to say.'

'You do?'

Mandy gave a slow tired nod, 'You're going to tell me to slow up with Jack, that he's not over his wife's death...'

'Not in so many words,' Jackie interrupted, 'I was going to say that until quite recently I thought Jack a shallow chauvinistic arsehole. I liked you, could see how you felt, and thought, how can I tell you?'

Mandy's face was wide awake, 'Well, tell me straight, why don't you?'

'Listen to me, and don't get all huffy, and yes you are. I've seen Jack in a different light these last few days. I've had cause to talk to people and his name was invariably involved in those conversations, and, I may have misjudged the man.'

Mandy sat back, her face a picture of astonishment, 'It doesn't surprise me, as Jack himself would say, he's an enema. Me, I think he aspires to being an enigma, but he's just a nice bloke rubbing along, living his philosophy, *misery is optional*. He is sensitive and caring, ugly as shit, but attractive at the same time, has a heart and it's big, and I want him to get to know me, but if he only half gets to know me, and over a time, I will be happy. He cares about what is happening to this country and I am even thinking of going on a demonstration with him, if the weather is fine; Jack's one that. But most of all, Jackie, I love the twat.'

'I know you do, Mandy, and I wanted to say he is clearly not over his wife. You will help him with that, because you are right for him.'

Mandy smiled and leaned forward, her elbows on the desk and her chin in her hands, she released a sigh. 'Thank you, I appreciate that,' but knew there had to be a sting in the tail and waited for it.

'Meesh is a different story, however. The other women are talking, convinced you will keep them safe, and I hope and pray you can. They will testify, so you have your man. They are however, fucked up, especially Meesh, seeing her own mother murdered, and maybe Biscuit as well. She will break, and we have to watch for the signs. She has bonded with Gail and her family, which is good, although it's chaos in that house. It's Jack, and you I worry about. Can you do what is right for the kid?'

Mandy still had her chin in her cupped hands, staring at this radiant and elegant black woman, hair in a croissant, 'What is right?'

'There are no rights or wrongs, just consistency, which has to come from Gail and her family, but I think, Jack, you, and now Dolly by the looks of it, will need to be there, as sort of, and I hate the word, Godparents?'

Mandy became animated, 'Oh well, Jack's your man there, him and Father O'Brien are as thick as thieves,' and she lifted her head out of her hands so she could cross her fingers and wave them in the air.

'All may not be what it seems. I think Jack likes Father O'Brien and they respect each other, and if Jack has someone to talk to, then that is good, after all, you have me.'

'And who do you have, Jackie?'

'I have Gill.' Mandy looked a bit taken aback. 'Don't look so shocked, if it wasn't that you have so clearly fancied Jack since I've known you, I would have had a go at you myself. Jack says you are a very attractive woman, he talked to me, he described your face with his eye shut, and that's how I know he loves you, because he described the woman I see.'

'I thought something had changed when Meesh said you told her Jack called you Phil, and it was funny.'

Jackie laughed, 'You know me well.'

'I've had my suspicions about Father Mike,' Mandy said, 'but maybe, seen in a prudential light, it is a good relationship.' PP she thought, but didn't punch the air, not wishing to show this woman who fancied her, she was as big a twat as Jack.

'So, too much happening? My advice, take it slow. Jack's like a dog on heat, but at least he's getting regularly injured and that will slow him down, but I can see by your face that may not necessarily be the case. Don't worry, let it happen naturally, and try not to let the wise head interfere too much. What's happening with the case now?'

Mandy blushed and Jackie had her confirmation, 'There's a press conference at five, watch that if you can, but we're all but done. We haven't caught the top men, but we'll keep trying. The spooks have the other bits, and Paolo's happy he has a nick, and a murder no less.'

'And Jack, what does he feel.'

Mandy sat back and thought, rubbed her tired eyes, 'Jack will not let it go, even if they bust him at the tribunal. God knows what he will do when he gets to sixty-five?'

'He will have you by then, what does he feel about the tribunal?'

'Frankly, Pugwash has him banged to rights. Jack says, you always come up against these expert committee men, practiced in the art of arse protection, manipulation, and nothing else. Jack's a doer, he acts, and sometimes he gets it wrong, but his motivation is always for the good, he has instinct, even though we take the piss out of his eye, the so-called twitching. Did you hear about the Osama thing?'

'Did I, it's all over the place, what a hoot.'

Mandy nodded and laughed with Jackie, 'Well, Jack is convinced that all is not right in that State of Denmark, and he refers back to his eye.'

'What do you think about his eye, Mands?'

'Did you not hear me? He's an ugly bastard, but I do not see the eye.'

Jackie's eyes rolled, 'No, you plank, thank the Lord I never got fixed up with you. I meant do you think he has intuition, and does he have a point about Osama's, and more to the point will you back him?'

'Yes, to all of those, except I would make a wonderful and supportive Dyke.'

'I know, and it's my loss, and Jack's gain.'

'I'll keep you posted just in cases, you know that's one of Jack's, don't you?'

'What?'

'Just in cases, from the film *Love Actually*; Jack loves Rom-Coms, the daft bugger.'

Jackie had a light bulb moment, 'I wondered why I had been saying it lately, Gill must have thought I was stupid.'

'I am sure she would never think that.'

Jackie stood, 'I must take Meesh back to Gail's.'

Mandy bounced into action and headed for the door, 'I'll wake Jack, he would hate to miss her.'

Jackie's face had a nonplussed grin, 'You were not kidding with the shushing, Jack's asleep in the deckchair?'

'No, he often has an afternoon kip.'

'Mandy, I take back all I said, you must need your brains tested.'

'I know, Jacks, isn't it lovely,' and like Tigger, she bounced off to the CP room, and Jackie looked on, a mixture of astonishment and a face like Eeh-Haw.

THIRTY-EIGHT

THE NEWSHOUNDS WERE POSITIVELY EXCITED, THIS STORY had everything; murdered policeman, sex slaves, paedophilia, skinheads and Nazis, and finally a shootout at the OK Corral. What would happen, Mandy thought, if they knew about the spooks and the drugs, which had to be omitted for follow up positions? Spotty opened the door and led the way, determined to at least give some semblance of control. His mum must be watching Mandy thought, tugging the Commander's sleeve, so Spotty was on his own, suddenly feeling conscious of his exposure.

It felt tense when Mandy and the Commander walked out, like a conductor and soloist appearing in front of an orchestra; an air of expectation. Spotty wanted to sit in the middle, bloody kids Mandy thought, and thought of Jack and his front, centre seat, gathered around the Telly in the CP room. Spotty did the introductions, hesitating over the Amanda, nearly calling her Mandy, he got through it and sat back, a mixture of relief and pride. His mum is definitely watching Mandy thought, a picture of Nobby on the naughty step forced itself into her mind, an unbearable desire to burst into hysterical giggles, then felt she might cry; she had never choked in a press conference, but here she was, choking.

The Commander picked up on what was happening, and so did Jack, who eased himself up and waddled down the stairs, through reception, along a number of corridors and entered at the back of the press room to stand beside Sitting Bull, who was nursing a newly acquired agitated expression; Jack was not supposed to happen.

The Commander was speaking of the past few days, 'Nearly a week has seen some dramatic events in Portsmouth, culminating in a shooting incident outside this police station last night when two gunmen fired at the Superintendent,' pointing to Mandy. He was intimating to the press *Go easy*, but Jack saw she was buckling. He walked deliberately through the crowd; Sitting Bull grabbing the air behind him. He kicked Bernie off his chair and swinging it up to the dais, he put it next to Mandy so his leg rubbed hers, she didn't resist. He raised his pink hand into the air and waved, 'Sorry I'm late.' For a few moments you could have heard a pin drop, before the whole house rocked with laughter, and Jack, never one to disappoint an audience, stood up, bowed, and waved his pink hand some more.

Back in the CP room Connie said, 'Jack got ping hand,' Frankie smiled, and Connie put her arm around her waist; those who were interested could see Connie snuggle in.

Jo-Jums did look, 'Fucking hell, Frankie, this isn't the back row of the pictures.' They all looked now, and Frankie kissed Connie full on, and a blushing Chinese girl emerged with a huge smile on her face. Jack would have looked at that and said, "What a team, make's you proud, don't it," Jo-Jums thought.

Meanwhile, Jack had just about finished milking the audience, Mandy pulling his trousers, he bent down, 'Steady on love, can't you wait until later?' Mandy laughed. It is said this is what endeared her to the viewing public, the clip shown over and over, but Jack said it was because they wanted to see a nice-looking bird undress him on national telly. He did eventually sit, and when a semblance of order returned, the Commander looked to Spotty, who addressed the press.

'I think most of you know Inspector Jane... I mean, Jack Austin.'

The journalists loved the joke, consummately delivered, so Jack waved his pink hand for the hell of it, this was like no other police press conference. Mandy summoned a calm pose, put her stopping the traffic hand up, her serious head on, and in a moment there was quiet. She spoke. 'The people of this City, this Police service and me, have cause to be grateful to this man today,' and she turned to Jack.

'Steady, babes, I've had me clap,' but he put his pink hand in the air and applied a cheesy grin. Jack could see the Chief at the back of the room with rolling eyes and would have loved to call out, "They will stay like that if the wind changes," but Mandy was continuing.

'Last Thursday, and following a long and careful investigation, Inspector Austin called a raid on the houses in north Portsmouth we have spoken of before.' She felt, her nose didn't grow, considered it already too big; maybe she had lied a lot as a kid. 'Sadly, we were not in time to save DS Smith and one of the women held captive, but as a result of this effort we have been able to frustrate a paedophile ring, and what is thought to have been a right wing disruption of this city. The detail of this will be in your press packs at the end.'

Spotty beamed so his mum would know he had done this bit.

Mandy continued, 'Inspector Austin took charge of the investigation that grouped the resources of the Serious Crime

Unit, Vice and Drugs, and within a few days an arrest was made and subsequently a man has been charged with the murder of the woman in the house. We expect to charge this same man with the murder of the policeman in a few hours' time.' This brought about shouts and hands up, and Spotty quieted them. Mandy continued, 'As the investigation developed momentum, so it became clear the Home Office would need to be informed, and Inspector Austin coordinated a strategy involving officers from MI5 and the French police, which will remain confidential for the time being.'

She paused, more scrambling to feet and shouted questions ensued. Spotty, rising to the occasion, put his hand up and with a brilliant dramatic effect brought them to silence, and to Jack's amazement and admiration, Spotty never said a thing; he nodded to Mandy.

'Finally, as Inspector Austin and I were leaving the station yesterday evening, a car pulled up and a gunman began shooting. If it were not for the observation and speedy reactions of the Inspector...' and she looked at Jack, this bit was replayed a lot on the telly as well, because it was clear in Mandy's eyes what she felt for him. 'If it were not for, Jack, I would not be here now. I commend also the bravery of Sergeant Barney Rubble,' a little titter among the audience, but they knew better than to disrupt, this was fantastic and it was clear she was stressed and not realised she had used Barney's nickname; what the hell was his name anyway Jack thought, but Mandy continued. 'These two officers approached the gunman whilst still firing; Inspector Austin disabled the car's rear tyres and as the driver tried to escape, the first gunman was pulled from the car, disarmed, and the sergeant disarmed the second gunman, the driver. Unfortunately, in the incident Inspector Austin was injured...' Jack waved his pink hand and gave another cheesy grin. Mandy continued, 'As you can see the Inspector has not recovered from the knock on his head when he tackled and arrested the murderer we have charged,' she laughed and the room joined in, as did the Commander.

Spotty saw his moment as Jack and Mandy gazed at each other. 'We can take a few questions; BBC yes?'

'Superintendent can you tell us more about the Home Office involvement and MI5?'

Her response was matter-of-fact, professional, she had regained her poise, 'I refer you to their spokesman.'

'Superintendent, can you say the investigation is now closed?'

Here Jack put his hand on Mandy's, and without thinking, she gripped it with her other hand; another shot repeated on TV. 'I'll answer this Amanda,' and Jack stood, faced the assembled journalists, waited for absolute quiet. 'We have opened a can of worms, arrested and charged a number of people,' Jack could see the Chief rolling his eyes at the back of the room and thought there's never a wind change when you want it. 'We have made significant progress, but there are people out there, powerful and probably well-concocted people...' a rumble of chuckling that confused him, '...people who have put into motion a plan, which has resulted in the murder of a fine young policeman. Four women and three children, that we know of, abducted, systematically abused, and sold like mediaeval slaves; at least one woman murdered...'

He paused, felt the pain of the victims, 'These kids and their mothers fell off the State radar, why? We will be looking into that and will not rest until we have those people responsible. I will not rest,' Jack stressed. 'Finally, there are other investigations ongoing that have been generated from this case. Despicable things have been done, things that just should not happen in our so-called civilised society, this Big bloody Society, and despite the cutbacks we have to weather, I say to you perpetrators...' and he paused again, and with his good hand he pointed into the TV cameras, '...I am coming for you. There are vulnerable people out there and we will not desert them, think on that.' He sat.

To a man and woman, the press corps were on their feet applauding. Jack thought they sensed blood, but Bernie later said the press guys were genuinely moved. Spotty calmed things down, 'I think we will call it a day there.'

But the press were not to be denied, and it was Bernie who shouted, 'Commander, is there a date for Inspector Austin's tribunal?'

Subdued, the press looked to the Commander, who looked over at Jack, apologetically, 'I am sorry to say, yes. Friday week, in a Guildhall committee room commencing at ten a.m.'

Questions addressed to Jack, 'Inspector, do you have anything to say to Captain Pugwash?' a ripple of laughter. 'Inspector?' Jack had gone into a dream, 'Inspector what do you say to Pugwash?'

'Jack, you don't need to answer that,' the Commander said, trepidation written across his face.

But Jack was on a roll, and Mandy felt scared for him, but strangely proud. He stood and waited, looked up at the ceiling, back down, and then spoke clear and strong, his eye directed into the BBC camera, *Know Thine Enemy.'* Jack grinned, waved his pink hand. Mandy jumped up to stand with him. The press corps stood and applauded, civilised and respectful. Mandy pushed him, to stop him waving his stupid hand around, making any more of an idiot of himself, and they made it to and through the door. Mandy leaned against the wall and blew all the air out of her lungs, took a deep breath and did it again. Spotty sauntered into the corridor, followed by the Commander who looked shattered, but he shook Jack's good hand, 'Heaven help us, Jack, my pension's in place, I hope yours is.'

They could hear Sitting Bull puffing and blowing, 'Sir, will you join me in the Community Policing room please?' Jack said as he turned and strutted off, determined to make it to the stairs before the Chief blew. He didn't hear the Chief blow, but he did hear Mandy running to catch him, she tugged his sleeve and he turned to face her, 'I know, I'm a total fuck-up.'

'Yes, you are, but you are my fuck-up, so shut the fuck up,' and she pushed him against the wall and on tip toes kissed him passionately. Eventually she came up for air, 'Fuck, I needed that,' lowered her feet, turned and led him by his good hand to the Community Policing room.

As they walked in, still hand in hand, the team were gathered around the TV, a look of worry and awe. Jack stood quietly until he had their attention, stepped forward, so he was on his own, 'In a moment the Chief and Commander will be through that door,' they were there already and listening, 'I fully expect to be bollocked and probably busted, if not by Sitting Bull then by Catkins Pugwash. I want you all to know this. I'm an old-fashioned copper. I believe in what is right and if that offends people, so be it.' He paused, not for dramatic effect, because he was emotional. He restarted, energised, 'If an officer cannot commit to these principles. If a police officer feels he has to watch his back all the time. If a police officer feels he has not the trust of his fellow officers. If a police officer has to sit and think what might be written in the minutes. If a police officer feels he cannot do his job lest he offend someone too fucking precious to be poufy footing around in this station, then, he is no member of the police force I want to be in.' A nervous titter.

'I'm a hothead, but I'm not a maverick. I'm a team player, and if it seems sometimes I am not conversing with the team, it's because I am protecting the team; my team. My team that I will fight tooth and nail for, and if all of this is not good enough for any one of you, and I will say that to the Chief when he gets here, then I will save Pugwash the fucking effort and resign here and now. I am proud of you people. We've been through a lot this last week. Lost a colleague, had to work long hours, Nobby on the naughty step, and to top that off, some bastard nicked my bike and its probably halfway back from France as we speak, filled with drugs,' he was breaking up, choking. Mandy went to move to him but he started up again. 'I'm sorry if I've let you down. I am knackered and I'm going home, and if you can all resist an "ooh err matron," I would like Amanda to come with me, if she will.'

He was unaware Mandy had stepped forward, it had been the equivalent of berserking and now, he felt exhausted, but it was Mandy's turn and clear for all to see. She touched Jack's hand to shut him up. 'You all know I love this man, and I will stand by him because of that alone, but I am proud to stand with him as a police officer, as a man, a real man, even if he is a feckin' eejit with a pink hand. He saved me yesterday, and he saved me just now on the podium, for that I love him more, but most of all, I respect him.'

There was a shout of "Hip, hip hooray, and for they are jolly good fellows", so old fashioned, but it felt right, though was short lived, a hush, the Chief had moved to stand next to Jack. 'And I stand with you Jack, and you all as well, so get back to work, and Jack take this girl home and get on with some fucking knitting.'

Jack nodded, his eye was red, 'Thank you, sir.'

'Don't thank me, we have Pugwash's tribunal to get through. Heaven help us, and save us from blinkered sailor boys.' The hornpipe dancing was lost on Jack; he was exhausted.

THIRTY-NINE

JACK GRABBED HIS JACKET, AND, LEANING INTO A SHARP bend and swerving to miss his messages, he followed Mandy into her office, squealing his tyres, flipping corners, 'School's out,' Jo-Jums called as he departed.

He parked his bike and shuffled to stand behind Mandy as she slumped in her chair, she rolled her neck and sighed. He placed his hands on her shoulders and began to knead. 'That's nice, don't stop,' he didn't, and he let her talk while he pressed the stress from her body. 'Christ, you can have days when nothing happens, and then you have a week like we've just had.' She leaned into his kneading, he worked a little harder and she responded. He leaned over and nibbled her lobe; the ebbing tension was replaced by building excitement. He kissed her neck and allowed his good hand to slide inside her blouse, his finger caressing the outside of her bra; her nipple reacted to the gentle grazing. A muffled moan, 'What part of let's take this slowly did you not understand?'

'Shall I stop?'

'No,' urgency in her command. She uncrossed her legs, slid

274

down in her seat and her skirt rode up. Jack was leaning over kissing her lips when a knock and the door opening caused Mandy to leap, the back of her head clunking Jack's nose.

Alice stifled a disrespectful guffaw, 'Sorry, Ma'am, message for Jack.'

'Alice,' Mandy was breathless, 'next time, wait until I say come, before entering,' she knew as soon as she said it.

'Talking to me, or Jack?' Jack could not resist a chuckle, even though he was concerned if he would need surgery on his nose, checking to see if it was bleeding.

'Droll Alice, I still have a bone to pick with you, kissing my man in a pub. What did you want Jack for?'

'I was undercover, Guv, and Father Mike's downstairs, he's left several messages.'

'It's only a few hours since his last confession!' Mandy leaned back in her chair and looked at his upside-down face, 'What is it with you and that Priest? Get rid of him, get back here, and this time we will lock the door.'

'I'll go then, shall I?' Alice didn't wait for an answer, she spiralled out and wafted along the corridor.

Jack shuffled to the door. 'Don't be long, ugly,' Mandy called, and Jack managed two fingers of his good hand behind his back and let the door close behind him, and they said he couldn't multi-task.

He heard Mandy chuckle and mutter, 'Multi-task?'

———

THE RECEPTION WAS TEEMING with old trout; women, all looking alike, having been trawled from the Women's Institute or the Knitting Circle, the twin set and pearls brigade. Father Mike was squashed against the far wall, looking distinctly discomforted. As Jack wriggled his way through the shoal of old cold fish, all moving and twisting in the same direction, Jack saw Hissing Sid raise his head above the shimmering sea of grey and blue rinse, 'Got a special on Cod and Chips, Sid?' Jack shouted.

'Ah, Inspector Austin,' and this caused the shoal to turn in unison, and as his head bobbed to the surface, Jack could see Sid grinning, a face like a cartoon rubber on the end of a child's pencil.

'Inspector Austin,' not a question but an instruction that could only be borne out of that middle-class confidence and arrogance that insists it must be listened to, and right now. Jack always said you heard people like this in John Lewis stores, talking loudly about knitting, sewing and even bra sizes. Jack knew this because he often took a detour through ladies' under-wear, had even developed a sideways glance almost indistin-guishable, allowing him a good look at the knickers and bras; an accomplished dirty old man.

Affecting a guttural theme from *Jaws* in his head, and in his best Captain Mayhap voice, Jack addressed the fish, 'Ladies, what's going on here, Aah Ha?' Okay, pirate voice.

A head fish emerged, and it reminded him of one of those ugly ones you see on fish stalls in European markets, 'Inspector Awstin, we are the representatives of the East Cosham Women's Guild.' Jack thought, not far off fart-faced Jam and Jerusalem. 'We need your assurance our policing will be increased so we can sleep safe in our beds at night.' Jack thought, the way you look, luv, I would say you're definitely safe. 'I beg your pardon Inspector.'

Sidling, squeezing, baby steps, Jack was slowly making his way to the door and Father Mike, 'Did I just say that out loud?'

Head fish returned to the surface, he noticed all the wrin-kles on her face and thought how come Mandy's wrinkles look lovely, 'You did, you rude man.'

The fun was dissipating, so he cast his net, 'Ladies, you need to be raising this with the Chief Constabule or your MP. Failing that I would suggest a word in the shell like of your dear Mr Mackeroon or his sycophant sidekick, Blott.'

'Blogg.'

'I beg your pardon?' Nearly there, Jack could almost reach out and touch Mike.

'It's Mr Blogg, and whilst we may not have voted for him, at least he is doing something to help us to turn the country around.'

Jack reached the door and looked pleadingly for Sid to press the release button. Sid was enjoying this contretemps with the fish people. Lady, how's your father, old boot Smythe, was still haranguing Jack and getting full vocal support from her fellow poisson preserve makers, while Jack was mouthing to Sid, 'Open the feckin' door.'

Sid leaned, 'The bike, Jack?'

'Alright, it was Nobby, but I said I would cover for him.'

'Nobby?'

Jack nodded, 'Now let us in.'

'What's the magic word?'

'Let us in pretty pleeeeease with brass knobs kind Sid the honest injun.'

The door fell open and Jack and Father Mike were sucked into the vacuum of the security lobby and then through to the interview room corridor.

'In here, Mike.' Jack went into the first interview room and there was Paolo, Jed Bailey, Buddha and Len, 'Len, Buddha, sorry.'

Heard as the door closed, "Lionel", "Whose fucking Buddha?", "You, I think".

'Let's try this one, Mike,' It was empty, and Jack thought, all this time he never knew where Dolly kept her aerosols, and all of a sudden thought of a deckchair song, 'Aerosols are cheap today, cheaper than yesterday,' Italian opera, nothing like it.' Mike agreed it was nothing like it. Irritated, Jack turned to Father Philistine, 'What's so important? I had a very important meeting on the go.'

'No, you didn't, you were fondling and kissing Mandy.'

'How the fuck?'

'I guessed, but right by the looks of it, 658 to 1, I think.'

'Bugger off 658, I still have three thousand from the other day.'

'I give in, now shut-up, I need to talk to you.' Jack applied his victory smile, wobbled his head and hummed "Doctor Who." 'Jack, I've had a message from Mickey Splif, Keanu is reporting, and you know what I think about that, but you may have had a point when your eye wrinkled.'

'Itched Mike, how many times, and then I get a sort of pain behind the loose skin, gives me Gyp as my Nan used to say.'

Matching Jack's irritation, 'Whatever, Jack. Del-Boy has a team in place, but we need to get Keanu out, it's not safe.'

'Shut-up, Mike, he's only working Saturdays.'

'He picked up some time after school, the point is, he's there now, and it's dangerous.'

The door opened and Mandy pushed herself in, observing two late middle-aged men face to face arguing in a tiny cleaner's cupboard, and thinking, this can only happen with Jack. 'A ménage a trois was not what I had in mind, but the room is so appealing, especially the smell, a girl could be tempted. Jack, you left me on the hook.'

Mike looked worried; welcome to my world Jack thought. 'Mandy sweet'art, I will manage your Artois's later, but for now the spooks have a set up at Osama's and we have to get Keanu out before they make the take down,' he looked at Mike, 'that's how the Yanks say it.' Philistine Mike was unimpressed, and embarrassingly for Mandy, Mike fumbled in his trouser pockets, seemingly for ages, causing them all to shuffle around. Eventually he handed a piece of paper to Jack; familiar she thought. Jack read and at the same time tumbled through the cupboard door. 'Mike you'd better go out the back way. Mandy, some things to sort,' and still a gangling stick man, he disappeared rapidly down the corridor. Mike left and Mandy caught Jack up as he held the door of the rear staircase for her.

'One day you are going to tell me about you and Jesus,' she said to his bouncy arse cheeks as they bobbed up the stairs.

'I heard that,' he said, puffing, looking back at a smiling beautiful woman with her tongue out.

FORTY

'ALICE SPRINGS,' HER HEAD POPPED UP, 'WE NEED Jo-JUMS back, now please.' Jack was issuing orders from the stair door-way, waiting for Mandy. 'Get Frankie and Confucius, I need them on the computers, if you could get into that now I would be most exceedingly obliged, my lovely.'

'I'm here, Jack,' a furtive Jo-Jums slipping from the tea room.

Alice had her hand up, 'Frankie and Connie are in the ladies locker room.'

'Well, get them out, this is urgent.'

'Do you have a twitch in your eye, Sir?'

'What's that got to do with the price of fish?'

'I was thinking back to when you stormed Osama's, know what I mean nudge, nudge?'

Jack caught on, 'Okay, knock a few times if you have to, but get them back here, blimey it's all going on here today.'

'Or not,' Jo-Jums said as a sheepish Wallace appeared from the tea room.

'Well, I didn't see that coming; Chop, Chop everyone,' and

Jack handed Jo, Mike's note. 'Get KFC to patch that into their box of tricks, sweet'art, and set up a command, Mandy will brief you. Wally, Nobby, arses into gear you're driving me to Osama's, and Alice, I need you to get Uncle Alfie to meet me there with a couple of reliable mates, atom bomb urgent, okay?'

Alice responded putting her jacket on, 'Jack, can I come with you? I'll call Oncle Alfie from the car.' Jack thought it looks like you're coming anyway, and he needed more exertion classes.

Jack kissed Mandy lightly on her cheek, 'Sorry about this, lover, keep something warm for me.'

'Hot water bottle?'

'Won't need it, love,' and having achieved the last word, he dashed off with Wally, Nobby, with Alice, following him down the stairs phoning her oncle. 'Wally, you got your car?'

'Yes, sir.'

'When this is over, I want you to tell me about you and Jo-Jums before I smash your head in.' Wally looked embarrassed, Alice took it in her stride.

More red faces from Connie and Frankie, but more Connie, Mandy thought. Jo-Jums passed the note to Frankie. Mandy spoke to the Chinese computer officer, 'Connie, it's a rite of passage, screwing in the locker rooms, and between you and me if this shite had not happened I would have been shagging on my desk, so, get on with your job then get home with Frankie and do it properly, okay?'

'Yes, Ma'am.' A crimson Connie went over to Frankie, the trouper, who put her arm around her Chinese partner, kissed her cheek, and commenced briefing. Frankie had already tapped in the codes, and on the screens they could see various views of Osama's Asian Emporium, and what looked like the bloke from the A34.

Not knowing how these things worked, Mandy took a chance, 'Del-Boy, is that you?'

'Ah, Miss Pumps, is Jack on his way?'

'He is.'

'Has he thought of a way to get the kid out?'

'If I know Jack, he will wing it, but it will be a plan, and will have as good a chance as anything else anyone can think of.'

'Yeah, that's Jack alright,' he chuckled knowingly. Jo and Mandy looked at each other quizzically, then responded to some shuffling noise and a little resistance somewhere behind Del. 'Mands, this looks like the bloke Jack asked to meet him, a Mr Fish.'

'Alfie Herring.'

'Sorry, sweet'art, didn't get that.'

She repeated, 'Herring.'

'Well, get deaf aids then,' and he laughed, looked at his Oppos beside him, who also thought it was a brilliant quip. Before Mandy could get to her repost, Del-Boy had turned his back and was talking to Alfie, when Jack appeared, stick man fighting the soreness.

'It's Jack, Mandy.'

And showing her irritation, 'I can see, you know.'

'Yes, but can you hear?'

There was a chuckle from KFC who were still tapping things and Mandy smiled. Jack turned and began to speak to a discreet mic and camera, a hearing piece to his ear, 'Mandy, Jo, can you hear me?'

'Loud and clear, Gobshite,' Mandy responded.

'Is that you, Jo?' Last word again, Mandy thought. 'Listen up, babes, Del-Boy has the con liaising with you and Jo, okay.'

'Okay,' Mandy looked to Jo, 'Con?'

'Prep some of the boys in blue, we'll need armed support, paramedics and ambulances, fire brigade, and Jo, no blues and twos. Connie, I hope Mandy has reassured you about rites of passage and all that, 'cause I need you focused sweet'art.' Mandy thought, good man, very thoughtful. 'Connie and Frankie, add this to your set up,' and he looked at another piece of paper, glanced at Del and read out some codes, 'your spook contact, he will tell you where to direct the armed support and where to stack the back-up, have you got that on screen?'

'Yes, we have contact now.'

'Okay, well, I'm going in with Alfie, so, Mandy, shut-up and listen, I love you very much and I'm ready, but I thought we might skip the pictures tonight, hope that's okay.'

Mandy sensed a tear tingle on her cheek, 'Got that, I love you too, and don't take any risks.'

Jack turned to a spook nearby and said, 'This thing's up the spout. If she gets back on the line tell her I said get another pair of stockings out of her drawer and make sure she has them on for when I get back.'

Jo-Jums put her hand on Mandy's shoulder as they watched Jack waddle up to Alfie and his cronies, and they sauntered and rolled jauntily to the shop, stick man incongruously following. As they got in amongst the street display stalls, two of the men started fighting. Jack got in-between, his Lowry arms wheeling and spinning.

'My God, what's happening?' Mandy and Jo could only watch. Jack was shouting, swinging the odd punch, they couldn't hear but they knew Jack, there had to be lots of swearing, as they bundled inside the shop.

Osama came out of the back as a shelf of eastern produce went west, 'Mr Austin, what the fuck, in it?'

'I'll tell you what, that oik there,' and one of Alfie's mates pointed to Keanu, shaking like a leaf, 'he's been knocking off my daughter, and she's only fourteen.'

Alfie faced the man up, 'Keep your fucking hands off, or you'll have to deal with me.'

'You don't scare me, Herring.'

Jack grabbed Keanu and pulled him aside, 'Get out and run at least two streets.' Keanu needed no further prompting, and the youngster shot out just as the bundle escalated. Alfie, Charlie, and some bloke Jack had never heard of, but looked like Plug out of *the Beano*, went at it hammer and tongs, more shelves went flying; magnos and rice Jack noticed. Mrs Ali was hitting Alfie with a stick. Jack grabbed her, she screamed, and Jack shouted to Osama, 'Get the fuck out now, in it,' and he dragged Mrs Ali as Alfie physically picked up Osama, knocking Jack over, causing him to release Mrs Ali, but she was collected by Plug and the other man, and they made their burdensome dash for the exit.

Back at the CP room, a stressed Mandy mumbled, 'It's Keanu, they've got him out. Come on, Jack.' They watched Alfie exit with Osama under his arm, the other two men carried Mrs Ali. 'Where's Jack?' There was a yellow then orange flash on all of four screens and the front of the shop blew out. Alfie and Osama went sprawling. Mrs Ali and the two men went down but seemed to be shielded as they had dragged the big woman to the hairdressers, still offering cheap manicures, 'Oh my God!'

'Mandy,' Jo looked. Mandy had gone rigid, blood visibly draining from her face, tears that at first welled, dribbled, then stood out like rivulets on her cheeks; she seemed not to blink, no breath. Out of nowhere a detached keening grew in intensity, a high-pitched wail came from her gut, and grew steadily in volume. Every woman converged on Mandy to offer support, hugged a screeching Banshee as the keening grew in intensity. Dolly pushed, her tiny body smothered Mandy, and together they dropped to the floor. Mandy was cradled by this thin and diminutive old woman, smelling of lavender polish and ever so slightly of wee.

The computers were spilling out detached voices, Del-Boy's, clear and in control. 'Jo, I need you, focus, back-up, fire brigade and paramedics now.'

Jo responded, 'On the way, Jack, what's happening?'

Del replied, 'Jo, the smoke and debris is just clearing and the place is afire. I'm sorry, Jack didn't get out, they must have blown themselves up.'

'Can you get in there?'

'Jo, we have to keep clear for secondary explosions, and there may be a shooter still active, it can happen.' Mandy heard and the wailing that had begun to subside, resumed, increased in volume and intensity. 'Fuck me what's that?' a shout from Del, 'armed backup, on my command, medic, and zoom a camera in on that movement.' A zooming picture revealed the smoking, blown out frontage.

'Someone's coming out. Oh Jeeez, it's Jack,' Frankie said. Mandy sprung up, Frankie called, 'Keep her back, looks like his skin has peeled off. Oh, Jack.'

There was another disembodied shout, 'Whose that fucking idiot, come back, lad.'

'Nobby,' nobody had noticed the Commander, 'Oh God, son, what are you doing?' On the screen they watched Nobby plough through debris, settling ash, and put Jack's arm over his shoulder, Jack was losing it, and Nobby was struggling. Mandy looked on, not breathing; the keening had stopped. Armed and shielded units began slowly to approach, someone else broke through the lines and they heard Del-Boy shout, 'Mike.' Father Mike reached them and with Nobby they had Jack back on his feet.

Dolly spoke, 'What has happened to you, Jack?' she was weeping. Jack raised his pink hand, now a singed, distorted shape, like a big drippy Halloween monster's claw; he was waving it.

An armed response officer reached them and reported back. 'Sir, I have Jack, he appears to be covered in what I think looks like, and certainly smells like, mango.' There was a roar of laughter as Jack stood erect and waved his drippy pink hand, the zoomed image showed him covered in a pulp of orange goo. There was blood, but it looked remarkably as though Teflon Jack had survived.

They reached Del-Boy, Jack waved a paramedic away, 'In a minute, mate.'

'Jack, you gave us a scare.'

'Del-Boy, is that thing working?'

'Yes, it's patched to Mandy and...'

Before Del could finish, Jack was speaking, 'Amanda,' he was breathy, but determined, 'close your mouth we are not a cod fish, get the stockings on sweet'art, I'm coming home.'

Del-Boy butted in, 'I was going on to say this is patched to your Nick and the Home Office, I do believe the Home Secretary is listening...'

Jack was completely unfazed, 'That twat. I never voted for you, and get the money back into the police you short-arse, baldy cretin,' then Jack collapsed, and paramedics swarmed.

Mandy screamed, 'Jack, you Gobshite, I'll tear your balls off one by one.'

Dolly pulled her arm, 'He's acting, look...'

Jack was winking and mouthing, 'Just rub-em a bit.'

Del-Boy came on screen, 'They're taking him to QA hospital, Mandy, I gather they know him quite well.' There was a murmur of laughter around the room, more of relief than jocularity. Jack was not on all cylinders, but firing, nevertheless. 'Mandy, it's time me and my team disappeared, be nice to meet up sometime. Frankie and Connie, good work, upgrades coming, so watch this space, your Comms will go down any minute.'

He turned to go but Mandy called out, 'Del, how do you know Jack?'

He looked back, 'Mandy, Jack and I go back a long way. I never thought he would get over Kate, but I think you have him there; bless you for that.' He turned to one of his men and Mandy could hear him saying he was ready. He swivelled back to the camera, 'Mandy, I'm off, I've a meeting with a widow, but one more thing.'

'Del?'

'Jack's not as tough as he says he is,' and he melted into the crowd, Del was gone.

'I've sorted bluebottle cabs, I'll get hold of Michael and Alana,' Jo said.

'What?' Relief, the Commander was making a twat of himself.

FORTY-ONE

'SAYS HERE YOU FELL OFF YOUR BIKE INTO A BOX OF Mangos?' the triage nurse was grinning.

'Jim, don't be a Pratt.'

'It's James,' he carried on with his checks.

'Jim get me sorted, I've a date with a beautiful woman.'

James laughed automatically but focused on Jack's vitals. Nurse Exactly was cutting away Jack's shredded clothes, cleaning him up. 'I used to like Mango, James, but mixed with blood, and what looks like rice, isn't doing me any favours right now.' James Mmm'd. 'What's this stuff?'

Jack stiffly raised his head, 'Mumbai Mix.'

'Don't you mean Bombay mix?'

There was a response from the next treatment bay, 'And that's how it all started, Bombay Mix.'

'Kipper, is that you? Exactly, can you pull that curtain back please?' The nurse looked at James who nodded, still focused on his analysis to which Jack was oblivious, which was worrying James. Exactly pulled the curtain to reveal Alfie Herring on the adjacent exam couch, 'Looks like you got smoked Kipper,' Jack remarked, and Alfie machine gunned a laugh. 'Steady, you nearly had me diving for cover.' Alfie laughed some more, and Jack thought it was a bit like being on the firing ranges.

Painfully, Alfie turned on his exam couch, 'Thank you, Jack.'

'Nurse, ask him who the Prime Monster is, I think he has a bonce injury.' More laughter from Alfie, and this was beginning to irritate Jack, a response James also noted. 'Kipper, laugh one more time like that and I will ask the nurse to pull the curtains, it's nearly my bedtime anyway.'

Jack's warning was not heeded, but Alfie was coming under control, chemically. 'Jack, seriously, thank you for saving Keanu for us.'

'You were there as well, Kipper.'

A short burst of gunfire but more subdued, 'Jack, it's you, and thank you for calling me Kipper.'

'Check his head, Jim.'

'James.'

'Thanks for the nickname, I mean, feel we have a bond now.'

''Kin hell, Kipper, you're a villain and I wear a white hat.'

'A white hat and a pink hand. Alice tells me if you don't have one of your nicknames, you're on the outside, Pugwash, brilliant; want me to have a word with 'im, subtle like?'

Jack eased himself up, propped on his elbow, 'Thank you, but leave Pugwash for now.'

'We all seem settled in here, how's he doing Jamie?' Mandy had arrived.

'It's James, not Jamie and, Jack, it is not Jim.' Jack noted Jim's irritability.

Mandy laughed, 'Sorry, Jim, I've been with him too long.'

Jack saw she had red rimmed eyes, washed out, looking her

age, and entering into the spirit, she whispered to Jim, who looked up, 'Right, Jane, let's get you upstairs.'

'Close your mouth, Michael, we are not a codfish,' she punched the air, and Jack thought she looked gorgeous, red puffed eyes, lines, age and all. His face must have conveyed that message as she responded with a warm smile; he melted, felt like crying. Mandy looked to Alfie, 'Mr Herring, ordinarily I would be very pleased to see you behind bars, but for now, I am grateful. Thank you for looking after Jack.'

'Kipper,' he said, and Mandy looked confused.

Jack flicked his head towards Kipper's bed, shrugged his shoulders, 'So what can I tell you, d 'you think it's easy,' back to Mandy and found she was peeping her head around two porters who looked like Mike and Bernie Winters. Nobody seemed to know them either, one short cheesy bloke, clearly the brains of the outfit, the other a gorilla with a grin going, "eeeeeH".

Jack's penny dropped, 'What's happening?'

Jim responded, 'Jane, you have a lot of minor wounds and you will need to be put out in order for us to treat you.'

'But I don't feel a thing.'

'We've anaesthetised the bad areas.'

'I think I would have remembered needles, Jim.'

'Alzheimer's, and you farted then fainted when you saw the needle.'

Through the machine gun fire, Jack could hear Mandy laughing, and a definite "eeeeh."

'Jamie darling, you've got potential,' Mandy said.

Jack lifted himself a little, 'Get me out of here, Bernie, eeeeh.' Nobody got the joke, but it didn't matter because Kipper laughed anyway, and Jack was grateful to hear the machine guns fading in the distance, like being taken from the battlefield.

Mandy caught up with the trolley, 'Jack, I'll be waiting for you.'

His good hand reached for hers, 'Amanda, I'm scared.'

'I know. I'll be here when you wake up.'

'What if I don't wake up?'

'Then I will fight Michael for your pogo stick.'

He grinned. 'You're definitely coming on, sweet'art.'

She smiled back at him, 'I heard you say to Dolly you thought I was past all that, and you were only interested because I wouldn't get PMT, well I've got news for you, we have the menopause.'

'Menopause, no sweat,' Jack beckoned her. 'This Sunday, I want our families together, Sunday Roast, you, your Liz and David, me, Michael, Colleen, Alana and whatshisname.' The lift bonged, "Doors Opening." 'No kidding, Tonto,' he said.

The nurse and Mike Winters laughed, Bernie went, "eeeeh," Mandy shrugged and leaned down to him as they waited outside theatre. 'Jack I will try, but you know Liz is not overly keen on you.' She noticed his eye swimming and figured it must be the pre-med he hadn't noticed being given.

'Amanda, it's time she grew up and accepted I'm not an arsehole of the first order,' referring to a quote from Mandy's daughter the last time they'd met.

'I'll try, Jack, I want her to see what I see.'

Jack made to look shocked his bits and pieces were exposed; it amused her, 'Amanda,' she bent down, 'tell the nurse I'm hurting, please.' She put her hand on his, thought of what Del-Boy had said, and kissed him, they started to wheel him in, 'Tell Michael you can have my pogo stick.' Last word again, she thought.

FORTY-TWO

Mandy insisted she was okay for the press conference, Spotty was waiting to get going. She detected a look of youthful yearning in his eyes, probably in his loins too, and remembered Jack saying what he was like when he was a youth, and how he felt about older women, except he insisted he didn't have spots. The Commander looked back, concerned, she'd not noticed they had gone in. She put one foot in front of the other.

'There will be a statement from Commander Manners, we will then take some questions,' Spotty turned to Mandy to seek a look of approval and mutual sexual attraction. She nodded and Spotty beamed. I bet he thinks he's in there she thought; God save me from men and spotty kids.

The Commander started, 'At the last briefing, Inspector Austin reported the investigation was proceeding on other fronts. Today our enquiries led us to a shop, the Asian Emporium in the north of Portsmouth, where a suspected terrorist cell had hidden themselves, holding the owners, Mr and Mrs

Ali, as emotional hostages. We believe they hold hostage elsewhere, the Ali's son, and we are looking for him; our thoughts are with Mr and Mrs Ali tonight. Mrs Ali is recovering in hospital, shock, and worried for her son. Mr Ali has a few broken bones as does a Mr Herring, a member of the public who assisted. We will take some questions.'

Spotty selected a BBC Journalist, 'Commander, is it true the owner of the shop is called Osama by Inspector Austin?'

The Commander metaphorically slapped his forehead, 'I see the subtleties of the investigation, and the Police results, are to be skirted over so we can get to the more salacious bits. It is important to say that Mr Ali has been known, affectionately I might add, as Osama for some time, and Inspector Austin is not responsible for the nickname. Apart from what the prejudiced or the politically correct amongst us may think, Mr and Mrs Ali, are English through and through, and take great pride in their absorption of the humour, and that includes affectionate epithets.' He resisted the prompts for more questions and carried on, 'I know also many of you will now want to move onto Captain Pugwash, regardless we have had an explosion in Portsmouth today and people have died, I have forever admired the incisive investigative skills of the British Press, but I tell you this, in this police station if you do not have a nickname, you feel left out. Myself, I am known as Good or Bad Manners, and the superintendent, as Mandy pumps or Mandy lifeboats.'

Mandy coloured, but could see the Commander was consummately defusing a hot subject. She thought of what Jack would say, "They know what you're known as anyway, it's never a secret". Spotty called on another question, and various others that enquired about the operation, the explosion, who they suspected as the terrorists, but inevitably it came back to the personal.

'Superintendent, can you tell us how Inspector Austin is, please?'

She adjusted her position in her seat, which did not disguise her internal discomfort, 'Inspector Austin is in the operating theatre right now, and I will be going back to the hospital just as soon as you have all of the hot gossip you need. His condition is not life threatening, although he was joking as he went in and I felt like killing him myself.' There was laughter, and the Commander nodded approval.

'Superintendent, how long is the investigation expected to last?'

She was settling into professional mode, 'If Inspector Austin was here, he would say to you, there is a child missing and others were hurt today, members of the public who had volunteered to help him regardless of the risk to themselves. Spotty here can give the names to you afterwards.'

The press laughed, and Spotty blushed, looked deflated, after all, his mum would be watching if she were not doing his tea. Mandy realised she'd let her guard down. 'I called Jeff, Spotty, to indicate to you all he is an integral part of our team, respected by Inspector Austin, a sign to everyone around the police station Jeff is one of us.' She went on, 'For those interested, Inspector Austin is calling Mr Alfie Herring, Kipper, and Mr Herring seems rather pleased with this.'

'Superintendent, you said you were going back to the hospital, is there any truth in the rumour that you and the Inspector are...are an item?'

She responded with a warm smile, 'I can tell you I am assisting Jane Austin with his enquiries, and find him quite arresting, and yes, I have an appointment at *Specsavers*.'

She stood to laughter, and left the room, the Commander taking her lead. Spotty was taken completely unawares and knew he'd missed his chance; Mandy walking speedily and deliberately on her way out of the building, and he thought, although she was older than his Mum, she was as sexy as anything.

FORTY-THREE

Mandy sat beside Jack's bed, a sensation of mixed emotions. She was angry, he had deliberately gone into a dangerous situation and made her worry; think he was dead. This powerful emotion of love towards him, how did that happen? How could this be, when all of her sensibilities said run a mile, but in her mind's eye she saw the truly good things about Jack that outweighed the fact he was a fat and ugly juvenile. Christ, she thought, even Spotty is more mature than him.

'Mum.'

Mandy turned, shocked from her thoughts by a familiar voice, her daughter Elizabeth at the end of the bed. Mandy stood and they hugged, 'Liz, I didn't expect to see you,' leaning her head back, but maintaining the embrace.

'I thought you might need me?'

'Darling, thank you, I do need you.'

'How is he?'

'Well, if he was awake, he would be arguing to take me to the pictures,' Mandy was emotional. 'He was lucky; shielded from the blast by a pile of rice sacks. He's had to have a million splinters removed, cuts sewn or taped, but he was so ugly before nobody will notice.' Jack was groggy, he heard, but carried on drifting. Mandy had Jack's good hand in one of hers and was holding her daughter's with the other. She sensed Jack was coming around, and speaking seriously to Liz, 'He will need another operation.'

Jack was taken aback, she felt an involuntary response in his hand. Oh no, I'm worse than I thought and heard Liz respond.

'Another operation?

'Yes, he's got a mango stuck up his arse.'

Liz laughed out loud and they both turned as Jack joined them, Liz, shocked to see his eye open, not so Mandy. They shared the humour together as the nurse shooed them away, saying she needed a moment with the Inspector.

'Mum, I'm sorry I called him an arsehole, you love him, don't you?'

She hugged her daughter, 'Liz, sweetheart, Jack is one of the most infuriating men I have ever met. Certifiable loony bin material, wretchedly sexist, but not, if you can understand that, and as soon as he graduates from junior school, I may seriously consider having sex with him. So, he is a lot of things, but he is not an arsehole.'

Jack was free of clips, thermometers, blood pressure cuffs, and the nurse was shaping to pull the curtains back, 'Can I get you a bed pan, Mr Austin, perhaps you can shit the mango out and save an operation?'

'If I do nurse be sure to stay out of the line of fire.'

Mandy whispered to Liz, 'Last word, he always manages it.' Mandy's phone rang, 'I'll take this outside or they get shirty.'

Liz held Jack's gaze, his head was clearing. 'I would like you and your partner to come and have lunch with me and my family this Sunday. Can you get up from Exeketer?" He called

Exeter, Exeketer, in his best country accent; thought it would make her feel at home.

Liz ignored his outspoken thoughts, 'What do you mean, my partner?'

'Liz darlin', you need to talk to your mum, it's hurting you're leaving her out,' he put his hand up to stop her talking, and coincidentally any passing traffic, 'she knows something and nothing, but you need to tell her before she asks, trust me on this one.'

'How did you know?'

Jack managed a patronising smile, 'Despite what your mum says, I notice things, what's her name?'

'Carly.'

'Okay, will Curly come up for Sunday roast?'

Liz chuckled into her chest, 'It's Carly, and she's been pressing to meet my family, and it looks like you might be a part of that soon, do you love Mum?'

'I do, but I've had my problems.'

There was a brief silence, Liz gathering her resolve. 'Getting over the death of your wife?'

He felt a pang in the pit of his stomach, bugger, still there, 'Bingo darlin', but I'm getting there, and I will do nothing to hurt your mum, you have to believe that.'

'I do,' a slightly uncomfortable silence, 'I'm sorry I called you an arsehole, Jack, but you are a juvenile.'

'And I'm too old a juvenile to change.'

Mandy bounced back, feigning more energetic bonhomie than she truly felt, 'Well, are we getting on alright, Liz what are your plans because I was going to get Jack some stuff then come back and sit with him.'

'Whoa Neddy,' Jack, who else could it be? He nodded to Liz, and Mandy turned to face her daughter.

'What?'

'Mum, can we go out, have a drink or something?' Mandy looked to Jack, seeking an answer that was not coming. 'Mum, I want to talk. I have something to tell you.'

'You have?'

'Yes, Mum.'

'Amanda, I need to sleep, can you tell all callers, including the Gnome Secretary, I'm retiring early, please.' Mandy looked at Jack quizzically, 'Go,' he said, his exertion lessons finally paying off.

'Liz, go outside, I'll be there in a minute, I just need to push that mango further up Jack's arse,' Liz stepped away looking distinctly edgy. 'I sense Jane Austin in this?'

'You need to talk to your daughter, and she will come on Sunday.'

'Will you be okay?'

'I still have my pogo stick, now bugger off and let me sleep.'

She kissed him firmly on his lips, lifted his good hand onto her thigh and rubbed it up and down. Jack could feel the suspender button and felt immediately aroused, mentally, the rest of his body was fast asleep.

'Bye darling,' and she spun on her toes and left, punching the air as she stepped out.

'What's that about Mum?'

'Last word Liz; 632 to 1.'

'Mum, you're getting as bad as him, and what's this about the Home Secretary?'

'Jack called the Home Secretary a short arse bald cretin on the video link today.'

'Is the Home Secretary short and bald?'

'Well, I would wager Jack thought he was talking to Bill Vague,' she flicked her hands, 'think Theresa Green was a little put out though,' he can't stand her, so no sweat there, and she put her arm around her daughter and hugged her.

FORTY-FOUR

THE DOCTORS RECOMMENDED JACK STAY IN HOSPITAL A few more days. 'Resistance is futile,' Jack said, and to demonstrate his wellness, he hopped off the bed and goose stepped up and down the ward, a finger to his top lip; Hitler in baggy pyjamas, bouncing floppy bits and pieces, and in his Nuremburg rally accent, he repeated, "Resistance is futile", several times. If it worried the Doctors, Mandy couldn't see it, because they shared the merriment with the nurses and other patients; Jack's audience.

Mandy was not convinced. She had tried to ask the Doctors, in an embarrassing roundabout way, if she could sleep with Jack, and the doctors conferred. "What do you think, is Jack up for a...?" and they made obscene hand gestures. Mandy had blushed like she was fourteen, and thought to herself, you are a grown woman, a Superintendent in the police no less. She tried to say she just wanted to sleep with him to make sure he was okay, and they conferred again, and it became clear Jack had endeared himself to all the medical staff. "What do you think, will Jack be able to get any sleep if this woman was next to him?" and they laughed again, but finally one Doctor succumbed to a medical response, saying, "He may get some flash backs, but we think this unlikely. We would have kept him in another two days, for complete bed rest, if you pardon the pun. Should you sleep with him?" and here they looked at each other and smiled, "personally, I think you need your eyes, ears, and brains tested, but medically, I cannot reasonably advise against it."

Oh how they had laughed, and how red she had gone. Now, here in Jack's living room, she looked around. David, Colleen, and Carly, who Jack was insisting on calling Curly, were getting on well. Where was Liz, she hoped she had explained about Jack and his nicknames to Carly? She had a flurry of panic, but then Liz came back with Jack, who went to the basket in the window and flopped on the floor to be with Martin.

Martin was not right, and neither was Jack.

Carly was clearly very fond of her daughter. How did she not see this, and how did Jack? She would speak to him, knew this would scare him shitless, and this did provide her with a lighter moment. The vet had said Martin needed time to get back to his old self, but Jack seemed oblivious, distant. Michael was getting the roast lunch going, but it would be closer to a dinner, but as Jack said, "Is anyone in a hurry?"

'Jack, can I have a word please?' she beckoned, and he followed her up the stairs to his bedroom, making moronic face gestures to his audience below. In his bedroom, 'Sit down Jack, tell me, how do you feel?'

Not even tempted to play the fool, 'Terrible.'

'Do you feel sick, are you in pain?'

'The pain is manageable, a bit tom and dick; it's something else.' She was worried, but kept her mouth shut, 'When I went into Osama's, it was you I was thinking about, and when I woke up in hospital after the operation, you were my first thought.'

'I don't understand, what are you trying to say?'

'I've held onto Kate all this time, it has been painful, but a comfortable pain. I got used to it. I've used that pain as a crutch, and now I have thrown that away and I'm scared. I'm afraid to heap myself upon you. I think I'm fucked-up, don't want to lose you, and I don't want to take advantage either. You're too precious to me for that.'

She looked at him intensely, saw something else, 'Jack, what is...?'

He got up and ran out, 'I'm going to be sick.' Brilliant, she thought, it's like dealing with a fucking kid, and she followed him into the bathroom and knelt down, her arm on his back, whilst he was sick, crying at the same time. She put a flannel under the cold tap, wiped his forehead and dabbed his mouth, stroked his hair.

Alana and Michael were at the door, 'Dad, you okay?' Alana asked.

'He's okay,' Mandy replied, 'the doctors said not to rush things, but you know your dad. Go back down, I have this one.'

'Okay, but call if you need us,' Michael this time.

Mandy flushed the toilet and got Jack to stand. She wiped his face and got him a glass of water, he rinsed his mouth, 'Tad wobbly on the pins, luv.'

'Let's get you into bed, a bit of a lie down and you'll be as right as rain.'

'Not much of a start is it?'

'Jack, we started ages ago,' Mandy said, helping him undress and into bed. She lay down beside him; he slept almost immediately. Propping her head on her hand and elbow she watched him breathe, like she used to do with her kids; knew this was a part of Jack's growth. She was touched he was concerned about her, and this was what she had been waiting for, not the words, but a physical sign he had moved on. Jackie had said to expect Jack to drop lower, before he would rise again, and she supposed the recent trauma of these past few days had kick-started the process. She reflected on all that had happened and thought, it's no wonder he's a shattered man.

After ten minutes she went downstairs and sat at the dining table, exhausted; she'd been through the ringer too, and needed to sleep, needed to look after herself as well. She looked up and there was everyone Jack had invited, Alana and Josh, Michael and Colleen, Liz and Carly, David and Father Mike who'd brought Meesh, who was on the floor cuddling Martin.

She asked everyone to sit around the table, Meesh climbed onto her lap and Liz sat next to her Mother, Carly stood behind Liz, her hands on her shoulders making small and gentle massaging movements. Mandy noticed it was relaxing her daughter, and getting pleasure from this woman's touch; she tried to put this out of her mind. 'Today was Jack being Jack,' she said. 'I know this is what he wanted, but he should have had a day or two more in hospital, he needs rest and so do I. Jack loves his family and he wanted the ones he loved the most to be here.'

Meesh looked up, sitting on Mandy's lap, 'Me as well?'

She smiled, 'You as well darling, Jack calls you Spesh, did you know that? He has a very big heart and loads of room in it.' She stroked Meesh's hair and the little girl snuggled up, mouthing the word Spesh and smiling to herself, listening to the resonance of Mandy's voice through her chest. 'Jack was likely going to give one of his lengthy and agonisingly poignant speeches, interspersed with mediocre, bordering on diabolical, jokes that we all love to groan at...' she trailed off and looked at Jack's children who knew she was right. 'Alana and Michael, your dad is racked with guilt that he is in love with me, and I love him. He feels he has deserted Kate. Father, he could be Catholic, so much guilt.' Mike gave a Gallic shrug, quite acceptable in the circumstances. Michael looked like he was going to say something but Father Mike put his hand on his arm. Mandy looked to Alana, she was crying. 'Your dad will need our help. When he wakes up he will pretend to be his normal self, a bit like today, larking about and joking in the hospital, but, and in the parlance, your dad is at rock bottom and needs our help to start the climb up. Superficially, he will appear no different, and to allow that illusion to be shattered would shatter him.

Alana, Josh, he loves you, and he's dug a big hole with you Josh. If he were here now he would say it was to bury you in, but he doesn't mean it. He can't get out of the hole, and we need to help him up. He has this Pugwash tribunal coming up, and we all know your dad is as guilty as hell. We have however, a very bright and expensive solicitor representing Jack, one Lionel Thackeray, whom Jack calls Len, and he is giving his services free for your dad, so, who knows. He will laugh off any verdict, but if it's bad, it will hurt deep, very deep, and we all know that too. So Father Mike, is he going to need help?'

Everyone on the table turned to Mike, 'He will, and he'll have it.'

Nodding, she turned to Michael, who still had his master chef apron on, 'I'm sorry about dinner Michael, but I'm exhausted. You all need to know I love Jack. I will continue to barrack and torment him in public, Christ knows why, he likes the banter, but make no mistake, I love him dearly, and I am going back upstairs now to lie with him and look after him until he's better.' She looked down at the little girl on her lap, finger tip tilted her head and looked into the devastating green eyes, 'Meesh sweet'art, you okay with the kids today?'

Colleen swept her off Mandy's lap, 'I think we should all go to the common and the seafront. Michael get your kite. Shall we fly the kite Meesh?'

'Yes,' excited, kids are easily distracted.

'Skittish things kites,' Colleen said.

Michael hit her over the head with a cushion, '*Mary Poppins,* Colleen, there is no hope for you?' Colleen grabbed a cushion, Meesh got a cushion, everyone got cushions, even Father Mike.

Liz hugged her mum, 'I love you, Mum.'

'I know, I love you too, and I want you and Carly to stay at my flat if you're not going back to Exeter today, you can have my bed, she looks nice, and you look happy. Does David know?' Liz nodded, still cuddling her mum. 'I need a little time, but your happiness is all I care about.'

She got up, dragged her hand across the shoulders of her daughter, looked for David but he was rolling on the floor singing, "Let's go fly a kite," with the rest, except Colleen, who was singing Jack's version "although the weather's shite," Martin looking like he was on the mend, barking and licking Meesh.

Mandy trudged the stairs thinking, Jack touches so many people.

FORTY-FIVE

HAD THE SPARROWS FARTED? BRIGHT SUNLIGHT JAGGED
through cracks in the thick curtains and burned Jack's eye.
Mandy was asleep, facing away, the warmth of her body
consumed him as he wrapped his good arm around and cupped
her breast. 'Mmmm, that's nice.'

'I must have dozed off, but I feel a lot better for it.'

Still sleepy, Mandy replied, 'I'd say, it's Tuesday, d'you not
remember the doctor?'

'No, what did he say?'

She stretched her neck and shoulders, allowed his other
arm and pink hand to slide under her neck, and put her hand
on top of his, holding her breast, and softly she spoke, 'Well, he
examined you, and asked me if you'd been blown up recently,
or maybe run over by a car, shot at, or knocked off a bike or
maybe all of these and I said yes, how perceptive. He said,
"Well, that could be it then",' she paused so he could laugh, and
she felt the juddering through her breast. 'He'd spoken to the
hospital, was worried about your head, but I was able to reassure him this was normal.' His fondling was affecting her and

she allowed her hand to wander. Jack seemed a lot better; they lay together as two nestling spoons, leisurely responding to each other's caresses, and with her hand she guided him. They stayed together like that for a little time feeling the intensity grow, Jack's good hand on her breast and nipple had done its work, she abandoned herself, and Jack followed.

———

MANDY NUDGED him awake with her knee, a tray of breakfast, lunch, or dinner, he was not sure, held out in front of her. He drank in the vision, she was wearing one of his shirts, it just covered her bum. He had always considered the sight of a curvaceous woman in a man's shirt sensual, his mind drifting to the sixties and posters of screen sirens; it stirred him sexually as an impressionable teenager, and still did.

'Is this breakfast, lunch or dinner?'

'Whatever you want it to be, courtesy of that amazing son of yours, cold lamb sandwiches, and I presume these disgusting red ones with beetroot are yours?'

'Lubbly jubbly,' Jack said, already with a mouthful. He was hungry, and they ate, comfortable together, and Jack wondered at this. Was it Mandy who made things seem right or was it they had grown together for a long time, and this was a natural extension of that growth? It was an indication of Jack's state of mind he did not begin to think it might be because of any contribution he made.

Whilst Jack had slept, Mandy had spoken several times with Jackie; she did not seem to mind. Jackie thought Jack displayed classic signs of a lack of self-worth, maybe due to illogical guilt about his wife's death, maybe reaction to trauma? She suggested that after a trauma, and often over a period of time, self-esteem can plummet, but with Jack it's disguised by humour, sensitivity to others, but not to himself. Mandy thought about his eye, or was it losing Kate?

'D'you want that last bit?' Jack asked, pointing. She smiled and shoved the remains of her sandwich into his mouth, and as he chewed she felt the vibrations of his noisy jaw and fumbling fingers on her chest, thinking, why can't men undo a button with one hand? She allowed Jack to make a fool of himself and get increasingly frustrated, thinking of David as a boy. She was forever sewing buttons back onto his school shirts because he couldn't undo them, remembered showing him how to turn the button sideways, aligning it with the slot of the button hole, and miraculously, the shirt would be undone; and here's another one. She dismissed the thought of Liz and Carly, two women who could undo anything; she needed time on that one, slid her hand under Jack's and undid the buttons, one hand; his hand slipped inside the shirt.

'How'd you do that?'

'I'm putting you on a course, how to undo buttons, and you still have to pass the bra strap test,' his reply lost in a mist as he explored her body.

———

IT HAD BEEN NIGHT, then dawn, and the feckin' birds whistled; Jack was not a countryman. He could hear the shower, seven thirty, he'd passed sparrow's fart again without waking; what is this woman doing to me? Mandy padded in naked, her hair wet, black and dangling like sore fingers and he realised he loved Mandy's face. He was, of course, remarkably stimulated by her body, she was gorgeous, a fulsome woman with curves, not like the stick insects that hang on the arms of famous people, which is why Jack thought celebrities were on the whole, thick; all that money and they get a stick. However, he needed only to look at Mandy's face and it did everything the rest of her body would do if he gave it a chance, which of course he would; there was no need to be silly. He watched as she rubbed her hair with a small towel.

'I won't offer a penny for them, I can see,' and she came over, kissed him, and her breasts swung pendulously in front of his face; no wonder women dominate men he thought. She sat beside him still rubbing her hair, her underarms showing a blur of shaved hair, her head on the side, she smiled, 'D'you know what I like about you, Jack?'

'My physique?'

'No!' and she laughed, 'you look at my face. I see you eye my backside and it makes me feel sexy, but I see you love my face and that's important to me.' She stood and put her bra on in a blink of his eye.

'How do you do that so quickly?'

'Practice. You just worry about the removal part.' She slipped on her blouse and a flowing, swirling skirt.

'Not coming back to bed then?'

'No, I'm going home to get some clean clothes and into the nick for a meeting with Jamie and Sitting Bull, we have the press at five.' She was over the top of him and he could not resist slipping his hand along the inside of her leg and letting it smooth its way upwards. 'You have a meeting here with Len, at ten.'

'You're not wearing any Alan Wickers,' he said, touching her in a way he had learned she liked.

'Jack you need to focus on Len, he can help you,' breathily said, as she leaned into him she pulled the bed clothes back and lifted her skirt.

'Len?'

'I was wondering if you heard me. He's offered his services to you, free, so listen to what he says. Despite you rubbing him up the wrong way, and despite his firm's unfortunate alliances, he's very good, and for some cockamamie reason, he likes and respects you. 'I'll see you later, and shower, you're rank.'

He had a sniff; she was kidding, that was just a manly smell, and while he had his nose out, he snorted her perfume wafts. He loved this scent on her, but preferred the smell of her when they woke in the morning.

FORTY-SIX

Ten, on the dot, Len parked his BMW behind Jack's garage. Jack nodded a wary greeting.

'Jane,' Len responded enthusiastically.

'Jane, I'm impressed.' Jack said, steering the solicitor through the garage to the house, 'I appreciate what you're doing, but I have to pay you something.'

'You can't afford me,' Len chirped, 'your fee can be you call me Lionel, how's that?'

'Len...' Jack's only functioning eyebrow went up.

'Just testing. I've done a lot of background on you, you're a real person, I like you, but you are in deep doo-doo.'

'Doo-doo?' Jack repeated, laughing, 'what school did you go to?'

'Winchester.'

'Thought so.'

'Can you work with a Tory boy?'

Jack grinned, he was relaxing, 'Half the police force is Tory or Masons, and I work with them. As Jesus said, "I come amongst you to put you on the straight and narrow".'

'Who told you that, Father Mike?'

'I believe it was, at my last confession.' How does he know about Mike, Jack thought. 'Coffee? I warn you, I make it very strong.'

'I like it strong.'

'Yeah but I'm not talking pansy arse Tory strong, I'm talking, Labour strong.'

'I'll give it a try and maybe sometime I can introduce you to the delights of Earl Grey tea.'

Warming to the banter, 'As a sophisticated socialist I have girl grey. Len, I think I might get to like you given a couple of lifetimes and another government.'

'Good enough for me, Jane,' Len said, putting his briefcase on the dining table, 'shall we see what we can do to get you out of the S H one T then?'

'Good man yerself, I'll bring the coffee.'

Jack returned for the coffee ritual, a tray with demitasse coffee cups and a formerly silver coloured, steaming, mocha pot. 'Lot of juice in this pot. Amanda says I have juice in things because I don't like change, but she's a girl, so wouldn't understand. No biscuits, my son hides them, says I eat them all, sorry. I thought I knew all the hiding places, but he's better at it than me.'

Jack poured Len his coffee and had a mixture of disappointment and admiration when Len sipped and said, 'Lovely.'

'It is, isn't it?' Jack responded, and allowed Len to lead off, may as well go down blaming a Tory for his downfall, Jack thought, and he projected himself into C&A's, a pint in his hand, cursing the Tory boy out of his depth, and the government of course.

'Jack, can I have your attention?'

'Sorry, son.'

'Pugwash is no fool.'

'Well he got to Captain in the Navy?' Jack smiled at his obvious point.

'Not much respect there?'

Jack extended his arms, palms flat on the table, he was going to make a serious point, already shaking his head, 'Respect for the front-line guys, but the martinet, pink gin, ward room, Wallah's, no.'

Len pulled a small sheaf of papers from his case and flopped them on the table, 'Pugwash's case; flawed.'

'Ah-so?' Jack said in Japanese.

'He argues emotionally, his hatred of you patent, claiming you leaked to the press, a cornerstone for dismissal from the Police Service.'

'Dismissal?'

'Did Mandy not say?'

Jack became introspective, 'I've been a bit out of it lately. She may have told me, but I have a blind spot on bad news.'

Len smiled warmly and Jack noticed it was compassionate, odd? 'Pugwash's blind spot is his prejudice, and this is also his Achilles heel?'

'Len mate, I'm lost, I'd be alright if I knew where the feckin' biscuits were.'

'The point is, and in your own parlance, you're banged to rights you insulted him in meetings, but that can be put down to the difference in your characters and the fact there is a clear dislike between you. The assault, I have written testimony he barged in on a minute silence for your lost colleague. What I am saying, Jack, is I hope to get you a wrap on the knuckles because Pugwash demonstrates his prejudice against you in his case, whereas you do not help yourself because of your foolish pride, which in both cases are human failings indeed, but I think I can turn it so you have the moral high ground.'

'Len, PP, you have style, if we can only get *Mary Poppins* in?'

'Well, there's still trouble brewing over Cherry Tree Lane.'

'Ha! Its official, I like you, you have cheered me enormously, and I am determined to get you out of that Tory party and over to Labour, they let Tofs in you know. I despair sometimes, but your company I believe I could tolerate.'

'Jack.'

'Yes, Len,' Jack was at the metaphorical barricades, flag forced into the wind, the noise and smell of conflict around him.

'Jack, when you have a moment.'

'Sorry, Len, back to work, eh?'

'No,' and Len smacked a labour party membership card onto the table.

'Len, I don't know what to say?'

'All evidence to the contrary.'

'But, in the interview room, you said you voted Tory?'

'I knew where you were coming from, and Buddha was a filthy paedophile, so I humoured you, within the scope of my representation of course, and it worked, did it not?'

'It bloody did that, son,' and Jack felt better than he had done for a very long time, his body coursed with energy, and felt the invigoration he usually felt after sex; he was alive.

'Jack.'

'Yes, my old china, Christ I didn't just say that out loud did I?'

'No, but I know one thing... actually two.'

'Okay, son, fire away,' just a little Riverdance, and Jack started dancing and listening, arms by his side, eyes down admiring his shuffling feet, thought he could have been a dancer, had even considered ballet, but his feet were too big for the poncy shoes.

'One, Mandy cares about you a lot.'

Jack stopped dancing and looked at Len. 'Second?'

'She has a point about your listening.'

'Ha,' and Jack leapt, bent his arms; he was doing "Step in Time," and Len enjoying watching, answered his phone on, "Let's go fly a kite, although the weather's shite."

'Len, what's that racket?'

'Should I offer you some guesses, Mandy?'

'Jack?'

'In one, he's still in deep doo-doo, but he's happy, seemed worried he had spoken some of his thoughts.'

Mandy hemmed, 'He does that.'

'Well, he did, but I said he didn't, I do not want to know about your sex life. Mandy, are you there?'

'Yes.'

'It's okay, I have finally started working with real people. I'm going to wrap up soon, but tell me one thing?'

'Anything, Len?'

'What comes after *Mary Poppins*?'

Mandy laughed and suggested he make a run for it.

FORTY-SEVEN

MANDY PUT THE PHONE DOWN, WISHING SHE HAD KEPT the conversation going so she could hear her plonker of a man happy in the background. I'll give this for Jack, she thought, when he bounces back, and she spent the rest of the morning, lunchtime and afternoon with a glowing sensation that made her want to step-in-time.

Jo-Jums led the team debrief, Paolo had wrapped up the skinheads, one or two leads but nobody was holding their breath. Chilly had caved when he learned the women were ready to testify; Mandy felt pleased Meesh could stay out of it. Jo-Jums had worked the conspiracy angle and determined there was a person or persons unknown who funded the skinheads, as well as an Islamic cell, maybe, as Jack had intimated, to generate street discord, codenamed Moriarty, currently reading Boratarty on the crime wall, in a box now, with lines coming out of it to other fields of the investigation; a growing web of intrigue. Finally, the drugs set up was to be allowed to run under Cyrano, this could be funding the conspiracy, and so may prove a better route to the instigators; a leg on the crime wall back to the spider.

Mandy reported to the Commander and Chief Constable and they decided how much to reveal. Spotty was called in for the latter part of the meeting. Mandy turned things over in her head, work, and personal thoughts. She had been flustered this morning, Liz and Carly still at her home. She had not allowed for the abandonment of youth, and her own confused feelings seeing her daughter happy with a woman. Most of all she thought about Jack. Worrying had clearly been a waste of time as Len had done the trick. She thought about the sex; there was time to work on that, but it was nice. Thought about him looking at her and how much she liked it, looked at Spotty, who was not so much leering as drooling.

'Mandy, want to share your thoughts?' The Chief Constable asked.

'I was thinking I ought to poke Spotty's eyes out.' The Chief, Commander and Mandy shared enjoying the bemused look on Spotty. 'Spotty, you will get better looking at women, but a tip, we always know, it's whether we allow you to continue to look.'

———

JACK WAS aware Michael and Colleen were hesitant around him. He reassured them he was now as right as rain, 'Well I would be if I could find the biscuits, and had a cup of girl grey to watch Amanda on the telly.'

'Sit down, Dad,' Michael switched the telly on and handed his dad the conch, the TV controller; "Whoever had the conch has control," he would say, "Lord of the Files." Jack turned the sound down on the telly.

Colleen sat on the settee, 'You okay, Jack?'

'Shush, I'm trying to listen where he's hidden the biscuits.'

'Oh, Jack,' and she rushed to his lughole, 'let's go fly a kite although the weather's shite,' she sung.

'Colleen, you're too smart for my son. How's your dad these days?'

'Pretty much as you, my mum stops him from punching Michael's lights out, but he knows I'm happy.'

He hemmed, 'It's hard being a parent.'

'Jack.'

'What?'

'The telly's starting.'

'Probably time to get your mum and dad round for dinner, what d'you think?'

Michael came in, 'Coooeeh light refreshments.'

'He does it better than you, and I will ask them.'

'Ask who what, babes?' Michael asked, setting a tray onto a side table.

'Jack wanted Mum and Dad round for dinner.'

'Yeah, what with Martin being with Meesh, we have a lot of food over,' Jack jibed.

'Oh good, I like my dad with a shiny nose,' Colleen quipped, and Jack thought last word, she is good, then turned his attention to the telly, his mug of girl grey and a couple of ginger nuts.

'Jack?'

'Sorry, I was thinking about Biscuit, it's his funeral tomorrow.'

'You going?'

'I am, darlin'...' his mind now pleasantly distracted watching Mandy, she'd let Spotty lead to stop him looking at her arse, thought, one arse man knows another arse man. He took a sip of his tea, dunked his ginger nut and saw a stunned Colleen. 'What? I didn't just say that out loud did I?' Part of the ginger nut fell into his girl grey, 'Feck.'

Colleen was not one to be deterred by a minor dunking incident, 'You did, and I will be keeping my arse out of your line of sight in future.'

'Too late, sweet'art.'

————

MANDY SUMMARISED THE BRIEFING NOTES, wrapped up the charges, and introduced the conspiracy thesis they had settled on. Jack had asked for a link to the local demos, and finally she reported that lines of enquiry were still open, principally looking for whoever set this in motion.

Mandy had arranged for Spotty to call on Bernie, who she had conspiratorially primed, 'Commander, can you tell us how Inspector Austin is please, I understand the request for the tribunal to be postponed has been turned down by the Chairman of the Police Committee?' a polite reference to Pugwash, also what she had agreed.

The Commander answered as agreed, 'Inspector Austin was blown up in an operation rescuing a young boy and two civilians. He slowly recovers and we have high hopes he will be back leading his team soon. We are, of course, disappointed the tribunal is even taking place, and the fact a postponement was not allowed...' he paused, '...it would be an understatement to say I am disappointed.'

'Superintendent, would you say this is a result?' a follow up.

'I'm pleased we have a number of perpetrators charged,' Mandy answered, 'but as Inspector Austin said the other day, the leaders are still out there, so success? No, we have a police officer's funeral tomorrow, another woman died, and there are women and children scarred for life. So, not a result, in so much as we will celebrate, more a catalyst to drive on.'

A BBC Journalist pushed, 'Commander, can you comment on how your ability to pursue this investigation will be hampered by the proposed spending cuts, and can you comment on the reported conversation Inspector Austin had with the Home Secretary?'

'The Police do not comment on Government policy.' The Commander responded, a chuckle from the journalists. 'Superintendent Bruce will answer the second part of your question.'

'Thank you, Commander,' Mandy paused. 'It is important to remember Inspector Austin had just been blown up, and it came as a surprise to him the Home Secretary had been listening in to what Jack thought was a personal conversation.'

'Superintendent, is it true he called the Home Secretary a "short arsed bald cretin"?'

She smiled and replied coolly, 'As I said, DI Austin had just survived an explosion and the fact he thought he was talking to Bill Vague is a reasonable mistake to make.' There was more laughter as everyone caught on to the subtlety of her reply. 'However, I can tell you when Theresa Green visited Jack in hospital, he was able to say he thought she had more hair than comes over on the telly,' the press were enjoying themselves. 'Seriously, and despite Inspector Austin's well-known political views, he appreciated the hospital visit from the Home Secretary and the encouraging sign was they shared a joke or two, his, and she laughed, so there may be something to worry about with the Home Secretary; he did say she had nice wellingtons, but he had just been blown up.'

Mandy stood and let Spotty lead them out. She knew Jack would be watching and he did not need to see a young lad leering at her bottom, that was his job, and long may it last.

FORTY-EIGHT

JACK WAS ASLEEP IN THE ARMCHAIR WHEN MANDY CAME in at about nine; is this prophetic she thought? So what if it was, the butterflies were fluttering, and in that she trusted. He opened his eye, she was on her knees, between his legs and looking straight at him.

'How'd you get in?'

'I cut myself a key.'

'Should I be alarmed?'

'Not unless you have someone else in your bed?'

'You're all I need sweet'art.'

She leaned over and they kissed, 'Right answer,' and they went up the wooden hill to Bedfordshire. Jack was out of practice on the bra strap, but there was time she thought, and he still had his pink hand.

———

THE NEXT DAY was Biscuit's funeral. Mandy stayed home with Jack, they cuddled and talked, Mandy about Liz and Carly, her feelings and asked how he knew, similarly with Frankie and Connie? "A twitching in his eye," he irritatingly said. She stroked and kissed it gently. 'It's like you're a Klingon?' Jo-Jums could speak Klingon, he told her. 'Tell me, Jack.'

'Luv, truthfully, I don't know, but I spent a lot of my younger life trying to figure women, even started reading *Venus and Mars* but had to stop.'

'The fact you started is impressive, why did you stop?'

Was she ready for his home-grown philosophy? Was he brave enough to impart it? Throwing in a contingency wince, he chanced his arm, 'Since the sixties, men, me in particular, have been trying hard to be what is now termed politically correct, to go out of their way to put themselves into the position of women and to understand them, presuming this is what women wanted? In my view, that's when men started to lose their identities as men. This is not a chauvinist argument, what women have achieved is right and proper and about time. My view is that if you can be a decent man, you can have a decent relationship with a woman, as a man, and we are different. I try to understand women, but it's an impossible task and has the potential to destroy a relationship, because it's a lifetime goal that may only partially be achieved. If you expect instant results, you are doomed. I tried, but never really understood Kate.' Mandy had a momentary flutter. 'Right or wrong, this is how I lead my life, how I have spoken to Michael and Alana when they asked,' he laughed nervously, 'what is it?'

She looked into his soul, 'Colleen and Michael have gone to school, we can make a noise.'

———

THEY SLEPT a little more and when Jack came back from the

bathroom, Mandy was awake, 'Give that week or two, sweet'art.'

'Jack!'

He smiled, having just demonstrated clear differences between men and women, 'Relaxacat, I've run you a bath in the other bathroom, it's ready, but I want to wash you.'

Mandy felt titillated, 'There's no time, but you once took a rain-check on my bath at home.'

'Taps in the middle?' and he put his head to one side and grinned, recalling the phone conversation outside C&A's.

'Do you want to stay at my place tonight?'

'Mandy, I would love to have a bath at your place, I've a feeling I might get dirty today.'

'Just get dirty tonight,' and she ran tippy toes to the other bathroom.

Returning she felt aglow from the bath and had a double take as she entered the bedroom, Jack stood, dapper, in a smooth, charcoal grey suit, white shirt and a black and white jazzy bow tie, a black silk hanky in his top pocket.

'Close your mouth, we are not a codfish,' he said.

'You look stunning.'

'So do you, luv.' She smiled and waltzed to where her own grey suit hung, and started to get dressed. 'I'll make some coffee, thought we could stop off somewhere for brunch as the sceptic tanks say?'

'Lovely, is that what the Yanks say?'

———

As MANDY DROVE OFF, she took Jack's good hand and put it on her thigh, a flutter of concern, ordinarily she would have to knock it off, not put it on. His hand was there now, smoothing and stroking, 'Sorry, luv, I was thinking about Biscuit, do I detect a button here?'

'It is a suspender button, Jack, do I have your attention now?'

'Mandy, it's not just sex, I love you, and I'm thinking of taking you on a date.'

She laughed into the steering wheel, 'A date? Now you're cooking.'

Jack put his serious head on, she noticed, and paid attention, 'Amanda, do you mind if I ask you something?'

She seized, 'No?'

'Do you fuck on your first date or do I go home and masturbate?'

'No hope of you growing up, I suppose?'

'What and lose my boyish charm.'

'I've got news for you, boy.'

Mandy turned down towards the Roman fort and the small village of Portchester; a nice pub for lunch.

FORTY-NINE

THEY WERE AT THE CREMATORIUM IN PLENTY OF TIME.
Mandy helped Jack from the car, he was still sore, they kissed
and she straightened his bow tie. 'You know you have style.'
She put her arm in his and they walked towards the chapel; the
first time I have put my arm in his she thought, and snuggled
into him.

'Cold?' Jack asked.

It was a glorious day, but there was a cooling breeze, not
quite summer. 'No, I'm feeling a bit Roman Candle, enjoying
the feeling of being with you, is that bad?'

Jack stopped and turned, 'Yes, you are a very bad girl.'

'Oooh, and what are you going to do about it?' Mandy
replied with a cheeky grin.

'Later.'

'Oh, I've gone all weak at the knees, Master.'

'A bit unseemly?'

'Hello, Sir, have you met my Master, Jane?' Mandy replied
to the Commander, 'you may not recognise him, a suit, bow tie
and no mango.'

'Poncey if you ask me,' the Commander replied, standing with Dorothy, his wife.

'Delores you look lovely.' The Commander went to correct Jack, thought better of it.

They headed towards a large gathering of blue uniforms which Jack thought should have been furtive guys in trench coats. Mandy peeled off to greet people, he felt a momentary panic, and Mandy noticed. Christ she thought, and pushed her way back and raised herself to his ear, 'I'm with you.' She felt him grip her arm; he's not even close, and then, of course, this was where Kate was cremated.

The cortège stopped at the approach road. Uniformed officers lined up behind for the last few hundred metres, and at a snail's pace, it eased to the chapel doors. The family stepped out of the following cars and Biscuit's widow walked determinably to Jack, a fixed stare before she slapped his face, hard. There was a collective intake of breath from mourners as she put her arms around his neck, hugged, and kissed him. Mandy heard what was whispered as she gently released the sobbing widow's arms. Jack blubbered also, a blossoming red mark on his good cheek.

The widow tugged Jack and started to walk back, beckoning Mandy to follow. She did, feebly, wobbling in high heels, whispering, 'What the fuck Jack?' He put his arm around her waist to steady her and they stood with the family. The coffin was hoisted on the pallbearers' shoulders and they processed.

In the chapel, Mrs Biscuit directed Jack and Mandy into a pew behind the immediate family; *Stairway to Heaven* played. Mandy whispered in Jack's ear, taking a discreet look back at Father Mike, resentful he was there, 'What did she mean Del-Boy had been to see her? You knew Biscuit, didn't you? That was why you were so upset, wasn't it?'

Jack nodded, he was crying, and Mandy felt simultaneously anger and guilt for tackling him. The Vicar was on his feet to start the ceremony. Jack thought this should have been Father Mike and looked around, saw Mike, and also the knob dignitaries; Top Cops, Councillors, at least Pugwash hadn't shown, he was worried about that and how he would have reacted. The ceremony stumbled on, and Jack was shaken from his thoughts when the widow got up to speak, her children clinging to the hem of her skirt, to be gently steered back to their seats by the sister. The commotion eased, and she spoke of Biscuit, a good husband and father, 'I had agreed the Chief Constable would say a few words, but it should be someone who really knew my husband. If Inspector Austin would do my family that kindness?'

She strode deliberately to Jack and Mandy thought she was going to slap him again, and thought, go for it girl. But the widow gently sought his hand, tugged, hugged and kissed him, as he stood. Mandy felt confused, jealous; how can I be so unreasonable? The widow sat, clutched her children as Jack made his way to the coffin and rested his hand on it, his good one, the pink one swung by his side. Mandy saw his pink hand, his eye, and all of his flaws, but most of all saw he was struggling to get going.

Then he did, 'I see the few people who knew, loved, and adored this very brave man. I see those who are here because they feel obliged, or have some other motive,' he was shaking his head. 'I knew Biscuit, and I'm wretched because I was not clever enough to save him; twelve hours too late, and I will take this with me until it is me up here,' he tapped the coffin, waited, as if he expected a response.

Mandy was crying, this is what he'd been carrying around with him, the feckin' eejit she thought, as he continued.

'It is rare we speak as coppers. We allow the fat cats to get their sound bites while those of us at the front line do the living... and the dying...' he looked at the coffin, through it, saw Biscuit lying there. 'They call us heroes. Lip service, that's all,' this was shouted and the congregation jumped at the shock of it. He calmed, took his time, 'We do what we think is right, and often in difficult situations, we do not complain...' he found more reserves of strength, '...we do nothing when comfortable politicians take away the resources we need to fight the growing battle against crime. Ours not to reason, but why?' shouted again, shaking his head. Jack looked directly at the politicians gathered at the back; '...Because the police do not comment?' he shook his head again, slowly, disgusted.

Mandy realised this is what he had been thinking about in the car. He began again, 'I look at your children,' and he made strong eye contact with the widow and her children, where his eye stayed, he spoke to them and Mandy thought this will be an abiding memory for them. 'I say to you, your dad was a brave and kind man, and you must grow up to be proud of him. He wanted to stop the cruelty to innocents. This was the essence of the man I knew, and I say again, why? Why are people so cruel to others? Why can't we just have a life free and joyful,' whispering now, 'a quiet life?' He raised his voice again and railed, 'But until we do, we have to fight against those politicians who take away the resources for this job...' his breathing was laboured, '...this pig of a job,' sobbing.

Mandy knew he was gone, and she left her seat just as Mrs Biscuit did, and together the two women walked him back to join the stunned congregation. The widow returned to the coffin, 'I say this to the man at the back trying to hurry me up. Fuck-off! You will wait for me, this is my time. My husband loved his job, and he loved and respected Jack Austin. It is important for me to say to Jack, there is nothing for you to feel guilty about. Biscuit would say "don't go Roman candle on me",' there was laughter, not from Mandy; Jack knew this man and that man knew Jack. 'We will have Brian's marker with the name Biscuit on it, because that was what Jack called him. I knew my husband was brave. I also knew he was going places he could not tell me about, he would not want you to feel guilty for what happened, Jack, but if it helps, I say to all of you here and now, I forgive this man as I forgive my husband. My children forgive you, Jack, and I charge you to get the bastards that did this to my Brian, their dad,' she stopped and whispered, 'Biscuit.' She kissed the coffin and angrily knocked the police cap off, another woman who had not wanted her man to be a copper, Jack had seen this before; Kate.

The vicar said a few things, the curtains closed and the congregation mechanically filed out. Mandy felt Jack was close to collapse, and then Father Mike was there. He's always there, sometimes she felt like cursing him, other times grateful, who the hell knew? She was not thinking straight, but he supported Jack physically, much as he did with Nobby outside the Asian Emporium. The widow insisted Jack stand with her at the external receiving aisle, Mandy and Father Mike bracing him. The widow had more strength than him; bloody typical Mandy thought, realising she was angry as she looked at Jack's face; grey, ravaged, but with a steely determination. She had seen this before as well, he knew something the bastard, he had seen something, but would he tell her, would he protect her like Biscuit tried to protect his family? This is not what she wanted, the fucking bastard.

The dignitaries filed and Jack's steely face became animated. He stepped out in front of the Leader of the Council and gripped his hand, pushed his head to the Leader's ear, there was hardness in Jack's eye, body language, stiff, erect and aggressive. The line stopped almost afraid of what they saw, this man who had given an impromptu and very emotional eulogy, who had spoken with a passion not all here recognised or could understand, wanted to understand even, and certainly not comfortable with. The handshake hurt the leader and he wobbled as Jack barged past to another Councillor who Mandy recognised but could not put a name to, people she did not know, but marked in her mind's eye to find out. This Councillor winced with the strength of the handshake, and looked equally frightened as Jack whispered in his ear. Words finished, Jack spun on his toe, and stiffly walked back to the widow and resumed his position as if nothing had happened.

Then it was Dorothy. She was crying, hugging the widow, onto Jack, followed by Jamie and Sitting Bull. They pulled him and Mandy to one side, but spoke only to Mandy, 'Get him better, we need him leading this one,' they hugged Jack in turn, these men normally uncomfortable with masculine personal space.

'The tribunal?' she whispered.

'We'll see about that, Mandy,' and they resumed their position in the shuffling line of mourners, looking at the flowers, and she knew exactly what Jack thought about that. He would have no flowers; "A cardboard coffin and chuck me in the sea". She looked at him as she heard his words in her head, and she wondered about his fascination with the sea. She thought about herself, something she had learned as a part of her life's survival pack; what had started out as a pleasant day, albeit the day of Biscuit's funeral, was now marked with more grief and sadness than she had bargained for, or more importantly, prepared for. She did not know whether to shout at Jack or hug him. In the end she did neither, she sat on a cold stone bench while Jack said his farewells to the family.

Father Mike eased up and sat beside her, looked into the space Mandy was staring into, 'He's just a man trying to do a big job,' he said, 'he's vulnerable, can you see that?'

She turned to him, and turned on him; a woman who was

hurting. 'No kidding, Tonto, and just who the fucking hell are you Mike? I know my man, and I don't need anybody telling me how to treat him, or whatever you think I should do. He is mine, and I will look after him, do you get that; you fucking, whatever you are, treble-sized twat?'

'Right answer,' Mike said, 'not the treble bit.'

Mandy was tempted to slap him, but there'd been enough of that today. She left Father Mike sitting on the cold bench and thought, serve him right if he got piles. She wobbled on her high heels over to Jack, took his arm and squeezed it. 'Hello you,' a warm smile, contrasted so much by the look he had only five minutes ago, and they headed for the car, her emotions bubbling, her stomach churning, nodding to people as they passed. He held the car door and she sat, not saying a word; brusque. Jack walked to the passenger side and settled.

Immediately, she turned on him, 'Jack Austin, never leave me out in the cold. I am your partner and I want to know everything. If you are going into a dangerous area, I want to know, so I can worry, do not protect me from worrying, got that, you bastard? I have a right to worry. Now if you want me, then you involve me in whatever this is, and use me. I'm a good copper and I can watch your arse because frankly you are far too old and you need someone.' He shaped to say something, but she came right back at him, 'And don't say I could watch your arse anytime, because I haven't got wide angle vision, now shut the fuck-up, we have a day and a half tomorrow and I am in the mood to shove a crate of mangos up Pugwash's arse, but in the meantime, put your hand on my suspenders, I'm taking you home for a bath... I feel dirty.'

FIFTY

Jack had never been to Mandy's flat and didn't get a chance to look around, the emotion of the day and the passion of the drive home could not be contained, and he had the bra test to pass; how many chances will he get? They began stripping each other's clothes off as they came through the door. She was pleased to see Jack tied his bow tie; she had always wanted to undo a man's bow tie, and then thought how can he tie that and not undo a bra? She would save that for later as he needed help with his trousers, shirt and even her clothes, because of his feckin' pink hand, but she was not going to let this spoil the moment. Mandy had him in just his socks, she in her underwear and she wanted to get lost in the moment, but they were making no progress to the bedroom.

'Jack, for Christ's sake, take me to the bedroom.'

'Where is it?'

'Oh, right,' she calmed, held him by his bits and pieces and with a disarmingly syrupy smile, 'follow me, darling.'

'Not much choice, darling,' mimicking her syrup, and she lead him down the corridor, opened the door, released her control and they bundled through, fell on the floor in a frenzy of pent up passion.

'Hello, Mum, Jack.'

Mandy screamed and frightened the bajeezers out of Jack, 'Shit, bang, fucking piss,' Jack screamed, covering his bits and pieces.

'What did you say?' and Mandy dissolved into hysterical laughter, as she looked up at her daughter in bed with another woman, Jack naked except for some stupid socks with, were those dogs and penguins, sidling like a snake on the floor back into the corridor to get his clothes.

Mandy got a dressing gown, silk, knowing Jack would like that, smoothed her apoplexy, still looking into the wardrobe, not really wanting to turn back to face the bed.

Mandy thought it would be Liz to make the first move, but it was Carly, who cleared her throat, and Mandy turned to hear what she had to say, 'Can I say, before we discuss this like grownups, those stockings and suspender belt are beautiful, and I want Liz to get some, do you have any spare?'

Mandy was in a dream and all she could think to say was, 'Discuss this like grownups?' and shouted, 'Jack, they want to talk about this, but not with you,' and she giggled, knowing if she did not control this now, it would never end.

'What?' Jack called from somewhere.

'Shall we have a cup of tea?' Carly still, will Liz ever say anything, ever, again.

Jack came back into the bedroom, his shirt and trousers crooked, 'Can you, err...my pink hand?' and he waved it about to demonstrate his disability.

'Come here, dipstick,' and she pulled him to her, and dressed him like a mum dressing a little boy coming out of the swimming baths. 'Now, put the kettle on.'

He made a silly face to the girls and went to go to the door and stopped, 'Where's the kitchen?' saw Mandy's exasperated look, was proud he didn't cower.

'This place is not so big you cannot find the kitchen.'

'I'm wary of opening any other doors,' good answer he thought, pleased he had restrained the gibbering wreck move he held in reserve for dire female emergencies. All three women looked at him, so Jack thought, Buzz Lightyear; 'To the kitchen and put the kettle on,' his pink hand leading the way, he glanced back for applause, and saw three stunned faces, two of which were peeking out from a hugged quilt. So he did what any mature man would do, disappeared down the corridor making whooshing noises.

'Well, Jack seems a little better,' finally, Liz said something.

———

JACK WAS EXPLORING THE KITCHEN, finding cups, tea, bending down to look in the bottom of cupboards, 'You got Girl Grey, babes?' then whooped, Mandy had goosed him; shocking but not unpleasantly so.

'We have unfinished business, Jack,' Mandy said.

'Shall I take the taps?' he grinned, she smiled her beautifully malevolent smile.

'Who's having what taps, Mum?' Liz appeared.

'Nothing, honeybun, let's have tea and talk like grownups, I'll sit Jack in front of the telly,' she laughed and dragged her hand over his dodgy eye, he was instantly mollified. Carly sat with Liz and Mandy noticed she pushed her chair close so their legs rubbed. God give me strength she thought, exactly what Jack does.

'Mum.'

Liz began to talk but Mandy put her hand up, 'Tea first.' It was quiet, so Jack slurped, Carly slurped, and then Liz, and

Mandy thought what the hell. It was the Chimpanzee's tea party, risky Jack, but well played she thought.

'I thought you'd gone home.'

'No kidding, Tonto,' it was Carly

'You know the Lone Ranger, Curly?'

'Is that where it's from? I heard you say it the other day and thought it was funny.'

'Thank you, Carly,' Mandy said, looking at Jack who applied a smug look, hummed, and tilted his head to Carly. She gathered herself, 'Look, it's okay, but can you tell me when you will be going home?'

Liz spoke, 'We thought we would wait for the weekend as Jack had his tribunal tomorrow, and you might need some support, and well, your bed is a lot nicer than the one we have at home.'

Mandy sighed and got up thinking, *Our bed at home*, was gone a little while and returned, dressed, and with a small case. 'Okay, Jack, I need a bath, shall we go?'

'What's with the bath, Mum?'

Carly nudged her, 'Your bath is lovely, the taps in the centre.'

'No kidding, Tonto,' and Mandy kissed Carly on her cheek, then Liz, and as she called to Jack to pick up the case, she said to Liz, 'I've left something on the bed for you,' looked at Carly, 'and Carly I suppose.'

'Good luck tomorrow, Jack,' both girls.

———

JACK HELD the car door for Mandy, she popped the boot and he put the case in then sat in the passenger seat, 'Permission to fondle your thigh, Captain?'

'Permission granted for diabolical liberties, this is a short drive.'

'What did you leave for Liz?'

'A pair of suspenders and some nylons, you see, for Carly as well.' They had driven no more than a few hundred metres when Jack's phone went; it kept ringing, 'Give it here.' Mandy said, looking at the number recognition, 'It's the Nick,' flicked answer, and passed the phone back.

'Despairing from Tunbridge Wells,' Jack answered, he listened, eventually worked out the call cancel; it was only big and in red, the twerp, she thought. 'Amanda, can you drive to the seafront please, I want to talk to you.'

'Jack, I want to get home,' and she turned to reinforce the sentiment, recognised his serious head, and steered toward the seafront, parked and cut the engine, 'okay, what?'

'I recognised the Head of Social Services and noticed he was close to the Leader of the Council. Did you see me go up to them after the service?'

'Yes, I think everyone did, I recognised the Leader but wasn't sure who the other man was,' Mandy replied, not so tetchy now.

'Would you like to know what I said?' it did not need an answer, 'I know.'

She thought about the answer, 'He did look shaken.'

'He must have been, because he just walked into our Nick and confessed to his part in the paedophile network, apparently claiming this and that but it's not going to amount to a hill of beans, been crapping himself since the bust on the house, I just tipped him over the edge.'

'What do you want to do?' she sighed, knowing bath time had been cancelled.

'Get Jo-Jums and Paolo to start the process and interview him, he's small potatoes, but he may lead us to Boratarty and then we might get the drugs, the skinheads, the Islamic lads, the women, and the children,' he groaned as he thought of the children.

Mandy began calling, 'And the rest, Jack?'

'We've been sniffing around, funding streams, terrorist activity, if this was the case, who knows, but one thing has led to another; something's not right.'

'We, Jack?' She got through, 'Jo, I'm sorry, raise Paolo and get back to the Nick, hang on I have Jack with me, he says get KFC in and they should patch through to that Del-Boy bloke for a briefing.' She listened then spoke, 'Yes he did say patch, and I've no idea what it means either, but the Head of Social Services has just handed himself in, confessing to the paedophile conspiracy. Jack thinks he's small fry but... hang on, Jo,' exasperated. 'What, Jack?'

'I said potatoes, small potatoes.'

'It's okay, Jack being juvenile, yes, no change there, thank you, I will take the Sainthood, yes, I will see Father Mike for it, now listen, get the team going, this is a big break, thank you.' She closed the call and turned, 'You were saying, is this terrorism?'

'Don't think so, you know Biscuit was a spook, following up the vice side as a possible funding stream?'

She put her hand on his to stop him, 'Biscuit was a Spook?'

He carried on matter-of-factly, 'Yeah, had a bead on Chilly, and it turned out the Head of Social was on his list as well, and today, I just pushed him a bit.'

'What about the Leader of the Council, you seemed to push him as well.'

'That was gut instinct, or I prefer to say twitchy eye. I don't like him, but it will be interesting to see what happens, someone is on him, but the Head of Social had problems about five years ago, and it all went away. I was curious as to why, and who helped him. There is no record, but the Spooks monitored and were able to suggest the Leader may have been involved somehow.'

'Who, Jack, who is on him?'

'One of Del-Boy's guys, it can't be one of ours, if we are wrong then we are there to be shot down, if you get my grift.'

Mandy looked pensive, 'I do, are we just inching up the chain or are we close to the top?'

'Inching love, and probably nowhere near the top.'

She thought for a bit, then took the plunge, and asked the question she had wanted to ask for a little time now, but was nervous of the answer, 'Jack, are you a spook?'

'Ha, at my age, babes? I'm seriously flattered.'

She was taken aback by the bombastic reply, but pushed, 'Jack, I am with you, I just want to know.'

He turned in his seat so his eye made contact, 'I was, Amanda, and now I'm a Community Police Officer, or at least until tomorrow, but you know how it is,' he flicked his hand, 'you never really leave.'

'Do I?'

FIFTY-ONE

Mandy took a call, 'Okay, Barney, I'll tell him.'

'Guess who?'

'Confession?'

'Confession.'

'Be back in a minute.'

'What was that all about Amanda?' the Commander asked.

'You don't want to know, Sir?'

After a short while, Jack returned from meeting Mike and went to KFC. The crime wall was being brought up to date by Nobby, Alice helping. Jack spotted *Sorry-farty* and laughed, Nobby reddened and the Commander sighed, realising he will spend his retirement worrying about his lad and the influence of Jane Austin.

'Jo with Paolo?' Jack asked.

'Yes,' Alice answered, 'interviewing.'

'Good, what we got, Connie?'

'Be on screen in minute, be patient, Jane.' Frankie looked at Jack, pulled a face and flicked her eyes, as if to say, coming on, eh.

Del-Boy appeared on the screen. 'Jack?'

'Yoh, bro.'

'Yes, well a little less of the Americanisms please, we have enough of that shite with the CIA,' Del said, and continued, he was outside the leader's house, 'no response, but would you Adam and Eve it, the alarm's going and someone has called the police, so we're waiting.'

Jack was stinging about his use of modern idioms, Mandy jumped in, 'Idiotisms, and yes, you did.'

Jack decided to focus; no time for childish remarks. The screen showed the boys in blue arriving, and eventually someone took the initiative to push in a door of the Leader's house. Frankie monitored local uniform radio and eventually heard what they had been expecting, a body had been found.

'Sweet'art, take that call,' Jack said to Mandy. 'I'll get Paolo and Jo out of the interview and get them to the scene, d'you fancy joining me in a little chat with the Head of Social Services, sort of like a first date?'

Mandy made the call, 'We have this one.'

BARNEY BUZZED Mandy and Jack into the interview suite, 'Which one, Barney?'

'Number two.'

'How appropriate.' Mandy felt a frisson of excitement, working with Jack; she'd been tagged with so much administration lately, and this was real police work, she thought, then thought again, I think? Jack held the door to let Mandy walk in first.

'Detective Superintendent Bruce and Inspector Austin have entered the room at seven forty-three pm,' Jo speaking for the record.

'Jo, Paolo, we need you to go to the Leader of the Council's house, looks like he's been murdered.' Jo and Paolo looked at Jack shocked, but not as shocked as Anthony Wolm, Head of Social Services. 'Paolo, okay if the Superintendent and I take over the interview of Mr Worm while you deal with the Leader?'

'Inspector.'

'Yes, Mr Worm.'

'It's Wolm, Inspector.' Jack looked at Paolo and winked.

'Okay, we're off then.'

Jack replied, 'And so are we, Paolo.'

Mandy opened up as Jo and Paulo left. 'Would it surprise you to know you have been on our radar for some time, Mr Worm?'

Worm looked up from his study of the table top, forlorn. 'No.'

Jack thought he's broken, we may need to build him up a bit, 'Of course, it seems you were only a peripheral player, and it will go well for him handing himself in, will it not Superintendent?'

'It will Inspector, the stuff on Mr Worm is not as damming as we have on some of the others.'

'You know about the others?' he mumbled.

'We know of them, and we know you escaped dying this evening. Lucky you came in, isn't it?' Worm nodded, as Jack opened the door and shouted for Barney, who, prepped, was there in a flash. 'Barney what're we like this evening?'

'Pretty full, Jack, you have a problem?'

'Well, I fear for Mr Worm's safety, if you get my grift?'

'I certainly get your *drift*, but nothing is one hundred percent.' They exchanged looks, picked up by Worm.

'Mandy, I think Mr Worm will talk to us, am I right, Mr Worm?'

'Yes, I will tell you all I can, please, keep me safe.' He looked truly scared. Jack thought, worm by name, but it's always the same with scum like this, fiddle kids and shit themselves when a grown up's on the scene. He looked guiltily at Mandy; he'd not spoken out loud, good.

'You heard the man, Barney, cell six one zero,' added 'F two X,' he was on a roll.

'That's the best we have, Jack.'

'Is the *Teasmade* working?'

'On the blink, sorry.'

'Shame,' Jack turned back to the interview table. 'Mr Worm, unfortunately, the Superintendent and I have a previous engagement tomorrow, the tribunal, but you would know all about that sitting on the police committee, wouldn't you?' Worm looked sheepish, a woolly worm Jack thought, and felt the laugh building in his stomach. 'The previous officers will be back to talk to you tomorrow, tell them all you know. We'll be on the dog and bone throughout the tribunal and will clear it to take urgent calls. If you need anything, they will get in touch with me, okay?'

'Yes, Inspector, thank you,' wondering what a dog and bone was.

'You've been read your rights, offered a solicitor?'

'Yes.'

Mandy spoke, 'Barney, look after Mr Worm, and if he needs us...'

'I'll be sure to phone, indeed, Ma'am,' and Barney took Mr Worm by the elbow as Mandy left and Jack followed.

'*Teasmade* Jack?'

'A *Goblin* one, darling,' Jack winked, and she blushed. 'Worm's ready to give us everything, let's hope it's more than we think. How about a nice murder scene, and then a bath?'

'Jack, you smooth bastard, you certainly know how to treat

a girl, but this does not count as a first date.' They briefed the Commander, told Nobby that Jo and Paolo need to see the end of the interview tapes before they have a go at Worm tomorrow.

'It's Wolm, Jack...' then Nobby realised.

The name on the board had changed to *Norafarty*. 'Bit past your bedtime, isn't it, Nobby?' Jack observed.

'Leave that to me, sir, I will see he gets an early night,' Alice Springs spoke for him.

'Mum gave me a get out of jail free card.'

'Nice save, Nobs.'

———

IT WAS clear the Leader of the Council had been murdered; clumsily, made to look like suicide. Jack suggested deliberately so, nobody queried the remark. Jack introduced Mandy to Del-Boy and out of earshot, 'Del, she knows, not all, but some,' and went off for a quick look around. Mandy took her eyes off Del for a second and saw Jack with two *Waitrose supermarket* shopping bags on his feet.

Del looked seriously at Mandy, struggling not to laugh, 'He's getting on, Mandy, and we need to look after him. He never was action man, was a back room Brainiac, and needs to take a back seat, his head still works though; just.'

'I know Del, fortunately, so do a few other bits.'

'Nuff said.'

'What's nuff said?' Jack was back shuffling his bagged feet.

'Nothing Jack, Del wants to know what Care Home you live in, thinks he might visit you, and the shopping bags?'

'For crime scenes, Der!'

'Jo, Paolo, you okay to take this on?' Mandy asked, trying not to laugh at her eejit.

Jo beamed, Paolo answered, 'We have it in hand, Ma'am.'

'Good, because I need a bath and Jack needs a seeing to, a lot on tomorrow.'

———

THEY GOT BACK to Jack's house, there were several notes from Michael plus some sandwiches which they ate and washed down with a cold beer each. They touched hands; quiet and intimate, no bath, they went to bed, cuddled and fell asleep, it felt natural and right and beautiful, Mandy thought.

Jack went to sleep.

FIFTY-TWO

'WHAT TIME IS IT?'

'Just after seven thirty.'

'When did Len want to meet?'

'Nine, at the coffee house,' Mandy answered, shaking her sleepy head to look at Jack, 'how do you feel?'

'Okay.'

She put both hands on his face, 'Whatever happens today, we...' and she emphasised, '...we, will be okay, you do know that don't you?'

'Yes, the one thing I do feel good about today.'

'Okay, let's get the bastards then?' Mandy said.

'Up-an-at-em atom ant.'

'What?'

———

LEN GOT JACK A DOUBLE ESPRESSO, an Americano for Mandy, calling back casual greetings. Jack drank the espresso in seconds, not good, and only warm. Mandy tapped him on the arm, 'Jack, Len's talking to you.'

'Sorry, miles away.'

'I said, I have submitted your defence, didn't bother you with it, guessing you had enough on your plate.' Jack nodded. 'Just follow my lead, okay?'

'Absolutely,' Jack replied.

Len suggested they go and Jack was out of his starting blocks, 'Is he okay, Mandy?'

She looked at Jack high-tailing along the crowded pavement, 'He's been through a lot, don't know what he will do if pushed,' and they trotted after Jack. As they rounded the corner into the Square, Jack stood rigid.

'Blimey, Len?' Jack exclaimed, faced by the crowd.

'I think your friend Bernie rounded up local support, though there is a bit of opposition, the East Cosham something, can't quite read their banner.'

'Pugwash, twin set and pearls brigade, dress like Margaret Thatcher and that's just the blokes,' Jack replied, muscling into the building.

The Guildhall manager welcomed them, 'Hi, Jack, see-'em off today.'

'Will do, Colin.'

'Is there anyone you do not know? Mandy enquired.

'Hi, Superintendent, we go back a ways,' Colin replied, 'Jack, they've changed it to committee room one, the public and press are to be let in.'

'What?' Len objected, 'This is outrageous, why were we not informed?'

Jack put his hand on Len's arm, 'Calm down, it's not Colin's fault,' and Mandy was amazed as he started talking to Colin about the Bournemouth Symphony Orchestra, 'Close your mouth darlin', and let's get up there.'

'See you at the concert, Colin,' Jack called back.

Colin was not finished, 'Will you be there, Superintendent?'

They stopped, Jack looked at Mandy, 'Berlioz, do you like him?'

'What piece Colin?'

'Symphonie Fantastique.'

'Fantastique, I'll be there.'

The lift doors opened, they went in and rose up, 'You like Berlioz?'

'No, who the fuck's he, some bloody French twat? Of course I know him.'

Jack pulled Mandy to him and kissed her, looked over at Len, 'Office banter, Len.'

'Office rocker more like,' Mandy told Len behind her hand, confident Jack wouldn't hear.

Pugwash was already in the Committee room, immaculately set up, uniformed and ready to go, the ugly sisters in the front row of the public area behind their hero. Jack went directly to him, hand out, 'John.' Pugwash, thrown by the gesture, stood and shook Jack's hand, an automatic reaction. 'Seaman Stains,' and confused, he followed Jack's eye down to the flies of his trousers. Jack laughed into his face, strutted back to Mandy and Len and slouched in his chair, lolled his head, looked at the ceiling.

'You could try not to lose the case before we start,' Len jibed, and Jack stopped his ceiling gazing.

'You said he was running this himself, personal you said.'

'I did, so what?'

Mandy stepped in, 'Jack's interview technique, has him rattled, ready to lose his temper.'

'Oh.'

Jack returned to the ceiling. The capacity spectators

quieted as the three adjudicators entered. The Chairman was Commissioner John Ball of the Met, his assistants, the Chief Constable of Hampshire, James Patterson and Edward Crawley, Chief Constable West Sussex; all good men, all straight as a dye.

The Commissioner kicked off, 'I find it unusual these proceedings are public. Had I been asked...' and he looked pointedly at Pugwash, '...I would have resisted. I feel obliged to ask if this is acceptable to Inspector Austin.'

Pugwash offered a feeble denial, Jack smiled to the ornate cornice, Len leapt to his feet, 'It is not acceptable.'

The Commissioner responded, 'And you are?'

'Lionel Thackeray, I represent Inspector Austin.'

The Commissioner nodded, looked knowingly at his fellow panellists, and with a smiley glance to Jack, 'Does he call you Len?'

'Aah, he does, Sir.'

'Thought he might,' and the Commissioner looked down from the raised platform that held the big desk, and to the almost comatose Jack, 'Jane, will you never change.' Mandy had her heart in her mouth, she'd already worked out the change of venue was likely down to him, and she kept looking to watch for Jack's mood and actions, but he seemed miles away, and had not answered the Commissioner. 'Okay, I shall call you Len if that is okay with you, Len.'

Jack whispered to Len, 'That will be fine, Jonty.'

'Ha, touché, Len.

Pugwash stood, 'Sir, may we start the proceedings?'

The Commissioner was not pleased, 'Captain, you are not on board ship now, these are civil proceedings that I suspect you have opened to the public, and I will see they are kept civil,' he chortled at his little joke and looked to his fellow panel members for a nod of approval; duly received. Pugwash sat, confounded.

'Okay, we'll start, happy Captain?'

Pugwash nodded and looked at the obese ugly sisters for support. Jack thought in a battle he would not want to be in the trenches with them for more reasons than one, not least there would be no room left.

The Commissioner started, waving a set of papers, 'I will not insult this tribunal by reading out this sheaf of charges, save to say we have read them, along with the defence papers, and have no immediate comment, except Captain, you have not addressed the charges to the officer I know. I will deal with that for you, please take notes.' Pugwash snapped up his pen, an automaton. 'It is not Jack Austin, but John, Peter, Joseph Austin, CBE, QGM.'

Mandy was amazed and turned to Jack. 'Sorry darling, my name isn't Jane.'

Mandy was not deterred and mouthed, 'CBE, QGM?' meaning, Commander of the British Empire and the Queens Gallantry Medal, but he was saved the need to answer.

The Commissioner continued, 'Now we have the name right, I understand it is the recommendation Inspector Austin be awarded the George Medal, recent events and all, we wish you well with that Inspector.' Mandy's jaw dropped, news to her, all of it. Jack was unmoved, having returned his gaze to the ceiling. 'Superintendent, when you are ready,' she apologised quietly. 'So, the charges, and he waved the pages at the gallery, I will ask you Len how your client responds?' Len was about to respond when Jack woke from his lethargy and put his stop the traffic hand up.

The whole room heard Mandy, 'Oh no, Mr Turnip.'

'Inspector, you have something to say?'

'Sir, the charge I am the anonymous source of stories to the newspaper, I would ask the Captain to produce evidence. The other charges are correct, but I plead extenuating circumstances.' The gallery murmured and the Commissioner frowned, looked to Mandy for guidance, she had none, other than she could recommend the ceiling, it had nice mouldings.

'Do you want to take a moment with Len?' the Commissioner.

'No, sir.'

'I am sure Len will detail the extenuating circumstances for you, but can you summarise please,' the Commissioner looked worried.

'Yes sir, I can,' but Jack said no more.

'Well, what are they?'

Jack leaned forward and looked directly into Pugwash's eyes, 'The Captain is a martinet and a twat, sir.'

There was an eruption of laughter and Mandy swept her hand to her mouth in horror. Jack held his stare with Pugwash, a picture of shock and awe, the smug look replaced by his more familiar, tight grimace. Mandy scanned the public benches, noticed Father Mike in the gallery, laughing with the crowd. What's he doing here, she thought?

'Yes, Mr Thackeray?' the Commissioner responded formerly to Len who had sprung to his feet.

'I ask you take into account my client has suffered many traumatic events this past few weeks, not least being in an explosion whilst rescuing a child.' There was a murmur of approval from the public gallery, and Mandy thought they are on his side at least, she cheered up ever so slightly, but Jack had glazed over.

'We are aware of the circumstances...' the commissioner commented, pointedly, '... and were amazed the proceedings were not postponed, is your client okay to proceed?'

'I would like a moment, I fear my client may be unwell.'

'Inspector, do you need a break?'

'Is there a *Kit Kat*?' Jack quipped, amusing the crowd.

'Jack?' Mandy thought she'd whispered, she hadn't.

The Commissioner sighed, and like Pontius Pilot before him, 'I'll take that as an okay, we will continue,' called on Pugwash who was up and poised like a terrier, but that is where the energy ended. The presentation of evidence from Pugwash droned, Len was up and down objecting, and it appeared Jack had actually gone to sleep. Pugwash eventually finished, formally submitted his evidence and the bench thanked him, looking like they were pleased it was over. 'Okay, I have the evidence of the Captain here...'

Jack's phone rang, 'Jonty?' Jack asked, waving the phone.

'Yes, Jane, you may.'

Jack gave the phone to Len who answered it for him. Jack took the call. There were two minutes while Jack spoke animatedly, even stood at one time, shouted the name "Barney" and "Feck the *Teasmade*" and "Worm" sat down, stood again, and Pugwash spluttered and protested.

The Commissioner lost it, 'Sit down, Captain.' The irony Jack was standing without being chastised was not lost on Pugwash. Jack did eventually sit and continued his phone conversation while the Commissioner berated the captain, 'We have been made aware there is something important happening, and I do not refer to this tribunal.' Pugwash demoralised and bemused, looked to the ugly sisters, but they were no help, trying to melt in to the background, impossible; they were the background.

Jack finished and Len cancelled the call for him. Pugwash was up, 'Sir, I want my objection formally noted.'

The commissioner had still to mellow, 'Should I formally note your error with the Inspector's name?' The chortling of the spectators was mixed with a tinkling, like breaking glass.

Jack had a text, and handed the phone to Len, and told him what to write in reply. That sent, Jack looked up to the front desk, a thumb up. Len switched the phone off, was tempted with a thumb, and chastised himself for coming under the Austin influence.

The Commissioner addressed the tribunal, 'We have read through both sets of papers and have the following comments. Len if you could hold your horses.' Len nodded, curious as to what was happening. The Commissioner continued, 'Captain, in your submission and presentation, you have not produced evidence the Inspector was the anonymous source for the newspaper article, and so, I am compelled to dismiss those allegations. I move on to the offence of insubordination to a senior officer.' Pugwash was not slow to show his indignation, but was put off objecting, 'Captain,' the commissioner asked, 'can you identify the senior officer please?' Len smiled, this was one of his. Pugwash stood, 'No need to stand Captain, unless you are planning to leave,' rumbles of laughter.

'Sir, I am not happy the way this tribunal is being run.' Pugwash expounded.

'Then make your complaints through the proper channels, we will assist you with our names, in the meantime, answer the question, who is the senior officer the Inspector is alleged to have been insubordinate to?'

'Me sir,' Pugwash stood to attention, felt the creases in his trousers, reassured, they were razor sharp.

'You, sir?'

'Yes, Sir.'

The Commissioner made a show of looking through the papers, and in an audible whisper, 'I can't see where it says the captain is a senior police officer, Chairman of the Community Policing Committee, but that is all.' He looked up to Pugwash, 'Captain are you a police officer?' Pugwash made to stand, 'No need to answer, we know you're not. We do not consider the reports you sent to us in any way substantiates a claim for insubordination, and so we dismiss this charge. However, you have a case for common assault. The Inspector admits this, but says you barged in aggressively on a *minute-silence* for a murdered colleague.' A sense of shock from the gallery. 'Your rights are clear if you wish to take this to the courts of law, but I tell you we will put up every officer I know against you, so, do you want to take this on?'

'No, sir.'

The Commissioner seemed satisfied, 'Okay, I understand that whilst we have been wasting our time here, the Inspector and the Superintendent have been doing their job; developments in the conspiracy case that has been prominent in both the local and national news. I am sure we will hear of this later, correct Inspector?' Jack nodded. The Commissioner looked at his fellow adjudicators and whispered, but it was clear they all agreed. 'It is the decision of this tribunal there are no grounds to substantiate the charges made and they are all dismissed. The Inspector may leave without a stain on his character.' There was polite applause, but the Commissioner put his hand up for quiet. 'We have looked into the background of the past few years and find that Inspector Austin has been treated unfairly by the Community Police Committee, and we reinstate him to the rank of Detective Chief Inspector with immediate effect.'

He allowed the assembly to absorb the news, raised his hand again, 'I would like to add my personal congratulations to the Chief Inspector and to say also...' he looked pointedly at Pugwash, '...the police force is not a place for politically ambitious laymen. It is a serious business, and at times, dangerous, as we have recently seen. We should be grateful to officers such as the Chief Inspector and the Superintendent, and we should not allow them to be used as political footballs for short-term political gain. This tribunal is closed.'

The committee room rose and there was great excitement, but Jack just sat, laid back in his chair, feet stretched out in front of him. The Commissioner approached, 'You have some very good friends Jane, please try not to make it too hard to help you, what do you say?'

He stood slowly, 'Nuff said, sir,' shook the Commissioner's hand, put his other hand on top of Jonty's wrist and they exchanged a look; Mandy had seen this before.

'You look exhausted.'

'I am completely shagged, sir, but Mandy and I have to go back to the Nick for a couple of hours, and then I shall be getting inordinately pissed with my friends at C&A's. You are welcome to join us, but I feel it only fair to warn you, I shall be plotting the downfall of the government.'

The Commissioner let his head roll back and guffawed, 'Knowing you Jack, you will succeed as well. I had a little whisper you will be awarded the GM and the Queen has apparently asked if you could try not to swear when you are with her this time.' Len and Mandy looked aghast, the Commissioner winked and shook all of their hands. 'Good defence papers, nicely handled Len,' and he left.

The room had emptied, except for Bernie. Pugwash had slunk away with his obese entourage, the room was noticeably lighter. 'Bernie, you are a revolting man, see you at C&A's tonight?'

'Wouldn't miss it for the world, can I have a quote?'

'An anonymous one?'

Mandy put her arm part way round Jack's waist and they walked. Colin was in the corridor, 'Back door?'

'Yes please.'

Len declined the party invite, 'I'm meeting friends at the Tate Modern.'

Jack, subdued, nodded approval, 'I like it there, and thank you, Len.'

————

THE TEAM SENSED a breakthrough and put Jack's jaundiced reaction down to the fact he looked exhausted. He shuffled off to join Mandy in her office, Jo-Jums and Paolo followed, and settled on the psychological chairs, while Jack took the PVC chair; the tree swayed hypnotically in a gentle breeze. Mandy took charge, 'What do you have, Paolo, Jo?'

'Coughed, Ma'am; we need to charge and dig more.'

'Paolo?'

'I agree, Worm and the Leader were middle men, we need to get what we can and see where it leads.'

Mandy dismissed Paolo. 'Jo, can you stay please.'

Paolo went to Jack, 'I heard, congratulations,' shook his hand and left.

'Will miracles never cease?' Mandy remarked, 'Jo, did you hear Jack is back as DCI?'

'I did.' There was no need for words, it was written on her face.

'I'm putting you up for Inspector, okay?'

'Yes, Ma'am, I'd be pleased to accept.'

'Finally, Jack and I are going to do the business on this desk,' and she patted the desk top, 'then a piss-up at C&A's, so round up the usual suspects.' Jo left.

'Jack, are you all talk?'

'What, the bit where I said I was bone-tired?'

FIFTY-THREE

IT WAS ONE OF THOSE MOMENTS IN EVERY RELATIONSHIP, and Jack offered no manly defence. Hidden depths? Mandy dismissed that thought as ridiculous, 'C'mon, let's get you home.'

She drove and he slept, answered a call with the hands free, 'Hi, Mandy, he didn't call, and his phone is off, how did it go?'

'Sorry, Michael, scot free and back to DCI.'

'What? Fantastic, is he there?'

She chanced a look, 'In a manner of speaking.'

———

MICHAEL HAD to shake his dad awake, then steer him to the front door where Colleen stood and waved. Mandy shrugged acknowledgement and allowed the engine to idle as she contemplated going back to her flat, a hint of despair as she pressed the accelerator; how did she feel about Liz and Carly? What was interesting was she forgot about Jack as her nerves increased about going home, for God's sake, she was a modern woman, wasn't she?

After parking the car in the basement garage she went up the lift and along the corridor, to the door of her flat; next dilemma. Should she ring the bell or use her key? She used her key but called out, 'Only me.'

Liz popped out of the living room and kissed her mum, 'How'd it go?'

On automatic, 'Teflon Jack, scot free and promoted back to DCI, how does he do it?'

Carly joined them in the hallway. 'He not with you?'

'Fast asleep, big drink at C&A's tonight, you're both welcome,' Mandy said.

Carly carried on, 'Mandy, I know only what I've learned in the past few days, but has Jack not been through more traumas in the past week than most people have in a lifetime, and is this not a bit of good news?' Mandy wondered if she did not have more questions than answers, and was going to say what the feck is it to do with you, but didn't. 'Can I ask why you look dejected, or do you feel left out?'

'Sorry?'

'Mum, Carly's a psychiatrist.'

'Oh, and I suppose you're going to analyse me and my difficulty in dealing with my daughter being a lesbian.'

Carly responded in her understanding psychiatrist voice, 'Yes, we should talk about that, but maybe a bath and a sleep would not go amiss?'

Mandy turned to Liz, 'I'm sorry, I can't explain what I feel. I have these crazy feelings about Jack, the ugly tow-rag, was hit on by a lesbian myself recently, and I want to say I am pleased for you, that I'm a modern woman and things like this are acceptable to me, as they are for colleagues and so on, but honestly, I'm having difficulty.'

Carly carried on, 'Liz should have talked to you before but...'

Carly's diatribe washed over Mandy, 'You know what really pisses me off? Jack guessed, before I knew.'

Carly hemmed, 'Deceptively, perceptive? I've not quite made up my mind. We have a bottle of wine and some nibbles, I can run you a bath and we can get a bit sloshed, then get really pissed at the pub tonight.'

Mandy sniffed, 'Sounds like a plan, just need time, I suppose.'

'Like Jack, getting over Kate?'

Feck me she speaks Mandy thought, 'Touché,' she replied, and went to the loo for a cry.

———

THE TAXI DROPPED Mandy off at Jack's at a quarter to eight and carried on with Liz and Carly to C&A's, another dilemma, should she open the door with her key or rap Kate's knockers? She was saved the decision as Colleen swung it open and asked if she was coming in?

'Is he up?'

'Michael's waking him, drink?'

'Glass of red?'

'Coming up,' and Colleen trotted to the kitchen. Mandy followed with hunched shoulders and feelings. 'Should be a good party, is he up for it, he looked all in when you dropped him off this afternoon.' Colleen took in the look of Mandy, 'What about you?'

'Mixed up.'

She handed her the wine, 'Jack, or Liz and Carly?

'Both,' quaffing; she was beyond sipping.

'Worried Jack's not over Kate, because Michael was

concerned for when he was at the Crematorium, we've not seen you since.'

She looked over the top of her wine glass, 'Jack was in a state, but how much was Kate or Biscuit, God knows?'

'Time again, isn't it?'

Mandy looked up, more animated, 'Yes, but I let go, and now I'm floundering. I'm not used to feeling helpless.'

'He's in for a Tom and an Eiffel, Mandy, you look good.'

This lifted her spirits, like father like son, she thought. 'Thought I'd dress up a bit,' she gave Michael a twirl.

'Top up?'

'Please.'

'To Teflon, Dad,' they chinked their glasses and sat back on stools. Jack appeared after ten minutes, wet hair, suit and open neck shirt, looking refreshed, and Mandy had to admit, gorgeous, if you could get past the fat ugly bit. Mandy however, had not slept, felt knackered, and was way past tipsy.

She stood to greet him. 'Haggly?' he asked, kissed her, and with his hand on her backside she allowed herself to be pulled to him, her concerns melted, thinking I was the one worried about his non-performance and it's as if it mattered not a jot to him. 'Alright sweet'art, not worried about this afternoon?' turned to Colleen and Michael, 'Couldn't get it up, a lot better now though.'

'Jack! You're embarrassing me.'

'Shouldn't I be embarrassed?'

'I've never seen you embarrassed, is it possible?' Colleen to the rescue.

'Well, the first time Mandy farted in bed.'

Mandy sighed, 'Shall we go?'

They walked to C&A's. It wasn't far, and the evening was mild if overcast. Mandy in a sleeveless dress, a shiny two tone blue, tiny cream knitted jacket, teetered on high heels. Jack raised his eyebrow, 'Had a couple of wines, while Carly, who is a trick cyclist I might add, sorted my head out about Liz being Lesbian...'

He interrupted, 'From the Isle of Lesbos.'

'Yes, Jack, you had resisted that for a long time and I was grateful. Had a couple with Michael and Colleen as they tried to straighten my head out about you. So, all in all, I'm ready for a few more and you may need you to carry me home, are you up to it?'

Michael shouted back, having listened in, 'We will carry you both home; you've earned this.'

'He has, and for a man who can't stand decorating, he's a list of decorations and about to get another, the George Medal, no less,' and Mandy gave Jack a sloppy kiss in the middle of the road, frustrating a car that wanted to get by; the driver froze from the Mandy stare.

'Dad, is this true?'

'Apparently, now shut-up, Let's have a drink.'

'Mandy, will you go to the Palace with him?' she detected a hint of panic, 'Mum went last time and said she'd never been so embarrassed in her life.'

Jack explained, 'The Queen farted in front of her, you know how Kate was when it was her turn.' They all groaned, and Jack stopped by the pub door. 'Let's not talk about this tonight, eh, that is embarrassing.'

Michael shook his dad's hand, 'Get here, you bleedin' eejit,' and Jack hugged his son. 'Funny, going in without Martin,' Mandy looked at him, how much did he really miss Martin? Colleen opened the door and dragged Mandy in, Jack followed with an arm around the shoulders of his son.

Bruce greeted Mandy with a hug and a kiss, both cheeks, a bit continental for a big beery man Jack thought, shaking Bruce's hand who held on and tugged him into the rear function room where he was greeted with an almighty roar, and the theme from *Captain Pugwash*, played by an Irish style band; squeeze box and fiddle player. 'I've seen you embarrassed now Jack,' Colleen shouted into his ear.

The band finished and Sitting Bull was standing in a clearing, a hushed expectancy,

'Detective CHIEF Inspector Jane Austin,' a cheer, 'your colleagues and friends have gathered this evening to say thank you, for being you.' More applause; Sitting Bull put his hand up. 'There's not much more to say except you are a real copper, and I'm right proud to call you colleague and friend.' Mandy thought to herself, "real copper?" she was not so sure, but let it go and walked up and kissed him to a resounding, "Oooh err matron".

That was it, and Jack grabbed the pint proffered by mein host Bruce and he downed it in one to the sound of *"Get them down, you Zulu warrior,"* wiped his face, turned the glass upside down on his head, drops of beer came out, and he burped, 'Beer shampoo.'

The band struck up with a jig and many people, not afraid to make fools of themselves, got up and pranced around like fools. Jack watched, Mandy slipped her arm into his, 'Okay?'

'I love you,' he mouthed.

'Me too,' she sloshed back.

FIFTY-FOUR

Coppers on a night off; the evening grew in intensity, laughter, dancing and drinking. Mandy's frequent kisses getting progressively wetter. Jack sang *Underneath the Arches*, the rugby version, to hoots of laughter, he finished, shouting, "Throw money, throw money," apparently his dad's, Uncle Peter, shouted that in the East End pubs.

Mandy seemed more relaxed with Liz and Carly, dancing and kissing, as was everyone comfortable with Frankie and Connie. For a bunch of pissed-up coppers, whose reputation to the public is not one of resounding tolerance, they took all of this in their stride. 'Makes you proud, eh girl, we've come a long way,' Jack said. The band struck up a reel and Mandy and Jack did their totally un-Irish, Irish dancing. Jack called it broken arm dancing and they reeled and swirled; Riverdance it wasn't.

There was a hush, then silence as the musicians reacted. Pugwash stood beneath a spotlight, his piggy eyes looking demonic; a red glint. Jack strode to Pugwash and held out his hand. The Captain ignored the gesture, was about to say something when Jack interrupted, 'You're either mad or you've got balls, and I had you pegged for a girl,' they stared; testiculating Mandy called it.

Blood boiled as Pugwash advanced out of the spotlight and closed on Jack, and through gritted teeth, finger prodding, 'I'm not finished with you, Austin.'

The assembled party, aware of Jack's berserking, readied themselves, but they needn't have worried because Mandy wobbled in, blousy and ballsy, and inordinately pissed. 'Threaten my man again and you'll have to go through me, you mealy mouthed fucking arsehole.' She was pushing and jabbing. Pugwash didn't know how to react, or even if he understood the slurred words, but he was getting both Mandy barrels and her intent was clear. He shuffled backwards, struggling to keep his balance. 'Fuck-off back to your tin pot boats and push your little sailor boys around. You're not man enough to stand in the same room with my man. Jack Austin is more man than you could ever be, so, unless you want a pair of stilettos up your fucking anally retentive arse, you'd better fuck-off, now.' She teetered, people shaped to catch her, but she held firm, ironically, steadied by her grip of Pugwash's jacket.

Pugwash broke the grip and did go, spluttering inanities, clunked on his head by a couple of well aimed stilettos. Jack slipped his arm around her waist, whispered, 'Are you shorter?' and turned to the crowd of hushed, inebriated, coppers. 'I am pleased to say we will not have to rescue Mandy's shoes from Pugwash's arse,' he pulled his other arm around, complete with pink hand, wrapped her up and kissed her for a very long time.

"Oooh err matron" resounded and the party resumed, and just past midnight Bruce called time for people to drink up. Slowly, people dispersed, calls of bonhomie fuelled by large quantities of alcohol, and "Watch out Moriarty", "Montyfarty" and eventually "Toryparty". Mandy was in a little crowd of Liz, Carly, Frankie, Connie, Jo-Jums, Dorothy, Dolly, Mike and

Alice, they were doing Jack's version of his aunts' East End dancing, skirts pulled up, legs bent, knees splayed, jogging up to one another, going backwards, to be repeated. Jack could not resist joining, as did Bruce; if you can't beat 'em.

It was one thirty when eventually they lefty the pub, and Mandy, propped by Jack, teetered along the pavement, the road and then the pavement. Liz and Carly hopped a cab with Mike, and Michael and Colleen walked ahead canoodling and giggling, previous offers of assistance forgotten. Mandy, decidedly green about the gills, was eying up a very comfortable looking privet hedge, when Pugwash jumped out from behind the corner of a house and punched Jack, full on the face. He staggered back as Mandy screamed and tumbled into the hedge. Jack reacted in his berserking mist and lunged, hurling punch after punch, most fortuitously hitting the mark. Pugwash hit the deck and was being repeatedly kicked before Bruce and Michael held Jack until he calmed. They could hear Mandy being sick, but where? Turning to the sound of retching and giggling, they saw her legs sticking out of a privet hedge.

Neighbours were calling out of their bedroom windows, letting them know the time. Jack thanked them, told them it was okay, he didn't have to be up in the morning, and had trouble not laughing when they said they had called the police. Michael and Bruce released Jack's arms and his eye followed their gaze to Mandy's legs, he thought her slender ankles looked lovely in the blue flashing lights. They began to drag her through the hedge backwards, but she was sick again. 'I think the sandwiches were off, Jack,' she called out, giggling and heaving.

'Jane,' a PC whose name Jack could not remember.

'Nick him,' Jack ordered, releasing his hold on Mandy and pointing to a groaning Pugwash, sat on the kerb. Mandy fell back screaming, laughing, sick; mentioned something about

Jack's multitasking abilities. He went back to Mandy, held onto the ankles for safekeeping but accidentally let them go again, as he explained the obvious charges to the policeman, 'Assaulting a police officer...and, the Superintendent and I may need a lift home. Now where is she?'

The PC handcuffed Pugwash to the lamppost and asked his colleague to stay while he dropped the Inspector and the Super home. Jack and the constable went into the garden, it was clear Mandy was not going to be able to manage unaided or back the way she went into the hedge, and when Jack and Mandy got into the police car, the neighbours seemed satisfied. Jack looked back through the rear window of the patrol car, saw Pugwash handcuffed to the lamppost, looking as if he was making love to a supermodel. Mandy spluttered a laugh, he'd spoken his thoughts, pulled her to him; imagined she smelled, as he felt around his bleeding nose.

The uniform helped Jack get Mandy out of the car, folded her over the garden wall; she was sick in the borders. 'She be alright, sir?'

'Fine, lock sailor boy up, our Nick, please.'

The PC disappeared and Jack helped Mandy through the door and up the stairs, straight into the wet room where she was sick again, mumbling something about one good turn deserving another; it was only a few days ago Mandy was holding him while he was sick; such is romance he thought. He took his pink hand off, flexed his fingers, they may be getting better, undid the long zip and pulled Mandy's dress off.

There was a tap at the door, 'D'you need a hand?'

He had Mandy's dress between thumb and forefinger, 'Thanks, Colleen, not sure what we can do with this?'

Colleen took the dress and disappeared. Mandy stood and fuzzed a smile, 'Managed the dress, hope for you yet, lover boy,' hiccoughed, slapped his face playfully, and grinned, which had a cartoon effect. Jack impressed further with the bra strap, off in less than twenty minutes, suspender belt, stockings and knickers; wrapped her in a towel, sat her on the toilet seat, nipped out and returned in his dressing gown, stripped off and went into the shower with her. She responded to him but he was busy cleaning and making sure she was okay, and eventually put her into bed, kissed her, and she was asleep; he cleared up, put his dressing gown back on and went downstairs.

'Feisty woman, Jack,' Colleen was sponging Mandy's dress at the sink. 'I'll drop this into the cleaner's tomorrow morning. She okay?'

'Yeah, think we all enjoyed ourselves, except for the Pugwash bits.'

Colleen leaned back against the sink, 'What will happen to him?'

'We'll put the frighteners on and let him go, but he's the sort to have another pop...' he shrugged. 'Thanks, Colleen, I'm off to bed, where's Michael?'

She pecked him on the cheek, 'Good night, Michael's in bed and probably asleep; settling down aren't we?'

'It's nice like that sometimes.'

She smiled, 'Night, Jack.'

FIFTY-FIVE

Jack spent the first couple of minutes of consciousness releasing his tongue from the top of his birdcage mouth; Mandy was still out for the count. He went downstairs, the clock approaching ten. Saturday, no pressure, just the nagging in the back of his head; the case, so many angles? He ruminated, staring into the kitchen wall tiles. Many times in his career he had come across different facets of human behaviour and crime, behind most of it, the seeking of power over others; robbing money or possessions, terrorism, religion even, and had said as much to Father Mike about the rise of the church in Europe, based hugely on fear rather than faith; afterwards he felt guilty. Standing by the sink, he thought this case, ironically, seemed to be not about seeking power, but demonstrating how powerless we are. But why, what for?

When he returned with coffee, Mandy was sitting up, the quilt tucked under her arms. He thought she looked lovely with privet in her hair; Roman, or was that laurel, no, her name was Amanda not Stan. 'You look like you've been dragged through a hedge backwards.'

'Thanks,' she replied, he kissed her and pulled out several twigs and spun them in the fingers of his good hand. 'Oh, how...?'

He eased her concern, 'Pugwash jumped me and the shock made you fall into the hedge, which, you found quite comfortable.'

'Oh God, I did, didn't I?' She tapped the bed, 'Get in, I want a cuddle with liberties.' He did, and the desk was forgotten, as were a lot of things, including the rest of the morning as they slept on.

The phone woke them, it was Meesh. Jackie was going to drop her down with Martin in about half an hour. They leapt out of bed, one bathroom each for some essentials, shared a shower, and Jack was downstairs for when Meesh knocked. The little girl bounded in, Martin, barking and running all over the place, followed up more sedately by the elegantly tall and slender Jackie. She had the look he had seen often in the past few days, but there was noticeably a more relaxed demeanour. She was in jeans and T-shirt, kicked her trainers off, not taking her eyes from his blossoming black eye. He greeted her with a peck on the cheek, one, but clearly she expected two and there was a stifled what do I do moment. Jack looked into her eyes that were a deep brown, and then just the whites showed. He went to plant the other kiss but Jackie had moved on, his lips brushed the croissant as it went by; Pratt he thought, Twat she thought; they nearly agreed on something.

Meesh was rollicking with Martin, 'They look good together,' Jack said, 'Martin's better.' He didn't say anything about Meesh, just tilted his head; how's she doing?

'Do I smell coffee?' Jackie asked.

Jack did the biz, mocha pot on the stove, turned back to Jackie, 'A minor celebration last night,' as if this explained everything about the way he was feeling, and looked, lucky he'd cleaned his teeth; something else they agreed upon.

'I know, Jo phoned.' The coffee bubbled and Jack got some cups; the playful barks of Martin stirred his butterflies. 'Strong black, and please, I've heard them all.'

'He will still make them. Hi Jacks,' Mandy appeared in one of Jack's shirts, kissed Jackie on both cheeks, bloody Europeans Jack thought, it's so confusing, it won't be long before they spend all their time bouncing from cheek to cheek. Hissing Sid said they were doing four in France now, but how he knew when the furthest he went was Brighton? He looked up, concerned he'd spoken; he hadn't.

'Seen Meesh?'

Mandy laughed, 'Yeah, had a cuddle, and Martin got jealous,' the barking explained, 'least he left my leg alone.'

They sat around the table, sipping coffee. Jackie broke the comfortable silence, 'You look washed out you two.'

'An understatement, what's up, Doc?' Mandy asked.

Jack looked naturally cautious, probably because Jackie was looking at him, 'Meesh is settling well at Gail's, a healthy bond developing, early days, we have a crisis to come, but I'm encouraged.'

Jack was impatient, 'Spit it out, Phil.'

Jackie snapped back, 'I want to leave Martin with Meesh a bit longer, and outside the office call me Jackie or Jacks, please.'

Jack looked to disguise the hurt on his face; Meesh was at the doorway listening. He'd forgotten this, kids, they creep up on you like Father Mike, and then, they know all your secrets. Power again, kids over parents, as the church over the congregation. Meesh was looking up at Jack, 'Can Martin stay with me, please?' No begging eyes or games, a plea from a child used to getting nothing she wanted.

He melted, 'Call Martin, we'll ask him.'

She did the imitation of Jack's discordant whistle, and Martin bounded in and sat beside Meesh's leg. Jack thought on that as well, as he addressed *his* dog. 'Martin,' his ears pricked, a sideways inquisitive look, 'Spesh would like you to stay with her, how do you feel about that?' Jack knew how to illicit a bark, and Martin complied. 'Okay, Meesh,' she looked on attentively, 'does Martin sleep on the bed with you?' She paused, thought it through, nodded as if this was wrong, but told the truth. 'Good, because I don't want him to be lonely at night,' she smiled with relief. 'Do you walk him and do you pick up his poo?'

She looked a bit iffy and Jackie intervened. 'She walks him with one of the others, often Keanu, and she's getting used to picking up the doings, aren't you?' Meesh nodded, a hint of a wry smile, a glance of thanks to Jackie.

Jack turned to Mandy who was looking lovingly at him, 'What do you think, Mandy, will you be able to part with Martin?'

Martin was at Wimbledon, flicking head to and fro. 'If Meesh is going to look after him, yes,' Mandy answered.

'Martin, will you look after Meesh as well?' Jack got him to bark. 'Well, that's settled, I will also call Phil, Jackie,' he looked up to Jackie, and she could not tell if he was hurt or just accepting this loss, his dog, and all of the other things in his life. Meesh looked surprised things had gone for her, a hug for Martin, she cuddled a portion of Jack's waist, then to Mandy, onto her lap and kissed her cheek, just the once. At a girl, how long before she becomes European Jack thought, wrenched in the heart department.

'Jackie, Jack is taking me on a date tonight, so if you would not mind dropping me home, I am going to kick Liz and Carly out,' and Mandy crossed her fingers in the air, 'sleep, and get ready.'

Jack could not disguise his shock, but Jackie was intrigued

having guessed the man had been cornered, 'That's nice, where are you taking her?' she grinned at Mandy.

Jack wondered if this was the time to have a fit, but his consequent vacant look seemed sufficient, as Mandy and Jackie shared a laugh at his expense, but he did recover the position by tapping his nose; that usually did the trick, and then he had a light bulb moment.

FIFTY-SIX

RANT AND RAVE, EIFFEL TOWER, BISH-BOSH, JACK WAS invigorated.

'Hi Jack.'

'Colleen, listen sweet'art I've not got my dressing gown, look the other way there's a luv.'

'C'mon, it's nothing I haven't seen before,' and she went down the stairs giggling, and he heard Michael asking what was so funny; he liked Colleen. Michael had asked why she didn't have a nickname, and Jack thought he had better think about that.

'Dad, why are you standing there with no clothes on?'

'Shite, son, I stopped to think.'

Jack to his son. 'I won't tell Mandy.' Jack was relieved, and Michael smiled at his dad's discomfort and wobbly bottom as he disappeared into his bedroom to be confronted with the next problem; no clothes. He resolved to ask Mandy to shop with him. Time she knew my waist size anyway he thought, there was no way to break that sort of thing gently to a woman; as if it will come as a shock to her.

Jack stood at the kitchen door looking at Colleen and Michael together, 'Dad, I know you're there.' He carried on and sat with them. 'What're you doing this evening, Dad?'

'First date with Amanda, and frankly, son, I'm nervous.'

'Leave it out, Dad.'

'No, Michael, Jack's right, this is important, even if it is arse about face.'

Jack looked askance, 'Did I just hear correctly?'

'Sorry, my language has deteriorated, my parents blame Michael but it's you, Jack,' Colleen explained.

'Of course,' Jack answered, proud, taking a bullet for his son.

'Where're you going?'

Puffing out his chest, 'Finest seafood in town, son, we love seafood, have that in common.'

'You do?'

'Yes, Colleen, we do.'

'Have you asked her?'

A confused look, 'No, a man just knows, male institution.'

'Do you mean intuition?'

'Maybe.'

'Dad, you always say for a port there's a dearth of good seafood restaurants.'

'Worse than that, son, this is a fishing port, not just your sailor boys here.'

'So, where're you taking Mandy?' Colleen asked, as apprehensive as Michael.

Jack beamed, 'Fatso's.'

Colleen had not heard of Fatso's, but by the look of horror on Michael's face, she guessed he had, 'Not sure I know that one?'

Michael felt he should enlighten Colleen, 'Fatso is a trawler skipper, and sometimes Dad goes to meet him, and his wife Maisie cooks on the boat.'

'My God, you cannot be serious.'

'Has *John McEnroe* walked in?' and Jack shifted in his chair to lecture Colleen on the culinary delights of fresh seafood. 'It's authentic, how many women get taken to such a unique place. The flavours are simple and sublime, from the net to the pot, to the plate, you can't ask for more, can you?'

But Michael thought you could, 'Maybe somewhere clean that didn't smell of diesel and fish guts?'

There appeared the look of a Mexican stand-off forming between father and son. 'Colleen, you've hooked yerself up with an unromantic bore. Expand your vision, son, there's more to life than bistros and wine bars full of postulating Tory tarts,' he jumped up before Michael could tell him it was posturing. 'Need a poo, where're your *Playboy* mags, son?'

Colleen looked shocked, 'Just kidding, Winders,' (said like Windows), it came to him in a flash, Colleen - *Windolene*, a patent window cleaner. Sentimental too, Jack's dad had been a window cleaner in Stepney in East London, had been known as Winders, Jack as Winder's Boy. This was not lost on Michael. At his granddad's funeral, his dad's eulogy emphasised how proud he was to be Winder's Boy.

'Dad?'

'Yes, son,' Jack was looking for something to read, eying the cornflakes box.

'Don't take the cornflakes to the toilet, and does this make me Winder's Boy?'

'Colleen, is he a man or boy?' distracted by the cornflakes.

'Definitely a man,' Colleen answered, confused as to what was transpiring between father and son.

'Then I would say you would be Winder's Man, leave me as Winder's Boy, eh?' he walked back, rubbed his son's hair, smiled, but Michael noticed the melancholic head as he turned, leaving Michael to do the explanations.

There was a tap on the door, 'Go away, contaminated area.'

'I know, it's coming under the door, I wanted to say you're a lovely man,' Colleen said.

'Only lovely?'

'Smelly as well.'

———

JACK WHISTLED, Mandy was in a lustrous crimson, silk or something swishy and shiny, full dress, just above the knee, short sleeves, V neck and a spanner bodice. 'Close your mouth we are not a codfish,' and Mandy mouthed, '532 nil'; Jack let her have that one.

Michael and Colleen looked at each other; Mandy noticed. She pecked Jack's cheek, 'Well, where are we going? I have to admit I have those first date nerves.'

'So do I,' Michael said.

'Seafood, darling, I know how much you like it,' Jack answered, giving his son a look.

'You like it, I'm okay with it,' did she notice Colleen's eyes go to the ceiling just then? 'Okay, seafood, whereabouts, Jack?'

'A surprise.'

'I bet.'

'Sorry, Michael, and are you rolling your eyes Colleen?'

'I'll check the front window for the cab,' Jack said, ducking for cover.

Michael sidled to Mandy, 'You love my dad?'

'I confess I do,' Mandy answered nervously.

'Then hang onto that thought this evening, he has a knack of screwing things up.'

'I know what you mean,' Mandy laughed, but did she really?

FIFTY-SEVEN

The Camber is a picturesque combination of Old Portsmouth working quay, and leisure area, at the mouth of Portsmouth Harbour; fishing fleet, Isle of Wight Ferries, private boats in the harbour and stacked on the quayside. "Nice pubs and okay restaurants," Jack would say. It was a warm evening, the buildings tinged red with the setting sun, and Mandy nestled into Jack, happy to walk, enjoying the moment. A girl, fifteen or so, dressed to kill, sashayed, "Allo Jack,' she tip toed, stretched and kissed him on his dodgy eye, 'noyce t'see yer,' and skipped off.

'Close your mouth,' Jack said. Mandy said nothing, she was processing information. 'I love it here, the sight, the smell, the people, the real ones not the wealthy buggers in their matchbox townhouses.'

'Admiring the view, Jack.'

'Fatso.'

Mandy followed Jack's eye to the fishing boat, low in the water beside the quay, 'Someone's shouting at you?'

'That's Fatso.'

She looked again, a scrawny man, probably fiftyish, tanned leathery skin, wrinkled face set with sparkly blue eyes, was grinning through a Spartan set of teeth, but seemingly distracted, intent on cleaning the deck like his life depended on it. 'Didn't expect you so early, I have to clean up, you know how Maisie can get.'

'I do, Fatso.' Mandy looked down to the working boat, to a joyful Jack, confident his nice surprise was filtering through, 'Freshest fish in town sweet'art, from the net to the pot, to the plate, no sauces, just good fish; sublime,' and he put his fingers to his mouth and kissed them away.

She was going to repost as soon as her speech faculties returned, looked down again at Fatso, two teeth visible in a black hole. 'Sorry,' he called out, 'Maisie'll be here soon with my clean vest.' Mandy only then noticed Fatso wore a formerly white vest, the material just managing to hold together, thick tufts of black hair sticking out through vast tears and sagging armholes; a gorilla, a thin one she thought, but a very close relative of the apes, nevertheless.

'Didn't tell yer, did he, honey?' A short, stout, matronly woman appeared, bottle legs planted akimbo, arms folded, just missing the rolling pin. She had a grimy apron over a black dress, but it was her hair on top of the round outdoor face Mandy noticed first; short, black, dressed like a man in the forties, slick with *Brylcreem*, she thought again, it was Hitler's haircut. As Jack lowered his head in what seemed like an accepted ritual, Mrs Hitler spoke, 'He's a daft bugger,' and she kissed him long and hard on his gammy eye. Jack looked nervous, a Mama-Mia holding her errant grown up child. Jack's face, still clasped, the woman turned to Mandy, but spoke to Jack, 'I know who this is, seen her on the telly, but, Jack, introduce me or I'll bat you into the harbour.'

'Maisie, this is Amanda Bruce,' he said, hesitantly.

'Amanda, Fatso and I welcome you, and more so because you mean so much to Jack. I think you'd better come with me,' Mandy was speechless, but Jack could see how much she was enjoying herself. Maisie tugged Mandy's hand as three teenage girls, teetering on unfeasibly high heeled shoes, in turn, kissed Jack's sunken eye, "Hoi, Jack" and they clacked and wobbled off, giggling and gabbling, strong Pompey accents, short skirts and skimpy tops.

Jack shouted after them, 'You'll get pneumonia of the arse dressed like that.' They looked back, giggled and wiggled their fingers. Mandy, trancelike, walked on with Maisie, Jack spoke to Fatso, 'Pint? The deck looks lovely, no need to get the Hoover out.'

Fatso nimbly scaled the rusty steel ladder fixed to the harbour wall and appeared at the top as Maisie and Mandy were disappearing into one of the large working sheds. 'Be in the Bridge, babes,' Fatso Shouted. The Bridge was the local pub named after a bridge that formerly crossed the harbour at this point.

The voluminous shed had a lofty ceiling, tin walls, slick concrete floor and expansive shallow china sinks; the smell more than suggested it was the fish gutting space. Pinching her nose, Mandy ducked into a changing room, 'Get that gorgeous dress off darlin', the boat'll not be as clean as it should.' Mandy stood her fishy ground as Maisie produced a set of overalls the same hue as Fatso's vest. 'I'll put the dress in this locker,' and Mrs Hitler had her undressed before Mandy could think, Isle of Lesbos? Boiler-suited and shod in huge trainers Maisie said were her little son's, did she say little, and looking like *Coco the Clown,* she followed Maisie. Despite assurances of cleanliness, the overalls stank of fish, diesel and male body odour, and a nauseous Mandy waddled after Mrs Hitler as she headed for the pub.

379

Jack's raucous laughter greeted Mandy and Maisie, he was at the bar with Fatso and six working men; this bar was for the Dockers in their working clothes. The tarts, as Jack called them, were in the other bar. Jack whistled, 'Here she is, better in real life than on the telly my girl.' Mandy admired his confidence, *my girl*. Eight men faced Mandy and grinned. Although she was about to chuck him in the harbour, she felt pleased Jack had the most teeth. The door swung and a Jack-the-lad and his girl bounced in, the man shook Jack's hand, Jack put his hand on the man's wrist, they exchanged a glance and the girl kissed his eye.

Maisie looked at Mandy, 'You need to be told a thing or two about your man, drink?' Before she could say, Maisie had ordered two port and lemons. Mandy thought, Port and lemon, boiler suit? There's never a hedge around when you want one. Strangely she enjoyed the port and lemon, and the edge, though not the hedge, was coming off.

'Having a good time sweetie; good,' Jack, oblivious of the chaos he was causing around him. 'Off for a gypsy's kiss, then something to eat I think,' he rubbed his hands, looked at Maisie.

'Got your favourite, Jack.'

'Lubbly stuff, Frau Fuhrer.'

Mandy thought, he calls her Mrs Hitler, am I thinking like him already? Oh please, no, a tiny despairing sigh picked up by Maisie who took her by the arm, 'Come on, they'll be some time weeing on each other's shoes,' and guffawed, more teeth than Fatso but not many more.

The tide was right out and it was a long way down the ladder. The combination of the port and lemon and clowns shoes meant she had to go very slowly, struck by the verticality. She rubbed her red rust hands on the overalls and felt instantly guilty; these were clean. Maisie was already down in the lower cabin, Mandy followed, impressed at how clear and clean it was, cosy, polished timber lined, but even Dolly's polish could not disguise the odour; fish and diesel. Mandy started to ask Maisie about Jack, but the clanking and rasping laughter suggested he was coming down the ladder.

Maisie signed, 'Tell you later' and took a call on her mobile. 'Darlin', you had a score yesterday. Come to the boat and get a tenner off your dad, he's had a few drinks with Jack.' She listened, 'Yes, here, and guess what, he's brought the girl off the telly. Clear as daylight darling, learning impaired, she's besotted with him,' Maisie laughed and hung-up. 'She said you should have gone to *Specsavers*,' Maisie said, as Jack and Fatso squashed themselves around the table, Jack beckoning Mandy to sit with him. She was not sure why, but she went, and he let her scoot across the bench seat and tuck herself in.

'Was that Dottie?'

Maisie busied herself, calling back, 'She's coming to see you, but just wants to scam a tenner off her dad and probably look gooey eyes at you Jack. He's a sucker Mandy, must be worth a tenner,' she carried on in the galley.

'Is he?' Mandy felt the boat move as another craft went by.

'Alright, babes? Wait till the Isle of Wight ferry, rocks like young-en then.'

'Oh great,' Mandy thought, definitely no hedges on board, she'd looked.

Maisie plonked down bowls of deliciously smelling mussels. Jack, using an empty shell as a tool, picked one which he proffered to Mandy, and like a child in a high chair, she opened her mouth and he dropped it in; minus the choo-choo train noise at least. She was taken aback, 'Gorgeous, eh?' Maisie enquired. They were; chopped shallots, white wine and steamed. She savoured the mussels and Mrs Hitler's warm smile. Jack rested his hand on Mandy's thigh and she picked it up and put it back; these were clean overalls.

'Sea Bass next, Jack, your favourite.'

This sorted his disappointed, bewildered face, "Andsome Fatso.'

Mrs Hitler mooned over her men; what is it with this ugly bloke, Mandy thought, I've got to get out of this. The boat swayed responding to a clumping on the deck, 'That'll be Dottie,' Maisie said, as the cabin door opened and down the narrow steps came a slim and beautiful young woman. Mandy thought early twenties, same dark hair as Maisie, but piled up on top, back combed, then dead straight to the sides, clearly the frame of Fatso but not the body hair, which Mandy was sure Dottie would be grateful for. She teetered in, pushing a barrage of perfume in front of her, clad in very tight jeans, a leather biker jacket and a Metallica T-shirt, high heel shoes; how did she get down the ladder?

'Mom, Dad,' and Dottie went straight to Jack, swivelled her hips and sat on his lap and kissed his eye. 'Oncle Jack,' broad Pompey accent; Oncle? Mandy thought, same as Alice says it.

'Dottie, this is Amanda,' Jack said from behind a cloud of lacquered beehive hair that tickled his nose.

Dottie leaned and shook Mandy's hand, 'Saw you on telly, didn't I?'

'Yes,' Mandy smiled, thinking why am I jealous?

'You look lovely, but Ted's overalls?' and she giggled, didn't wait for an answer, looked towards Fatso, her mission recollected, 'Dad, lend me a tenner please?'

'Lend?'

'Give, Dinlo,' and she tittered.

Fatso gave her a tenner and Dottie lifted off Jack's lap so he could get a tenner out as well, 'There you go, and don't get pissed.'

'Jack, you daft bugger, this is for cocaine,' and she pocketed the money and wiggled her fingers goodbye and was off up the stairs, and Mandy could not help envying her youth and her bum, looked at Jack; I'm off to the Isle of Lesbos, pretty sure Jackie would take her.

Maisie told Jack to sit next to Fatso then squashed in beside Mandy and pointed to the stair, 'That, sweet'art, is why Jack is here, and why he has only one eye.'

'Maisie, shut-up being a drama queen and get the sea bass, me taste buns are going on strike waiting.'

Maisie ignored him, 'Buds, and, Mandy, you need to fall in love with a man like him, warts, gammy eye and all. He's a royal pain in the arse but will always be welcome here. He saved that girl and got his eye for the pain.' She pointed to the stair again, 'Our little Dorothy, from the *Yellow Brick Road*, love that film, don't I, Fatso?'

Fatso had a hopeless expression. 'She does, drives me up the bleedin' wall, but there's no doubt she loves it,' he looked glum at the prospect of watching the film again.

Ignoring that the film was *The Wizard of Oz* Mandy looked at Maisie, averting her eyes from Jack, 'Was he not glassed in a pub fight?'

'Is that what he told you?'

She looked taken aback, and not for the first time that evening, 'Err, no, it's what is said. I've known Jack for nine years, well, you never ask do you, and that is what I thought, or was told.' She felt nervy, the ground shifting below her feet, which was the Isle of Wight ferry leaving.

'Darlin', I'll cut a long story short,' and Maisie put her fat arm around Mandy's shoulders, very familiar, and Mandy stiffened.

'Please, Maisie.'

'Shut-it, Jack,' Maisie's watery eyes looked directly at Mandy. 'Dottie would've been twelve,' Fatso nodded. 'A serial rapist was attacking young girls in Portsmouth and Jack was on the case.' She picked up the corner of her grubby apron and dabbed her eyes, 'Well, as I say, long story short, he had our Dottie in that shed,' she pointed to where Mandy had just changed. 'Jack got to him before he could do anything, praise God,' they both crossed themselves, and Mandy thought more bloody Catholics, they've all come out of their priest holes lately.

'Jack got Dottie away, but it turned into a very nasty fight, rolling out onto the quay; you know about Jack and when he blows?' Mandy nodded. 'Well, eventually they fell off the quay and onto the deck of our boat, and before Jack could do anything the bastard had his eye out with a boat hook. God knows where Jack's strength came from.' They crossed themselves again, mentioned Mary and Joseph. 'Jack was still going at the bloke, stir crazy, beat the man terrible and threw him overboard and blow me down if the bugger couldn't swim; he drowned. Divine justice is what Fatso and I call it, but Jack dived in and tried to find him even though blinded in one eye. So there you have it sweet'art, and that's why, whenever he comes down here, and whenever he meets a woman from the fishing families, they kiss his eye, as revolting as that is,' and she screwed her face up in mock distaste. 'It's our way of thanking him, as is this little meal, many before and I hope many to come, with you as well, but maybe dressed for it next time?' she smiled, it was warm and caring.

It remained quiet around the table for what seemed like an age, then Jack piped up, 'Well, so much for Jackanory, where's the fish?'

Maisie got up slowly and as she went to the tiny galley, she allowed her hand to stroke Jack's eye and looked at Mandy as she did it. Mandy could say nothing, looked at Jack, and he did a, *So what can I tell you* shrug; Gallic? Who cared, she was fed up with fucking shrugging as well. Mandy followed Maisie, there was barely enough room for the two of them in the galley, comfortable with silence, but eventually Maisie spoke in a gentle voice that belied her frame, 'He's brought you here because he wants us to meet you. That makes you special, even Kate didn't come here, but by then she was fed up with him being a copper. Still, he could have said you were going to dine on a fishing boat, and I suspect you wouldn't have worn that dress, but if I'm any guess of a man, and I know our Jack, he thinks you're gorgeous in Ted's overalls.'

Still Mandy said nothing, helped to carry the sea bass to the table. Steamed, simple as Jack had said, with salad. She would never have believed this or anything like it had you told her beforehand, but she enjoyed the fish and the conversation, drank the wine that had miraculously appeared; it was good, dry, and crisp. She was well and truly lost for words, could only listen and admire the effrontery of Jack, conversing as if nothing had happened, conscious that all the time she was watched by Maisie; weighing her up. The conversation ranged from Jack lambasting the government, naturally, to the state of fish prices, fish stocks and the Solent generally; the amount of dickheads that should not be on the water. Mandy gathered Fatso was the latest in the line of many generations of Fatso fishermen.

Mandy only spoke when Jack asked about *Tracy Island*. '*Tracy Island*, that's *Thunderbirds* isn't it?'

Jack elucidated, 'It's what the local fishermen call Spitbank Fort sweet'art, because of all the comings and goings, helicopters, speedboats, the lot.' He explained, 'Spitbank Fort is the first in a series of Napoleonic Forts outside the harbour, in the Solent. We've looked at it as we've walked the seafront,' she was dumbstruck, which Jack mistook for the need of further explanation. 'Over the years it's been various things, but now it's a conference centre, retreat type of place, apparently doing well.'

Fatso joined in, 'It's not Spitbank that concerns us, it's No Man's Land fort.'

And for the benefit of Mandy, Jack explained, her eyes not having to travel far to reach the cabin ceiling, 'A similar fort, but further out to sea, about a mile, you can see it but it's not as prominent as Spitbank, converted into a house wasn't it Fatso?'

Fatso nodded, 'Dead luxy an all, two helicopter pads and everything. Word is the bloke went bust, it's on the market, but that's where the activity is. We don't mind, but it's the eejits don't know the water and the rules. Doesn't stop the helicopters though, they go in and out as frequently as they do at Spitbank, probably doing another conference thing, if the other one is successful.'

'Probably,' and Jack leaned back, put his arms out, stretched, retracted them and rubbed his belly, 'bleedin' 'andsome Maisie, enjoy that, luv?'

Mandy had regained some of her composure, managed a stare at Jack that would tear yer skin off that miraculously morphed to a sweet smile when she turned to Maisie. 'I did, it was delicious, Maisie.'

'Well, you're welcome anytime, preferably without Jack,' and she guffawed along with Fatso. 'We've another bottle of wine?'

'Perhaps not, Maisie, we had a skin full at the Pugwash do last night,' Jack said, yawning.

'That bloke's a maniac, Jack, watch him. We could have a word if you like?'

'I'll do the watching, Fatso, and you'll have to line up behind Kipper.'

They went up to the quayside, the ladder a lot shorter, the tide had risen. Jack hugged and kissed Maisie and went to Fatso who was talking to the cab driver. Maisie looked at Mandy nodding towards Jack, 'Lot to take in?' Mandy nodded back.

'Give him time, despite all you see, he'd rather not have the attention, well not in the way you're thinking. He's a tosspot bloke, and that is how he wants to be. He can come down here and be a tosspot, because all the blokes down here are tosspots; fits in perfect, know what I mean?'

Mandy smiled but her heart was not really in it, 'Why does he not say?'

'He's embarrassed. He's the sort of bloke things happen to, and between you and me, Kate never wanted to come here, as I said. She hated Jack being a copper and after what happened, Dottie an all, she wanted him to take retirement. It was the only thing he stood up to her about, being a copper,' and she tapped her nose. What was that Mandy thought? 'It's what makes him the man he is. The rest, a little boy, God love him. Take your time and you'll get to know the man we know. I have a nose for these things.'

Mandy replied, 'I'm just not sure, Maisie.'

Maisie hugged her, 'Whatever, sweet'art.'

FIFTY-EIGHT

Mandy wandered into the forecourt garden, kicked her heels while Jack paid off the cab and fished for his keys, 'You're quiet, babes.'

'For God's sake, Jack, the only reason I'm here is because I did not have the heart to kick Liz and Carly out of my flat. I don't know you. You close yourself to me so I can't find out about you. You tell me nothing unless I ask directly, and then I have to ask the right question. In your mind you think you've bestowed some sort of honour on me by taking me to meet your friends this evening, which I appreciate by the way, but why the bloody hell could you not tell me, and a first date, and in a bloody dress?'

'Ah, it's the dress, we'll pick that up tomorrow and you can return Ted's overalls then, no need to worry.'

She looked at him in amazement, 'It's not the dress or Ted's fucking overalls. Who are you Jack, John, Peter, Joseph, CBE, QGM and soon to be GM if you don't fart or swear in front of the Queen, I haven't a clue!'

He was riled, 'You said, you wanted to go on a date and get

to know me, so I took you to people who know me best; speed it up!'

Not for the first time that evening she was dumbstruck. There was logic in what he said, and had she known beforehand, she would have been thrilled at meeting Fatso and Maisie, but would certainly have dressed differently, but still, a first date?

'Messed up, thought he would?' They both spun to face the front door.

'Michael, how long you been there?'

'Long enough to know dad's in deep doo-doo.' Jack looked at his son, worried he'd become a Tory over night; doo-doo? 'Get in, Dad.'

He followed Mandy who followed Michael. Colleen was standing at the foot of the stairs and received Mandy's stare with a degree of stoicism Jack ordinarily would have admired if his head had not been hung low.

Mandy stopped in front of Colleen. 'You knew.'

'About the fishing boat, yes, but didn't know how to tell you. Having said that, and apart from the smell, the boiler suit has a certain modishness.'

'Colleen, I like you, but don't rely on that in court.'

Michael appeared with a bottle of wine and four glasses, 'Let's talk about this like grownups.'

Colleen and Mandy said, almost at the same time, 'What's Jack going to do?'

Stilted laughter over, they sat around the table, Mandy in Ted's overalls, Colleen and Michael looking smart and casual, Jack wearing a mixed bag of clothes, none of which went together, and a frown that did not help his looks at all.

'May I talk please?'

Michael nodded to Mandy, 'Engineering has the con.'

Mandy could see how this was funny, but didn't feel like laughing. 'Michael, what do you know about your dad?'

Silence, Mandy folded her arms, and Michael looked at his dad, his head in his hands. 'I think dad has told Alana and me everything. He trusts us to keep his life, where appropriate, discreet. I asked him if I could tell Colleen, and after a while he agreed.' Jack looked at his son, nodded, and Mandy noticed the assent. 'Dad was a spook, high level, strategic not field, and was awarded the CBE on retirement. We suspect, but do not ask, he's still involved. He wanted to become a copper which, with the help of his many Whitehall friends, he was able to do here on the south coast, getting in at Inspector level. He got his eye by rescuing a kid down at the fishing quay. You've now met the parents, if not Dottie herself; he got the Queen's Gallantry Medal for that. Yes, he embarrassed Mum at the Palace, they never spoke about it, but the row went on for weeks, Dad more worried about what Mum thought than the Queen. He was scared of Mum because he loved her, because I think, he struggled to be himself with her, he wanted to be what she wanted, he tried, but an impossible task. He could not keep up with Mum's intellect, and to be fair to Mum, it's not what she wanted.'

'I didn't tell you that.'

'Dad, I'm alive, have a brain, eyes and ears. Mum wanted you to give up the police.' He looked at Mandy, 'She'd had enough of him getting hurt, was sick of worrying. Mum said when he was a spook he never got into action, but in the police he did, he's like a trouble magnet. Mum wanted him to have a 9-to-5 job, argued he was inept, and it frightened her.'

'Son, that's unfair on your mum.'

Michael gave him a look that Mandy would have been proud of, it shut him up. 'Dad, Mum used to say you were like a ship and we lived in your bow wave. The rest you know,

Mandy, except as kids we love him, just as he is, and always will. We worry, of course, but he is doing what he wants to be doing, we miss Mum terribly, but she was different, and towards the end, Dad and Mum had grown apart.'

Jack lifted his head, 'Grown apart?'

'Dad.'

'I'm sorry, sorry if I worry you too.'

Colleen looked lovingly at Jack, 'If I might say, and I know you know this Mandy, he's a kind, gentle and generous man and for that I personally would allow an element of dipstick crap, but what would I know, I love his son, and he's not much different.'

Michael stemmed the tittering Colleen, 'Mandy, the trawler is the key to dad. We stayed up because we knew he would blow it, we wanted to help smooth things over, he can never do anything on his own, it's why he's a team player. We thought you would see that.'

Mandy eventually broke the silence, 'Yes, well', she sighed, 'I knew he was a tosspot right from the start, and to let me go to a trawler in that dress thinking everything will be okay, frankly, he deserves to be in the dog house big time.'

Jack lifted his head, 'I wonder how Martin is?' Mandy was tearing his skin off with her eyes, 'Our first row, Amanda.'

'Yes, Jack, now shut-up and get up those stairs.'

'Amanda.'

'What?'

'Will you take a shower, you smell of fish guts and diesel.'

FIFTY-NINE

ONLY A REFRACTED LIGHT CAME THOUGH THE EDGES OF the curtains, accompanied by a chill; Mandy guessed a sea mist. They cuddled, the night had been about reparation. "Probably why people courted, to get to know one another", Jack had said. Mandy derred. She was wearing one of Jack's shirts and lay facing away. He wrapped his arm around her and gently didn't undo the buttons; she did it for him. 'I'm definitely putting you on that course, how to undo buttons, bra straps, for the inept male,' she turned, and the passion was released in a frenzy.

———

ABOUT MIDDAY, Jack and Mandy shared brunch with Colleen and Michael, the mist was breaking and the sun brightening, all seemed right with the world for Jack, just the nagging in the back of his mind, the case, something pushing to the surface; the raison d'etre? Jack had a light bulb idea, 'Walk down the seafront?'

The bulb dimmed upon Mandy's reaction, 'Taking me for a

walk, so this is what Martin feels like? Okay, but the boiler suit might attract attention?'

'Just when you thought it was safe to go in the kitchen,' Jack mimicked the deep throaty film trailer voice in his head, unfortunately, out loud. However, slowly the glacier retreated and Liz and Carly came over with some clothes, Carly laughing heartily at the trawler date; Mandy guessed she was the more masculine of the two.

The sun grew steadily stronger, sluggishly burning the mist off the coastline, generating a late spring feeling where the warmth is relished, making the body feel rejuvenated. Leaning on the promenade railings, it was Mandy who mentioned the forts; *Tracy Island* was obvious, nearby and clear, wisps of mist trailing the battements. Jack pointed out No Man's Land Fort. It was distant, and in the mist, impossible to look at in any detail, a grey mass. They decided to walk eastward and kept the fort in their line of vision. The early afternoon was filling up with walkers, some with dogs, a lot with kids and some on their own. The odd jogger came by making Jack jump and Mandy refrained from mentioning hearing aids, she was still sore, and watched him looking at her face to see if things were okay; like he would know?

They strolled, and at each seafront feature, Jack regaled Mandy with stories of Alana or Michael, when they were small, the pier, Alana wanting to play the revolting machines, Michael wanting to fish and Jack, ironically, hating to touch a wriggling fish. Mandy melted a little more each time, and squeezed further into him. Canoe Lake, where Alana was good at crab fishing, fished out with bacon on string, often with Jack nursing a hangover from the previous rugby day. The rampart mound, part of the old Lumps Fort that edged the Park of Canoe Lake, the model village on top, and they made plans to bring Meesh. They walked beyond the model village and via the walled Rose gardens, climbed a steep rampart to achieve glorious views out to the Solent, and settled on a solitary bench, legs squashed together, a few mmmm's as the sun warmed their bodies, the mist fading; they enjoyed the intimacy.

Jack, looking out to sea, 'No Man's Land fort, has me thinking.'

The fort was still shrouded and she wondered how long he'd been thinking this, and was it while she was trying to discuss how she felt about the previous night, but let it go. 'How so?' and waited for the Japanese joke, but it never came.

'What d'you say we get KFC onto it, pass a message up the line, if you get my grift? All that activity, what's happening?'

'Jack, I think I like you involving me, and yes.' She had his attention, and in a mellow tone, 'Will you talk to me about yourself, not now, over time? I won't pressure you, and I won't try to change you, and maybe, I can talk about me?' The mellowness ramped up, and took him by surprise, 'What do you know about me?' She answered for him as he blinked his immediate response, 'Nothing, you act on blind faith, are you not even curious?' he was quite shocked by her vehemence.

Turning, so his good eye faced her, he tried not to show his own irritation, 'I know you're from a small village in Surrey, your dad was a doctor, Mum stayed home, and eventually drank herself to death.' He squeezed her hand as she reacted, 'Your dad was cold; you and your sister had to fend for yourself. You were a high achiever, your sister in your shadow for which you still blame yourself. It would be nice to meet your sister, her husband and family, they're only in Sussex, yes?'

'Yes, outside Brighton, carry on, you're amazing me,' had she mellowed, he was buggered if he knew, but carried on.

'You got a first-class degree in sociology at Exeter and you're pleased Liz is there doing the same, but worried because David is at Nottingham, which is a pretty hairy city even if you forget Robin Hood.' She chuckled at the obvious joke. 'David will be okay, but you worry about Liz, maybe now you won't so much. You married a copper because you got pregnant with Liz. He was a tow-rag, but you held it together for the sake of the now two kids, but when he started to hit you, thank God, you kicked him out.'

She winced at the memory, and he squeezed her hand.

'I'm not sure if you know where he is, but he eventually dried himself out and is living in Birmingham. He sees David occasionally, Liz doesn't want anything to do with him; hopefully that will change, both are nervous to tell you he got in touch. This may also explain why you're wary of drink; your Mum, and your husband. You don't drink much, why you were not used to the drinking the other night. You had so much to cope with by evening, a drink seemed like a way to deal with it. It never is by the way, alcohol's a mood enhancer, think about it, you were uncomfortable, Liz, me, your life; a turmoil of emotions.'

She was dumbfounded, again. He was tempted with codfish and mouths, aware he had some scoring to catch up, but chose to carry on. 'You brought your kids up by yourself and made your way in a tough career for a woman, despite all of that, you are not a feminista, although you will fight tooth and nail for your equal rights, me too incidentally, I just happen to be a man who feels men have lost their way.'

She interrupted him with a hand gesture, 'Jack how d'you know these things? Oh Christ, you didn't have your spook friends...?'

He stopped her, 'I pestered your kids, remember Liz, arsehole? She thought I was stalking you. In a way, I suppose I was, it's how I know your perfume is Opium.' Mandy had a strange look on her face, stunned, curious, relieved the shite in her life had been uncovered and he was still there. 'So you see, I know a lot about you, but not in an intimate way, and I want to, but it will be me as a man, not a great thinker, not Mr Sensitive perceptive guru, just an ordinary bloke in love with a beautiful woman, can you live with that? I hope you can.'

She was looking out to sea in a dream which was broken in a way only Jack could do, and after such beautiful sentiment and words.

'Right then; pictures?'

She turned to face him, and taking his face in her hands, she kissed him, 'No love, let's go home and go to bed, courting is temporarily suspended.'

SIXTY

Monday Morning

'SID, YOUR FAMILY, THEY ARE WELL?'

'Tolerably well, thank you.'

'Cod and chips twice,' and Jack bounded up the stairs where Mandy was waiting.

'I was talking to you and you weren't there?'

'Sorry sweetness, bit of banter with Sid, not quite himself?'

'Oh? I'm going to brief the Commander on your thoughts,' Mandy said.

'Our thoughts Mands, dynamic duo, and before you ask you're Dobbin,' he crossed his fingers and put his hands in the air so she couldn't argue.

She stood hands on hips and shook her head, 'Get in Batman, and be good.'

Jack looked at his desk, a note from Father Mike, a computer code for Frankie and Connie; they were used to this now. Other chaos notes didn't look interesting so he balled them up, threw, and missed the waste bin, wheeled himself to the basket, retrieved the ball of paper, looked around, nobody looking, moved the basket closer and had another go; missed again, blamed his eye and left it for Dolly.

'Kids okay, Jo?'

'Just a bloody nuisance.'

'Briefing at nine?' Jack was swinging in his chair.

'Sure,' Jo didn't even look up, 'anything cooking?'

'Maybe nothing.'

'I've amended the crime wall, Jane,' a pensive Nobby said.

Alice looked at Jack then smiled at Nobby; something has bloomed in the chalk and cheese department. He sat legs out, swinging more vigorously in his chair, thinking of the weekend.

Jack jumped up, 'Shitehawks, Pugwash, what's happened to him?'

Nobby answered, 'Alice and I interviewed him the next morning. Somewhat distracted by Alice's attire, he coughed, and is recommended to be bound over to keep the peace.'

'Nobby, Alice, a result,' he pondered, 'Nobs lad, did Alice deliberately wear these clothes?'

'No sir,' Nobby replied, a picture of innocence, admired by Jack, 'we were going out afterwards. Pugwash seemed unstable to us.'

'Did you file a cautionary report?'

'I did.'

Jack spun a full round, 'Well, we have our arses covered in true Pugwash fashion,' he tapped his gammy eye.

Throwing up noises greeted Mandy as she entered with the Commander, 'I would like to thank you all for the hedge in my office, it will come in handy when I have to look at Jane,' and they settled around the chaos table.

'No Cyrano?'

'No Commander, we're treating the drugs as a separate issue, remember?' Jo shrugged; her head in her notes.

Jack smoothed the Commander's feathers, 'Keep us posted Jo, Mands and me will need bikes from Hogwarts soon. I'll be the one wearing the Lycra of course, nothing like a pert arse on a bloke, eh, Mands?'

Mandy looked aghast, whilst the rest of the squad asked to borrow Mandy's hedge. 'Nobby, what do you have?'

Nobby strode purposefully to the wall, 'I temporarily changed Moriarty back to Moriarty,' laughter, Jack approved. He ran through the spider's web, how he had reorganised the wall, 'I'd like to add a personal thought please?'

'Rock-on, Nobs,' Jack answered, and Mandy felt like Spotty losing control.

'Alice and I think the Islamic thing may not be terrorism, the bombers were likely naive youngsters allowed to believe they were an Al Qaeda cell. Maybe the objective was public demonstrations stretching the police resources, fear amongst the Islamic populace?' Jack stopped swinging, 'We've learned that Osama's son, Tahir, is not the only child missing, seems the community is too scared to say anything.'

Jack leaned forward, 'And?'

'We think they've been taken for the paedophile ring. We would like to get a *Hearts and Minds* team in, to gather information locally.'

'Paolo?' Mandy asked.

'I preferred NoraFarty,' another joke from Paolo? 'We agree. Worm is singing, and Frankie and Connie are convinced it was the Leader of the Council that saved him five years back, and they're trawling social services computers, looking for tie ups, common themes.'

'Connie?'

'We look for where records been deleted. We have Del shit-hot programme for getting deleted file.' Frankie smoothed her thigh, Connie correspondingly warmed. 'We'll plug in what we get from the Asian community when we get it.'

'Anything else, Frankie?'

'Our feeling is this is small, local, and relatively new, which is encouraging.'

Mandy gave Jack a wide berth as she headed to the crime wall. He thought she looked gorgeous, as she went by, just out of reach. 'Okay, so when Jane's stopped staring at my arse,' the team chortled, Jack smiled. 'Jane and I also feel this is local, but where? Connie, Jack gave you some stuff this morning, Coastguard, air traffic, we may have something to look at?' She waved at the wall, 'Nobby, KFC will have pictures of No Man's Land fort, aerial as well as estate agents pictures; it's currently for sale. Jo-Jums add this to your list, we need to know if this has legs and if not, bin it quick. Any questions, no, Jane, summary please.'

Jack skipped to the wall, 'There's a lot of activity at this fort and our kids may be there,' an aerial view of No Man's Land Fort was now up. 'My instinct is to go in, but we have to build a case. Of course we may be wrong, in which case it was Mandy's theory,' and he rolled up in a pantomime laugh. Jo looked at Mandy; Jack was more over the top than normal.

Mandy answered Jo's looks, 'Leave Jack to me, any thoughts on the set up?'

Jo reacted, 'Paolo, your team, if the kids are there how do we get them out? Scenarios as soon as you can. If the kids are there and they disappeared off the social services radar, where are the mothers? Think about that too.'

Mandy and Jack made to leave, Frankie stopped them at the door, 'The fort has been let on a temporary, renewable licence for the past eighteen months, and was recently renewed for another twelve.'

Mandy responded, 'Check with the agent, are they allowing interested purchasers to see around?'

———

JACK WAS BACK at his deckchair, 'Connie does that computer do cinema listings?' and before he could get to sleep she handed him a sheet of films; he knew she would be good. KFC had six computers now, courtesy of Del-Boy; Jack called it silicone galley. Mandy, tip toed past the deckchair and looked at each screen, two processing information, three others chuntering, one had a fixed aerial image of the fort and a box image in the corner. 'What's in the box Frankie?'

'Spitbank Fort, Del thinks it might be worth monitoring both forts while we're at it.'

'Do we need permission?'

'Ma'am, I get the impression Del-Boy has all the permission he needs.'

Mandy hemmed, Jack stirred, 'He's thinking sea and air movements coming in under cover of approved traffic to Spitbank.'

'You were listening?'

'Not very good tip toeing Mandy, I could help you there, I used to do ballet as a boy.'

Connie spun, 'Jack, you ballet dancer?'

'He's pulling your leg,' Mandy replied, enjoying Jack's exaggerated hurt face.

Frankie worked the oracle, 'Mandy, we have the plans of the fort. Nobby and Alice have set up a separate board over there,' she pointed to where they had opened up some of the wonky screens to the Sissies.

'Alice, Nobby, what are you doing?'

'We're looking for areas where prisoners could be held, fastest access routes, and evacuation scenarios,' Alice replied.

Jack responded, 'Jo-Jums, keep the Commander and Chief briefed, Mandy and I are going fishing. Frankie, Del-Boy will give you a secure line, satellite cover of the Solent and that sort of stuff, no ship to shore, or mobiles, we have to assume a degree of sophistication,' amazed eyes focused on Jack. 'What?'

SIXTY-ONE

'HEARD IT WAS GOOD FRIDAY, APART FROM PUGWASH.'

'It was Sid, where were you?' Jack was leaning on the reception counter, Mandy pacing, excited.

'My daughter's not well.'

'Sid, I'm so sorry, can you say?'

'She found a lump.'

Mandy thought, Oh no Jack is bound to make a joke, but he didn't, 'Buzz me through.' He did, and Jack put his arm around Sid's shoulder.

Mandy thought she saw a frailty in Sid she'd never seen before.

Jack spoke as soft as he could, so they heard in Australia, 'I'm sure it'll be okay, anything you want, just ask,' and Jack picked-up the phone, nothing.

'You have to press the button here.'

'I know that, I was using dramatic irony.'

Mandy and Sid looked at each other, "dramatic irony"? Sid pressed the button.

'Hello, can you put me through to Brenda please?' Jack

paused, 'I don't know her second name, don't hang up... Sid where's the switchboard?'

'Down the corridor turn left, carry on, it's at the end.'

'Sid, you're going home, your wife and daughter need you.'

Sid went to contest, but Jack had already disappeared down the corridor. Mandy and Sid looked at each other; 'Oh no.'

Jack found the door, 'Hi, Jane.'

'Yo, Nylon, who's answering the dog and bones?'

It was Brian, shortened to Bri, hence Bri-nylon, a material from the sixties only Jack remembered. Mandy was at the door shaking her head, 'We have a rule not to disturb telecoms during a shift,' but Nylon made the mistake of looking at the room as he spoke, and Jack went in.

'Good morning, I'm DCI Jack Austin, who answered the phone just now when I asked for Brenda?'

A comfortably plump woman, short bottle legs that swung on her chair, mid-forties, raised her hand. She had frizzy hair, everything except the blue rinse, but definitely modelled on Margaret Thatcher, blue, knitted jersey suit with a Beatles collar, purple shiny blouse with an enormous bow; Jack took in this vision of Jam and Jerusalem, 'Your name please?'

'I am not sure that is important to you, Inspector,' a confident snotty reply.

Jack brought his body up, the room was claustrophobic and he had assumed a hunch as an involuntary response, 'That would be Chief Inspector, and if I ask you your name, you tell me,' calm, but Mandy knew he would blow.

'Mrs Margery Clements.'

'Well, Mrs Clements, you are not up the knitting club now. This is a police station and we do serious business here. If I ask you to do something, I do not expect to be questioned. I do not expect to be hung up on. You may think you're doing your bit, but this ain't fucking Dunkirk.' Here it comes, Mandy thought. 'We need serious people here, not people playing at *Watch with Mother.*' He was wound up and everyone, including Mrs Thatcher, knew it. Margery made to reply, his hand stopped her, 'Well Margery, let me tell you something, Brenda is the PA to the Chief and we have a big operation going on in this nick right now, and because you are so up your own arse, I cannot speak to him on the phone. I don't give a toss about your Big Society. I don't give a toss about your sensitivities or Blogg and Mackeroon. If you want this job, paid or not, then do it properly, otherwise get thee to a library woman.'

He turned to go but stopped, Margery looked traumatised, she was going to crack and Jack had not even reached ballistic. Mandy got ready to step in. Jack carried on, 'Remember me when I phoned in and you would not give me the telephone number of a police officer. You hung up several times.' She went to speak, but Jack was rising to a crescendo, Mandy edged closer. 'Shut the fuck-up woman.' He spent a little time calming himself, straightened his clothes, a gesture to smooth his ruffled inner self, and when he resumed, he was respectfully hushed. 'The policeman I wanted to get hold of was not in the pub, as you thought all coppers do cause it's what they do on the telly, he was murdered that night.' He allowed the shock to get to her, 'You should know that even if you had managed to get off your fat arse and give me the number, it might not have saved the man, but we will never know that will we?'

Margery burst into tears, mumbling something incomprehensible. Oh Christ, Mandy thought, and what Jack did amazed her, but should not have as it was typical of him. He approached Margery, who seemed to have melted into her chair, crouched and put his arm around her. 'Now, take a break, smoke a fag if that's what you do, or go and inhale some of the passive smoke, which Nylon does nothing about,' he looked at

Nylon sternly. 'When you've got yourself together, let's start again, and do the job properly. Can you do that for me, Margery?' She sniffed and nodded, 'Good, Nylon, a cup of splosh for Mrs Jam please.'

Jack left and Nylon went to Margery, 'Okay, Margery, do as Jack says, he called you Mrs Jam, it means he's accepted you, okay?' She rose from her desk, nodded and sobbed into Nylon's handkerchief, which Mandy would not have touched with a barge pole, and thought what was is it with men and their hankies, but Mrs Jam took it; well, she supposed that was two big lessons for this Big Society woman.

The door banged open and everybody jumped, Jack was back, and shouted, 'Nylon, get a replacement for Hissing Sid, he's going home right now, and we ordered a bluebottle cab feckin' ages ago, I've a good mind to switch my loyalty to another nick.'

SIXTY-TWO

JACK REASSURED SID AT HIS COUNTER, AND MANDY FELT unusually sorry for this man she had in the past vilified.

There was a uniform at the door, 'Jack, we're not your personal taxi service.'

'No, you're mine!'

'Superintendent, yes, ready when you are,' a stiff reply.

'Sid, Jack and I need to go, the cabbie's getting snotty.'

'I'm okay, Ma'am, thank you.'

'Shut up, go and see your girl and give me cod and chips twice,' Jack said, injecting some solemnity.

'Heard you the first time,' said by rote, but it brought a smile to Sid's face.

———

'WHERE TO MA'AM?'

'My flat it's...'

'We know, Ma'am,' Bobby, the uniform turned. 'Blues and twos, Jack?'

'Brilliant, go for it, Bobby.'

He started for the switch, but Mandy stopped him, 'We do not need sirens or flashing lights to take me home, bloody kids.' Bobby made a face to Jack in the rear view mirror. 'I saw that.'

They finished the journey in relative silence, except Bobby turned out to be a Millwall fan, an exiled Londoner, and they chatted about the Lions, mentioned for the umpteenth time the two corners they got against Man U in the FA cup final.

'Jack, tell us how you had pie and mash and green liquor while you watched it,' Mandy said, sarcastically.

'She's got your number, Jack,' and Bobby smiled to himself, saw the look on Mandy's face in the rear view mirror. 'Sorry, Ma'am.'

JACK AND BOBBY waved goodbye like two kids as Mandy headed to the front entrance of her block of flats. 'Wait here.' He waited and Mandy soon reappeared in jeans and sweater, carrying a holdall bag, she was always quick; Jack liked this.

'Liberties, Ma'am?'

'Permission refused,' she started her car, 'and take that sulky look off your face,' she said, as she drove off, 'you may take minor liberties.' After a while, 'You amaze me, Sid and Mrs Jam. Jack you are well on your way to becoming an enema.' Jack took the opportunity to slip his good hand between her legs, taking advantage of the good mood, but he'd pushed his luck.

They were quickly in and out of Jack's, and headed to the fishing quay, along the seafront, looking out to the forts, 'Are they there?' Mandy asked.

'If they are, I will kick myself, waiting to go in, what kind of torture will those kids suffer while we get our ducks in a row?'

At the Camber, Maisie kissed Jack's eye, 'Let's get you two sorted,' steering Jack and Mandy to the shed. Mandy choked on the acrid aroma. Jack told her that after a while you get to like it. I don't think so, a strange man, she thought. Maisie handed out thick, fish-and-diesel-smelling jumpers, slick yellow trousers and sea boots. 'It's a nice day, do we need all this?' Jack asked.

'Nice inland, but choppy and breezy on the Solent,' Maisie answered. 'C'mon, Fatso wants to catch the tide.'

Jack watched Mandy waddle, 'Don't say a thing,' she could see him with the eyes in the back of her head.

Maisie waited at the ladder, 'Well you might pass from a distance, but up close you are two town softies. Del-Boy looks the part,' she flicked her head to the boat, high in the water.

'Del with us?' Mandy asked.

'He insisted, wanted to meet you again, sort of like a second date.'

She put her arm a little way around him and in pretty please speak, 'Jack, can we have our third date on dry land?'

And with a show of more confidence than he felt, 'Already working on it sweet'art. Toss-up between the pictures or a dirty weekend away in Exeketer, nice hotel, dinner with Liz and Curly Friday evening, and then, just you and me, babes.'

'And *Top Deck* shandy, Jack, sounds lovely, surprise number three today.'

Jack watched Mandy struggle to swing her leg over the steel ladder, resisted the obvious joke, trying to remember the other two surprises.

Fatso called for Jack to get a move on, 'Jack, the tide is turning.' Jack looked, couldn't see anything turning. Little Jack, named after Jack, just twelve and shaping up to be a cross between his Mum and Hagrid, slipped the mooring ropes and they felt the boat move with the building current, before Fatso gunned the engine.

'Ahoy, Del Boy.'

'Captain *Birds Eye*,' Del responded.

'Now that was funny,' Mandy said, with a smirk, felt the swell, wobbled and sat down'

'Just turned into the main channel, the ferry causing that, luv,' Maisie said, busying herself in the galley. Del-boy joined them around the table for coffee. Mandy had only managed a brief assessment of Del the other evening, he was smaller, slighter than her first impression, the boyish charm was there with his floppy blond hair, but there was steel in the pale blue-grey eyes, which gave an impression not to mess with him. Little Jack appeared, shook Jack's hand, other hand on the wrist, and they exchanged a look, and he kissed Mandy on the cheek, which surprised her.

'He's the cheeky one, Mandy,' Maisie said.

Mandy didn't mind the kiss, she was more interested in his feet, they were huge; it was his trainers she had worn the other night. Maisie, swaying with the boat, handed Little Jack two mugs of steaming hot chocolate. He took them, turned to go up the companion way, never spilling a drop, grinning with a full set of very white teeth; well there's a difference, she thought.

SIXTY-THREE

'THE BOAT IS BEING TRACKED BY SATELLITE AND RELAYED to the CP room,' Del said.

Jack got up, 'I'll go and wave.'

'Sit down,' Del-Boy said, 'we also have cameras on the boat sides so we can review the fort. The approach by sea is the landing stage, or by air, two helipads. The property is leased on licence, which allows for viewers in the last quarter period, but not before then.'

'Any sign who's renting it?' Mandy asked.

Del's teeth gripped his bottom lip, 'Shell Company in Belize, agents don't give a toss, take their money and run all the way to the bank.'

'Any agency has to inspect the property?' Mandy added.

'Done last month. Wouldn't mind betting they didn't go, took the cash anyway, this is a private renter who wants no disturbance.'

'I bet,' Mandy remarked.

The cabin door opened and Little Jack, with his high

pitched voice and occasional croak, heralding manhood, sung down the stairs, 'Coming up off Spitbank.'

Maisie gathered the mugs, 'Try to look like you know what you're doing, Jack,' and she kissed his eye to compensate for the hurt look.

Up on deck, Del chastised Jack for waving to the satellite, his wave received in the CP room, everyone gathered, waiting for a second, which happened when Del's back was turned. 'I know you just waved again, how do you put up with him, Mandy?'

'I always wanted more children, Del.'

The power of the sea around the base of Spitbank fort impressed Jack, he was not a man of the water, thought he might prefer to come in on the helicopter, but then he was not overly keen on flying either.

Del interpreted Jack's thoughts, 'You will not be going in.'

'Of course I'll be going in.'

Del showed resolve in his boyish face, 'Jack, I had my balls chewed off for letting you go into Osama's. I'm sorry to say, even if you had the training, which you don't, this is a young man's game. I'm serious.' Jack mumbled an irked reply. Mandy could see a testiculating standoff in the making. 'I'm not changing my mind.'

They were like kids arguing in the playground, probably Jack's influence, Mandy thought, 'I don't want him anywhere near if something goes off.'

'Amanda, I don't think you should be telling me what to do?' Jack said, wobbling his head in that way you either thought endearing or infuriating, Mandy experienced both of these feelings at various times and chose, this time, to be endeared, but not to show it.

Del looked for some fishing jobs while Mandy noticed Jack disappear up a ladder to the wheelhouse; she joined him. The boat swayed more, higher up, but slowly she was getting her sea legs. Jack though, was looking green, 'Diddums feeling Tom and Dick?' and she chucked him under the chin.

Jack sighed and gave her his best patronising look, 'Mandy, I'm a natural Mariner,' he was queasy, but recalling *Moby Dick,* or was it Tom and Dick, he decided to be Captain Mayhap. He looked up, then down, Mandy had left and was now, on deck, knitting nets; "Always been a patronising Sod, Jack", Kate's voice said in his head, shite, where did that come from. They were passing No Man's Land fort. Jack was not sure what he expected, but in his mind he thought he might find an excuse to go in; there was nothing.

'I'm taking her to Langstone Harbour, out of sight, sit there for a while then return with the tide, okay Jack?'

'Aye-aye, Cap'n,' Jack decided to stay with Fatso.

'What's up, you going to be sick?'

'Err, no, what's that bobbing?' he pointed.

'Loose mooring buoy?'

Fatso handed Jack binoculars, 'Fuck me, it's a body.'

Fatso shouted through the wheelhouse window for little Jack to get the gaff, as big Jack dashed past Mandy, 'Close your mouth, we are not a codfish,' he managed to say just before he dived overboard and fecked as he surfaced, it was freezing, but a couple of strokes got him to the body of a young boy floating on his back. Jack detected movement of the blue lips, grabbed the shoulders, kicked his legs as the boat edged beside them. Little Jack bounced Jack on his head with the gaff, 'Oi, watch it.' Del-Boy looked over, 'He's alive, just,' spluttering and swallowing more water than he felt he should; thought about his salt intake as he guided the gaff to the boy's T-shirt, and he was hauled out of the water.

Jack made his way to a ladder hanging over the side. The cold water had chilled his bones, he grabbed at the ladder, his grip slipped, grabbed again feeling every minute of his sixty years, his eye misted, his energy ebbed, and his mind conjured a picture of Hastings where as a young lad he had fought for his life in the sea, scrabbling and panicking, pushing off submerged rocks. Jack knew he was giving up; he never deserved to survive Hastings. If he'd given up then, he would not have had all the responsibility he felt as a kid and since; so tiring. He opened his fingers, slipped the ladder rungs, and felt a sense of rapture; no more responsibility.

SIXTY-FOUR

He woke, and this surprised him, 'Oi, Maisie, what're you doing?'

Maisie was stripping his clothes away and rubbing him vigorously with a towel. 'Shut-it, you're so much trouble,' he felt admonished but couldn't understand why. Maisie had him down to his pants. This could be embarrassing he thought, but marvelled at the strength of Mrs Hitler as his body warmed.

'How's the boy?' Jack's teeth chattering.

'Hypothermia most likes,' Maisie said, 'air sea rescue's coming, but because of cutbacks, it's from quite a distance and where's an air ambulance going to land, only the coastguard could pick the lad up off the deck.'

'Let me see him.'

The boy was with a wet Mandy. Jack crouched, quickly kissed Mandy on the way, he still had not connected Mandy had dripping hair. 'Hi, fella, can you open your eyes for me? I'm Jack and this is Mandy. We know a little girl called Meesh. She survived just like you will. Hang in for me son.' The boy's

415

eyes flickered. 'Good lad, come on, tell me your name, give me the eyes again.'

Del was back, 'We've ship to shored, air sea need at least twenty minutes, air ambulance is going to land on the fort in five. We've called for clearance.'

As Little Jack secured the boat at the fort's jetty, a man appeared at a door, high in the fort's side. Del had the lad in his arms and Fatso helped him onto the jetty.

Maisie thrust a new Jumper and what looked like Ted's old trousers for Jack. 'Where's Mandy?'

'She's followed them to look after the boy.'

Getting into his new clobber, 'Christ, Maisie, call this in, we may need back-up.'

'It's done, and you need to rest.'

'Do I bollocks,' Jack, brooking no argument, appeared to stop and think; the connection, Mandy saving him was made. He felt light headed as he looked up and could hear the helicopter. He had sodden trainers, short, greasy, baggy trousers, a sort of three quarter length that he instinctively knew would make him look fashionable if it were not for the thick baggy, knitted jumper. This all hampered him as he clambered over the rail to get to the steps of the landing stage, thinking all the time, blimey I'm cold. The noise of the sea crashing on the fort base was deafening. He made his way up the steps from the landing stage to the door, they were steep and slippery.

Maisie was calling, 'You need to rest.'

He did need to rest, felt it, but carried on up, talking to himself, 'Blimey this is fucking steep, and why am I swearing, cause its bollocking cold that's why.' He did eventually reach the door, it was shut, why lock the door? He looked up to the sky and waved and pointed to the door. In the CP room they had followed everything, had already alerted a back-up squad in a third helicopter, which was on the way.

Jack felt Maisie pulling him to one side, 'Move over,' and he worried she would open the door and he would look silly. He looked silly anyway, fashionable, but silly, but he was only temporarily relieved.

'What you got there?'

'We carry small amounts of explosives, just in cases.'

'*Love Actually*, Maisie?'

'Yeah, Fatso likes it, but I can take or leave Hugh Grant, know what I mean.'

Jack relaxed against the rough-hewn stone wall, it felt comfortable. 'I do, I like him in some things, but others, I'm not sure.' He recovered his senses just before he was going to talk about Bridget Jones, Maisie was ignoring him, busy, something pushed into the lock?

'Stand away.' He had hardly moved when there was a bang and the door swung open. 'I'm going back to the boat, d'you know how to use this?' She thrust an old fashioned pistol at him. He'd had a little small arms training a long time ago, he was a big leg man really. 'You take the safety off here, and that bit,' she pointed to the muzzle, 'is the dangerous end.'

He gave a despairing look at Maisie and took the pistol, 'I will not ask where the gun, or the bomb, came from.'

'It was just a little plastic. Now, get up there, just in cases.' She went back down the steps, sprightly leapt onto the boat, and released the mooring ropes. Little Jack had the helm and he let the boat slip into open water.

'Brilliant,' he shouted 'you leaving me here?'

'Get inside, you Wally.'

'Righto, Maisie,' and Jack put the gun in the huge pocket of the trousers, poked around the voluminous void that had swallowed the weapon, and had to go to his shin to get it; 'feck if I need to get this in a hurry' and slowly he climbed the steep stone steps inside the doorway. He was knackered, if he was honest he was a tad out of condition; no cycling you see. The noise of the sea was so much louder in the narrow stairway, echoing, cave like. This may account for why nobody came when Maisie banged on the door, so to speak, could have a problem later, "Explain blowing up the door, Austin," he could hear it now. He girded his loins; 'Never before has a man's loins been so girded,' he said out loud, making himself laugh as he walked out into a voluminous space. Jack remembered the pictures and plans this morning, a central court with a vast glass roof. It was bright, his eye smarted and was blurred, a combination of sea salt and the brilliance of the sun, 'Can't see a bloody thing. Mandy, you there?'

'Jack, there are men with guns pointing at you and us,' Mandy answered.

He put his hand to his ear, 'What? Think I've got sea in my ears.'

'Deaf aids?' Mandy shouted.

Jack banged the side of his head, 'Nope, can't hear,' then rubbed his eye, 'my eye's stinging, is that air ambulance here, they might have some ointment,' heard her groan. Jack crouched and felt the smooth polished timber floor, simultaneously taking a surreptitious look around. He saw two men with hand guns, probably fifteen metres away, he had heard another helicopter landing and hoped it was the back-up. 'This is nice, big space, lovely floor,' he looked again, he could see no other armed men, just Mandy, Del, Fatso, and the boy looking lifeless on the floor about five metres from the gunmen. He hoped the gunmen would be amateurs, here to fiddle kids, the thought riled, and he crossed his fingers and put his hands in the air, feckin' eejit, as if that would help.

'You know what, Mands, this reminds me of when I did ballet as a kid, we had a big studio like this,' and Jack rose, springing as he did, arms outstretched, called out 'Jetty' and was off the floor. 'An elegance in the lines of the body you see, babes,' he shouted. 'Now, Demi-Point,' and with his left foot planted firmly on the floor, he brought his right leg up, bent it, then pointed his toes, in and out repeatedly. 'See the alignment, luv, Feckin' eye hurts. Rond-de-Jambe-a-Terre,' and he started walking like an effeminate donkey in a circle around the room, his legs pointing, toes outstretched with each step, 'Eat your heart out Darcy Bussell,' he knew Mandy would appreciate the PP reference. He came close to the gunmen, whom he hoped were confused, as he dare not look. 'Battement-Fondu,' he called collapsing, 'dying Swan, babes,' waving his arms above him whistling what he thought was *Swan Lake* but was actually *Bob the Builder*.

He thought he heard Mandy say "feckin' eejit". 'Philistine!' he shouted. He was in the pose for a short time while he farted, important when doing Battement-Fondu. 'Et finale, Battement-Frape, STRIKE,' and Jack all of a sudden transformed his dying builder, leapt and smashed into the first gunman, then the second, a gun fired, Del-Boy moved in, the armed back-up from the second helicopter, arrived and cable tied them. Jack was writhing on the floor.

'Oh Christ,' Mandy said, kneeling beside Jack as he screamed. 'Get the boy off to hospital, Del, this dozy bastard has shot himself in the foot, and not for the first time.' One of the tactical support guys had the boy, taking him up the stairs to the air ambulance. Del was directing others to secure the fort. The power of Jack's screaming was winding down to a more accustomed moan, 'Shut-up, Jack, you're embarrassing me.'

'I'm embarrassing you?'

'Yes, you're on camera, the armed units carry cameras.' She looked up to where a support officer stood, his helmet and vest cameras pointed at them. Mandy spoke to the cameras, 'I've looked at his foot...' serious face, '...I'm sorry to say, Jane Fountain will never dance again.'

Back at the CP room there were roars of laughter, the Commander saying to Frankie, 'I hope you got all of that recorded, this is going to run and run.' The hilarity stilled to stunned silence as a naked boy was brought up from the bowels of the fort. Mandy left Jack propped against the wall and went to the boy, he was barely alive; 'Air ambulances, paramedics, Jo.'

The tactical helmet looked up, 'She said they're already despatched and will begin lifting off in convoy as needed. Our helicopter is going back to the common to free up a pad.' She heard it take off as he spoke and another taking off after, presumably the first air ambulance, 'Ma'am, they're asking if Jack should go next?'

He did look pale, 'Kid's first,' Jack said.

There were now three children lying on the floor, she decided to stay with them, was able to offer some comfort. Paramedics and a doctor were triaging, talking into radios; "Malnourished, beaten, drugged but vitals okay," then onto the next one, same report, one unconscious, "take him first".

Mandy's tears stung, there were now five children, a sixth being brought up the stairs. Del appeared with a very small girl and he laid her over to one side, called the doctor over but he knew and shook his head; seen by the team in the CP room. Dolly was there, they let her stay; it was Dolly after all. The Commander called her to him and he put his arm around her, 'Bad business, Dolly.'

'Yes, but you've got to them. God love 'em.'

Jack was feeling woozy, his foot funnily enough was not so painful; must be shock? He felt his vision going. He pulled the gun from his pocket, the safety was bloody broken. A man appeared from a side door and shot at the support officer who fell backwards, another bang, Jack had levelled the gun, fired, and the man dropped; a hit in the arm. Mandy dived for the gun as it skittered across the polished floor. The tactical was okay, a hit in the vest. Mandy had the gunman with his own gun trained on him, 'Good shot, Jack,' she could not disguise her amazement.

Del Boy had Mandy mic'd with her own camera and earpiece, she was speaking with Jo-Jums, 'Two more kids to go, that will make, twelve in all? Then Jack...' but Del signalled, they'd found five more children. 'You heard that Jo? And tactical have captured three gunmen, one with a wound to the arm, courtesy of dead eye dick, if you pardon the pun.' Mandy was feeling light headed, but recovered her poise; she was the officer on the ground. 'We'll need police cover at the hospital, Jo, for the shooter, they appear to be rank amateurs, but you never know.'

Jo was speaking again, 'One of Paolo's men is on his way to interview the guy Jack shot, see if he can get anything before they put him under. We have meat-wagons on the common to pick up other suspects as the helicopters bring them in. How many men were found down in the rooms with the kids?'

Mandy responded professionally. 'We now think four men and two women, we're still searching, it's huge.' Mandy felt sick, always did when women were involved in things like this, she felt the nurturing instincts of women would always out, but sometimes, it just didn't.

Jo interrupted Mandy's train of thought, 'Mandy, Frankie has rerun the shooting in slow-mo and is convinced there were two shots. Jack doesn't look so good, can you check him over?'

Mandy looked, Jack was pale, she turned back to camera, 'I think stage fright has just hit him, this was his first performance of *Bob the Builder*.' She called to the Field Doctor, 'Can you look the DCI over please?'

'Will do, gunshot to the foot?'

'Yes.'

The doc looked, 'Lot of blood for that.' Mandy heard this and panic hit the pit of her stomach. She heard the Doc call "next ambulance" as he laid Jack down, then to his radio, 'Gunshot to the abdomen, tertiary to foot, we'll need a theatre straight away.'

Mandy sunk to the floor beside Jack, 'Fuck you, Jack, what have you done?' His eye had gone to the top of his eyelid. The paramedics ushered Mandy to the side as they set up a drip, applied field dressings and heaped him onto a stretcher and up the stairs, amazingly fast. 'He's scared of flying,' mute words, only heard in the CP room.

'Mandy, listen to me,' it was Jo, 'we need you to secure the scene. More people are on their way, scenes of crime, forensics, you must keep the cavalry from the evidence, okay?'

Mandy was still in her nightmare, but Jo was speaking sense, 'Yes,' and looked around her, as if leaping into action, but in truth she was stunned.

Jo looked to break the spell, 'Alice is on her way to the hospital and will meet Jack. She will stay with him until you can get there, do you understand me? You need to be there for the time being.'

'Yes, Alice?'

'She insisted,' Jo answered. Mandy was dry crying, holding her breath. Jo continued, 'There will be more helicopters coming and going, you can hop one of those when you're able to. We will clear it to take you to the hospital.'

'Okay,' Mandy replied, holding the sobs back.

Fatso was beside her, 'He's a tough bugger, Mandy, do your job,' and she dabbed her eyes with his filthy hanky.

SIXTY-FIVE

THE FORT WAS SYSTEMATICALLY CHECKED, TWO MORE MEN found, 'The feckin' weasels,' Mandy said, now deep inside the bowels of the fort confronting the horrifying sight. Perimeter cellular rooms set up as bedrooms with cameras; bare, seedy and dirty, a central control room; bile etched her stomach lining. Focused and in denial about Jack, she called for the tactical lads to stop and went up to one of the men, held by the arms. She looked straight at him, a wimp, a weasel, a slimy fucking bastard, and she spat in his eye. She moved onto the next man, made of sterner stuff, 'You, I will see in an unprotected cell. You will feel how those kids felt, and you will feel it over and over and over again, as the kids felt it over and over,' and Mandy spat in his face as well. She turned to the tactical guys, 'Don't you dare wipe that spit off their faces, I want it to sting like acid, I want it to burn through to their skulls, do you hear me?' She looked at them, Mandy shouted, near screaming, 'Do you hear me?' The prisoners flinched.

'Yes, Ma'am,' the officers shouted.

Mandy did not hear the shout of approval from the CP room.

'Erase that, Frankie.'

'Yes, Commander.'

Satisfied the rooms had been secured, Mandy went back to the upper areas. As she got to the glazed courtyard Jo called, 'Mandy, Jack is in theatre, prognosis, fifty-fifty.'

Mandy felt a lump in her throat, 'Thank you for being honest, Jo,' and she leaned against the wall, picturing Jack dancing around like a fool, heard the shot, just the one, but there had clearly been two. 'Jo, will you let Michael know, Alana, Dolly, Jackie and Meesh please.'

'Already done, Dolly is here, we're getting her a bluebottle cab to the hospital, we've got a message through to her son Andrew.'

'Thank you,' she felt an arm around her, it was Del-Boy.

'Mandy, we need the helicopters. Jack has a ten hour proce-dure, can you go back with Fatso and Maisie.'

She opened her eyes and saw Fatso and Maisie, their open, honest faces, pleading for her to come back with them.

Jo again, 'Mandy, all helicopters have been commandeered. Go back on the boat, Jack is in good hands and there is nothing you can do, we will keep you informed, and I promise, if he deteriorates, I will fly a fucking helicopter myself and pick you off that boat, okay?'

'How was Michael?'

'He's worried, of course, sends his love, and said to say they're always prepared, and you would understand.'

She nodded, 'Jo, phone Liz at my flat, tell her I need her please.'

'Who's driving?'

Maisie decided not to make a joke, 'Little Jack.'

'Is he okay to drive?'

Maisie had her fat arm embracing Mandy's shoulders, 'Fatso will take over in a short while, Little Jack knows what he's doing.'

'Thank you for taking me home.'

Maisie was mothering and smothering. 'Darlin' we are proud to have Jack's girl with us.' Mandy nursed her sweet tea. Little Jack came on the intercom, she was aware of his high pitch voice and the sudden deep croaks, 'Just heard they've changed Jack's thing to eight hours not ten, so that must be good, eh?' Fatso acknowledged the message, she was reminded of Jack's frontier gibberish.

'Darlin', he will be okay, want a drink?' Maisie asked.

Mandy recoiled, 'Oh no, my mum used to drink at times like this and she would get plastered, my sister and I had to fend for ourselves.'

Maisie tried to conceal her sense of horror, 'What about your dad?'

'Didn't give a shit.'

'Sounds tough. Fatso, take over from Little Jack now, please.' Fatso got up, stretched over his wife and put a hand on Mandy's shoulder, she found it reassuring, thought if only her mum and dad had done that.

'Only a few days ago Jack was blown-up, I'm not sure I can take this, Maisie?'

Maisie tightened her embrace, 'I know, I know...' rubbing Mandy's shoulder, and then her back. Mandy thought, I bet Jack is like this with his kids. 'Babes, as I said, Jack is the sort of man things happen around. Don't ask me why, it just does. Ordinarily you meet Jack and you would peg him for a girl's blouse, that's what Michael calls him.' She stopped talking, took her arm away and turned Mandy to face her. 'Listen to me, you love that man, I can see, but you need to think about yourself as well, many women don't, but you must, because he's a big man in every sense of the word. I've seen women drive themselves into the ground through the love of a man. Don't get me wrong, he is kind and considerate, will be there for you all the time, it's just...' and flicked her hands, '...things happen around him.' Mandy raised her face and looked at a woman who clearly loved Jack. Maisie talked some more, 'Look at us, my Fatso could have been shot today. We were there because we will do anything for Jack. We love him, but we come from a different angle, babes, you understand what I say?'

'I understand how you feel and why, but why is Jack with you?'

She gave a short, wry laugh, 'Darlin', you do not know the half. He loved his wife, but it was not what I would call an equal love. He worshipped her, forgave her everything, did whatever she wanted, except the one thing she really wanted, he would not give up the police. This became worse after my Dottie and his eye. We got to know him because the rows began, and often he would come to us. Suppose he felt a bond, I like to think so. He even slept a few times on the boat. Kate couldn't stand this, nor could she understand the kissing of the eye.'

'I must admit I have a little difficulty there.'

'I know, but you have to understand the fishing families are close, have been for generations, and we are not best loved. Jack did a big thing for us. He gave up something big, and for us. It's our way to show we do not forget, the women especially, we feel it with a child. That's why it happens. The men just shake his hand and have the male thing of looking each other in the eye, don't ask me how it works, but it does; never understood men.'

Fatso was on the intercom, 'Coming into harbour, the Police have a car for you, Mandy, Bluebottle cab with blues and twos, said you'd know what they meant?'

Mandy nodded and smiled, 'It's what Jack would have said.'

Maisie squeezed and nodded, looked Mandy in the eye, 'Go for him, darlin'.'

'I will.'

'Do me one thing, eh?'

'What's that?'

'Stay in touch, it will be down to you. Jack will go one hundred per cent for you and he will be putty in your hands, so I ask you, woman to woman, please keep in touch and try to understand the eye thing. Most of all, stay in touch, because Jack is useless like my Fatso, but if you go with Jack you will need an army of support around you, and we can do that for you, will do that for you,' she shrugged, 'and we want to see him as well. Let's not forget that.'

'I would like that, thank you.'

The intercom again, 'Berthing babes.'

'Think he's talking to you,' they both smiled at the feeble joke.

'Let's get you changed, you want to look good for him when he wakes up, the little tow-rag.' Mandy managed a chuckle, when she thought she would never laugh again, but this short, stout, working woman, Mrs Hitler, did it for her. They climbed the dock ladder and Mandy followed Maisie into the shed. S stopped and smelled. 'What is it?' Maisie asked.

Looking around her the inside of the bleak, utilitarian shed, Mandy answered, 'Jack said there will come a time when this smell will be nice to me, I laughed, but now I like it.'

'It's the association for Jack, friends and seafood, I sometimes think it's mainly the seafood, but I live in hope.'

'I see that, can see how Jack steps aside from the material world like he does.'

Maisie was effusive, 'Mandy, that man embraces life, and that is how I know he will be okay, that, and he will know you are there for him. You are aren't you?'

'I am, Maisie.'

SIXTY-SIX

Mandy emerged from the shed in her red dress and Maisie shooed her to the police car, 'Hospital, Ma'am?'

'Yes, Bobby, thank you.'

'Blues and two's?'

'Give it all you got,' Mandy replied, holding back her sobs. They took off with the sirens and lights going, and Mandy slumped into the rear seat, she was exhausted but jumped with a start and put her seatbelt on, thought of Jack, then looked out of the window. Bobby was talking but she hadn't noticed, 'Sorry, I was miles away?'

'I said Jack will be alright, he may look like a wet rag, but he's made of strong stuff, Millwall you see, breed 'em tough down the Den.'

'Do they, I hope so.'

'How is he really, Ma'am?'

She sniffed, 'Not good, and I'm scared shitless.' She felt the car surge as Bobby leaned on the accelerator. She was glad, looked out of the windscreen, people moved their cars out of the way. 'Can you put me through to the CP room?'

'I can.'

Jo-Jums picked up, 'Mandy, how are you, where are you?'

'As well as can be expected I suppose, I'm on my way up to Jack, what's the news?'

'Not much more, chaos downstairs as they bring the bastards in, crime scene is set, 17 kids in all, one dead. The one in the water makes it eighteen, he's still hanging on, a tough cookie. Seems he was being delivered by boat early this morning and gave them the slip, was clinging to the side of the fort but eventually slipped in. Lucky you came along when you did.'

'Keep me posted, I need to stay active.'

'Understood,' Jo replied, 'by the way, one of the kids was Osama's, so tell that to Jack when he wakes, it will cheer him up.'

'I will, and Jo, you've done brilliant today.'

'Thanks, Liz, with Carly, Dolly, Michael and Colleen are there, Alana is on the way with Josh, Alice said she's staying, and the Holy Ghost is floating up on his own steam. Mandy, give Jack our love.'

'I will, I'm here, thanks for the chat.'

The patrol car pulled up at the casualty Porte Cochere. Mandy looked lost and Bobby got out and helped her to reception, made the enquiries. He came back and took her by the arm. 'This way, Ma'am.'

'Bobby, you can call me Mandy.'

He tightened his grip as he felt her falter, 'Thank you, but on duty...'

He guided her through the corridors, up in the lift, "doors opening," 'No kidding, Tonto,' she said.

'Sorry, Ma'am?'

'Nothing, Bobby.'

Bobby left her at the theatre waiting area. Michael got up to hug her, Alice was standing aside, eyes red raw. Michael let Mandy go and Colleen hugged her. Her dam burst as she bent to cry into Dolly's shoulder. 'There, love, get it out of your system, our boy will be alright you'll see,' Dolly guided her to a low bench and they sat down.

'What time is it?' Mandy asked.

'Seven thirty,' Michael said, 'he's been in for seven hours he's....' Michael stopped, there was a Doctor standing in surgeons' blue scrubs. Mandy's heart sank.

'Jack Austin's family?'

'Yes,' Michael answered, 'How is he?'

'We've finished the major procedure, a lot of damage which hopefully we have repaired. We are doing his foot now, one and half hours I'd say, he is critical but it went as well as can be expected,' and he left.

Liz arrived and hugged her mum, 'Sorry I've been difficult.'

'It's okay, Mum.'

They hugged like they would never separate, then the practical Mandy surfaced, 'Michael, ring Alana and tell her he's out of danger, no need for her to drive fast. I will phone the station.'

'I'll go back now he's okay and tell them,' and Alice left.

SIXTY-SEVEN

JACK WAS IN INTENSIVE CARE, THERE HAD BEEN complications, but he had a fighting chance. Mandy dozed fitfully in the chair next to his bed and woke with a start as he touched her hand that was draped across him.

'Jack.'

She moved her chair closer and rested her head onto the bed, he stroked her hair and whispered weakly, 'Did we get the bastards?'

'We did.'

His voice was hardly discernible, 'Moriarty?'

'Probably not.'

'The boy in the water?' he opened his eye, she had made sure she was positioned so his good eye could see her.

'Critical, but will make it.' He responded with a gentle nod. 'They found Osama's son. They want to come and see you, probably shove a mango up your arse, that's what I would do; feckin' ballet.'

'You didn't believe me?'

'No, and I still don't, you were making it up.'

'You will never know.'

'Ah, but I will, the tactical support had cameras and you are on film and going around all the nicks as we speak, you will be a laughing stock if I have anything to do with it, you scared the living daylights out of me.'

'You love me though?'

She gripped his hand and pulled it to her cheek, 'I love you deeply,' he seemed like he was losing the little energy he had and she wanted him to shut-up, but he wouldn't.

'We got them, went around the houses, but we got them. Mike says, "Know thine enemy", they should have listened. He drifted off mumbling about Moriarty and whose enemy he was, was he an enemy at all? This confused Mandy. She rested her head beside his hand. Jack looked out across the bed, the walls slowly disappeared and everything seemed bleached, his eye felt dodgy, all was a bright misty white, except for the lustrous crimson that was Mandy's dress.

Mandy fell into a deep sleep. She did not hear the beeping monitor change to a single tone, nor the staff of the ICU run to the bedside with the crash cart, nor the tinkling glass sound, a text message on Jack's phone she had in her hand bag. Later she would read that message:

Get well soon Jane
Round 2
Angels and Virgins
Do you know thine enemy Jack?
Mor.

THE END *or is it...?*

Book 2 - Kind Hearts and Martinets
Can, Can't, Will
Irony in the Soul

DEAR READER

Dear reader,

We hope you enjoyed reading *Cause and Effect*. If you have a moment, please leave us a review - even if it's a short one. We want to hear from you.

The story continues in *Irony in the Soul*.

Want to get notified when one of Creativia's books is free to download? Join our spam-free newsletter at http://www.creativia.org.

Best regards,
Pete Adams and the Creativia Team

ABOUT THE AUTHOR

Pete Adams is an architect with a practice in Portsmouth, UK, and from there he has, over forty years, designed and built buildings across England and Wales. Pete took up writing after listening to a radio interview of the writer Michael Connolly whilst driving home from Leeds. A passionate reader, the notion of writing his own novel was compelling, but he had always been told you must have a *mind map* for the book; Jeez, he could never get that. Et Voila, Connolly responding to a question, said he never can plan a book, and starts with an idea for chapter one and looks forward to seeing where it would lead. Job done, and that evening Pete started writing and the series, Kind Hearts and Martinets, was on the starting blocks.

That was some eight years ago, and hardly a day has passed where Pete has not worked on his writing, and currently, is halfway through his tenth book, has a growing number of short stories, one, critically acclaimed and published by Bloodhound, and has written and illustrated a series of historical nonsense stories called, Whopping Tales.

Pete describes himself as an inveterate daydreamer, and escapes into those dreams by writing crime thrillers with a thoughtful dash of social commentary. He has a writing style shaped by his formative years on an estate that re-housed London families after WWII, and his books have been likened to the writing of Tom Sharpe; his most cherished review, "made me laugh, made me cry, and made me think".

Pete lives in Southsea with his partner, and Charlie, the star-struck Border terrier, the children having flown the coop, and has three beautiful granddaughters who will play with him so long as he promises not to be silly.

Printed in Great
Britain
by Amazon

32341547R00265